I0611435

Blacklist Protocol

By

Alex Clifford

Blacklist Protocol
Copyright © 2008 by
Alex Clifford

All rights reserved

No part of this book may be reproduced or transmitted in
any form or by any means, electronic or mechanical,
without the written permission of the publisher, except
where permitted by law.

Library of Congress Catalog Card Number – Pending

First Printing

Published by

Cogwheel Press
P.O. Box 9592
Ketchikan, AK 99901

For a personalized copy order directly from

Cogwheelpress.com

ISBN: 978-0-578-00218-7

Acknowledgements

This book is dedicated to my father who taught me to go after my dreams and my mother who was there to pick me up. It is also dedicated to my sister, Robin, who always spoils me, and my brother, John, who is always looking over the horizon.

Special thanks go to Nancy Phillips for her input on the first draft, author friends Becky Cantrell and Debbie DiGiovanni for their help with subsequent drafts, and of course, Melissa Weidow, for all the fine-tuning.

More than ever, I owe everything to my wife, Jennifer, who puts up with my daydreaming, late nights, and busy weekends.

Disclaimer

The characters and situations in this book are fictional. Any reference to real people or circumstances is purely coincidental.

Look for other books by
Alex Clifford
along with other titles at
www.newonlinebooks.com

Day after day, day after day,
We stuck, nor breath nor motion;
As idle as a painted ship
Upon a painted ocean.

-Samuel Taylor Coleridge
The Rime of the Ancient Marine

1

There's nothing like a rowboat in the middle of an intersection to screw up the Friday morning rush hour commute. The high and dry craft was blocking northbound traffic where Warner Avenue merges with Pacific Coast Highway in Sunset Beach and had already caused one fender-bender when a white Chevy Tahoe swerved to miss it and sideswiped a dark green minivan full of school children. The situation had now deteriorated into a horn honking and middle finger waving contest. As Officer-in-Charge of Port Security for San Pedro Harbor, I should have been at the Coast Guard base on Terminal Island a half-hour ago because I'd finally gotten the call I'd been dreading- a seven hundred foot long tanker loaded down to her marks with premium unleaded gasoline was burning in the harbor. I knew the day a major disaster hit the port was coming sooner or later, and now that it was here, there was a feeling in the pit of my stomach like a mongrel dog feeding on road kill. It didn't take a genius to figure out I was going to have a shitty day and to make matters worse, nobody was willing to leave their vehicle to help me get my boat back into the bed of my pickup truck.

"How about a little help?" I hollered to the guy in a silver BMW that was about four feet from the boat and honking his horn. He flipped me off and mouthed words I couldn't hear because he had his windows rolled up.

Normally I can handle the boat by myself at the beach by dragging it across the sand, but asphalt was a different matter. If somebody would just grab the other gunwale we could carry it across the intersection and have it in the back of my truck in thirty seconds.

My cell phone rang and when I stopped dragging the boat to answer it, a fresh round of horn honking and middle finger waving broke out.

"Commander Stanton," said my yeoman, a strapping and diligent kid named Clifton Jenkins who was a mere six months removed from life on a farm somewhere in Nebraska or Iowa. "Admiral Ballard called again from Alameda. He said he's been on the horn with the President and wants to know why you're not at the base or answering your cell phone."

My cell phone had been tied up because I was looking at live pictures on-scene Coast Guard personnel were sending me of the disaster in progress. The tiny screen showed images of angry yellow flames billowing skyward eight or ten stories high and even with low-grade cell phone video, it was plain to see that the hellfire had completely enveloped the British-flagged vessel.

"Tell the Admiral that I'm stuck in traffic and he can't reach me on my cell phone because I've been talking on it."

"I'll tell him that, but Commander Stanton, the Admiral sounds really pissed. Maybe you should call him."

"He's always like that." I grabbed the boat and started dragging it again with my free hand. "Tell him I'm busy right now and I'll call him just as soon as I get to the base."

When I'd finally wrestled the boat into the truck, I secured it in place with ropes from the bow and around the seats - something I'd failed to do back at the beach because that's when I got the first call about the incident. My mind was reeling when I heard from the

Coast Guard duty dispatcher that initial reports indicated a speedboat had fired four rockets at the London based Whitehall Lines tanker, *M.V. BELEZA*, while she was outside the breakwater entrance and that the vessel had proceeded into San Pedro Harbor engulfed in flames. With a million other thoughts racing through my mind as I left Bolsa Chica State Beach after my morning rowing session, I'd failed to fasten the surfboat's tie-downs. When the red light at Warner Avenue turned green, I'd stabbed the gas pedal to the floorboard, dumped the clutch, and when the truck hurtled forward, the boat slid out like it was on greased skids. In my rearview mirror I saw commuters dodging it like it was some sort of alien spacecraft, which in the middle of morning rush hour traffic on Pacific Coast Highway, it was.

The motorcycle cop that showed up to sort out the mayhem was satisfied with my military identification and hasty explanation so he let me go without taking a report. It was another twenty minutes of stop and go traffic before I arrived at the Coast Guard base's front security gate. The sentry on duty waved me through even though I was out of uniform and wearing a set of saltwater soaked Coast Guard Academy Rowing Team sweats.

The *Beleza* disaster happened in full view of the Coast Guard's Reservation Point base on Terminal Island. The 18-acre facility is strategically located at the east entrance to the main shipping channel for San Pedro Harbor and is a collection of World War Two era stucco and red tile buildings kept current with endless coats of white paint. The extravagant and immaculately manicured lawns are generally considered a waste of prime commercial real estate worth in the neighborhood of twenty million dollars an acre.

As I pulled around the main building to the rear parking lot, I noted that the two medium-endurance cutters normally berthed at our dock along San Pedro's main shipping channel were underway and at the scene providing security and firefighting assistance to the burning tanker. All seven of the smaller Sea Marshal patrol craft used for routine harbor reconnaissance had also been manned and were up to their eyeballs keeping sightseeing civilian boaters at a reasonable distance. As I got out of my truck, I paused for a moment to stare at the stricken vessel that was listing severely to starboard and exhaling a massive amount of sooty black smoke that rolled skyward, overwhelming the horizon like an approaching Kansas thunderstorm. The tanker looked even more out of place in the harbor than a rowboat in the middle of the intersection during rush hour.

To make firefighting efforts even more perilous than they already were, the first brutal Santa Ana condition of the season had kicked up last night. The October high-pressure area over the Mojave badlands was funneling hot, dry wind through the canyons to the east in excess of sixty miles an hour, fanning brushfires and forcing the temperate marine layer far out to sea while depositing a layer of desert dust on everything downwind. Airborne dust particles, refracting the sunlight, turned the morning sun blood red, giving a prophetic suggestion of events to come.

There was bedlam inside the building as on-duty personnel scrambled to handle the situation and arriving off-duty personnel reported for emergency duty assignments. The Coast Guard Captain of the Port, Capt. Robert Boyle, had left for Washington D.C. on business earlier in the week, and as his second-in-command, I was in charge. Yeoman Jenkins handed me a stack of messages and followed me as I unlocked my office door.

"Who's the duty officer this morning," I asked as I pushed my door open.

"Lieutenant Bailey."

"Get him on the phone, I need a status report."

"The harbor has been shut down, sir."

"Just the entrance or the whole damn harbor?" It was no easy task closing San Pedro Harbor. The bustling commercial enterprise consisted of over 40 miles of waterfront and 26 cargo terminals that handled more than 6,000 ship movements and 500 billion dollars worth of cargo last year.

"No ships coming or going and all cargo operations have been suspended."

"Good. I still want you to get him on the phone."

"Her."

"Her?"

"Yes," Yeoman Jenkins said. "Lieutenant Bailey is a *her*."

"Very well, then get *her* on the phone."

My shoes and socks were still wet from wading in the surf and I peeled them off when I sat down at my desk. When my phone rang, I was expecting it to be Lieutenant Bailey on the other end so I answered, "Stanton, talk to me."

"Damn you, Jared," bellowed Admiral Ballard. "Where the hell have you been?"

Officers who served under Admiral Harold Ballard called him 'Hard-Ass Harry' behind his back, a nickname he got as a young Ensign and was proud to have. He had been an All-American defensive end on the Coast Guard Academy football team in the mid-seventies and lived his life with urgency like his team was down by one score when there were only two minutes left to play in the game. Admiral Ballard was a team player, but you damn sure didn't want to be on the wrong side of him.

"Sorry sir, but I got stuck in traffic. I got here as fast as I could."

"I'm not interested in excuses, Jared," Admiral Ballard said with enough volume that I had to hold the phone away from my ear. "I want to know why in the hell I heard about this incident from the Commandant back in Washington before I did from an officer under my command in San Pedro?"

"Sir, I…"

"The way it works is that I get the call from one of my officers and then I call the Commandant to explain to him what has happened." Admiral Ballard paused to breathe. "I shouldn't have to explain to you, of all people, that when I can't answer the Commandant's questions about an incident because I haven't even been told about it, that I'm not going to be happy. Not happy at all."

"Sir, I…"

"A turd in the punchbowl, Jared. That's exactly what this is."

It was common knowledge that the Commandant of the Coast Guard would be retiring within six months and that Admiral Ballard, in charge of the Eleventh District based up the coast in Alameda, was in the running for the soon to be available position. Unfortunately, in the military it doesn't matter how many 'atta-boys' you have in your personnel file, just one 'oh-shit' can ruin your entire career.

"I hand-picked you for the job and I don't mind telling you I took a lot of flack for my decision…your grades and conduct weren't the best at the academy and you had a few mediocre officer performance evaluations, not mention that you quit the Coast Guard once to have your little fling over at the FBI."

"Yes sir."

"The reason I chose you to head up port security down there is that you're not a strong book person. Your job requires thinking and street smarts, *not* going *by the book* all the time. I had a lot of officers apply for your job, damn fine officers, *by-the-book* officers. I selected you over them because I thought you would figure out what needed to be done and then do it without wasting valuable time looking it up in the manual."

"Yes sir."

"I was on the phone with the President and I felt like a damn fool. The President doesn't want another fiasco like the World Trade Center. Elections are next month and he wants this contained right damn now. I assured him we had top-notch officers and men on the scene and that the situation was under control, even though I'm getting the feeling that it's not under control at all."

"Well, sir…"

"I'm on my way to the Alameda Air Station as we speak and going to catch a plane down there. Meet me at the Santa Monica Air Station with a helicopter in one hour, I want to see that damn ship and I'm personally taking charge of this situation."

"Yes sir."

"I heard we lost a Sea Marshal on that ship this morning."

"I'm still checking on that." I ran my finger down the duty roster and saw that Lieutenant Rita Velasco had led this morning's boarding team with Marshals Bennet and Kuhn but I hadn't heard yet which one was the casualty.

"Well, I've confirmed it. We lost a Sea Marshal and I sure as hell don't like to lose anybody under my command. You better get your head in this game and get it in quick. There's no time to lose."

"Yes sir."

"The President has locked down every goddamn harbor in the country until we get a handle on this. Do you have any idea of the economic impact that's going to have? The elections are next month and we've got a turd in the punchbowl. Right now that punchbowl is San Pedro Harbor."

"I'll see you in one hour, sir."

"The media is going crazy with this. They've already got helicopters flying overhead, sending video of that burning ship to every television set in the country. Shut down that airspace."

"I'm on it."

"The damn newscasters are saying this means another war and this country can't afford that type of talk. Jared, you get this thing under control or it's your ass."

2

Yeoman Jenkins stuck his head into my office. "Your chopper is ten minutes out, Commander, and there's a guy from the FBI waiting to see you."

"Give me a minute and then send him in."

Lieutenant Ann Bailey had briefed me on this morning's tragedy and furnished me with a copy of all the official Homeland Security communiqués we'd received so far concerning the *Beleza*. I hadn't read them yet because I'd gone to the locker room to take one of the fastest showers of my life and change into my Coast Guard short-sleeved working blues so I could meet Admiral Ballard in something other than a damp sweatshirt and sweatpants with a hole in the crotch. The helicopter ride to the Santa Monica Air Station would take about fifteen minutes and I could read the Homeland Security messages on the way. I was shoving the paperwork into my briefcase when my office door opened again.

The FBI agent that came through the door was wearing a white Panama hat, yellow flowered Hawaiian shirt, and white chinos. I didn't recognize him at first. The blue eyes looked familiar, but the leather sandals, dark curly hair pulled back into a ponytail, and the diamond earring stud threw me off.

"You're a Commander now?" he said, more of a statement than question. "Not bad. Small office though." He surveyed the converted storeroom that served as my office and then flashed me a broad arrogant grin.

"Mike Dillon." His voice had triggered my memory and I leaned back in my chair without getting up to greet him. I knew Mike Dillon all too well. We'd crossed paths a few years back when I did my ill-fated four and a half year stint with the Bureau. He was one of the new-breed the FBI had been hiring since the Department of Homeland Security reorganization - Ivy League types, born with silver spoons in their mouths and more valuable for their political connections than their professional ability. Mike Dillon had a reputation for being a first-class brownnoser when I'd known him and the fact that he was standing in my office meant that my day was going from bad to worse.

Mike Dillon pulled up a chair and sat down across the desk from me. "How do you like working for the Sea Scouts again?" he asked, flashing me another grin that I desperately wanted to wipe off his face.

As the only armed service to reside outside the Pentagon, the Coast Guard has always been considered the military's redheaded stepchild, complete with typical redheaded stepchild complaints - lack of love, respect, and financial backing. For years the Coast Guard's role had been to thwart smuggling and act as a merchant shipping inspectorate under the Department of Transportation, but now organized under the Department of Homeland Security, the Coast Guard has the lead role in defending 9,500 miles of this country's coastline and rivers as well as more than a hundred commercial shipping ports from any vessel that comes over the horizon posing a threat, either because it's decrepit and may spill something into the water or because it's involved in criminal activity. Protecting the nation's coast is a daunting task and just looking at my office set-up clearly illustrates just how far behind the curve we are in meeting the challenge. Port security for San Pedro is run from a converted storeroom without windows and my yeoman, for lack of adequate workspace, is still parked at a small desk in the hall outside my office like a schoolboy who has been expelled from his classroom. The Coast Guard needs a lot more money, personnel, and equipment, but is always at the bottom of the list when Congressional appropriations are handed out.

"Nice outfit," I said, surveying Mike Dillon's undercover clothes. "Have you been working up in Hollywood?"

He ignored my question. "You look like you put on some weight. You must have finally quit smoking."

"So much for the pleasantries, Dillon. What are you doing here?"

"I'm taking point on the investigation of this morning's tanker bombing," he said with a smirk.

"I thought you were working out of Washington, riding a desk on the Wall Street insider trading investigation."

"You're out of touch, Stanton. I've been with the Domestic Security Task Force for more than a year now."

"That's the Bureau for you. Fuck-up, move-up."

"You should know all about that."

"I'm surprised you even stayed with the Bureau after what happened in Hoboken. You were walking around with your tail between your legs like an egg-sucking dog," I shot back just to wipe the smirk off his face. It worked.

Mike Dillon grinned but his eyes told me it was forced. "Maybe we should talk about you and what happened in Boca Raton."

I started shoving papers in my briefcase again. "I'd love to shoot the breeze with you about old times, but duty calls."

"Can you confirm or deny that the tanker this morning was hit with shoulder-fired rockets?"

"I can neither confirm nor deny those reports." I snapped the locks closed on my briefcase.

"Then what do you know about the attack?"

"Not much."

"Why do I get the feeling you're not being cooperative with this investigation?"

"It's not that I'm being uncooperative. It's that the smoke hasn't even cleared and we're only beginning our investigation. There's not a lot to tell you yet."

I started around my desk but Dillon blocked my path.

"You don't like me do you?"

"Don't take it personal, it's not so much you as it is guys like you that I can't stand."

"What do you mean?"

"They name streets after people like you," I said. "One-way."

"Screw you, Stanton," Dillon said as I pushed past him. "I'll be reporting that you're not cooperating with the inter-agency investigation."

"Knock yourself out."

"I'm in charge of this investigation and we're going to have to work together whether you like it or not."

I started to tell him that Admiral Ballard and the Coast Guard were going to be in charge of the *Beleza* investigation, not him or the FBI, but I decided it would be more fun to watch him get chewed out later when he clashed with the Hard-Ass Harry Ballard.

My hand was on the doorknob when Dillon said, "I heard you lost a Sea Marshal this morning."

Mike Dillon's eyes were full of vengeance when I turned to face him. The smile he'd worn into to my office was nowhere to be seen.

"You must be getting used to it by now," he said.

If I didn't already have enough problems to deal with this morning I probably would have knocked him on his butt.

"The difference between me and you, Dillon, is that I didn't blame somebody else for my own fuck-up."

Dillon clenched his jaw shut. "I've checked with Homeland Security and the ship this morning wasn't on your Blacklist. Why did you have three Sea Marshals aboard?"

"Are you trying to tell me how to do my job?" The Coast Guard has to monitor over six thousand vessel movements each year in the Port of San Pedro alone, not to mention every other port in the country. A majority of freighters we get here are loaded in third-world countries and a significant amount of the cargo they carry comes from cities and towns scattered hundreds of miles from the nearest seaport. It's impossible to track everything being shipped out of remote foreign ports due to the sheer volume, so Coast Guard Headquarters developed a Blacklist to prioritize monitoring of ships.

"You have a protocol for using the Blacklist."

"And we followed it." Profiling isn't legal so we call it something else. Vessels on the Blacklist usually have a record of safety or criminal violations, or else have been red-tagged by Homeland Security because of intelligence information. Ships arriving in San Pedro that are on the Blacklist get extra scrutiny, but foreign registered tankers carrying gasoline are ready-made bombs and don't need to be on the list because they're always a priority.

"Why were your Sea Marshals aboard that ship this morning?"

I started out the door without answering.

"Why wasn't the ship on the Blacklist?" he demanded.

"You're in charge. You tell me," I said to him, then walked out of my office.

***

The orange and white Coast Guard MH-68 helicopter slowly circled the *Beleza* as Admiral Ballard and I surveyed the wreckage through our binoculars. Aft, on the starboard side, the ship had a gaping hole in a cargo tank about twenty feet below the main deck, just forward of the scorched and mangled superstructure. The fire had been extinguished and the gasoline cargo was no longer escaping from the hull, but the superstructure and crew's quarters were heavily damaged and still smoldering, emitting both white and black smoke which meant the fire was still being fought with water from inside the vessel. Six fireboats were on station around the stricken tanker, their water cannons spraying water skyward in all directions in case the cargo caught fire again. A large seagoing salvage tug idled outside the security perimeter established by Coast Guard vessels, waiting for clearance before pulling the *Beleza* from the mud bank and into safer waters.

Despite the gusting Santa Ana winds, the helicopter pilot expertly maneuvered toward the starboard bow of the *Beleza* and hovered while Lieutenant Velasco was hoisted from the main deck in a basket. She scrambled into the chopper and her eyes widened when she realized Admiral Ballard was aboard.

"Sir," stammered Lieutenant Velasco, unsure if she should shake hands or salute the Admiral. Her orange Sea Marshal coveralls were smoke streaked and a perplexed look overwhelmed her subtle Asian features.

When I took her elbow to guide her away from the open door I noticed that her shortly coiffed raven was scorched at the ends and the right side of her face was bright red with several blistered burns.

"I want to know what blithering idiot brought that ship into the harbor," bellowed the Admiral, trying to be heard above the turbines and rhythmic beating of the rotors. Dressed in working blues, it was apparent the former All American kept himself in good physical condition. He pulled his dark blue Coast Guard baseball cap tighter over his gray hair so he wouldn't lose it out the door. His penetrating cobalt blue eyes focused on Lieutenant Velasco while he waited for her answer.

"The harbor pilot," she said.

"What in the world was he thinking? I'll have his license for this!"

The chopper's crew chief labored to slide the door shut and when it was closed we could finally hear one another without yelling.

"What the hell happened out there today?" Ballard asked.

Rita grabbed an overhead handhold to steady herself as the aircraft began moving. "It all happened so fast, Admiral. I was on the radio reporting to the dispatcher that we'd completed our inspection and were inbound and then the next thing I knew I was on the deck and flames were shooting through the wheelhouse."

"Did you see anyone firing rockets at the ship?" he asked.

"I didn't see a thing. There was a dull thud and a few seconds later a huge explosion and then there were flames and the smell of gasoline everywhere."

"Why did you let the pilot bring it in the harbor?" he asked.

"I didn't. It was pretty confusing after the explosion and the ship was already heading for the breakwater entrance. The helmsman and the third mate were blown out of the wheelhouse and so the harbor pilot went over to steer the ship. When I saw what he was doing, I ordered him to turn around and head out to sea."

"Why didn't he?"

"He said there wasn't enough room to make the turn and that the only thing keeping the entire ship from blowing up was our speed through the water because the burning gasoline was trailing behind us."

"What did the Captain of the ship say when you ordered the harbor pilot to turn around?"

"He was out of it, sir. He'd been drinking tea before the explosion and for several minutes afterward, he just walked around with a teacup handle between his thumb and forefinger like he was still holding a full cup of tea. All he could say was, "Bloody hell. We're bloody-well on fire."

"Lieutenant, I still can't believe you just let that harbor pilot bring a burning tanker full of gasoline into this harbor."

I could see Lieutenant Velasco's eyes narrow. She was trying to be respectful, but she wasn't about to let Admiral Ballard intimidate her. "Admiral, I drew my weapon and put it to his head and told him to turn the damn ship around."

"What did he do?"

"He told me to go ahead and pull the trigger, I'd be doing him a favor because were going to die anyway. Then he told me our only chance was to run into the ship up on the mud bank in the outer harbor while keeping the engines on full ahead. He said with any luck the propeller wash would keep the bulk of the fuel behind us so it didn't consume the entire ship."

"He told you to go ahead and pull the trigger?"

"Yes sir, he said to pull the trigger because I'd be doing him a favor."

Admiral Ballard crouched and moved forward to signal the pilot to take us back to the Terminal Island base. Lieutenant Velasco took a seat across the aisle from me and took a small plastic bag of ice from her jacket pocket to put on her facial burns.

"Go over to sick bay as soon as we land," I told her. "You need to have those burns treated."

Admiral Ballard sat next to me and when he caught her eye, he gave the exhausted Sea Marshal a fatherly nod. She flashed him a weak smile and hung her head. Tears crept down her cheek and when they reached her burns, she wiped them away with the back of her hand.

I couldn't help feeling bad for Lieutenant Velasco. As the Officer-in-Charge of the Sea Marshal unit that was under my command, she'd lost Marshal John Bennet in the fire and Marshal Joyce Kuhn had been life-flighted to Our Lady of Mercy Hospital in critical condition. To top it all off, I was going to have to tell her about Mike Dillon being assigned to the case. I'd heard about the Hoboken incident involving her and Dillon, and although I didn't know all the intimate details, I was pretty sure he was the last person on the planet she was going to want to run into today. I knew how I felt when Mike Dillon rubbed my nose in it about Boca Raton this morning so I could only imagine what she would be going through when she found out he'd been assigned to the investigation. Everybody has something in their past they'd like to forget, but Boca cost me my marriage and my wife's life and that's a tough one to get past.

Admiral Ballard leaned over and said in my ear, "If these assholes start attacking ships outside the harbor like this, we're going to have a damn tough time stopping them!"

3

By noon I knew there was no way I'd make it to the Dodgers' game tonight. It was the end of the regular season and I'd scored a ticket just four rows behind the home team dugout for this evening's match-up against the Cardinals. The Dodgers weren't going to the playoffs this year and some of the new players, just up from the minor league affiliates, were getting their first shot at competing in the show. Because most of the regular fans had given up on the team sometime last a month, I was finally able to get a great seat. All week I'd been looking forward to drinking beer and eating Dodger Dogs at the game, then spending the rest of the weekend getting over the indigestion.

Rita Velasco hadn't been warned about Mike Dillon coming to the meeting. After we'd returned to the Terminal Island Base in the helicopter, she'd gone straight to sickbay to have her burns treated and then back to her cubicle to file a report. We were on our way to Admiral Ballard's meeting in the conference room when we ran into Mike Dillon marching down the corridor with four other FBI agents in tow. They formed a wedge, like geese flying south for the winter, Dillon leading the way. They were all dressed alike in the FBI uniform of the day - dark gray suits, light blue shirts, black ties and government haircuts. Mike Dillon had lost the ponytail and earring he'd been wearing when he was in my office earlier today.

Admiral Ballard, who fancied himself a prospector of underdeveloped talent, had personally lured Rita Velasco away from the FBI. She was half Southern California Latino and half native Vietnamese, inheriting only the best genes from both her mother and father. She was tall, good-looking, and had enough brains to graduate from UCLA Law School with honors. Her mother died from cancer while Rita was still in grade school, probably caused by exposure to Agent Orange in Vietnam, and her father spent twenty-five years drinking himself to death, a predictable result of the two tours he did as an Army Ranger. The FBI recruited her straight out of law school and she had a promising career at the Bureau until her involvement in a botched undercover assignment in Hoboken that resulted in the death of a fellow agent. The Bureau's internal investigation uncovered the affair between her and Mike Dillon and they were reassigned to paper-shuffling jobs in different sections. The Coast Guard was Rita's second chance, and from what I'd seen of her work, she was making the most of the opportunity.

Rita was still in the set of orange Coast Guard issued coveralls she'd worn aboard the *Beleza* this morning and as a result of what had transpired aboard the ship, her clothes reeked of smoke and were streaked with soot and grease. I glanced sideways to catch her reaction when she first saw Dillon. She was deadpan.

"Look what the cat dragged in," she said, stepping into the center of the corridor to block the FBI procession.

Mike Dillon appeared stunned and came to an abrupt halt, causing the agents behind him to bump into each other in a comical chain reaction. I could tell by the look on his face that he didn't recognize her, and from what little I know about women, my guess was that wasn't a good thing.

"Rita?"

"Lieutenant Velasco."

"Excuse me?"

"You can call me Lieutenant Velasco."

"Of course," he said. "I didn't recognize you at first, it must be the uniform." He looked her up and down and then flaunted a boyish smile; the kind of smile a kid gives his mother when he gets caught throwing rocks at the neighbor's cat.

"Yeah, must be the uniform," she said, shuffling her feet. "Why are you here?"

"I'm in charge of the investigation on that tanker attack this morning," he said. "Are you involved in that?"

Rita took a step back so he could look at her. "Why do you think I look like this?"

One of the agents started to laugh and she glared at him.

"And if you think you're in charge..." she said, and then brushed past him without finishing her thought.

***

"Let's get one thing straight, right here, right now!" bellowed Admiral Ballard.

The conference room was packed and in chaos. There wasn't much standing room remaining for the personnel still trying to squeeze in. The bulk of the crowd stood in the corridors, looking through the glass panels that formed two adjacent sides of the conference room. Admiral Ballard stood at the head of the large rectangular table and I sat to his immediate right. Senior personnel from Customs, Immigration and Border Protection, Bureau of Alcohol, Tobacco, and Firearms, as well as local law enforcement also sat at the table. Less senior agency personnel lined the walls.

Admiral Ballard dispensed stern glances around the room, his bushy eyebrows twitching almost comically. He was quite an imposing figure in the conference room; his massive frame decked out in dress blues, campaign ribbons, and gold stripes. He brushed his short, thick gray hair back with one hand and waited for the room to grow quiet.

"When I call a meeting," Admiral Ballard said in a quieter tone, allowing a pregnant pause before he spoke again. "I don't expect to be kept waiting. I know we're all busy, but there's a lot of ground to cover and time is of the essence."

"I'm sorry, Admiral," said Dillon, who had taken a seat on the Admiral's left, directly across the conference table from me. "But we had a few…"

"I'm not asking for excuses," said the Admiral. "And I don't want them."

"But we had…" Dillon protested.

"If you can't be on time, I'll be glad to call your office and arrange for someone else to attend these meetings!"

Admiral Ballard broke into a pep talk that was condescending at times. He outlined the chain of command for the multi-agency task force that was being set up under the authority of the Department of Homeland Security. He announced that he would personally be heading up the task force. Dillon tried to object but was quickly admonished. The incident had taken place at sea, inside territorial waters, and was within Coast Guard jurisdiction. The matter wasn't negotiable.

"I wanted to stay longer," Admiral Ballard said, looking at his watch. "But we got started late here and I have a conference call with the Pentagon. Commander Stanton is the Officer-in-Charge of Port Security and he'll finish this meeting. He is reporting directly to me. Any questions?"

Attendees in the conference room looked at each but nobody volunteered to raise a hand.

"Good. Commander Stanton…the meeting is yours." Admiral Ballard abruptly gathered up his briefcase and made his way through the crowd.

Murmurs broke out as soon as the Admiral left the conference room and in short order the murmurs grew into another dull roar. Many attendees took the Admiral's departure as a sign that nothing of significance was going to happen so they began to filter out a few at a time.

I slid my briefcase to the head of the table, faced what was remaining of the crowd, and waited for it to get quiet again. Rita Velasco moved from a spot along the wall to the seat I'd just vacated and in my peripheral vision I caught her giving Dillon an icy stare.

"Is that guy for real?" muttered Dillon to the FBI agent next to him.

"As a matter of fact he is." I leaned toward Dillon, speaking softly so the others in the conference room wouldn't hear. "Let me assure you that Admiral Ballard has more horsepower than you can even imagine. My recommendation is that you be on time, or don't bother coming at all."

Dillon started to say something to me but then changed his mind and pretended to search for something in his briefcase.

I gave a brief overview of what the Coast Guard had pieced together so far, which wasn't much. Four rockets had been fired from a small speedboat as the British-flagged tanker, *Beleza*, entered San Pedro Harbor. Two rockets struck the ship, the other two missed high and wide. The Navy had expert underwater teams searching the bottom of the ocean for the two rockets that missed the ship and when they were recovered we could identify the source. The *Beleza* had a total of eighteen cargo tanks, but luckily, only one had been breached. Approximately five percent of the vessel's eleven million gallon cargo of premium-unleaded gasoline had been lost. Pollution was minimal because the fire consumed the bulk of the spill. Eight lives had been lost, including one Sea Marshal.

Eighteen had been injured, twelve seriously. Salvage operations were under way. Things could have been worse. A lot worse.

"We've located the speedboat involved in the incident," Dillon said as he stood up to address the conference room. "I'm Special Agent Mike Dillon of the FBI. We had a report that a boat left the scene of the tanker attack and traveled up the coast. That boat was run up on the beach fifteen miles from the scene of the attack, Redondo Beach to be exact, and then intentionally set on fire to destroy evidence. Four adult males were seen leaving that scene in a white Dodge minivan. Witnesses got the license plate number and we have crime scene personnel analyzing the remains of the boat. We should also have more information…"

"Thank you for your briefing, agent Dillon," I said, cutting him short and motioning for him to be seated. "Let's just say the investigation is ongoing and leave it at that."

I tried to move the meeting along by quelling interruptions and stressing that the current incident had been contained. Extra Coast Guard patrols, cutters, and personnel had been assigned. All agencies were to remain on heightened alert status. Yeoman Jenkins passed out copies of the incident document listing personnel and phone numbers of those assigned to the multi-agency task force. The task force would meet twice daily at 0900 and 1600 in the conference room and I stressed the importance of being on time.

After the meeting was dismissed, the whispers of the conference room grew into a thunderous cacophony in the corridor.

Dillon remained behind and stood next to the conference table.

"Is there a problem already?" I asked without looking up from the paperwork that I was loading into my briefcase.

"There's always a problem. That's why they hired us."

"Don't be a smart-ass, Dillon. If you've got something, let's have it."

"Look, about the minivan there's a problem and I didn't want to bring it up at the meeting. I wanted to you to give you a heads-up in person."

"You're going to do something for me? What's your angle?"

"It has to do with Rita."

"Leave her out of it," I said, moving closer, invading his personal space. "Don't even start that shit."

"It's not what you think."

"And what do I think?" I asked, moving a little closer. Mike Dillon stood about six foot two, close to my own height, but at thirty-eight years old, I had a good five or six years on him.

"Just listen to me." Dillon took a step backwards. "The minivan belongs to a guy named Astal Kamran. He reported it stolen ten days ago."

"So?"

"He's a lawyer. He has an office in Harbor City."

"So?"

"He went to law school with Rita."

"Where are you going with this?"

"He's a criminal defense attorney, but he does a lot of immigration and naturalization work. He's Iranian. Actually he's American, born here, but his parents are Iranian immigrants. The Bureau has had their eye on him for awhile."

"Go on."

"Actually it's not him we've been looking at. It's some of his clients. He represents a number of illegals that are being detained by Immigration...expired visas and whatnot."

"And so?"

"Rita shows up on his phone records. And she's been to see him."

"She's not involved in this." I studied Dillon's eyes. "How do you know all this anyway? Have you been following her?"

"I'm not saying Rita is involved in the attack. All I'm saying is we're looking at Astal Kamran because of who he represents, and she's been talking to him. This morning his minivan was used as a getaway car after the boat was burned on the beach. I just wanted to give you a heads-up. That's all."

"You're up to something."

"Look," Dillon said. "I just brought it up in the meeting that we had the license plate number because it's already common knowledge now. I didn't want somebody else blurting out this guy's name. Rita could look bad."

"So now, all of a sudden, you're concerned about Rita's welfare?" I did the math in my head. The Bureau had moved fast. They got a license plate number and in just a few hours had checked out the owner and found out it was somebody who was already under surveillance. "Have you picked this guy up?

"We've got him."

"What does he have to say?"

"We're working on it."

Dillon was playing his cards close to his chest. I looked at his eyes again to see if I could read more into what he was telling me. How did this all fit? First Dillon shows up in my office wearing undercover clothes and now a friend of Rita's from law school was linked to the attack of a ship outside harbor.

"That's all? You're working on it?" The Bureau had been watching Astal Kamran before this morning, Dillon had said that much. But what else did he know that he wasn't sharing with me?

"I'm just handling things down here in San Pedro. Somebody else is doing Astal Kamran's interrogation."

"Why are you here?"

"What do you mean?"

"It's an easy enough question, Dillon. Why did the Bureau send you?"

"I told you, I'm with the Domestic Security Task Force and I was assigned here this morning."

"I'm not buying it. The Bureau separated you and Rita and now out of the blue, you show up."

"I had no idea she was here. I didn't even know she was with the Coast Guard."

That sounded like bullshit, but then again, he did appear surprised to see her in the corridor before the Admiral's meeting.

"There's something you're not telling me."

"Come on, Stanton. I don't have time to argue with you about this. Believe what you want to believe, but you have bigger problems than me because this thing is far from over, it's just starting."

"Meaning...?"

"I'm telling you that it's just starting. Nobody smuggles just four rockets and extra Coast Guard patrols and cutters won't stop it. Next time it'll be a lot worse."

As much as I hated to admit it, Dillon was right. A few lightly armed Coast Guard Sea Marshals in rubber boats weren't going to stop an organized attack on San Pedro Harbor. Any attack on the port needed to be stopped long before it arrived. Good intelligence and undercover work were the things that would provide port security. After what happened this morning, it was obvious that more than a few things had fallen through the cracks somewhere along the line.

"What do you know about the weapons that I don't?" I asked. Dillon wasn't sharing everything with me. He wouldn't.

"This could have been a test," he said. "To see how we reacted. Or a diversion, to get our attention on something else and away from the real threat."

"So you're looking at this guy that had his minivan stolen?"

"Astal Kamran? Yes and no. We're looking at him, but we also have several thousand others all over the country we're keeping an eye on. It's just that his vehicle was involved in the getaway. I'm not sure what that means, but Rita is part of this whether you like it or not, and sooner or later, her association with Astal Kamran is going to be made public. "

"I'll handle it."

"Okay." Dillon stood up to leave.

"So you really think this is just beginning?" I asked. "That there's really more to this than we've seen so far?" I tried to read something, anything, in Dillon's face but got nothing.

"Ask yourself the questions. Why this ship, why here, why today? What were they trying to accomplish?" he said. "Damage to the tanker and its cargo was minimal. So did they fail today or did they succeed?"

Dillon started to leave.

"Dillon."

"Yeah."

"You never did say why you were already here. What were you really working on?"

"That's right," he said, the shit-eating grin back on his face. "I never did say."

I watched him as he walked away. Through the glass I could see him chatting with the other four agents who had been waiting in the corridor. He glanced over his shoulder at me one more time and then disappeared down the corridor with the other FBI goons in tow.

An older gentleman in a neat gray business suit had been waiting outside the conference room for me to finish talking and as I stepped into the corridor he approached me. "Commander Stanton?"

"Yes," I said, politely offering a handshake.

"I'm Larry Jackson. I represent the Pacific Shipping Association."

I'd been to quite a few luncheons sponsored by the Association, but knew Larry Jackson by name only. The Pacific Shipping Association had established itself as a major player in West Coast ports by bringing more than two hundred independent shipping companies and agencies under one roof. The Association handled the negotiation of longshore contracts, pilotage and wharfage fees, tugboat contracts, and other similar related shipping expenses on behalf of its members. The smallest companies in the Association were charged the same rates for services as the largest companies, thereby leveling the playing field. The Pacific Shipping Association had offices in all the West Coast ports and brandished quite a large stick in local port politics.

"Glad to meet you," I said. "I don't think we've met, but you do look familiar."

"I don't think our paths have crossed yet, Commander. I spend quite a bit of time of my time overseas on business."

"What can I do for you, Mr. Jackson?"

"The Association is very concerned about what happened today."

"I can understand that," I said politely. It went without saying that a lot of people were concerned about what happened today. I glanced at Larry Jackson's watch. He wore a gold Rolex with diamonds. Jackson had cool hazel eyes, neatly knotted navy blue silk tie, expensive suit, and razor cut hair with the gray colored out of it. Manicured and buffed fingernails. Jackson was smooth. That much was for sure. I glanced down to check the shoes, they tell a lot about the man. Larry Jackson wore a very nice pair of Italian loafers.

"Any interruption in port operations could be quite costly to the members of the Association," he said, his eyes avoiding mine. He held out a business card while looking straight through my chest.

Larry T. Jackson, President, Pacific Shipping Association. The business card also indicated that Jackson was a member of the law firm of Ward, Pierce, Jackson, and Pierson. Admiralty Law was their specialty.

"I appreciate your concern, Mr. Jackson," I said. "Rest assured, the Task Force will do everything it can to make sure there are no disruptions in port operations."

Jackson's faced pinched. "I'm concerned that all the extra security precautions are going to cause unnecessary delays to cargo operations in the port."

I started walking down the corridor toward my office and motioned for Jackson to walk with me. "We'll do what we can to keep delays to a minimum," I assured him. "I can appreciate your concerns, Mr. Jackson."

"I'm afraid that's not good enough, Commander." Jackson stepped in front of me. "I would like your guarantee that operations will not be affected by this incident."

"Excuse me if I'm being blunt, Mr. Jackson, but the Coast Guard doesn't make guarantees. We can't possibly…"

"I don't think you understand, Commander. A delay for one of our new containerships can cost the owners over a hundred thousand dollars an hour. It's after two o'clock right now and the port has been closed all day. The meter is running, Commander Stanton, and we've already lost millions."

"I understand that, Mr. Jackson, but given what happened this morning certain extra precautions must…"

"I'll be taking this up elsewhere!" He huffed, then turned on his heels without speaking again and stormed down the corridor toward the exit.

I stood stunned as he walked away. That was odd. What was that all about? Why did Larry Jackson have such a short fuse? The President had closed the harbor, not me.

Yeoman Jenkins handed me another stack of messages as I walked past him and closed my office door. I set my briefcase next to the government-issued gray metal desk and slumped into the matching chair that killed my back. Someday I'd buy a better chair with my own money. The Excedrin was in the top desk drawer and I washed three of them down with the last of the cold black coffee left in my cup from this morning. I didn't have a headache yet, but under the circumstances, I felt obliged to take the cure as a precautionary measure.

My office had previously been a storeroom down the hall from the port operations communication center. Before September Eleventh, the Coast Guard rented office space in a downtown Long Beach bank building, but for security reasons, had now moved everything to the Terminal Island. New facilities were under construction at the base, but due to the protracting bidding process and complicated government specifications, all the buildings were behind schedule and office space inside the Terminal Island facility was still at a premium. The storeroom had been given a desk and chairs, phone line, several file cabinets, and then assigned to me with the explanation that I'd be spending the bulk of my time in the field anyway.

I was thumbing through my messages when Rita Velasco came into my office holding a large styrofoam cup of coffee. She sat down in one of the two chairs in front of my desk, took a sip of coffee, and winced when the scalding liquid burned her lips and tongue. She slouched in her chair, still wearing the same dirty orange coveralls.

"You okay?" I asked.

"Yeah." she said, casually blowing small puffs across the surface of the coffee.

I thumbed through more messages.

"No," she relented. Her eyes moistened.

"It's been a bad day," I offered.

"Bennet..." she said, wiping a renegade tear from her cheek with the back of her hand. "He was married, two kids. Last week he asked me if he could have today off so he could go on a field trip with his son but I couldn't give it to him because we're short-handed."

There really is no way to describe the feeling when you think you're personally responsible for another person's death. Rationalization, attributing it to fate, and repression just don't seem to work. The guilt clings to you like an evil stench, penetrating your very soul. Unfortunately, I know the feeling all to well.

Right now wasn't the time to go into it with her, but I made a mental note to get her some counseling after we got past this incident.

"What did they say about your burns?" I asked.

"They're not bad." She touched her right cheek with her fingers. "The one on the back of my hand bothers me the most. I didn't realize it was there at first."

"Take care of those. They can be bad news."

"Yeah."

"Anyway, Admiral Ballard handled informing Bennet's wife," I said. "He talked to her personally, got in a car and drove over to their house right after we got off the chopper this morning. He's good that way. You wouldn't know it by the way he acts, but he's actually pretty good about things like that."

Rita stared at me across the top of her coffee cup.

"Sorry I didn't get a chance to warn you about Dillon."

"Why did they send him anyway?" Her almond eyes narrowed. "Out of all the agents working for the Bureau, why did they send him?"

"I didn't ask for him. That's for sure."

"He didn't help. I mean, with Bennet dying today and all. I didn't need to be reminded about what happened before…"

"The Admiral was impressed with the way you handled things today. He asked me to write you up for a commendation."

Rita nodded slightly and pursed her lips as she blew across her coffee.

"I don't like the fact that Dillon is here anymore than you do. But somehow, Admiral Ballard found a way for the Coast Guard to be in charge of this investigation and as a result, we're going to have to work with him. Bottom line, the Coast Guard just doesn't have the investigative resources to handle this incident by itself and we're going to have to work with the Bureau."

Rita sipped her coffee.

"That's why Admiral Ballard hired you and me," I said. "He needed our training, experience, and our ability to work closely with the Bureau on things like this."

Rita looked at the floor and I knew what she was thinking because I'd heard the scuttlebutt, too. Other Coast Guard officers were saying that Admiral Ballard had recruited a couple of FBI rejects to head up port security. Most of them didn't even know that I had graduated from the Coast Guard Academy in New London and did eight years active duty before leaving the Coast Guard for the FBI. Maybe they'd heard that Rita and I had been taken out of the field, put behind desks, and given dead-end jobs analyzing data. How could I even begin to explain to other Coast Guard officers the bureaucratic behemoth that is today's FBI? The Bureau is a quagmire of internal politics, private agendas, and personal empire building. However, in the end, Admiral Ballard knew he had to hire from outside to get experienced law enforcement personnel qualified to meet the expanding role of the Coast Guard.

Rita Velasco was a perfect example of the politics inside the FBI. She was blamed for the improper affair with her supervisor, Mike Dillon. The 'good old boys' at the Bureau just couldn't blame Dillon for taking up with her. Hell, she was young and gorgeous. It couldn't possibly be Dillon's fault; it had to be that she initiated the relationship and was trying to sleep her way into a promotion.

"You're not responsible for what happened to Bennet today," I said. "And as far as what happened between you and Dillon, I consider that water under the bridge."

"I know, but still..."

"Look, I worked with Admiral Ballard years ago when the Coast Guard was stealing the FBI's thunder on those drug busts off the Florida coast. The Bureau was under a lot of pressure from Congress because the Coast Guard was upstaging them. We were hitting them right in the old budget appropriations. Anyway, my point is this that Admiral Ballard's goal is to have the Coast Guard take the leading role in security of all the ports nationwide, and we're in on the ground floor. Forget about what happened when you were with the FBI and forget about Dillon. You've got a great career right here."

Rita nodded.

"The Admiral wants the port open by five o'clock today," I said. "Our orders are to keep all small craft at least a quarter-mile from inbound and outbound ships."

"We don't have enough boats or personnel to do that."

"I know. Concentrate on keeping civilian boats from loitering at the harbor entrance for now. The Admiral is talking to the Navy about getting a few ships to patrol a little farther offshore for us."

"I'll have to cancel days off and schedule some double shifts."

"Do what you have to do to cover it," I said. "There's something else."

"What?"

"There are probably more weapons somewhere in the harbor, and if that's the case, we need to find them before they're used again."

"Is that what you were talking to Dillon about? What did he say?"

"Not much, other than he thinks the attacks are just beginning."

Rita took a sip of coffee and thought for a moment. "I know some guys, longshoremen that work down on the docks. I went to high school with them and if any illegal arms came across the dock or are in a warehouse somewhere, they may have heard something."

"That's a start. See what you can find out," I said. "Look, I have a lot to do here, so…"

"Sure," she said, rising from her chair

"By the way, I need you to bring that harbor pilot in for an interview, the Admiral is livid because he brought the *Beleza* inside the breakwater."

"Do you want me to get him now?"

"The sooner we get his statement the better."

"I'll take care of it." She started for the door.

"One last thing…" I said, watching Rita's face to gauge her reaction. "They found the owner of that getaway van today. Turns out it belongs to a friend of yours. Astal Kamran."

Rita Velasco's jaw dropped.

4

Rita called my office to let me know she'd arrived with Captain Thomas Hannigan, the harbor pilot that brought the *Beleza* inside the breakwater this morning. On the way out of my office, Yeoman Jenkins handed me a priority weather advisory issued by the National Oceanographic and Air Administration detailing a developing storm that would be impacting high seas shipping. I didn't need a NOAA communiqué to tell me that late season hurricanes in the eastern North Pacific are typically the most violent. I knew the storms normally brewed at sea off the coast of Central America in the northern portion of the warm equatorial countercurrent and were caused by the annual change in seasons. The weather of the longer, warmer days in the southern hemisphere collided with the weather systems of the shorter, cooler days in the northern hemisphere and created an area of intense meteorological instability. On Friday afternoon, while the Santa Ana winds dominated the weather pattern in Southern California, the sea west of Costa Rica was hatching the most brutal hurricane of the season. Hurricane Kendra.

I knew where to find Captain Hannigan as soon as I heard Hard-Ass Harry's voice.

"As of this moment," thundered Admiral Ballard. "Your license is suspended!"

"You can't suspend my license without a hearing," protested Captain Hannigan. Without his Coast Guard issued pilot's license, I knew Captain Hannigan couldn't work.

"Your license is suspended until the hearing," Admiral Ballard said. "Then, your license will be revoked. Permanently!"

Hannigan sputtered and tried to object. He acted like he was being choked and tugged at the yellow tie he wore with his navy sports jacket, light-blue button down shirt, and gray slacks.

"The Coast Guard issued your license and the Coast Guard can suspend or revoke it as the circumstances dictate," explained Admiral Ballard. "You flagrantly violated a direct order by Lieutenant Velasco and your license is suspended on that basis."

Hannigan surrendered his license to a young ensign that stamped, *SUSPENDED,* across the front of the document and then handed it back.

"Ain't this just ducky," muttered Hannigan as he looked at his now worthless license.

"You might want to consider legal representation," suggested Admiral Ballard.

"Great."

"We're done here," Admiral Ballard said. "Commander Stanton has a few questions for you."

Hannigan's face was flushed with anger and the burns on the right side of his face were already crusted over yellow and orange. His lips were pursed together like he was getting ready to whistle and the muscles in his jaw undulated involuntarily, his blue eyes filled to the brim with indignation. I'd seen a lot of anger in my life and I could tell that Hannigan was a man about ready to go off.

Admiral Ballard had thrown his weight around and got away with it. I'd need to approach the harbor pilot with a little more care.

"Good afternoon, Captain," I said, thrusting a hand toward Hannigan. "I'm Jared Stanton. Port Security."

Hannigan was hesitant to shake hands, but I left my hand extended, waiting for him to respond.

"I'd like to thank you for coming in. Hopefully you can help us sort through exactly what happened this morning. We'll try to make this as quick as possible, I'm sure you have other things you'd rather be doing."

Hannigan's expression softened slightly with my somewhat gentler approach and he finally shook hands.

We walked down the corridor to my office without talking and after we sat down, I had Yeoman Jenkins bring us cans of cold root beer from the vending machine down the hall.

"Admiral Ballard can be a little abrupt," I said in my best calming tone that was cliché good cop, bad cop. "But every harbor in the country has been closed since this morning, and under the circumstances, I hope you can understand his actions."

It was almost time for the afternoon Task Force meeting and Hannigan's interview would have to wait. I hoped keeping him in my office would give him a chance to cool down a little before we tore him apart again.

"We've got a few questions we need to ask you about this morning's incident, we're still trying to piece together exactly what happened," I said. "We'll need a little more space than I have here because the FBI will be sitting in so I'll have to see if the conference room is available."

Hannigan's faced pinched again when I mentioned the FBI. "Do I need a lawyer?"

"I really don't think so, Captain Hannigan," I said, trying my best to keep him at ease. "Admiral Ballard did what he had to do, but our questioning is not going to be about whether your actions were right or wrong. You'll have a hearing at a later date. My focus is going to be on how and why the *Beleza* was attacked this morning."

"You're sure I don't need a lawyer?"

"This is a criminal investigation, Captain, so unless you are part of some criminal conspiracy or activity involving the *Beleza* this morning, I don't think you'll need a lawyer."

"Fine."

"Let me check on that conference room and we're waiting for the FBI investigators to show. Make sure to let Yeoman Jenkins know if he can get you anything else."

***

At precisely 1600 hours, Admiral Ballard commenced the Friday afternoon Task Force meeting that wasn't nearly as well attended as this morning's soiree. After another short pep talk in which he told everyone the situation was under control and that the harbor would be open within the hour, Admiral Ballard handed the meeting off to me again. He excused himself, saying he had another commitment.

I detailed the extra patrols outside the harbor and explained the quarter-mile safety zone for inbound and outbound ships. Dillon couldn't wait for his chance to talk and quickly gave an update on what the Bureau had learned so far. He informed the Task Force that several minor radical groups had claimed responsibility for the attack, but the Bureau didn't consider any of their claims to be credible. The owner of the minivan had been picked up for questioning, however the vehicle had been reported stolen ten days earlier and the suspect's alibi for Friday morning seemed to check out. As far as the speedboat, very little remained other than the cast iron engines. The fire, using gasoline as an accelerant, had been extremely effective in destroying the fiberglass hull and any other evidence. Identification numbers on the engine blocks indicated

General Motors had manufactured them and the history of the engines was presently being traced.

The meeting only took fifteen minutes and with little else on the agenda, I scheduled the next update for 0900 Saturday morning. When the conference room cleared, I sent Rita Velasco to bring Captain Hannigan from my office.

"So what's going on?" inquired Dillon.

"I'm bringing in the harbor pilot that was on the *Beleza,*" I said. "I can't wait to hear his explanation about what happened this morning."

"What do you know about him?"

"Not much, other than that Admiral Ballard just suspended his license. He looked pretty mad when I saw him and he's likely to be a little hostile. I've worked with these merchant marine types before. They seem to think the Coast Guard is out to get them and they're generally a little paranoid."

"Do you want me to run him through the computer and see what comes up?"

"I guess it wouldn't hurt."

Dillon turned to one of the junior agents standing behind him, whispered something, and the agent promptly left the room.

"Good afternoon again, Captain Hannigan," I said, advancing a firm handshake as Rita escorted him in. "Please make yourself comfortable. We have a few questions for you."

"Great, suspend my license, then ask questions," grumbled Hannigan.

"Please, have a seat," I said again when he remained standing. "Would you like a cup of coffee?"

"No," grunted Hannigan, taking a chair on my left near the head of the table.

Dillon slipped into a chair directly across from Hannigan.

"Please, Captain Hannigan, try to understand the urgency of this matter. I'm not here to judge your actions as a pilot, that's not my job. I'm with Port Security and I'm trying to find out if you have any information that can help us get to the bottom of the attack on the *Beleza*."

"Sure."

"This is Special Agent Dillon of the Federal Bureau of Investigation," I said. Dillon and Hannigan shook hands across the table, exchanging cautious acknowledgements.

"Be careful with those burns," I said to Hannigan in my good-cop voice. "They can be a lot of trouble."

Hannigan just nodded and looked impatient.

"Anyway, Captain Hannigan, if you could tell us about this morning, anything unusual or out of the ordinary. Any detail, no matter how small, may be significant," I said.

"Okay," he replied, retrieving a small black leather-bound notebook from the left breast pocket of his navy blue sports jacket.

I leaned back in my chair, trying to indicate to Hannigan that this would be a relaxed meeting.

Hannigan opened the notebook. A laminated card marked the page where an entry for the *Beleza* had been made. "Let's see what I've got."

I glanced at Dillon who sitting upright in his chair with his arms crossed against his chest, a hostile expression plastered across his face.

"*Beleza*. British flag," read Hannigan from the small black notebook. "Sixteen thousand horsepower diesel engine. She's six hundred and eighty-seven feet long and came into port with a deep draft of thirty-eight feet. I picked her up at the sea buoy and was scheduled to take her to Berth 164, port side alongside. Two tugs were assigned for docking and I boarded her at 0718."

"May I see that?" I asked.

"I didn't make any other entries after that," said Hannigan as he slid the book and bookmark to me. "It got kinda' wild."

"I'll bet," I said, thumbing through the small notebook. It was full details about ships Hannigan had piloted. Dates, times, places, vessel details. Pretty routine. The bookmark was one of Hannigan's business cards that had been laminated in plastic. On the backside of the card, laminated inside the plastic, was a feather. Unusual.

I passed the notebook and bookmark to Dillon.

"Did you notice a speedboat in the area?" I asked.

"Yes. As a matter of fact, I did." Hannigan paused and was deep in thought for a moment. "White hull with blue trim I think. Maybe red and blue trim. I didn't take much notice at the time."

"Nothing seemed unusual?" I asked.

"Well, it seemed funny to me at the time that a boat like that would be out that early on a Friday morning."

"What do you mean?"

"Well, it looked to me more like a Saturday or Sunday afternoon boat."

"A Saturday afternoon boat?"

"Yeah, kind of a sport boat, like one of those Cigarette-type ocean racers. Only smaller, maybe thirty feet long. You see a lot of them out on the weekends, usually in the afternoon when the weather is nice. They'll take a run over to Catalina Island, or maybe race each other."

"And that's unusual?" I asked.

"Sure."

"How so?"

"Sometimes I see commercial or private fishing boats out there in the morning, but boats like that aren't usually out that early in the day, especially during the week. That's all."

"Anything else unusual?"

"When I first saw the boat, it was crossing my bow from starboard to port. From my right to left," said Hannigan as he looked over at Dillon and paused. "I thought that might be a problem at first, but then they turned around and made a few circles. I figured one of them lost a hat or they'd dropped something over the side."

"How many people were in the boat?" I asked.

"Seems like I saw two guys, can't be sure, though."

"Just two?"

"Yeah, a guy driving, and another guy in the passenger's seat, maybe leaning over the side. That's all I remember seeing."

"Anybody else?"

"I don't recall seeing anybody else. As soon as I knew that the ship was going to clear them all right, I forgot about them. I got busy after that."

"Any unusual radio transmissions?"

"The radio frequencies are recorded in case of an accident."

"We have the recordings, I just wondered if anything seemed unusual to you."

"Other than what I've told you? No."

"What happened next?" I asked.

"Pretty routine, until the explosions."

"Did you realize that you were being fired on by rockets?"

"No. Not at all. The ship's captain thought that the pump room exploded and that seemed realistic to me."

"How about after the explosions? Anything unusual?"

"Are you kidding me? The whole damn thing was unusual."

"I can imagine," I said "But maybe you heard something on the radio, or saw a rocket fly by the wheelhouse and you could describe it. Maybe someone in the crew said something strange. Anything at all that struck you as unusual."

"Yeah, there was one thing I thought was a little unusual."

"What was that?"

"Flames."

"Flames?"

"Yeah, flames," Hannigan said. His eyes narrowed and he made a sweeping motion across his body. "Flames came in the starboard door, went all the way through the wheelhouse, and out the port door. That was unusual as hell."

One of Dillon's agents poked his head through the door and motioned to him.

"Maybe this is a good time to take a break," I said. "Captain Hannigan, are you sure we can't get you a cup of coffee?"

Hannigan rolled his eyes. "How long is this going to take?"

"Not long," I said, following Dillon into the corridor.

Dillon was already deep in conversation with the agent when I closed the conference room door.

"I want more on this," Dillon said. "Get Interpol on the line and tell them what we have here. We're going to need dates, times, names, all of it. Got it?"

The agent nodded, did an abrupt about-face and hurried down the corridor.

"What's going on?" I asked.

Dillon looked smug. "Looks like your Captain Hannigan has ties to the Irish Republican Army."

"What?"

"Yeah, he's red-flagged. His name popped right up. We're getting full details from Interpol, but we need to take a hard look at him."

"Hannigan?"

"Think about it," Dillon said. "Irish Republican Army, British tanker, the political turmoil in Ireland is heating up again. It's no secret that the IRA has been trying to bring outside political influence into their dispute. Hannigan pilots the ship in, it explodes, and then he ignores Coast Guard orders to turn around." Dillon raised his eyebrows at me.

"Somehow, I just can't see Hannigan being involved. He doesn't seem the terrorist type."

"And exactly what is the terrorist type?"

"Not Hannigan," I said. "Besides, I thought I thought the IRA had a truce with the British."

"Officially, maybe," Dillon said. "But there are still militant factions, authorized and unauthorized, that are still extremely active. If you were still with the Bureau you'd know that."

"I don't see it. And if you had Hannigan red-flagged in your system, why did you keep to yourself. We gave the guy a license to bring ships in and out of the harbor, hell, we're supposed to know every time he even gets a parking ticket."

Dillon just shrugged his shoulders. "We just got something else. Some old intelligence from the C.I.A."

"About what?" And what do you mean old intelligence?"

"About an arms sale that took place about four months ago. It included some shoulder fired anti-tank rockets and a vague reference to San Pedro Harbor."

"And I'm just now hearing about it? Who's been sitting on this? I never heard anything about it."

"I'll have to make a call and get the details. Seems someone passed the intelligence to the CIA and they sat on it, waiting for something else to reference it with. Apparently, the Agency didn't know if the intelligence was legitimate, so they didn't pass it along."

"Do they think arms sale and the *Beleza* attack are linked or not?"

"I don't know, I'll make the call after we finish with Hannigan," Dillon said. "I want to see his reaction when we link him with the IRA."

I followed Dillon back into the conference room. Rita Velasco, wearing a clean set of orange Sea Marshal coveralls, came in the conference room and sat on the other side of the table from Hannigan, leaving an empty chair between her and Dillon. She sipped hot black coffee from a large white ceramic mug.

I asked Hannigan a few more routine questions but he seemed irritated and didn't add anything substantial to what he'd already said. However, during the last set of questions, I did notice the eye contact between Hannigan and Rita. Sometimes Hannigan would look over at her and she would look down, pretending she hadn't been looking at him. I wasn't quite sure what to make of that. They had survived a tanker fire together this morning. Was that it or was there more going on?

As soon as I ran out of questions, I laid my pen on the table beside my notepad, signaling Dillon that it was his turn to question Hannigan.

"Captain Hannigan, I have a few things I hope you can clear up for me," Dillon said.

Hannigan rolled his eyes and slumped in his chair. He looked like a bored child in the principal's office.

"Do you know a John Hannigan?"

Hannigan grew alert.

Dillon waited.

"How about a Paul Hannigan or Jennie O'Leary?"

Hannigan sat up. Cleared his throat but didn't speak.

"Come now Captain, don't be coy. Sometimes I ask questions I already know the answers to." Dillon waited.

"Well, if you really did know the answers," Hannigan said, finally responding to Dillon. "You wouldn't be asking the questions."

"I might surprise you. So, do you know these people or not?"

"If you are talking about my uncle and cousins, then the answer is yes."

"See," Dillon said in a condescending tone. "Now we're getting somewhere."

"And just exactly where is this going?" Hannigan sat forward in his chair and looked uneasy.

"Are you aware of your family's ties to the Irish Republican Army?"

Hannigan didn't respond.

"Do you need me to repeat the question?" pressed Dillon.

"What does their business have to do with me?"

"Well, a British tanker was hit by rocket fire this morning. The IRA has been known to commit such acts of terrorism."

Hannigan's eyes narrowed.

"And you just so happened to be the harbor pilot on that British tanker," Dillon said. "I'm wondering if that was a coincidence."

Hannigan said nothing and wore a blank expression on his face.

"How familiar are you with your family's ties to the Irish Republican Army?" asked Dillon.

"I consider it their business. They don't consult me, I don't offer advice."

"How about assistance?"

"What are you saying?"

"Are you involved with the Irish Republican Army, Captain Hannigan?"

Hannigan stood up. His face was red and pinched, his jaws flexed involuntarily.

"What are you saying?" blurted Hannigan. "That you think I'm some sort of Irish suicide bomber?"

"Please sit down, Captain Hannigan," I said.

"I think I'm done here!" Hannigan said, piercing me with his blue eyes. "I came in to answer a few questions and I now I'm accused of being a suicide bomber." Hannigan grabbed his notebook from the table and moved toward the door.

An FBI agent that had been standing in the corridor moved to the doorway and blocked Hannigan's exit.

"Please sit down, Captain Hannigan," I said again.

"Am I under arrest?" Hannigan's eyes were narrow dark holes, his face flushed crimson.

Dillon and I looked at each other.

"Not at this time, Captain," I said. "But I wish you would sit down so we can finish."

"If I'm not under arrest, this is finished! Admiral Ballard suggested I get legal representation. Now I know what he was talking about."

I stood up up. "Please, Captain…"

"I'll tell you something," snarled Hannigan. "If you're looking to hang this on me, you're barking up the wrong tree. You guys don't have a clue who did this! You have nothing!"

Hannigan glared at the FBI agent in the doorway, muscled his way past, and marched down the corridor toward the exit.

"Well now…" I said. "It appears our Captain Hannigan is a little touchy about his family history."

5

"Admiral Ballard was just on the five o'clock news." Dillon was standing in the doorway to my office, leaning against the jamb.

"Is that right?" I pushed aside the thick stack of phone messages I'd been working my way through without much progress.

"He must know something we don't know," Dillon said. "He announced that we're close to resolving the *Beleza* incident and that the harbor is already open again."

"That's good news. He must have heard you've got Astal Kamran in custody."

"Are you interested in taking a ride?"

"Where?" I asked.

"Manhattan Beach."

"What's in Manhattan Beach?"

"The owner of the boat used in this morning's attack?"

"You tracked the engine numbers already?"

"Sure, but we had a little help. The San Pedro Police Department had a boat owner report his boat stolen from Cabrillo Marina last Sunday and the California Department of Motor Vehicles lists engine serial numbers for all boat titles. It wasn't too hard to compare the list of stolen boats with the DMV data."

It was clear to me that the FBI was way ahead of the Coast Guard on this one. Hell, I was still trying to return phone calls from this morning and Dillon's crew had already made significant progress tracking the boat used in the attack. I wasn't sure why Dillon was including me on this instead of keeping all the information to himself. The Bureau is pretty territorial when it comes to sharing credit and it instills the same philosophy in its agents. I didn't trust Dillon as far as I could throw him and figured that it had something to do with Rita or the possibility that I had something he needed and he was just trying to stay on my good side.

I grabbed my cell phone and stood up. "Your car or mine?"

The black Ford Expedition careened through rush hour toward Manhattan Beach while I braced myself in the back seat and Dillon tapped on his laptop computer in the front passenger seat. One of Dillon's clones, probably fresh out of the Bureau's offensive driving school, was behind the wheel.

"Here's what we have on the boat owner," Dillon said, reading from the computer screen. "His name is William Hansen, 44 years old, six-foot, 200 pounds, brown hair, brown eyes, lives at 432 Pacifico Azule in Manhattan Beach. He owns an auto body repair shop, married, two teenage daughters, fifteen and seventeen. He has a yellow 2007 Corvette convertible, a blue 2008 Chevy Tahoe, and a red 2008 Mustang GT that is probably the oldest daughter's since she has three tickets in it. There's also a new black Jaguar that his wife is probably driving."

"What about the boat?" I asked.

"We checked the engine numbers and it's the boat we're looking for. It was a 2005 twenty-eight-foot Donzi, twin 300 horsepower Chevrolet engines. That thing should have run at least 75 miles-per-hour."

When we drove up, William Hansen was standing in the driveway of the large blue and white metal sided building that served as his body shop. He had a clipboard in hand and was giving a middle-aged brunette woman a repair estimate on her red Porsche 928 with moderate front-end damage. The neighborhood was semi-industrial with a carpet and flooring store on one side and a wholesale plumbing supply on the other. After Dillon flashed his identification, Hansen quickly finished up the Porsche estimate and escorted us to his office near the rear of the building. It was late and most of the employees had cleared out for the day. The interior of the shop had about fifteen workstations with vehicles in various stages of repair. Body-filler dust mixed with cleaning solvents and the smell of wet acrylic paint hung in the air like a toxic cloud. A lone employee continued to hammer out a dented front fender on a late model Dodge convertible as we walked past. Near the office, a high school aged kid with baggy pants and a backwards baseball cap pushed a broad stiff bristled broom that sent dust billowing ahead of it.

Hansen had Labrador Retriever brown eyes, leathery skin from too much time in the sun and perfect teeth that were very white. "This must be about my boat," he said as he sat in his black leather high-back office chair and motioned us into the chrome and black plastic covered chairs stationed in front of his desk. A mound of paperwork covered with a dense layer dust obscured his workspace. Car parts in cardboard boxes filled the corners and several calendars with bikini-clad women were strategically hung on the walls.

"What makes you think this is about your boat?" Dillon asked.

"He's with the Coast Guard, I recognize the uniform. Why else would the FBI and the Coast Guard be in my office unless it was about my boat?"

Dillon was silent for a moment before he opened a manila file folder and casually looked at the contents. I glanced over and could see that the folder contained a copy of the theft report taken by the

San Pedro Police and a half-dozen or so photographs of the burned out boat on the beach.

"We found your boat for you," Dillon said as he handed William Hansen one of the photographs.

"Holy shit!" William Hansen said, his eyes wide as he looked at the picture. "Are you sure this is my boat?"

"That's your boat," Dillon said. "And it was used in the attack on a tanker outside San Pedro Harbor this morning."

We were both carefully watching William Hansen's reaction to the news about his boat.

"Are you shitting me?"

"The FBI doesn't shit anybody, Mr. Hansen." Dillon said. "I can assure you of that."

"How…why? I don't understand…"

Dillon studied the police report for a moment. "You reported your boat stolen on Sunday?"

"Yes, sir." William Hansen's demeanor had suddenly changed to submissive.

Dillon glanced over at me. He'd noticed it as well.

"Were you behind on the payments?" Dillon asked.

"What? No. Why?"

"It's a question we always ask in a situation like this," Dillon said. "It's common for an owner to be behind on the payments or just want to get out from under the debt so he makes his boat disappear and collects the insurance. You did have insurance didn't you, Mr. Hansen?"

"Of course I had insurance and no I wasn't behind on the payments."

"Why were you selling the boat?"

"What does that have to do with anything?"

"Mr. Hansen, twelve people are dead and millions of dollars of damage were sustained in the harbor this morning and your boat was used in that vicious attack. We're trying to determine how your boat got into the hands of those perpetrators. You can answer our questions here and now or you can put on a set of handcuffs and take a ride. The decision is yours."

"I'm sorry, I just don't see why I'm selling the boat has anything to do with what happened."

Dillon waited for a moment and when William Hansen didn't answer he nodded to his clone that was standing near the door. The clone took a set of handcuff from inside his jacket and started across the room.

"Okay, okay," William Hansen said. "That shit isn't even necessary, I'm selling the boat because I wasn't using it much anymore. It was a family toy, my daughters used to like to ride in it and liked to go fast, but they're older now. Hanging out on the weekends with their father isn't cool anymore, they want to spend time with their friends, that's all."

"That's all?" Dillon asked.

"That's all. I wasn't using it and the slip rental is close to six hundred dollars a month, plus insurance, and then gas at the marina is over five bucks a gallon and that thing sucks gas like it's going out of style."

"How long have you had it up for sale?"

"A couple of months."

"Anybody looking at it?"

"A few people, but I'll be honest, with the price of gas these days, I haven't had a lot of interest." William Hansen looked at the photograph of his boat again. "Wait a minute, you don't think I had anything to do with that tanker this morning do you? I saw it on the news this morning, but I didn't know my boat was involved."

Dillon's cell phone buzzed and he checked the text message. He didn't respond to William Hansen's last question, instead he said, "I'll need a list of the people that looked at your boat."

"I'll have to find my notes, it might take awhile."

Dillon handed him a business card. "Call me with names and phone numbers when you get the list put together," he said and then stood up to leave.

"By the way, Mr. Hansen," I said. "I was wondering why you kept your boat at Cabrillo Marina. Isn't King Harbor closer? Or even Marina Del Rey?"

Hansen blinked and pursed his mouth unconsciously.

"I don't know," he said. "I guess Cabrillo was just more convenient, and it has nicer facilities."

"Okay," I said. "I was just wondering."

Dillon motioned me toward the door.

"One more thing," I said. "What was the range on that boat with the tanks full of gas?"

"I don't know. Maybe about 150 miles if you took it easy, more like 40 or 50 if you we're getting on it."

William Hansen escorted us out of his body shop and back to the parking lot.

"Where are we going now?" I asked when we were back in the black Ford and had the doors closed..

"Cabrillo Marina," Dillon said. "I had a couple of my guys check it out and they're keeping a couple of employees after work so we can talk to them. What did you think of Hansen?"

"More convenient to keep his boat in San Pedro? I don't think so," I said. "Since when is a forty-five minute longer drive in traffic more convenient? There's something he's not telling us."

"That's exactly what I'm thinking," Dillon said.

To get to Cabrillo Marina we took Pacific Coast Highway through Hermosa Beach and Redondo, and then drove along the coast on winding Palos Verdes Drive. Near Point Vicente, I could see the outline of Catalina Island, some twenty-six miles distant. The indigo-blue sea was flat calm and lily-white cumulus clouds lingered where the water kissed the sky.

When we finally stepped out of the black Expedition at Cabrillo Marina, the sky overhead was almost blue again and the sun hung above the sea like a giant reddish-gold ball. The faint aroma of the beach told me that the Santa Ana condition was weakening. The return of the nurturing marine layer was an innuendo that danced on the breeze.

Cabrillo Marina is named for Juan Rodriquez Cabrillo, the Spanish explorer that in 1542 led the first European expedition to explore the west coast of what is now the United States. The area's abundant palm trees go nicely with the white stucco and red tiled roofed buildings that are in keeping with the local Spanish theme. The marina, home to more than 300 yachts, is on the lee side of San Pedro Hill that shelters it from the prevailing westerly winds that often reach gale force in the afternoon and is protected from ocean swells by a massive stone Federal breakwater. Fort MacArthur Military Reservation borders the marina to the west. The fort is minimally manned these days, but during World War Two, the facility was strategic to the defense of the commercial harbor and stored ammunition for the gun emplacements on San Pedro Hill. To the east of the marina is the coal terminal at Berth 49. Much to the dismay of everyone in the area, copious amounts of black soot settles over the yachts, palm trees, and buildings every time a ship loads at the berth.

The pretty girl behind the desk in the marina office had long brown hair, doe eyes, and three piercings in each ear to go with her pierced tongue. She didn't look old enough to be out of high school. She looked bored when we first walked in but perked right up and it was obvious that she was very impressed with Special Agent Dillon of the Federal Bureau of Investigation.

"I'll pull the file," she said, fluttering her eyelashes. She used long strides and too much hip on her way to the file cabinet.

Dillon and his clone exchanged acknowledgements and smirks.

"Here it is. Slip E-8. The boat's name is 'Why Not', a twenty-eight foot Donzi. They had a thirty-five foot slip," she said, sliding the file across the counter toward Dillon, leaning in so she could look at it with him.

"Why would he have a thirty-five foot slip for a twenty-eight foot boat?" Dillon asked. "Don't you charge rent by the foot?"

"Yes, we charge for the boat length or the slip length, whichever is longer," she said, leaning even closer to Dillon. "I don't know why they rented a thirty five footer, it doesn't say anything about it here. Maybe that's all that was available at the time they moved their boat here."

"When did they move the boat here?" I asked.

"June," she said. She giggled and gave Dillon a come hither look. "That's my name, June."

Dillon repaid her with his patented smile.

"What marina did they move the boat from?" I asked.

"We don't keep track of that."

"Who is Paul Hansen?" Dillon asked, reading from the file.

June leaned in closer and looked at where Dillon was pointing with his finger.

"That's the guy that's been paying the slip rental," she said.

Dillon gave her a confused look.

"The only reason I know him is because he comes in and pays cash for the slip rental. Most other people just send us a check in the mail, except when they're late, then they come in person. But hardly anybody else pays with cash. They always write a check or use a credit card."

Dillon smiled at June.

"Cash?" I asked.

"Yeah, he always has a roll of bills in his pocket. He must have a couple of thousand dollars on him when he comes in here."

Dillon motioned to his clone and pointed to the information in the file. The agent wrote Paul Hansen's name and address in his notebook and went to the car to run it on the computer.

June walked us down to the dock and showed us where 'Why Not' had been moored. Trash blown into the water by the Santa Ana winds floated in the empty slip. Mooring lines, with one end made fast to their cleats, had been cast off the missing boat and left dangling in the water.

By the time we returned to the marina office, Dillon's man had the information on Paul Hansen written on a note pad. Paul Hansen turned out to be a used car salesman from Long Beach with two arrests for driving under the influence and three arrests for misdemeanor possession of controlled substances. He was also William Hansen's half-brother.

"Looks like we should pay him a visit," Dillon said.

"Funny he didn't mention his brother," I replied.

Dillon asked June for a list of people keeping their boats at the marina. It took her a few minutes to print out a copy of the file and then she handed it to him with a smile and a fluttering of eyelashes.

"You're a piece of work," I said when we walked out of the marina office. "Don't you ever quit?"

Dillon agreed to drop me off back at the Coast Guard base while he had his clones checked out Paul Hansen in person. I was going over the tenant list from the marina while Dillon played on his computer in the front seat.

"I wonder what real the range is on that Donzi?" mused Dillon. "With extra fuel tanks the Hansen boys might be making jaunts down to Mexico on the weekend. Maybe to smuggle a few kilos of weed or run a few guns."

"Well, well, well," I said. "Look what I found."

"What's that?" Dillon turned around and faced me in the back seat.

"Hansen's boat was stolen from slip 'E-8'. Guess who has a boat in 'F-7'?"

"Tell me."

"According to this marina map," I said. "It's almost directly across from the 'Why Not'."

"I give up," Dillon said. "Who is it?"

"Captain Thomas Hannigan."

6

The frozen fried-chicken dinner had been in the microwave oven for less than a minute when my doorbell rang.

"I thought you might like to get a beer," Dillon said.

"Shit, now you know where I live." I held the door open but kept Dillon on the front porch.

"Well? Do you want to get a beer?"

"Drinking muddles my already poor judgment. What do you want?"

"I have a few things I want to talk to you about. I could get a beer and you could have something milder," he offered.

"I don't feel like going out. What do you want to talk about?"

"Come on, Jared, it's Friday night. Live a little."

"I don't know how to tell you this, Dillon," I said. "But I really don't like you very much."

"All right, I did a few things I'm not very proud of, I'll give you that, but that was years ago. How long are you going to hold a grudge?"

"It's not a grudge. I just don't trust you because you've always got an angle you're playing."

Dillon counterfeited an innocent expression like he couldn't believe what he'd just heard. "What do you want from me?"

"Straight answers, for one thing."

"Like what?"

"You never did tell me what you were working on and how you got out here so fast," I said. "I know you were undercover on something. What's the big secret?"

"I can't tell you."

"Have it your way." I started to close the door in his face.

"Okay, okay," he said. "I'll tell you."

Dillon stood frozen on the front porch and I opened the door a little more.

"I'm not supposed to say anything, so you didn't hear this from me." Dillon looked down and considered what he was going to say. "Have you heard about the civilian vigilante groups guarding the Mexican border?"

"What about them?"

"It started in Arizona a couple of years ago and now it's spreading to California. The people in Arizona weren't very happy with the job the Border Patrol was doing, they felt the illegals were draining state financial resources, so they organized themselves into vigilante groups and started to protect the border by turning Mexican Nationals back."

"And so?"

"So the vigilante groups are arming themselves and the Border Patrol got concerned and asked the Bureau to check it out."

"You're telling me the Bureau assigned a team from the Domestic Security Task Force to investigate a bunch of American vigilantes at the border?"

Dillon nodded.

"And that's what you were working undercover on?"

"I was in San Diego when I got the call about the *Beleza*, that's how I got up here so fast. Can I buy you a beer now?"

"Nah."

"I have a few other things I want to talk to you about," he said. "I've made a few phone calls. Since we're not going out, are you going to invite me in?"

"Keep talking."

"Homeland Security wants to send a couple of their people out here from Washington and I need to talk to you about Admiral Ballard." Dillon paused and weighed his next words carefully. "Look, Jared, we're working together on this thing whether you like me or not, you're just making things harder by being stubborn."

You can't always pick the people you work with and I knew it. I might have to work with Dillon, but I still didn't trust him. Curiosity and a sense of duty got the better of me so I opened the front door and motioned him inside.

My place was modest by Huntington Beach standards. It was an older ranch style house and the living room had a built-in fireplace with a massive wooden mantle, dating the house to the late 1940's or 50's, before air pollution regulations in the Los Angeles basin when fires could still be used to provide warmth in the winter months. Since I live alone, my place is pretty barren. Near the fireplace, along the far wall, I have a well worn but serviceable brown naugahyde recliner from Goodwill that faces a small television and a DVD player that sits on a coffee table under the front window.

The microwave was still humming in the kitchen and I went to shut it off.

"Do you want something to drink?" I hollered as I extracted chicken platter. When I poked at the chicken with a finger I found it soggy and lukewarm. The mashed potatoes looked like something the dog did on the carpet.

Dillon didn't answer and I heard the old wood floor creak. Opposite the front door, just off the living room, are the bathroom and two small bedrooms. One bedroom is where I sleep and the other set up as an exercise room. When I came out of the kitchen I caught Dillon snooping around.

"Do you want something to drink?"

"How about a beer?"

"I don't have beer."

"What do you have?"

"Not much. Water, tea…orange juice."

"Orange juice."

Dillon walked over and surveyed the large wooden desk that filled the small alcove next to the kitchen. The desk, also from Goodwill, held the telephone, my unopened bills, car keys, and a couple of month's worth of dust. There were two framed photographs almost completely obscured by stacks of paper.

"You're kind of nosey."

"Sorry. Habit I guess."

"Ice?"

"Sure."

 "So, you wanted to talk about the Admiral?"

Dillon touched the framed photographs. One was a wedding picture of Elisha and me; the other was of Elisha reclining in the bow of my grandfather's rowboat.

"Here you go," I said, offering him the glass of orange juice and turning the photographs face down. "Come on in the kitchen and have a seat. I don't have much furniture in the living room yet."

My kitchen isn't much either. There's a small wooden table with four chairs in one corner. The turquoise tile on the countertop was popular during the era the house was built. The dirty dishes in the sink are as recent as last week but the refrigerator and gas range are genuine antiques.

"Nice place," he said. "Do you rent or own?"

"Rent," I said as I sat the chair that left my back to the wall. "I can't afford to buy around here." I wasn't particularly fond of the house, but it was in a quiet neighborhood and less than fifteen miles from the Coast Guard base. So far, the reasons to move hadn't outweighed the reasons to stay.

Dillon sat with his back to the counter, looking into the living room.

"How long have you lived in Huntington Beach?"

"Since I moved out here a couple of years ago," I said. "You told me that you wanted to talk about the Admiral."

"Sure, among other things."

"Look, if you're here to talk about you and Rita, forget it. I don't want to hear any sad stories about how you still love her and she should give you another chance. Tell it to your shrink."

Dillon tried not to look wounded by my comment.

"What about the Admiral?"

Dillon paused, started to talk, and hesitated once again before finally speaking.

"I just think it's odd that he is heading up the task force, that's all," he said. "I mean...the Bureau has superior resources. The Coast Guard's investigative resources are limited at best."

"Maybe," I said. "But it has nothing to do with resources. It has to do with politics."

"You didn't hear this from me, but some of the people at Bureau feel he's too much of a cowboy."

"Meaning?"

"They think he's reckless, that he shoots first and asks questions later."

"I think *they* might be a little bent out of shape because the Coast Guard has jurisdiction and *they* get to play second fiddle on this thing."

"Well, I think the investigation is going to be hurt by having the Admiral in charge."

"The Admiral won't hurt the investigation. It's too important, he'll stay out of the way and leave the work to us."

"What do you mean?"

"You're a smart boy. Think about it," I said. "Admiral Ballard wants to be the next Commandant of the Coast Guard. He sees this as his ticket."

"And what if it doesn't turn out the way he hopes?"

"He'll blame it on the Bureau and CIA."

"He'd never…"

"Let me tell you a little bit about Admiral Ballard," I said, swirling the orange juice in my glass. "He was a legend at the Coast Guard Academy, he played football there."

Dillon leaned back in his chair and sipped his drink.

"I was assigned to a cutter in Florida and the captain of that ship played football at the Academy with Admiral Ballard." I said. "This guy played on the offensive line and told me the story. He said one day this scrawny, raw-boned kid showed up to practice. The coach said the kid was going to play defensive end and the captain just laughed. He said he outweighed the kid by eighty pound or so, and on the first play from scrimmage, he knocked Ballard on his ass."

"So Admiral Ballard played football," Dillon said. "I'm not impressed, a lot of guys played football in college."

"He said he tried to help Ballard get up, but Ballard didn't want his help," I said, ignoring Dillon's comment. "Ballard just gave him a dirty look, and on the next play, Ballard had this guy on *his* ass."

Dillon looked impatient.

"My point is this," I said. "The guy told me that Ballard didn't look like much of a football player the first day he met him, but Ballard put on a little weight, some muscle, and he ended up as small-college All-American. Ballard's got heart, and you don't want to be between him and what he wants. You'll end up on your ass."

Dillon was silent.

"What do you make of the interview with Hannigan?" I asked, signaling the end of our discussion about Admiral Ballard.

"Odd," Dillon said. "And I got a little more information on him. It turns out he's been to Northern Ireland five times in the last two years, and maybe some more times we don't know about. His uncle, John Hannigan, has been in prison in England and is known to be well connected to the trade of illegal arms."

"What do you make of the feather he had for a book mark?"

"I don't know. I've never seen anything like that. Could it be some sort of Native American thing?"

"Could be, but I don't think it fits."

"I'll have one of my guys look into it and see what he can come up with," he said. "There must be some significance to it. Why else would he have it enclosed in plastic?"

"Or we could just ask Hannigan and see what he has to say."

"That's a thought. But would he be honest?"

"Why wouldn't he be?"

"He failed to mention that he has a boat in the same marina and across the slip from the Donzi used in today's attack."

"Maybe he didn't know about it."

"I don't believe in coincidences."

"How about Rita and Astal Kamran?" I said. "I know this conversation is going there sooner or later. Let's clear the air right now."

Dillon was silent.

"Look, I know thousands of people and I deal with new people every day," I said. "I've known people that got murdered, people that got killed in car wrecks, people that cheated the IRS and went to prison. That doesn't mean that I had anything to do with any of it. Hannigan works in the harbor and has a sailboat. A boat was used in the attack this morning and that boat was in the same marina. Maybe it's coincidence and maybe it isn't. Rita went to UCLA Law School, but then again, a lot of people went to UCLA Law School. Just because somebody she went to school with had his van stolen doesn't mean she's involved. We have to separate these things out."

"You're conveniently forgetting that Hannigan has family ties to the IRA and that Rita's been talking to Astal Kamran on the phone."

"Hell, Dillon, I've got three brothers on the East Coast and I don't have anything to do with what they're involved in...and I grew up with them. You're talking about Hannigan's uncle in the old country. There may be something to it, but I think it's a reach. As far as Rita's concerned, you even said yourself that you weren't looking at Astal Kamran as a suspect but some of the people he represents, and this may come as a big shock to you, but defense lawyers often have dealings with criminals and immigration attorneys deal with foreigners."

Dillon started to say something but I could tell by the expression on his face that he changed his mind.

"What else have you got for me?" I asked.

"I made a call and got more information about that arms sale. It turns out the initial report was from Israeli intelligence. They were monitoring arms sales to the Palestinians and came across some SEP DARD 120's, French anti-tank rockets."

"Anti-tank rockets?"

Dillon nodded.

"The DARD is able to breach the front armor of a main battle tank so the hull of a ship would be a piece of cake," he said. "They think that these are some of the munitions that were shipped out of Iraq after the fall of Saddam and made their way to Syria. Intelligence reports show that once the munitions got into Syria and out to the coast, they could move almost anywhere in the world undetected. A lot of those arms are still being funneled back into Iraq, but some went up for sale on the open market. "

"Bad news."

"Yeah. But there was something interesting about the sale," he said. "The buyer of the SEP DARDS wasn't one of the usual players the Israelis watch. He was dressed like a Palestinian, but had some sort of a European accent, or maybe Baltic. The report also made reference to there being twenty-eight rockets and several hundred kilos of explosives."

"Twenty-eight rockets? That means there's definitely more out there somewhere!"

"That's what I'm saying."

"Twenty-eight rockets is kind of an odd number isn't it? And what makes you think they came from Iraq instead of somewhere else?"

"The number is odd, and the seller was Syrian so that's why we're thinking they were originally Iraqi."

"You said the seller was Syrian?"

"Yeah. We know the French had been selling arms to Iraq before the war. The rockets probably came from some of the Iraqi Republican Guard that fled to Syria. A lot of that stuff has been showing up lately, mostly in Africa though."

"Anything else?"

"Yeah, there where some vague references to San Pedro Harbor. The report didn't specify if San Pedro the target or a shipping point."

"Where were the rockets coming from?"

"The buy was made in Algeria, the port city of Arzew. It's near Oran. The French have been out of Algeria for years, but some of the old arms dealers still have connections on the continent. Israeli Intelligence lost an agent on this one, but passed along what they knew to the C.I.A."

"Algeria?" I asked. "How long ago?"

"Four months ago."

"And that's it? Nothing else?"

"Not until this morning when the *Beleza* got hit by rocket fire."

"You said the buyer was European? Are you thinking he's Irish?"

"Could've been," he said, finishing the last of his orange juice. "Who knows? But it puts a different twist on Hannigan's actions today, doesn't it?"

Dillon rattled the ice in his glass and I went to the refrigerator for more juice.

"They're really pushing me to make something out of the guy with the minivan," Dillon said.

"Astal Kamran? Why?"

"It works. He's an Iranian lawyer that represents detainees and illegal immigrants."

"I suppose it doesn't hurt that he's Iranian…and you know how the administration is looking to hang something on Iran, even though I'll bet you that most of Kamran's clients are from Mexico and Asia."

"Turns out this guy loaned out the minivan a lot. My guys talked to the parking lot attendants. Kamran kept his van in a commercial lot near his office and paid for parking by the month. The attendants said that other people have driven the van in the past. Kamran could have loaned it out, then when it went bad, reported it stolen."

"Went bad? What do you mean?"

"Well, suppose he lent the minivan to a client, something illegal happened, and when he found out about it, he reported the van stolen so he could distance himself and not appear to be involved as an accessory."

"I don't know," I said. "The guy is a lawyer, a UCLA graduate for crying out loud. He's got to be smarter than that."

"What did Rita say about him?"

"Not much. She told me that she knew him from law school and they used to study together. She's talked to him a few times since she came back here from the East Coast. They've been to dinner a few times, as old friends. She seemed shocked that he was involved because she knows that he loves this country, and she can't imagine him doing anything to hurt people. Supposedly, he believes in the American way of life, especially the freedom and opportunity he has here, and that's why he's helping the people he represents. He thinks they're not getting a fair shake."

"Saving the down-trodden. A real patriot," he said and then snickered softly. "Rita can be naïve sometimes."

"Don't start that shit now, you've been doing good."

"Anyway," he said, changing the subject away from Rita. "There's a lot of political pressure to solve this thing quickly."

"Get to the truth quickly or hang it on some poor sucker quickly? Like maybe somebody from Iran? That would be convenient."

"What are you saying?"

"You said there was a lot of pressure to solve this quickly," I said. "That could be for one of two reasons. First of all, they may want to get who is really behind the attack so more of the same doesn't happen. The other reason they might want to wrap this up fast is that they can conveniently blame somebody before a detailed investigation is completed."

"You make it sound like some sort of government conspiracy. You're not one of those people that thinks our government brought down the World Trade Center buildings just to blame terrorists are you?"

"That's not what I'm saying. You told me the Bureau thinks Ballard is a cowboy, but it sounds to me like the Bureau has a posse ready to lynch the first person that even looks remotely guilty. I'm just wondering why the big hurry."

"Maybe to prevent more attacks?"

"To do that you have to get the right people and the rest of the rockets. I get the feeling that it's politically expedient to hang Astal Kamran for this and blame Iran."

"I don't see it that way. The Bureau wants to stop more attacks and we're going to press hard on anybody involved, that's all."

"That's all? Aren't people in this country getting a little tired of our politicians crying wolf? Sooner or later, people want to see a wolf, and I'm guessing Astal Kamran is that wolf?"

It was obvious my comments rubbed Dillon the wrong way.

"So, if you have a theory on this, what is it?" he asked. "Or is it just an act of terrorism? Pure and simple."

"Obviously it's terrorism of some sort. But to figure who and why, you're going to have to look at the big picture."

"Meaning what?"

"Global transportation. Six hundred billon dollars a year worth of commerce flows through Southern California ports. The Panama Canal is obsolete now, that's why we gave it away. They use the land bridge instead of the Panama canal."

"Land bridge? What do you mean?"

"If you want to ship a television set from Japan to Europe, you put it in a container and send it by ship to San Pedro where you take it off the ship and put it on a train. The train takes the container across the United States and then on the East Coast it's put on another ship going to Europe. It's faster and cheaper that way. They have a land bridge across the United States, there's no need for a canal in Panama anymore."

Dillon thought about it.

"Remember several years ago, when the Pacific Shipping Association locked out the longshoremen on the West Coast?" I asked. "There was a labor contract dispute over automating terminal facilities."

"I remember. It made national and international news for weeks," he said "The White House finally had to step in and end it. The ports were only closed for ten days, but it cost billons of dollars and cargo was backed up for months."

"That's right."

"So, you think somebody saw what happened then and decided to do this?" he asked. "Are you saying that you think they tried to shut down San Pedro Harbor by blowing up a tanker at the entrance?"

"That would be my guess."

Dillon silently considered what I'd just said.

"So, if you're right, we have the how and why. Economic terrorism by attacking ships coming into our harbors," he said. "All we need now is who?"

"There's something about today's rocket attack that's been bothering me," I said.

"What's that?"

"How does a speedboat pull up alongside a ship the size of the *Beleza*, fire four rockets, and then manage to only hit it twice? Those rockets were fired from pretty much point-blank range."

Dillon shrugged his shoulders. "I don't know."

"Me either."

Dillon looked at his watch and stood up. "Thanks for the orange juice."

"Don't mention it."

"Mind if I use your toilet before I go?"

"Right through there," I said. "But you already know where it is."

Dillon glanced in the bedrooms before closing the bathroom door.

When he came back to the kitchen he asked, "Are you sure you don't want to go out for a beer?"

"I thought you had to be somewhere else."

Dillon walked out on the front porch and I held the door. He hesitated, turned, and started to say something.

"Don't even say anything about her." I closed the door in Dillon's face and watched through the small window in my front door until he drove off.

After I was sure Dillon was gone, I went to the desk to stand Elisha's pictures up again. Something inside me died the day she passed on. The shrinks tell me it's okay, that I'm still grieving. But I'm not sure how much longer I can live life just going through the motions. More days than not it is almost too much work to breathe. The pills help a little on especially bad days but I don't like how they make me feel, my mood improves but I feel sluggish and tired.

Why did I put her pictures facedown when Dillon was looking at them? Why didn't I want him to look at her?

I jumped when the phone rang and grabbed it before it could ring a second time.

"Are you busy, Commander?" asked Rita Velasco.

"I was just going to eat dinner," I said, putting Elisha's rowboat picture back where it belonged. "Why?"

"This afternoon you said there might be more rockets in the harbor and told me to check it out. I've been talking to one of the security guys down here and there's something I think we should check into."

"Where are you?"

"Berth 224," she said. "The Malaysia-Pacific Container Terminal."

7

It was half past ten and I was sitting in the front seat of a white Ford pickup truck with Rita Velasco and Eddie Taylor, an old high school friend of hers, eating burritos and guacamole from the Mayan Café, occasionally taking a sip of tepid black coffee that he poured into our foam cups from a large stainless steel thermos bottle he kept on the floorboard.

The high-pressure area over the desert had moved eastward, taking the arid winds with it, and the resurgent marine layer hung like a silvery veil over the halogen light standards inside the Malaysia-Pacific container terminal. The impudent dampness sought out every crack and crevice in the seaport, turning the residual layer of desert dust to dank grime. Foghorns that marked the main shipping channel bleated mournfully like lost sheep, their signals reverberating up and down the rows and stacks of shipping containers on the dock, the sound being scattered in a hundred different directions at once.

Eddie had backed the Malaysia-Pacific security truck into the shadowy southeast corner of the container terminal so we could watch the chain link fence in two different directions during his scheduled dinner break. He shut the motor off but left the rotating amber beacon on top of the truck going so he could advertise our presence and it cast an eerie glow in the fog-darkened corner of the shipping terminal.

When I'd met her at the front gate, Rita briefed me on Eddie Taylor. She explained how they'd grown up in the same Torrance neighborhood and were once close friends, but they hadn't seen a lot of each other since high school. She explained how she'd gone to college while Eddie went to work on the docks as a longshoreman. They would sometimes run into each other in the old neighborhood over the holidays, but they'd been out of touch for the last several years until they met up again at the Renaissance Fair in Hermosa Beach this summer. They caught up on old times and promised not to be strangers now that they'd found each other, but of course, that didn't happen. Rita knew Eddie was working security on the docks but had to call his parent's house to get his cell phone number.

The reflection of the rotating amber beacon oddly illuminated Eddie Taylor's slightly feminine facial features. He wore his blue security officer uniform, black steel-toe work boots, and blue nylon jacket with the Malaysia-Pacific security logo. A white baseball cap with the same security logo was jauntily pushed back on his head.

Rita wolfed down the last of her burrito and wadded up the paper wrapper before putting it in the right-hand pocket of her black suede jacket. She'd changed out of her regular Coast Guard uniform and was dressed in dark civilian clothes and a pair of black Tony Llama cowboy boots.

"You don't mind working nights all the time?" she asked Eddie.

Eddie swallowed another bite of his burrito.

"Nah, kind of used to it now," he said.

Rita drummed her fingers on the dashboard.

"I'm going home when everyone else is going to work," he added. "I kind of like that."

"Are you getting anti-social in your old age?" she joked.

"No. It's just that it makes me feel like I'm getting away with something. Kind of like ditching school and going surfing."

"Ditching school?" she laughed. "That takes me back."

"Yeah, don't tell me you never ditched school?"

Rita laughed harder and shook her head.

"Really?" he asked. "No wonder you always had good grades."

"If I remember correctly," she said. "You were always ditching class to go surfing."

Eddie laughed to himself and studied the fence in both directions for a few moments. "I probably shouldn't tell you this," he said. "Especially in front of your boss."

"Tell me what?"

Eddie hesitated and took a sip of coffee from his cup.

"Tell me what?"

"That the only reason I even went to school at all was because of you."

"Me?"

"Yeah."

"Why?"

"I'm over it now, but in high school, I had a big crush on you."

"You're kidding me! But you were going out with Yolanda, you even married her."

"It's true. I had the biggest crush on you, but you scared me to death."

"I never knew!"

"Yup. I never missed American History class because I sat right behind you. History was first period and then I'd cut out and go surfing."

"But we were friends, I mean, we hung out together and all, but you were going with Yolanda. I never knew, Eddie!"

Eddie smiled nervously and checked the fence in both directions again.

Silver mist floated through the open windows of the truck. Rita drummed her fingers on the dash, shivered, and then pulled her suede jacket tighter around her chest. The silence was awkward.

"Yeah, we were friends," said Eddie finally to break the lull in conversation. "I remember we used to have a lot of heavy conversations. All of us, the whole group."

Rita forced a timid laugh.

"Like what?" she asked.

"I remember we had a lot of discussions about God."

"Yeah?"

"You hated that Catholic girl's school your aunt kept putting you in. You kept running away and coming back to our school," he said. "You were adamant that there was no God. You insisted that we were nothing more than tail-less monkeys clinging to a piece of dirt being hurtled though space."

"Yeah, well I had a lot of anger back then," she said. "I was mad at my mother for dying, mad at my father for drinking, and mad at my aunt for putting me in a school where the nun's were shoving God down my throat. I was especially mad at God for the way my life was going."

"So," he said. "How are you doing with your anger these days?"

Rita looked at Eddie and just rolled her eyes. The amber beacon reflecting off the mist gave Rita's brown eyes an eerie yellow glow.

"Do you still surf a lot?" she asked, changing the subject.

"Sure." Eddie hesitated slightly at the sudden change in the direction of the conversation. "Sometimes I'll stop by the beach in the morning after I get off work. If the surf looks good I'll catch a few waves before I have breakfast. I've been to Hawaii a few times, but that's another story."

"Hawaii, hunh? For competition?"

"Nah, I'm not that good."

"Hey," she said. " I just remembered, we had our ten-year reunion last month. Did you go?"

"Nah, I skipped it."

"You didn't go? Why?"

"I don't know. Didn't feel like going, I guess."

"Because of Yolanda?"

"Maybe."

"How long have you been divorced?"

"Five years," he said. "Did you go to the reunion?"

"No," she said.

"Why not? I thought for sure you'd be there. Maybe to see if The Albino was there," he chortled.

"The Albino?" she asked.

"Yeah, The Albino, you know, that guy you went to the prom with."

"He wasn't an albino!"

"He looked like one," laughed Eddie. "He thought he was too good for everybody else. Mister 'more-money-than-you'. He was stuck up."

"He wasn't stuck up, and he was blonde, not albino."

Eddie chuckled and Rita elbowed him in the ribs.

"I don't know why you even went out with him, his parents didn't like you. You were too dark."

"He was nice," she protested. "And his parents were nice to me, too."

"Sure," he said. "Mister Harvard, better than everybody else."

"All right, have it your way," she said, glancing over at me. "Let's drive around and see what's going on. I'm sure Commander Stanton has heard enough about our high school days. "

"Sure." Eddie started the truck, turned the defrosters on to clear the windshield, and began to drive slowly down the south fence line toward the water.

"Albino."

"Was not!"

"Was too!"

Rita elbowed him again.

Eddie stopped the truck at the water's edge and looked up and down the misty channel for a few moments. There weren't any ships at the dock tonight and most of the overhead halogen lights had been extinguished as a power saving measure. He made a right hand turn and slowly drove down the dock along the water.

"Tell Commander Stanton what you told me about the undercover U.S. Customs guys," she said.

"Undercover?" Eddie coughed up a mock laugh. "There's no undercover on the docks. Everybody knows everybody. Those guys stick out like a sore thumbs, everybody knows they're undercover Customs agents."

"If everybody working on the docks knows that Customs is working undercover," I asked. "Do they know what Customs is looking for?"

"Sure," said Eddie. "They're trying to find out where all the missing containers are going and looking for drugs."

"Have you heard about this, Commander?" Rita asked.

"I know about it," I said. "Most of the undercover agents working for Customs are overseas and they do their best to find out what's going into the shipping containers before they're loaded onto the vessels. We get regular intelligence reports and if anything is questionable, it's reported to the CIA and then we're notified so we can add the ship to our Blacklist. Customs has added extra undercover agents in San Pedro because for the last eight or nine months there have been more discrepancies at both the Malaysia-Pacific and Korea Lines terminals."

"What kind of discrepancies?" she asked.

"Discrepancies on the cargo manifests," I said. "Each container has a cargo manifest listing the contents and weight of the cargo. Customs randomly checks containers here in San Pedro and finds that ninety-eight or ninety-nine percent of the time the manifest is accurate. Lately there have been more discrepancies, almost like somebody is trying to find out how close we're checking what's coming into this country."

"What constitutes a discrepancy?" she asked.

"Significant difference in either weight or contents," I explained. "For example, Customs might open a container and find it's full of linens and towels instead of wicker furniture like is reported on the manifest. Sometimes the weight is off by several thousand pounds from the declared weight. When Customs questions the shipper on the discrepancy, they say it's just a clerical error."

"So what's the problem with an occasional clerical error?" she asked.

"It's happening so much lately that we think they might be testing us," I said.

"Who exactly, is testing us?" she asked.

"Who knows," I said. "There are thousands of containers on each ship arriving here and the contents of each of those containers belongs to a different shipper and receiver. The ship owner only knows what's in each container because of what's reported on the manifest for that particular container. If the manifest is inaccurate...well, then who knows what's actually inside?"

"So what about the missing containers?" she asked. "Sea Marshals only escort the ships in and out of port so I hadn't heard there was a problem with missing containers or discrepancies once they got to the dock until I talked to Eddie tonight."

"The ship owners are complaining that containers are disappearing from the dock after they're unloaded from the ship," I said. "Some valuable cargo has come up missing and they're going crazy because the terminal is fully computerized and nothing comes or goes unless it's checked out the front gate. So unless the containers are hopping over a ten-foot chain link fence all by themselves, there's a problem."

Eddie made another right turn and stopped between two long rows of containers stacked between six and eight high. After checking both right and left between the rows, he resumed our patrol.

"So, Eddie, you said you had a theory on how the containers are getting out of here," she said. "Tell him what you told me."

Eddie took a sheet of paper off the dashboard and handed it to her. "These are the containers that we're looking for tonight," he said.

Rita looked at the sheet.

"There must be thirty containers on this sheet," she said.

"They lose containers here all the time. That's one of my main jobs here, to look for the lost containers."

"I don't get it," she said. "How do they lose so many containers?"

"Malaysia-Pacific has ten to fifteen thousand shipping containers in here at any one time, and sometimes, some of 'em get misplaced. You know the old saying, 'shit happens'."

"How?"

"I'll show you how the terminal is organized. Then you'll understand," he said. Eddie began using his hands to point as he talked and drove. "They have twelve rows, starting with number one at the water's edge, number twelve near the street. Then the containers are in stacks, 'A' starting in the south, through 'R', at the north end of the terminal. Each stack is two containers wide, five long, and up to eight containers high. That's as high as they can stack them here with the equipment they have here."

"Okay," she said.

"Containers waiting to be loaded on a ship are stacked at the north end of the yard and the ones coming off the ships are stacked at the south end."

Eddie took the paper back. "Now, let's take this container for example, TVU2786643. Its location is Row 4, Stack F, Number 18, which is first row high, number four, dockside. Get it?"

"Okay," she said, appearing to be a little confused.

"But it's not there, that's why it's on the list," Eddie said.

"So where did it go?" I asked, wading into the conversation.

"I don't know." Eddie smiled at us. "Let's go see if we can find it."

Eddie turned left and drove between rows three and four, stopping at stack 'F'.

"Let's go." Eddie got out of the truck, leaving it running and with the emergency brake on. "Bring your flashlight."

Rita and I piled out of the front seat and caught up with him.

"See," he said, pointing to a container on the second row up with his flashlight. "That's not the right container." He checked the number on the container again and then compared it to the number on the sheet of paper.

Eddie laughed to himself.

"Now there's another container in the wrong spot," he said. "It's supposed to be in '28', one row up, but '18' isn't there to set it on." He made a note on the sheet of paper.

Rita followed with her flashlight as Eddie checked the surrounding stacks of containers. He walked slowly, shining his flashlight left and right, up and down, on container numbers, occasionally checking the paper in his hand.

Eddie giggled out loud. "There it is," he said. "See."

We looked at the number being illuminated by Eddie's flashlight. TVU2786643.

"How'd it get over here," she asked.

Eddie shined his flashlight around the stacks of containers, stopping several times to look at a number.

"My guess is that they needed the container that was under this one, so they moved it from 4-F-18 over here to 5-G-21, right here on the corner, then either forgot to move it back to the right location or they forgot where they put it."

"Is it always this easy to find them?"

"Usually. Every night they give me a list of containers that are missing and I try to find a few of them. It's been my experience that these lost containers show up all by themselves in time, so I don't work too hard looking for them. I just do a few every night to make it look like I'm really doing something. I usually do it when I get sleepy and need to walk around a little."

"How do the containers get found all by themselves?" I asked.

"The forklift operators are supposed to check the container box number against the location numbers when they move them and make a list of containers they find in the wrong spots so the computer can reconcile it. That way, the lost containers find themselves."

"But not always, right?" I said.

"Not always, sometimes the wrong container gets put on a ship and sent to the next port. Then it takes them a while to find it and send it back."

"Well, what prevents them from picking up the wrong container and just driving out of the terminal with it?" I asked.

"That's next to impossible. The containers are almost always lost inside the terminal…or put on the wrong ship."

"Why is it impossible to take the wrong container out of the terminal?" she asked.

"Too many checks and balances. The container has a number and also a bar code. When a driver comes into the terminal with an empty truck and chassis to pick up a container, he shows his paperwork to one of the longshore clerks at the gate. Then he drives his truck over to the loading zone while a terminal forklift operator gets the right container and loads it on his empty chassis. After it's locked in place on his chassis, the truck driver goes back to the front gate where they scan the bar code and check the container box number and make sure they match up. There is also a scale and the clerk checks to make sure that the weight of the container matches the weight as shown on the paperwork."

"So people aren't just driving out of here with the wrong containers?" I asked.

Eddie seemed amused at the naiveté of my question. "No," he said. "That doesn't happen."

"How do the containers end up on the wrong ship, or is it more like the wrong containers on the right ship?" I asked.

"Both. Well, that end is more complicated. It gets crazy around here when they're loading or unloading a ship. A lot of times guys are working double and even triple shifts, so human error is a factor. They may load a thousand or more containers on a ship during a single eight-hour shift, and of course they have a lot of things to consider. Time is money, as they say, and sometimes they're loading containers on one part of the ship and unloading them on another part."

Rita and I looked at each other as Eddie waved his hands and explained.

"They can't just load containers on a ship and go," he said. "The weight has to be distributed just right. You can't have too much weight high or low, left or right, or to the front or back of the ship. Then they may be loading containers for four or five different discharge ports, so they can't put the containers for the first port under the ones for the second port or they'll have to unload the whole ship to get to them. It gets really complicated."

Rita looked baffled. "It sounds complicated," she said. "How do they figure all that out?"

"A computer. A very big and very smart computer. It tells them what container to load where and in what order."

Eddie motioned us back to the truck.

"Okay," Rita said. "If it's all computerized, how does it get messed up?"

Eddie pointed to the paper in his hand.

"Easy. It's human error most of the time. For example, the computer says it's time to load the container that's stored at 4-F-18 on the ship. So they get the container, and they're supposed to check the number, but sometimes it looks similar or they're tired or something, and the wrong box that was in the right location is loaded. That's all."

"And it turns up later?"

"Sure, eventually," said Eddie as he got in the truck. He waited until Rita and I climbed into the cab until he resumed his explanation. "Sometimes a container that's supposed to be on the ship doesn't show up on time," he said. "Maybe the truck bringing it to the terminal has a flat tire...or gets stuck in traffic on the freeway and it misses getting loaded on the ship altogether, which creates another problem because all the containers are stacked one atop another and if one doesn't show up, you can't just have an empty spot, it has to be filled with a substitute, then they have to rush around and find another container to put in its place that has a similar weight and destination. Like I said, it gets crazy around here when we have ships at the dock."

We met another security truck on patrol. Eddie hung out the window and joked with the other driver, spreading rumors and gossip. The other security man wanted to know why he didn't have a good-looking woman riding with him all night long, too.

"I'll see what I can do for you," joked Eddie.

The other guy laughed. Eddie offered to check the perimeter fence if the other driver would check the wharf line. They waved to each other and drove off in opposite directions.

"Who was that?" asked Rita.

"Frog-eyes."

"Frog-eyes?"

"Yeah."

"Why do they call him frog-eyes?"

Eddie thought about it. "I don't really know. I think he got the name when he worked in the shipyard."

"That's a weird nickname."

"Yeah, most nicknames are weird."

Eddie suddenly pointed to a fog-shrouded car parked outside the security fence. He eased the security truck up to the car parked on the other side of the fence, keeping it in the beam of our headlights. The driver of the car turned the interior dome light on. San Pedro Police Department.

The officer on the passenger side of the patrol car squinted into our headlights and waved. Eddie saluted back by flashing his high beams and we continued our patrol.

"Do you ever have people breaking into the terminal?" she asked.

"Sure, sometimes," said Eddie. "Kids usually. Or gang-bangers. They'll cut through the fence, or climb over it, and then open up some of the containers. Usually they're looking for stereos or televisions, that type of thing."

"Is it a big problem?" I asked.

"Nah, we don't lose too much, mostly just have to fix the fence or replace locks on the containers. Vandalism mostly. That's why we patrol with the beacon on. They see us coming and they split. We make regular patrols, so they don't have a lot of time to look through the containers. They usually don't get away with much of anything"

Rita yawned.

"Bored?" Eddie asked.

"No, just wishing I was home in bed."

Eddie parked the truck in the southeast corner of the terminal again and emptied the last of his coffee into our cups. The two-way radio in the truck squawked and Eddie answered it. "Code four," said a female voice.

"Gotta' go to the front gate," he announced.

"What's up?"

"Don't know," he said. Eddie gulped the coffee from his cup, put the truck in gear, and raced through the terminal. When he pulled up to the front gate, Eddie asked us to stay in the truck. We watched as he went to the guard shack and talked to the longshore clerk through the window. After a few moments with the clerk, Eddie climbed up on a truck being detained at the gate and leaned in the window to talk to the driver. The driver got out and he and Eddie walked around behind the truck. They were gone a couple of minutes, there was a brief discussion with the longshore clerk at the gate office, and then Eddie began talking to the driver, using his hands to give directions.

"What was that?" asked Rita when Eddie climbed in the front seat again.

"Some guy dropping off an empty container. The numbers on his paperwork didn't match the numbers on the container, so I had to check to make sure there wasn't a bomb or a dead body in the container, that's all."

"He can do that? Just drop off the wrong container?" I asked.

"Sure. He probably just hooked up to the wrong one at Wal-Mart where they unloaded it. No big deal. The clerk is going to make a correction in the computer."

"Don't they keep better track of the empty containers?" I asked. "It seems kind of lax to me."

"Sure, but they're a big pain in the butt?"

"Why?"

"There's so darn many of them, they don't have room to store all of them."

"Why are there so many empties?" Rita asked.

"Well, just look at the huge trade deficit this country has," he said. "How many trillion dollars? They ship a lot more goods into this country than they ship out. That means there's a lot of empties on our side of the ocean to deal with."

"You know, a lot of the missing containers are the empty ones," I said.

"Like I said, they aren't missing, just misplaced."

"How are they different than the loaded ones?" I asked.

"A lot of the empties go in for repairs. If they get damaged somehow during shipping while they're full of cargo, they have to fix them before they can fill them up again. The forklifts poke holes in them all the time and they can lose track of them at the repair facility, or sometimes if the damage is too bad, they just total them out and scrap them. Or sometimes, when a ship sails, they'll just throw a bunch of empties on top at the last minute just to get them out of the terminal and nobody takes down the numbers. They need to get them on the other side of the ocean so they can fill them up again. We usually find them when they arrive full of cargo the next time. That's how it works, full containers come in to port, and empty ones go out. Big trade deficit."

"How many empties are we talking about?" I asked.

"Well, I think they figure that for every full container that comes into port they have between two and three empties that need to go out."

"That many?" Rita asked.

"Yeah, and the empties are a real pain in the ass. They're stacked everywhere around the port. They even have places you can buy them for personal use and somebody on the City Council wants to make homeless shelters out of them. On this side of the ocean we have too many, on the other side they don't have enough and we can't ship them back fast enough, so they just manufacture more new ones and fill them up. Then we end up with even more empties over here."

I thought about what Eddie had just told us. "Let me ask you this," I said. "What would have happened just now if the number on that supposedly empty container had matched the number on the paperwork?"

"Nothing. He would have driven into the terminal and dropped it off, that's all."

"And nobody would have looked inside to see if anything was in it?"

"Nope. No reason to, a forklift operator would have taken it off his chassis and added it the stack of empties."

Rita and I looked at each other and the mongrel dog began to stir in the pit of my stomach. It was going to take me awhile to process everything Eddie Taylor told us tonight to see where it fit, but I knew the system was flawed at best, and somebody had figured out how to exploit those weaknesses. The more I thought about what had happened today and what Eddie told us tonight, the more the dog howled and I was guessing he was howling because it wasn't going to be long before something else happened. Something big.

8

It wasn't long before I found out what the dog was howling about. The phone call came at a little after one o'clock on Saturday morning as I was trying to fall asleep. The events of the day wouldn't quit playing over and over in my head. I'd tried warm milk and counting sheep and found those methods useless, and although I didn't have any bourbon in the house, I was tempted to make a run down to the liquor store. It didn't take a rocket scientist to figure out Saturday was going to be a long day and that I was going to need some rest just to get through it, but the pressure of trying to fall asleep and the nagging feeling that I was missing something obvious had been keeping me awake.

It took me five rings to reach the phone in the living room. "Commander Stanton, this is Chief-Petty-Officer Burke, sorry about waking you up, Commander."

I'd rather be called a thousand times for something trivial than not be called the one time when I was really needed. Besides, I wasn't sleeping anyway. "No problem, Chief, what's going on?"

"We found a body, sir."

"A body? As in a dead body?"

"Yessir."

"Where'd you find a body, Chief?"

"Floating under the Vincent Thomas Bridge, sir. We were on harbor patrol and watching a containership undock from Berth 227, and as soon as the ship got underway, the body came floating up in the ship's propeller wash."

The Vincent Thomas Bridge spans the harbor's main shipping channel from San Pedro to Terminal Island and at least a couple times a year somebody commits suicide by jumping from it. Normally I wouldn't be that interested in a floater because in addition to the suicides, bodies turn up at the rate of two or three a month and are usually gang or drug related homicides. The harbor is a good place to dump a body because it saves the four or five hour drive out to the desert to find an isolated place for a shallow grave and the currents in the harbor move the body around quite a bit before it has time to decompose enough to come to the surface.

"Maybe it was a jumper from the bridge," I said.

"I don't think so, sir."

"Why not?"

"I'm no expert, sir," said Chief Petty Officer Burke. "But he sure looks like he's got a gunshot wound to the back of his head and most of his face is missing. What do you want me to do?"

"Where's the body now?"

"We've got it on our boat."

"Call San Pedro Police, it's their jurisdiction. Tie your boat up at Berth 227 and I'll be there in twenty minutes."

"Yessir. Should I call Lieutenant Velasco and have her come down, too?"

"No, let her sleep for now, she'll be down there by six anyway."

"Yessir."

"One more thing, Chief."

"What's that, Commander?"

"Don't let that ship leave the harbor until we identify the body. Have them anchor near the breakwater until we clear this up."

"Yessir."

While getting dressed I thought about the body. Berth 227 was a few docks seaward of the Malaysia-Pacific Terminal where Eddie Taylor worked. The body probably didn't come off the ship in question because it takes a couple of days for a corpse to become a floater and if somebody from the ship ended up in the water, we wouldn't find the body until after the ship was long gone. The gunshot wound sounded like an execution and that was typical of a violent gang related homicide. San Pedro gangs prefer drive-bys, saving the up-close and personal executions when a special message needed to be sent.

The surfboat was still in the back of my truck and I briefly considered taking it out and setting it on the front lawn but decided not to waste the time. Traffic was heavier than I expected on Pacific Coast Highway for this time of night. Then again, it was a weekend and the drunks were out in full force. The lights of Huntington Beach disappeared in my rearview mirror as I reached the isolated stretch of highway near Bolsa Chica State Beach where I liked to row in the morning and I spooned the window down to let the smell of the surf inside the cab of the truck. The early morning mist made oncoming headlights seem brighter than usual and I'd have to squint until they passed.

Suddenly I missed Elisha. The middle of the night is the worst. During the day I'm busy enough to keep my mind occupied, but at night, when things quiet down and I'm alone, I start to miss her, and then the guilt attacks. I can't escape the feeling that I was responsible for her death. I try to tell myself that it was the cancer that took her, but the guilt tells me the only reason the cancer took her was because she didn't want to live and the reason she didn't want to live was because of my affair. I rationalize by saying the affair was part of the undercover assignment, like trying the cocaine just to show everyone you're not a cop, but then I hear Elisha say that an affair is an affair. A rose by any other name is still a rose and bullshit by any other name is still bullshit. It doesn't matter what I tell myself; in my heart I know she's right.

A set of headlights swerved into my lane and I instinctively jerked the wheel to the right without checking the lane next to me. Fortunately it was empty. I honked my horn after the fact and in my rearview mirror I could see the car weave back into its own lane. Stupid drunk. Where are the cops when you need one? Adrenaline rushed through my veins, the damn car didn't miss me by more than a foot, and then suddenly I knew what had been bothering me but hadn't been able to put my finger on. Eddie Taylor said it was 'next' to impossible to get a container out of the terminal because of the checks and balances. That meant it 'was' possible to smuggle a loaded container out and Eddie Taylor knew how it could be done.

***

The body was nude, bloated, blanched-white, and Chief Petty Officer Burke was right- most of the guy's face was missing. Uniformed San Pedro Police officers swarmed the deck of the Sea Marshal patrol boat but the homicide detectives hadn't arrived yet because early Saturday morning is prime time for the inebriated and dysfunctional members of our society to interact with tragic consequences. I'd seen my share of floaters pulled from the straits between Florida and Cuba- refugees that didn't make it because their boats sunk, or sometimes bullet-riddled and heavily tattooed Cuban prison escapees that somebody wanted to keep out of our country. This floater had a couple of tattoos on his forearms, but what surprised me most about this body was that Special Agent Mike Dillon of the FBI was kneeling next to it.

Dillon poked at the body with a ballpoint pen. I wasn't sure what he was checking for, but from the look on his face, he wasn't enjoying a moment of it. I'm sure seducing beautiful young women that worked for him was more to his liking.

"You do go out on Friday night after all," Dillon said as he stood up.

"Technically, it's Saturday morning," I said.

"Not until the sun comes up," he replied, wiping the pen with a tissue and returning it to an inside jacket pocket. "We gotta stop meeting like this."

"Works for me."

"What did you find out at the Malaysia-Pacific Terminal," Dillon asked.

"Not much," I said. Son-of-a-bitch, I thought to myself. Dillon either followed me or had my phone tapped. I hadn't said a word to him about going to the terminal and yet he knew I was there. I was about to pass on what Eddie Taylor told me, but since the bastard had been in my harbor less than twenty-four hours and already had a tail on me, he could go pound sand for all I cared.

"What do you make of this?" Dillon asked as he pointed to the nude floater.

"I guess he doesn't have any identification in his pocket," I said. "Until we know who he is, I won't know what to make of it."

Dillon leaned in and looked at the remains of the floater's face. "I don't think he has enough left to get dental records and the fingerprints are going to be too close to call because he's been in the water so long. These tattoos may be all we have."

The tattoos were distorted because of the bloating, but since only the forearms had tattoos, I didn't think the floater was a gangbanger. If he were, he would have ink on his back and shoulders, but he didn't. I got a big whiff of rotting corpse and moved around upwind.

I wondered how Dillon got here before me. Burke called me before notifying the San Pedro Police I got dressed and came straight here. If the police department called Dillon, he must have been somewhere close. His clones were missing so maybe he had a stakeout going on in the harbor he wasn't telling me about. Son-of-a-bitch.

Dillon started to say something but the blast of a ship's whistle stopped him. We looked up and saw that a huge black-hulled ship was approaching the Vincent Thomas Bridge from San Pedro Harbor's West Basin area. The tugboat made fast on the vessel's port bow sounded its shrill whistle, followed shortly by the rumble of its diesel engines and a cloud of black smoke. We could hear the tugboat's towline creak, groan, and pop as it took a strain and began to push on the freighter's hull. The change of direction was almost imperceptible at first, but slowly the huge vessel lined itself up with the main shipping channel on its way to sea. When the ship was in position, the tugboat sounded its whistle again and the towline went limp. It only took a few minutes for the ship to pass us. Dillon stood in awe of the vessel that was over three football fields in length and over twenty stories tall.

"Korean Expeditor," Dillon said, reading the name off the stern. Black smoke burbled from the ship's smokestack. "Big damn ship, they don't look that big until you get up close. Where's it headed now?"

"Probably San Francisco," I said. "Then back to the Far East."

"That ship must have just left the Korea Lines Terminal," he said.

"That's right."

Ship traffic had been backed up outside harbor because of the delay yesterday and was struggling to get back on schedule. Time is money in the shipping business and a ship the size of the Korean Expeditor must have an exorbitant hourly rate. With the delay, things were probably even crazier than usual around the terminals. Eddie Taylor said it was hectic inside Malaysia-Pacific whenever ships were at the dock. Could the added confusion be a diversion?

The black Ford Expedition I'd ridden in last evening pulled up to the dock and one of Dillon's clones got out. When the passenger door opened I was surprised to see Ron Butler, the senior U.S.

Customs officer for the port of San Pedro. Dillon's clone escorted Ron Butler down to the deck of the patrol boat and they viewed the floater together.

"That's him," Ron Butler said, looking like he was on the verge of vomiting. "That's Mick Biller."

I stared a hole in Dillon. "This guy's a Customs Agent?"

"Looks like it," Dillon said, trying his best to look innocent.

I wasn't buying it. Dillon got down here before me and then had one of his clones bring Ron Butler down to identify the body. Even with the floaters face blown off, Ron Butler knew who it was right away.

"All right, Dillon, what's going on?" I asked.

"Mick Biller was working undercover at the Malaysia-Pacific Terminal and he's been missing since Wednesday."

Nobody told me that a U.S. Customs undercover agent had been missing since Wednesday. Why wasn't I in that loop? I worked with Ron Butler all the time and he was on the joint agency task force for the *Beleza*, so why hadn't he bothered to tell me one of his agents was missing?

"How did you know it was Mick Biller?" I asked Dillon.

"I didn't."

I grabbed a handful of Dillon's jacket. "Listen to me you piece of shit," I said. "You had a damn good idea this floater was Mick Biller because you dragged Ron Butler down here in the middle of the fucking night to identify the body. You were working me, saying we couldn't identify the body because the teeth were gone and the fingerprints were no good, and the whole time you knew damn well who it was."

Dillon took my hand from his jacket. "Calm down, Jared. Shit, you're freaking out, get a grip on yourself."

"You asshole."

"Look, Jared, Ron Butler told us he had a missing agent, I don't know why he didn't tell you, but hell, you're with the Coast Guard, we're the FBI."

"We pulled the body out of the water for you."

"I know, I know," Dillon said. "Good work."

"How'd you know it was Mick Biller?"

"We had a description and knew Mick Biller had tattoos on his forearms. It was just a lucky guess, that's all."

"Lucky guess my ass, Dillon," I said. "You holding out on me."

Dillon didn't have a response but backed away. Maybe he thought I was going to knock him on his ass. If that's what he was thinking, he was reading me right.

I climbed up onto the dock from the patrol boat and headed for my truck. I'd had enough for one night. Something big was going down and I was being kept on the outside. There's no doubt in my mind that Mike Dillon and the FBI knew a lot more about this than they were telling me. I felt like a doll being dangled from a string, and Dillon could jerk that string anytime he wanted.

The only thing I had going for me was what I'd learned from Eddie Taylor tonight. But was Eddie Taylor holding out on me? Probably. Why would he open up to a guy like me the very first time he met me? He'd said there weren't any secrets on the dock and everybody knew who the undercover Customs agents were. Did Eddie Taylor know Mick Biller was missing, or more importantly, did he know Mick Biller's face had been blown off? He'd slipped up when he said it was 'next to impossible' to get a loaded container out of the terminal. Eddie Taylor's slip up wasn't much to go on. I was going to have to make the most it.

9

The Dodgers beat the Cards by a score of five to two last night. Some new kid named Greg Thomson went three for four at the plate with two home runs and a double for the Dodgers. I was sorry I'd missed it.

Mario poured me a twenty-four ounce coffee and then put the cream and sugars it for me while I checked the box score in the Los Angeles Times. Mario tried to pass himself off as an Italian even though he was Pakistani. He ran the local corner market, together with his wife and two sons that did their best to infiltrate the surfer crowd in Huntington Beach.

"You want the paper, too?" Mario asked.

"Why not?" I said as I handed him a five.

"Yesterday's ship fire is very big news," Mario said. "They had a special report on the television last night."

I closed the sports section and looked at the front page. One of the local television traffic helicopters had taken aerial photographs of the *Beleza* billowing smoke and they were plastered all over the front of the paper.

Mario handed me my change. "Terrorists," he said as he shook his head. "Very bad people, very bad."

I didn't know if Mario's coffee was going to be enough to wake me up this morning. Caffeine can only do so much when you only get two hours of sleep at night. I folded the paper and put it under my arm as I walked back to my truck. I wasn't sure why I bought it or even when I'd have time to read it today.

It wasn't until I was driving past the beach that I remembered I still hadn't taken the boat out of the back of my truck and I wondered how long it was going to be before I had enough free time to go rowing again.

Saturday morning traffic on Pacific Coast Highway was pretty light and I sipped my coffee and half-listened to a sports radio talk show while I drove toward Terminal Island. A few people were on the streets getting an early start to their day, but most Southern Californians were still at home trying to figure out what to do with a day off. Must be nice.

It was a quarter past seven when I got to my office and Admiral Ballard was waiting for me.

"Sleeping in, son?" he asked.

"I didn't get home until three," I said, trying not to sound defensive.

"Making any progress?"

"The shit just keeps getting deeper. Besides the *Beleza* attack yesterday, late last night we found a local Customs agent floating in the harbor that had been shot in the back of the head execution-style. I know the FBI is onto something big, but they aren't telling me what it is. The Customs guy had been missing for several days and the FBI knew about it, but they kept it to themselves. So when you described the situation as a turd in a punchbowl, you pretty much summed it up. They're keeping me in the dark and it's starting to piss me off."

Admiral Ballard looked at me for a moment. "Have you ever worked with mules?"

"Mules?" I asked. What was he talking about? I definitely needed more caffeine because I'd lost the drift of the conversation somewhere.

"My granddad raised mules when I was a kid," he said. "Do you know what a mule is?"

"I've heard of them, but I've never met one in person."

"A mule is half horse and half jackass," he said. "A female horse is bred to a male ass and the offspring is a sterile hybrid."

"Sure," I said, not having a clue where Admiral Ballard was going with this.

"The FBI is like a mule. It's a stubborn, sterile, hybrid that has the worst qualities of both parents. The FBI is half law enforcement agency, half intelligence agency. Half jackass and half just plain horse's ass."

I needed more coffee.

"Listen, Jared," he said. "I know it's hard dealing with them sometimes, but that's what you've got to do. Just like a mule can't help what it is, the FBI can't help what it is. Our job is to protect this port, and we have to rely on intelligence we get from the FBI as well as what Customs and the CIA can furnish us. It would be nice if everybody worked together but that probably isn't going to happen."

If this was the Admiral's pep talk, it wasn't working.

"I need your gut feeling on this, Jared," he said. "I'm flying to Washington this morning for a meeting at the Pentagon to draw up an action plan for the President. I've read the intelligence reports concerning the Algerian arms sale. Could those weapons be in San Pedro in spite of all our precautions?"

"I'm afraid so, Admiral." I quickly briefed him on my tour of the Malaysia-Pacific terminal, Eddie Taylor's explanation of cargo operations, and then the unfortunate fact that it was no big secret that Customs was undercover on the docks.

Admiral Ballard was silent for a moment. "I want the *Beleza* moved, it's a damn sitting duck where it is. If those weapons are somewhere in this port, they may come back to finish the job. If that happens, there's going to be hell to pay, and we both have our butts on the line."

"I'll see how the salvage operation is going and get her to the dock as soon as possible so they can discharge what's left of the cargo."

"It's the weekend and you're going to have a lot of yacht traffic coming in to get a look and take pictures."

"We're on it, Admiral," I said. "Nobody's getting near that ship."

"Good," he as he stood up to leave. "Military Intelligence at the Pentagon thinks the arms may have been smuggled in a few at a time instead of in just one big shipment. We can't let our guard down, Jared. We have to stop this."

Today's Blacklist was on my desk. I ran a finger down the first column and picked out a ship due to arrive at the Malaysia-Pacific Terminal tonight. "The *Pacific Venture* is coming in tonight by way of the Singapore Straits. Customs put her on the list for a discrepancy in Kuala Lumpur."

"Good. Hit her hard, we need to send these people the message that they can't smuggle weapons into this port. I don't care how long it takes, Jared, find the rest of those damn rockets!"

"I'm on it, Admiral," I said. "Have a good flight."

Admiral Ballard paused at the door. "You have my cell phone number. If anything happens, make sure I hear about it from you and not the Commandant this time."

A few seconds after Admiral Ballard left my office, Mike Dillon walked in. I wondered if he'd been listening at the door because he had a strange look on his face.

"Captain Hannigan is gone," Dillon said.

"What do you mean?"

"We went to his house last night to ask him a few more questions but he never came home. We showed his picture around and it turns out that Captain Hannigan was one of the people that looked at the boat the Hansen brothers had for sale. We checked the marina this morning and Hannigan's boat is gone."

"Maybe somebody at the marina saw him leave."

"We asked around, nobody saw him come or go. You need to find him."

"I need to find him?"

"That's right, you're the goddamn Coast Guard, Jared. One of the prime suspects in the attack on the *Beleza* is out there somewhere on his boat and it's your job to find him."

"Have you got a description of Hannigan's boat?"

"It's a thirty-four foot sailboat. White with blue trim."

"No problem, Dillon," I said. "There are about forty thousand sailboats that fit that description in Southern California and we've got several thousand square miles of water to search. We'll have that done for you in no time."

"Those rockets may be on his sailboat and we need to find it."

"I'll alert the Sea Marshals to be on the look out for Hannigan and his boat."

"That's it?"

"That's it. Unless you've got a better idea."

Dillon shook his head. "We had him right here yesterday and we let him walk out the front door. We never should have done that."

In twenty-twenty hindsight, Dillon was right. Given the circumstances, we should have done more than just suspend Captain Hannigan's license and let him go. If Hannigan had some of the SEP DARDS on his sailboat, it was going to be like trying to find a needle in a haystack.

10

At the Saturday morning meeting I laid out the plan for the raid on the *Pacific Venture*. The Coast Guard would stop the ship well out to sea, somewhere off Anacapa Island, and secure it with a Sea Marshal boarding team from one of our patrol cutters. Once the Coast Guard boarding team completely secured the vessel, additional teams of agents from the FBI, Customs, and the Bureau of Alcohol, Tobacco and Firearms would be flown to the ship in helicopters and the *Pacific Venture* would be held at sea until all Blacklist discrepancies were resolved.

It was hard to get a read on this morning's meeting. Yesterday there was a lot of confusion and noise. Today the tone was hushed, maybe even somber, and of course there weren't as many attendees. Ron Butler from Customs was at the meeting and he looked rough, like he hadn't slept all night. I didn't get many questions or a lot of discussion about tonight's raid, everybody seemed relieved to be doing something instead of just waiting for another attack. After setting the agenda for this afternoon's meeting when the plans and personnel for the raid would be finalized, I adjourned the morning meeting. Agent Mike Dillon hadn't said a word the whole time we were in the conference room and he followed me back to my office.

"Why the *Pacific Venture*?" he asked as he sat in a chair across the desk from me.

"Why not? It's on the Blacklist and detaining a vessel at sea is within our protocol."

"You were at the Malaysia-Pacific Terminal last night and now you're stopping a ship scheduled to dock at that same terminal tonight," he said. "It seems curious to me."

"It doesn't hurt that Mick Biller was undercover at Malaysia-Pacific and he ended up dead," I said.

"Do you even know why Customs red-flagged the ship?"

"Does it matter?"

"I checked into it, Jared," Dillon said. "Customs flagged the ship because of four containers being trans-shipped from India. Four containers out of four thousand aboard the ship, and Customs is only disputing the declared value of brassware and rattan chairs inside those containers so they can charge the importer additional duty. Customs was going to wait until those four containers were unloaded from the ship and were on the dock before opening them up for inspection. Now you're holding the *Pacific Venture* and its entire cargo at sea."

"Like I said, it's within our protocol."

"Bullshit."

"The ship is carrying containers from India. You don't think it's possible a nuclear device is planted inside one of those containers?"

"We would know about that."

"Like we knew about the rockets?" I asked.

Dillon didn't have an answer for that one.

"What about the Donzi used in the *Beleza* attack?" I asked in a less accusatory tone. "Did you ever find the brother that was paying the slip rental in cash?"

"He's a used car salesman and had yesterday off but he wasn't at home when we checked. He's supposed to be at work today and we're going to run him down this morning."

"How about Astal Kamran, the guy that had his van stolen?"

"We're still looking at him. He's got an airtight alibi for yesterday, and the paperwork is in order as far as the theft report he filed with the Harbor City Police Department, but that doesn't mean he doesn't know who took the van. Of course he's not doing anything to help himself."

"What do you mean?"

"He won't give up any information on his clients, he says it's a violation of their civil rights. A bunch of baloney if you ask me."

"So you still have him in custody?"

"It's not custody, it's questioning."

"Ah, questioning," I said. "Be careful, sometimes there's a fine line between questioning an torture."

Dillon frowned at me and got up to leave. "I still don't know why you picked the *Pacific Venture*."

"You know what they say in poker," I said.

"What's that?"

"Trust everybody in the game, but always cut the cards."

Rita Velasco had been waiting for Dillon to leave and they exchanged glances but not words. Rita looked exhausted and the burns on her face appeared a little better than they did yesterday.

"Aloe Vera," she said when she caught me staring at her face. "It really works. I have a plant at home." Rita held clutched a styrofoam cup full of steaming black coffee with both hands and blew small puffs across the surface of the liquid to cool it.

"You look tired." I said. "Did you get any sleep last night?"

She just rolled her eyes. "Sorry I missed this morning's meeting, I was on an inbound passenger ship and it was running late."

"No problem. I guess you heard we found somebody from Customs floating in the harbor last night."

"I heard." Rita sipped her coffee and showed absolutely no emotion.

"You need to get some rest this afternoon because we're going to have a long night." Rita stared at me over her coffee cup as I explained the plan for tonight's raid on the *Pacific Venture.*"

Rita had the thousand-mile stare going. She was over-tired and over-stressed and if my guess was right, she was afraid to go to sleep. I'd seen it before. The guy that brushes my teeth in the morning has that same stare a lot of times.

"I can't take this afternoon off," she said. "I'm short of people for the duty roster."

"I'm not asking you to get some rest, Lieutenant, I'm ordering you," I said. "Assign Sea Marshals to security of the *Beleza* until we get her out of port and we'll also need five more from your squad for the raid tonight. You're taking the afternoon off because you're working with me tonight."

"I don't have enough people," she said and I could see her eyes get moist. She gritted her jaw to fight back the tears. "They've been working straight through without any rest."

"I know. Rotate them as best you can so everybody gets a few hours sleep, but you need some rest, too. You can't do it all yourself," I said. "I'm going to need you clear-headed when the shit hits the fan, and I don't know if that's going to be in ten minutes or ten days, but I'm going to need you, so pace yourself."

"Yessir," Rita said as she stood up to leave.

"I'm not kidding," I said. "You need sleep."

"Sure."

***

After making two phone calls, I learned that the *Beleza's* underwriter, Lloyds of London, had inspected the vessel earlier this morning. The salvage company had pulled the tanker from the mud bank Captain Hannigan put it in yesterday and had already covered the breach in the hull with plywood. They'd fastened stainless steel bolts to the hull of the ship with epoxy, attached the plywood with nuts and washers, and then painted it to match the rest of the vessel. A Sea Marshal that saw the *Beleza* after the repair said that to the untrained eye the ship didn't even look damaged. The *Beleza's* owners were flying in additional crewmembers this afternoon to replace those killed or injured and the ship was scheduled to shift to her unloading berth later this evening. With any luck, in a little over twenty-four hours, the crippled tanker would be leaving San Pedro and going to shipyard somewhere for repairs.

I still wasn't sure if the *Beleza* was the specific target or just a target of convenience. One thing was for sure. If somebody got another shot at her before she left San Pedro, both Admiral Ballard and I would take the fall for it. It had been over twenty-four hours since the initial attack and we still didn't have much to go on. All we had so far was the remains of the speedboat used in the attack and the license plate number of the minivan used to escape the scene when that boat was destroyed on the beach. Both the boat and the minivan had been reported stolen well before the attack on the *Beleza* and it wasn't at all unusual for stolen vehicles to be used for committing crimes. But why did Captain Hannigan bring a burning gasoline tanker into San Pedro Harbor and run it up in the mud. Better yet, where was Captain Hannigan now? If he'd been keeping shoulder-fired anti-tank rockets on his sailboat, they were sure to be in somebody else's possession or at the bottom of the ocean by now. Intelligence reports indicated a lot more weapons than those used in yesterday's attack here in San Pedro had been purchased overseas and shipped in this direction. If those weapons already came through the port in a shipping container, they could be on a truck to anywhere else in the country by now, and that meant that every port in the country was under the same risk to shipping as San Pedro. Not since the German U-Boats of World War Two had there been such a threat to American shipping along our coasts. No wonder

Admiral Ballard was flying back to Washington for meetings at the Pentagon.

"I guess our little talk yesterday didn't do any good."

I looked up to see Larry Jackson standing just inside my office.

"Good morning, Mr. Jackson. What can I do for you?"

"You can explain why you held one of our ships inside the breakwater for three hours last night. That ship will now miss the tide in San Francisco and cost us another twelve-hour delay. All told, that ship is now a full day behind schedule because of delays in this port."

"Well, Mr. Jackson," I said. "That ship was detained because a body was found in the water near the vessel and that body turned out to be a U.S. Customs agent."

"What does that have to do with the ship?"

"The body was found in the immediate vicinity of the ship right after she departed her berth. We detained it as part of our investigation and we cleared it as soon as possible so she could proceed to her next port."

"But ultimately, Commander Stanton, you found the ship had absolutely nothing to do with the body. Can I expect you to hold up international shipping every time somebody from the homeless shelter ends up dead and floating in San Pedro Harbor?"

"The man we found was an undercover U.S. Customs agent, not somebody from the homeless shelter."

"This time maybe, but you know what I'm talking about, Commander," Larry Jackson said, his tone poisonous. "Just a few weeks ago two bodies were found in the harbor and they were from the homeless shelter on 25th Avenue right here in San Pedro."

"I remember."

"I'm filing a complaint with the Federal Trade Commission, Commander. You give me no choice. Ships are being unnecessarily detained due the incompetence of the Coast Guard."

"That's a bit extreme."

"Is it, Commander Stanton? The Coast Guard didn't protect the *Beleza* yesterday morning and now due to your incompetence, ships are being unnecessarily delayed. I am an expert in admiralty law and I'm going to protect the rights of the shipping association."

"Under the circumstances, Mr. Jackson, I think that maybe…"

"I will be filing that complaint first thing Monday morning, Commander Stanton," Larry Jackson said as turned to leave. "Good day."

11

Rita Velasco and I rode with Mike Dillon and two others FBI agents in the third of the three Coast Guard MH-68 helicopters being used for the vertical insertion. She'd arrived just moments before we took off from the Coast Guard base for the raid on the *Pacific Venture* and even in the soft red light inside the chopper's main cabin, she looked beat.

The sun and moon were on the far side of the earth and if not for the lighthouse on the high northern bluff of Anacapa Island, the sea and sky would be an eternity devoid of light. The smooth, breezeless ocean blended into a vague horizon of nothingness and the stars were no more than twinkling pinpricks of light on black velvet.

Rita caught me looking at her and she flashed me a spousal-like glare before turning her head to look out the window. I wondered if it was something I'd said or done or just that she knew I knew she didn't take any time off this afternoon liked I'd told her to do. Any other time, I would have pulled her from the duty roster for few days so she could get some counseling. Just living through the hell-fire on the *Beleza* was traumatic enough, but she also had to cope with the guilt that consumes an officer when somebody under his or her command dies in the line of duty. Even Admiral Ballard was struck by Sea Marshal Bennet's death and he was way up the chain of command. Rita was Bennet's immediate supervisor and she'd made out the duty assignments for the *Beleza* so I knew she was playing it over and over in her mind. If she had to do it all over again, knowing what she knew now, she would have done it differently, and understanding Rita like I do, she would have traded places with Bennet or Kuhn in a heartbeat. Now she was playing the no-win game in her head. Shoulda, coulda, woulda, but didn't. To add insult to injury, she had to ride in the same helicopter as Mike Dillon.

Rita leaned her head back and closed her eyes. I wanted to do the same thing. What I really needed to do was go home and crawl into bed for twelve hours but the *Beleza* incident had turned into a bigger circus than anyone could have anticipated. Tugs had moved the damaged ship to her unloading berth late Saturday afternoon and the event drew huge crowds. Thousands of pleasure craft jammed the port's waterways and the Harbor Freeway had been backed up for miles with weekend looky-loos trying to get a glimpse of the ship. We needed the fireboats to use their water cannons just to clear a path in the shipping channel ahead of the mammoth gasoline tanker that was making international headlines. The crowd hadn't been friendly, their behavior bordering on hostile. There were plenty of protestors with picket signs that didn't want the ship in the harbor at all and they were mixed in with boatloads of drunken gawkers that threw empty beer cans at us when we asked them to back away from the ship. I'm not sure how many arrests the SPPD patrol boats made, but the Coast Guard had been undermanned in a big way. With any luck, by tomorrow afternoon the *Beleza* would be headed out of San Pedro Harbor and once she was clear of the breakwater she would be somebody else's problem.

Our chopper banked to the left and slowed and out the window I could see that the lead helicopter had turned its landing lights on and was hovering above the *Pacific Venture* in preparation for debarkation of the boarding team. We were barely moving now and

I had a good view as the first chopper discharged its team and cleared the ship. We drew closer as the second chopper moved into position and when it was finally clear we approached the ship. Shipping containers were stacked eight levels high above the main deck of the *Pacific Venture* and our pilot expertly flew the MH-68 less than a foot above the top row of boxes. It was a tense moment because if the ship rose on an ocean swell and the helicopter made contact with the top row of boxes, the landing gear would easily puncture the thin metal roof of a shipping container and the pilot would lose control of our aircraft. When the pilot had our chopper in position, the crew chief signaled us and we unfastened our safety harnesses and moved single file toward the exit. Mike Dillon was the first to step from the chopper to the ship and the other FBI agents followed him.

I stood in the doorway and waited for Mike Dillon to look back at me. When we made eye contact I turned to the crew chief and yelled, "Take her up, Chief. I'm staying aboard."

Dillon mouthed words I couldn't hear because of the engine and rotor noise but his one-finger salute said he was less than pleased with me. Rita and I moved forward to our seats and she sat across the aisle from me again and as soon as she had fastened her safety harness she looked at me and grinned. The chopper quickly climbed to flight altitude and headed back to the Coast Guard Base. I leaned my head back and closed my eyes. With any luck I'd be able to grab a ten-minute nap before we got back to the base and had to go to work.

****

A pink shaft of light in the eastern sky proclaimed the arrival of Sunday morning. Rita Velasco and I were dressed alike in our longshoremen disguises- black Frisco jeans, long sleeve Hickory shirts, and Carhartt jackets. We were getting enough double-takes that I knew we weren't fooling anybody but at least we didn't stand out like we would in Coast Guard uniforms. Rita huddled against the pre-dawn chill while chatting with two undercover Customs and Border Protection agents. We stood on the east side of a stack of empty containers in the Malaysia-Pacific Terminal and drank coffee and shivered and waited for the sun to come up. Rita brushed her hair back with one hand and then tugged the Dodger baseball cap low across her forehead in a feeble attempt to conserve body heat. She shivered and began dancing from foot to foot trying to keep her feet warm. One of the Customs agents poured her some more hot coffee from his thermos bottle and she blew small puffs across the cup of steaming liquid while cradling it with both hands.

I'd hoped we would run into Rita's friend Eddie Taylor but apparently he had the night off. Eddie and his security truck would make us more mobile inside the terminal, not to mention a little warmer. No such luck today.

"About damn time," Rita said when the first golden ray of sunlight pierced the cobalt sky.

Longshoremen arrived at the terminal to start cargo operations on the *Pacific Venture* only to find out the ship was delayed at sea and since they had nothing else to do they milled around on the dock and drank coffee and ate doughnuts while they waited. Two Sea Marshal patrol boats motored slowly up and down the channel in front of the Malaysia-Pacific Terminal. Shortly after sunrise, forty uniformed Customs and Border Protection agents descended on the terminal in force, opening containers and double-checking paperwork. It was no undercover operation.

About twenty minutes into the raid, walkie-talkies squawked and the Customs agents we were standing with bolted for Malaysia-Pacific's front gate. Rita and I followed them at a jog and when we caught up we found an inbound truck had been detained. I smelled what was inside before I saw it. The fecal stench hung like a toxic cloud at the back of the opened container. Border Protection had eleven men from inside the shipping container sitting cross-legged on the ground near the front of the truck. Two brave but stupid agents searched the back of the truck for people or contraband and after completing the search, one of the agents dropped to his knees and vomited on the ground. I peered through the open doors and saw several white buckets the men had been using for toilets and a few blankets on the floor. Nearly empty jugs of water were sitting on the ground by the back of the truck next to a large cardboard box with sacks of tortillas and partially filled coffee cans of rancid pinto bean slop. I'm not sure how long those poor souls been stuck in the back of that truck, but I knew what they'd experienced was one hell I didn't want to visit.

This bust was clearly outside the jurisdiction of the Coast Guard but I moved a little closer to the main conversation so I could eavesdrop. I stood near one of the Border Protection agents as he phoned the details in to his office. The truck was supposed to be empty and had come across the border from Hermosillo, Mexico by way of Mexicali and a government van was coming to pick up the men so they could be processed at the Terminal Island Immigration facility.

Admiral Ballard was in the middle of Sunday brunch at Washington D.C.'s downtown Hilton when I called him on my cell phone. I brought him up to date on the *Beleza* as well as the morning raid at Malaysia-Pacific. I had to move farther from the truck during the conversation because the stench was making me gag.

"Are you sure that truck was coming from Hermosillo?" Admiral Ballard asked.

"That's what I heard but I haven't actually seen the paperwork," I said. "Why?"

"Something about the town of Hermosillo came up in one of our meetings yesterday, the Agency is running that operation and didn't say much, but I do remember them mentioning the name of that town. But, hell, we have about two million pieces of intelligence to sort through and it's going to take some time. The rest of those weapons are still in the breeze as far as we can determine and the President is scared shitless that there's going to be another incident any minute."

"Admiral, they're moving the truck right now, but I'll stay close to this investigation and if you hear any more about what's going on in Hermosillo let me know."

"Just make goddamn sure nobody gets another shot at that ship while it's still in San Pedro, Jared," Admiral Ballard said before he disconnected.

***

"You set me up!" Dillon said. He was in my office, sitting behind the desk with his feet up when I walked in.

"Well, hello Agent Dillon. Having a nice day?" Rita and I had just come back from the Malaysia-Pacific operation that was still in progress and while I changed into my working blues in the locker room she'd caught a ride up the channel on a patrol boat to check on the *Beleza's* cargo operations. I wondered how Dillon got into my office and if he'd had enough time to go through my unlocked file cabinets.

"You asshole," Dillon said. "You knew, didn't you?"

"I heard you got stuck on the top row of containers and couldn't get down. I would have thought the ship had a ladder for you to use."

"We froze our butts off out there and that raid was a waste of time. We couldn't find a damn thing on that ship while it was at sea."

"I know, but if I would have tried to talk you out of going, you'd have thought I was trying to hide something."

"That raid was your idea."

"Yeah, but I told the Admiral it was yours."

Dillon scowled. "That was a waste of time and manpower."

"Yes and no," I said. "It had the desired dramatic effect."

"Dramatic effect my ass, and I suppose making me look like an idiot didn't hurt, did it?"

"That's the first time we've put that many people on a ship with helicopters, normally we just board the ships from one of our cutters. We'll have to make some changes to our vertical insertions if we do that again," I said. "Can I have my desk back?"

Dillon was slow getting to his feet. I'd screwed him over, but I hoped that now he would have a little more appreciation for the difficulties the Coast Guard faced on a daily basis.

"Look at it this way," I said. "At least you got some experience. Now you know how these raids go down."

"Here's your vertical insertion." Dillon gave me the finger. "Hannigan is still missing."

"He hasn't turned up yet?"

"No. His boat isn't at the marina and he hasn't gone back to his house. I think he's taken a powder on us."

"Did you tell him not to leave town?"

"It didn't seem necessary at the time."

"Did you ever turn up anything on that feather he was keeping in his black book?"

"Not yet. A couple of old Japanese customs is all, but I don't think they really apply to Hannigan."

"So all we have on Hannigan is that a few of his relatives are with the Irish Republican Army?"

"Not to mention he brought a burning British tanker into to San Pedro Harbor and ran it aground. I'd say that qualifies him as a person-of-interest at the very least and now he's on the run."

I was tired from being up all night and my thinking was muddled and slow but I couldn't get that stupid feather out of my mind. Why would Hannigan have a feather sealed in plastic? Was it from a pet bird or something? Why carry a stupid feather. Pictures of kids, a wife, maybe even a dog I could understand. But a feather?

"How long have you been here?" I asked, again wondering if Dillon had time to rifle through my files.

"I got back just before you did, I was trapped on that stupid ship the whole time," complained Dillon. "Why?"

"Have you heard about the eleven Mexican nationals that Border Protection grabbed up this morning?"

"No, I haven't heard a thing. What happened?"

"While you were on a surprise inspection of the ship, Customs and Border Protection agents tore the Malaysia-Pacific Terminal apart. They turned up eleven 'illegals' in an empty container."

"An empty container?"

"During the raid they were checking everything that came in or went out of the terminal. First thing this morning they opened a container as it came through the front gate. The paperwork said the container was supposed to be empty, but it had eleven people, some food and water, and it stunk like the inside of outhouse. Those poor bastards."

"And they were trying to drop it off at the Malaysia-Pacific container terminal?"

"That's right."

Dillon looked confused. "Why are they smuggling illegals into the container terminal? Wouldn't they be trying to smuggle them out if they came in on a ship?"

"That's what I don't understand."

"Where was the container going? To some other port?"

"No, it was just going to be stacked with the other empty containers in the yard."

"That doesn't make sense."

"It doesn't make sense to me either."

"Where are they now?" Dillon asked.

"They're at the detention center here on Terminal Island. I was going to head down there and see if the Border Protection boys turned up anything when they processed them. Do you want to go with me?"

"I guess," he said. "Even though I'm getting that fucked feeling again."

I signed out a dark blue Plymouth sedan from the Coast Guard motor pool and Dillon along with one of his agents, a new kid he introduced as Gregg Wyatt, rode with me. It was the first time Dillon had introduced any of the other agents working with him. The gate guard dutifully made a note on the log sheet that he kept on a clipboard and then waved us off the base. I made a left on Seaside Avenue and immediately got into the far right lane. About a quarter of a mile later I made a right hand turn into U.S. Border Protection's Terminal Island Service Processing Center.

"I'm here to see Terry Baldwin," I said to the elderly Latino security guard sitting just inside the massive smoked glass front doors.

"Go ahead, Commander Stanton. Nice day isn't it?"

"So far, so good," I said.

The guard delayed Dillon and Gregg Wyatt while he carefully checked their identification.

"They're with me," I said over my shoulder and the guard waved them through.

Terry Baldwin was in her office yelling into the phone when we arrived. She was in her late forties with blue eyes and medium length blonde hair that was pulled back and held in place with a silver and turquoise hair clip. She wore a black skirt with a white cotton blouse and her face lit up a little when she saw me. Terry Baldwin had obviously been quite good looking in her youth. But that was mostly behind her now. Too many hard miles and too many years of working for the government.

"I don't give a damn. I need it and I need it now. Fax me the whole damn file," she said. "They just walked into my office…okay…just send it, bye."

"Shit," Terry Baldwin said, making an obscene gesture at the phone on her desk before motioning for Dillon and me to sit down.

Agent Gregg Wyatt waited in the hall and I made the introductions.

"What was that all about?" I asked, pointing to the phone on her desk.

"That was the Eloy Detention Center over in Arizona," she said. "One of the guys we picked up this morning spent a few years in a correctional facility."

"You don't say," I said. "What for?"

"Well, he's a pretty bad seed. We've been throwing him out of this country for the last twenty years. I'm trying to get some more information on him but the girl that handles those things in Eloy is having a baby, so the whole freaking office is in turmoil."

"I've heard that song before," I said. "So what do we have here so far?"

"Well, we got this Flavy Lopez, Flavino is his first name," she said. "And we got Salvador Lunes, and the other nine are first timers."

"They didn't have any identification on them when we found them. How do you know who they are?"

"We ran their fingerprints, and we had Lopez and Lunes in the system," she explained. "Flavy Lopez has a record about four feet long. A lot of petty stuff. Whenever he got in trouble, the courts would just turn him over to us and we'd deport him. They did that several times, but then there was selling of controlled substances and resisting arrest, felony assault on a police officer and attempted murder in Phoenix. He cut a Phoenix police officer up pretty bad. We held him at the Eloy correctional facility for a couple of years, and then the whole September Eleventh thing came up and they had to cut him loose. We deported him again and then he turned up four months ago in Nogales. Now we have him here."

"How about the other guy?" I said.

"Do you mean Lunes?" she asked.

"Yeah."

"Not much on him. No criminal record. We've picked him up a couple of times in raids, auto repair places I think. That kind of stuff, you know, working without a green card. But he doesn't have a criminal record."

"And how about the others?" I asked.

"They're just kids," she said. "It's their first time through the system as far as we know. We don't have any of their fingerprints on file. I'd say they were all between fourteen and seventeen years old. Just kids. If I had to take a guess, I'd say that Lopez and Lunes are escorting them somewhere."

I looked over at Dillon to see if he had any comments.

"Nobody's talking," she added. "I think they're scared to death of Flavy Lopez to tell you the truth."

"Do you have the cell wired?" I asked.

"Yeah, and we got somebody in the same holding cell, too. We put a couple guys in there ahead of time, somebody that speaks their language. Didn't do much good, Lopez knows all the tricks. He kept telling the kids not to talk."

"Can we take a look at them?"

"Sure, follow me," she said as he started down the corridor, tucking her blouse into the back of her skirt as she walked.

Terry Baldwin led us to a small room full of video monitors. Two middle-aged male uniformed Border Protection officers sat at the control console drinking Pepsi and talking about the strengths of the San Diego Chargers and the team's prospects for the Superbowl this year. They casually greeted Baldwin and went back to their conversation.

"Here," she said, pointing to the monitors. "We have two views."

"My guess is that would be Lopez," I said, pointing to one of the people on the screen.

"Yeah, and that guy over here, that's Lunes," she said, pointing to another man.

"And nobody's talking?" Dillon asked.

"No," she said. "We interviewed them one at a time when we processed them, but we couldn't gets names or anything."

"Any idea where they are from?" Dillon asked.

"Mexico," she said, grinning at me.

"Any idea from where in Mexico?" he asked.

"Like I said, nobody's talking," she said. "But Customs tracked the container they were in and it crossed over the border from Mexicali last night about ten."

"Mexicali?" I asked.

"Yeah," she said. "Down near El Centro."

"El Centro?" Dillon looked puzzled.

"Yeah," she said. "El Centro. It's in the Imperial Valley, a big agriculture area just north of the Mexican border here in California." She looked directly at Dillon. "You must not be from around here."

Dillon said nothing.

"Do you suppose they're farm workers?" I asked.

"That's what we wondered. But, why would they end up here?" she said. "I could see somebody smuggling them over the border, that happens every day, but they were taken right through El Centro. The driver could have just stopped at a truck stop or on the highway, open up the door, and let them scatter through the lettuce fields, or even some dark side street in the middle of town."

"It doesn't make sense," I said.

Terry Baldwin shrugged her shoulders. "Flavy Lopez has to be up to something more than smuggling farm workers."

"How about the truck driver?" Dillon asked. "What does he say?"

"We don't have him, L.A. County Sheriff has him," she said. "We couldn't hold him. He's got a green card and everything is legal. So other than having eleven Mexican nationals in the back of his truck, he hasn't done anything wrong as far as Border Protection is concerned."

"What did he say when you questioned him?" I asked.

"He claims he picked up an empty container in Hermosillo and his paperwork said to bring it to the Malaysia-Pacific terminal to drop it off and that he didn't know what was in the back, it was supposed to be empty as far as he knew. He thought it was empty because that's what his paperwork said, and besides, it had a Mexican Customs seal on it and he didn't break it, which makes sense. U.S. Customs said they checked it through at the border and put another seal on it. They didn't look inside, just saw the Mexican seal, added one of their own, and then waved the driver through."

"Mexican Customs sealed eleven men in the back of a truck?" Dillon asked.

"It's hard to say who did what on the other end," she said. "All I know is what turned up here."

"Wait a minute," I said. "Hermosillo to San Pedro by way of Mexicali? That doesn't sound right."

"Yeah, seemed a little fishy to us, too," she said.

Dillon looked lost. "I don't get it," he said. "What are you saying?"

"Hermosillo is in Mexico," she said. "But the fastest way from Hermosillo to San Pedro is to come across the border in Arizona at Nogales, then take the freeway up to Phoenix and then take I-10 west to San Pedro. Mexicali is quite a few hours out of the way if you're heading to San Pedro from Hermosillo."

"You said Lopez turned up a few months ago in Nogales?"

"We just processed him thru the border on a day trip, no charges were pending and he stayed out of trouble."

"You just let known felons across the border for day trips?" I asked.

"I don't write the regs," she said. "All I know is we have him now."

"So, exactly where is the truck driver now?" Dillon asked.

"The L.A. County Sheriff has him at their Lomita station."

I studied the video monitor.

"Where's the truck?" I asked.

"The Sheriff's office impounded it," she said.

"Anything unusual about the truck that we should know of?" I asked.

"No," she said. "It belongs to Oaxaca Trucking, a Mexican company based in Hermosillo."

"Waahack...?" Dillon said.

Terry Baldwin laughed. "Oaxaca," she said. "You pronounce it 'waa-hawk-uh'."

"Waa-hawk-uh?"

"Yeah, and other than being a piece of junk, all the licenses, permits and insurance are current. Everything else is legitimate," she said and shrugged her shoulders.

I studied the video monitors again. "How long are these guys going to be here?"

"How long do you want them here?" she asked with a devilish grin. "It'll take a couple of weeks to deport the kids unless you want us to hold them longer. But Lunes and Lopez, well, we might want to hang on to them for a while. At least until we can figure out what they're up to."

One of the officers at the control console stood up and finished the last of his Pepsi. "Well, at least they aren't fighting anymore," he said. "I gotta go pee." He started to leave.

"Wait," Terry Baldwin said. "What do you mean fighting? What fight?"

"Right here," said the agent. "This guy right here, got up and grabbed this kid by the throat and then hauled him over to the bench and made him sit down next to him. Got in his face really bad. The kid was crying."

"That's Flavy Lopez," she said to me. "What else happened?"

"Nothing, he just got in the kid's face, smacked him around, and then it was over with. Now they're sitting together just fine. No problem."

Terry Baldwin shook her head in disgust. She went to the console and started pushing buttons. She rewound the tape on one of the monitors, leaving the other monitor showing what was currently going on in the cell. When she got to the part of the tape showing the scuffle, she played it forward. The sound had been turned down and Baldwin turned it up so everyone could hear. The kid asked Flavy Lopez a question and Lopez came out of his seat, grabbed the kid by the throat, hit him several times in the face, and then took him across the cell where he slammed him down on the bench.

"What did the kid say?" I asked.

"Let me play it back again," she said.

This time Baldwin turned the volume all the way up and listened closely. The kid said something and Flavy Lopez immediately got up and grabbed him by the throat, slammed him on the bench and got in his face. After that, the kid looked scared to death.

"What did the kid say? I couldn't hear it," I said.

"It sounded like he said he was hungry," she said. "And he wanted to know how much longer it would be before 'El Jefe' would come for them."

"El Jefe?" I said.

"Yeah, it means 'The Chief'," she said. "Or it could mean 'The Boss'."

Dillon and I looked at each other.

"So all we know is that they were coming here to work for somebody called the boss," Dillon said. "That narrows it down."

"You said this guy, Lunes, worked in auto repair?" I asked.

"I think that's what's in his file," Terry Baldwin said. "We get so many of these guys through here that it's all kind of a blur."

"Could it have been auto body repair?" I asked.

"Could have been," she said. "I'm not sure."

Dillon and I looked at each other again.

"You don't suppose he was working for Hansen do you?" Dillon asked.

"It's a long shot," I said to Dillon and then turned to Terry Baldwin. "I'd like to find out when and where he was picked up the last time and who he was working for."

"Sure," she said, looking at her watch. "But it's going to have to be later, I have a meeting to go to."

"Sure, give me a call. If I'm not around, leave me a message," I said.

"No problem," she said. "Just out of curiosity, who's Hansen?"

"The guy that owned the speedboat used in the attack on the tanker Friday morning. He owns an auto body repair shop up in Manhattan Beach."

"Okay." She wrote Hansen's name on a piece of paper from the desk, then folded it in half. "I'll check out this guy Hansen for you, too. I'll see if we have anything on him."

"Thanks," I said. "I appreciate it."

"No problem," she said, smiling at me. "I still want to go rowing with you sometime."

"Sure," I said. "When we get past this, okay?"

***

Mike Dillon wanted to check out the operation at the Malaysia-Pacific Terminal to see what he'd missed earlier and since we were in the immediate area, the three of us stopped to find out if there were any new developments. Customs had the U.S. Department of

Agriculture assisting them with the inspection of the containers that came off the *Pacific Venture*. The plan was to x-ray each container as it came off the ship, but the x-ray machine broke down and it would be several days until the required spare parts arrived. That meant that unless each container was completely unloaded, only the contents at the back of the container could be checked. Contraband could easily be stowed at the front of a container or in the middle of the contents. We nosed around for about an hour before we got bored and drove back to the Coast Guard base.

I dropped Mike Dillon and Gregg Wyatt off at their black government Chevy Tahoe in the parking lot and headed for my office. It had been a little more than forty-eight hours since the initial attack on the *Beleza* and we had made exactly zero progress in the investigation. A clue here and a clue there but nothing matched up. We had no substantial suspects, other than Hannigan or Astal Kamran and they were both long shots at best. Worst of all, we didn't have any idea if there were more weapons in the port or where they might be. It was just past eleven in the morning now and my stomach growled and I tried to remember the last time I'd eaten anything. I sat down at my desk and one of the petty officers from the communication center brought me a stack of phone messages he'd taken while I was out. The top message was from Larry Jackson complaining about delays on the *Pacific Venture*. Big surprise. I'd half expected him to be camped out in the corridor waiting to chew my ass. The next message was from Terry Baldwin. She'd left a message saying that a lawyer came by the Processing Center just after we'd left to expedite the deportation of the eleven Mexican Nationals being held. Terry Baldwin took the man's name down for me.

Astal Kamran.

12

Astal Javad Kamran.

That's the name that came back when Linda Lonseal, a reserve deputy for the San Bernardino County Sheriff's Department, ran the vehicle identification number on the white minivan. Sergeant Hiller had assigned her the lowly task of running all the license plate numbers of the vehicles through the computer and when the Arizona license plate number didn't match the description of the vehicle, she ran the VIN from the tag on the dash. She told me she felt like she'd hit the jackpot on a as Vegas slot machine. Not only did the vehicle come back as stolen, it had an 'All Points Bulletin' issued by the United States Department of Homeland Security.

I was interviewing Deputy Lonseal and Mike Dillon was doing his best to get the low down on the Sheriff Department's Sunday morning sting operation at the Fontana salvage yard from Sergeant Shaun Hiller. The Channel Seven news cameras were a major distraction to Sergeant Hiller and I wondered if he was the one that had tipped off the reporters about Astal Kamran's van being recovered.

I wasn't sure why Mike Dillon invited me come with him to the Fontana auto salvage yard because after what I'd done to him earlier, I should have been on his shit list. He'd told me that his other agents were tracking down leads on Captain Hannigan's whereabouts and used car salesman Paul Hansen's involvement with the 28-foot Donzi 'Why Not' owned by the half-brother. I suspected that Dillon was onto something linking Captain Hannigan and Paul Hansen with the weapons and he wanted to keep me out of it. But then again, maybe it was because he needed a convenient place for the FBI helicopter to pick him up. He'd been in San Pedro when he got the call about Astal Kamran's minivan being recovered sixty miles to the east in the high desert town of Fontana and the Coast Guard base was the government's closest and most convenient heliport.

The sun was a brutal orange ball suspended in the hazy blue Fontana sky like a giant heat lamp. The auto salvage yard appeared to be about ten acres in size and was full of junk and wrecked cars. Several large corrugated steel buildings were in the center of the yard and a dozen or so metal-shipping containers were stacked neatly along the back fence line. Rancid motor oil, spilled antifreeze, and transmission fluid discolored the dirt underfoot and made it stick to the soles of my shoes. It had been ten minutes since the FBI chopper dropped us off fifty yards outside of the facility's ten-foot high chain link fence in a field of weeds. The rotors had thrown up enough dirt to blot out the sun and I still had dust grating inside my eyelids. Sweat was already beginning to trickle down the back of neck and from between my shoulder blades. Cool Pacific breezes don't reach this far inland.

Deputy Lonseal was straightforward in answering my questions and I was watching the interaction between Dillon and Sergeant Hiller out of the corner of my eye. The trouble with inter-agency cooperation is the diversity of personalities and agendas involved. The more I listened to what Sergeant Hiller was saying the more he sounded like Mike Dillon. Hiller was blowing his own horn loud enough for the news reporters to hear him and Dillon lingered in front of the television cameras a little too long giving his very best performance as FBI-agent-in-charge of the situation.

"Why don't we see what else is going on here," I said to Dillon, thinking it a wise move to talk things over out of earshot of the reporters. "I don't have all day."

Dillon and Sergeant Hiller pried themselves away from the press and we walked over to the largest building. It had four overhead garage-style doors and they were wide open. A total of seven vehicles in various stages of assembly were inside. Five heavily armed San Bernardino County SWAT team officers had eight suspects handcuffed and sitting cross-legged on the concrete floor.

"We've been watching this place for a couple of months," explained Sergeant Hiller. "A lot of the higher end vehicles in the county have been disappearing."

"And they were coming here?" Dillon asked.

"We were aware of some unusual activity at this site and when we could get a warrant, we decided to check it out," Sergeant Hiller said.

Dillon surveyed the inside of the building for a moment and then said, "Let's take a look at the minivan you found. You can explain as we walk."

"Sure," Sergeant Hiller said, leading us back into the yard. "Anyway, like I was saying, we've been losing a lot of high end vehicles in the county."

"High end?" Dillon asked. "What do you call high end?"

"Mercedes, Porsche, Cadillac, Jaguar, sometimes a few Suburbans and a Ford Expedition or two. All newer models."

"And what led you here?" Dillon asked.

"A tip from a local citizen down the street, an old guy that has lived here for years. He said he's awake most of the night and that he's noticed a lot of activity here at all hours of the night and thought that it was unusual. So we started watching it and sure enough, cars were going in and nothing was coming out so we figured it was a chop-shop operation. We took down license numbers of vehicles going in and when they came back as stolen, we had enough for a search warrant and here we are. We ran the license plates on the cars that still had plates on them and most of them are stolen. We're still running VINs on the cars with no plates."

Dillon was making notes on a spiral pad and nodded his head for Sergeant Hiller to continue his explanation.

"Then the minivan turned up," Sergeant Hiller said. "That's when I called my Lieutenant...and he called you."

"Who owns this place?" Dillon asked.

"Same guy for the last forty years," Sergeant Hiller said. "He's seventy-eight now and he says his nephew is running it with a few of his friends."

Astal Kamran's minivan was parked next to a small beat up camping trailer with two flat tires. FBI crime scene personnel had just arrived and were unpacking their equipment.

"Whew!" Dillon said as he looked at the interior of the van. " It looks like they've been living in there."

Junk-food wrappers, empty soda and beer cans, blankets, and pillows littered the interior of the minivan. The ashtray was over-flowing with cigarette butts. Body odor and the lingering smell of marijuana emanated from the dark blue cloth upholstery.

"This is just like we found it," Sergeant Hiller said.

"Who do you have in custody?" Dillon asked.

"We have eight guys, all green cards from Mexico."

"Let's have a look at them again," Dillon said. "What can you tell me about the owner's nephew?"

"We don't have him in custody and we don't have any idea where he is. His name is Alex Burke. Did a couple of years up in Lompoc for car burglaries and petty theft."

Sergeant Hiller led us into the other steel building he thought served as a parts warehouse. I walked over to a Porsche. The trunk lid, doors and most of the interior had been stripped from the vehicle. Several other vehicles were in the warehouse and obviously in various stages of disassembly.

"Selling parts?" Dillon asked.

"No sir, I don't think so," Sergeant Hiller said.

"No?" Dillon asked. "Then what are they doing with these cars?"

"My theory is that they are rebuilding these things."

"What do you mean rebuilding them?"

Sergeant Hiller beamed. "I think what they've been doing is stealing vehicles, stripping them down and dumping what's left of the bodies on the street somewhere. They carefully label all the parts from each vehicle and store them in the shipping containers. When we find a stripped out and abandoned vehicle on the street, we have it towed away," explained Sergeant Hiller. "Then somebody buys the stripped out body for next to nothing from the insurance company, and since the Vehicle Identification Number is never removed, they can get a salvage title to it. Then they bring the bodies back here, put the same engine and transmission back in using the very same nuts and bolts, and then the interior is put back and the doors re-hung. For a couple of thousand dollars worth of time and trouble, they have a forty or fifty thousand dollar vehicle with a clear title."

"What about the minivan?" I asked. "If that's what they're doing here, the minivan doesn't seem like it's a vehicle they'd want for this operation."

"No. I think they were just using it for transportation," Sergeant Hiller said. "You can't get more low profile than a white minivan in San Bernardino County."

"What about the suspects you have in custody?" Dillon asked. "What do you know about them?"

"Like I said, they all have green cards. Nobody has a record, at least not under the names we have for them. It seems like the older guy is in charge. We frisked them all and we found this notebook on him." Sergeant Hiller handed Dillon a cheap red covered notebook.

Dillon thumbed through the notebook and I leaned in to look at it with him.

"What makes you think he's in charge?" Dillon asked.

"I don't know, just that he's older and the way that the others keep looking at him to see how he's reacting. It's just a guess, but I'm pretty sure he's the guy in charge of them."

"You're probably right," Dillon said, looking at more pages in the book.

"So Dillon, what do you think?" I asked.

Dillon pursed his lips. "I don't know. I was hoping there would be something in this notebook that would help. It just looks like notes about what they need to finish building the vehicles and some type of numbering system about where each vehicle's parts are stored."

"What's that doodling?"

"I don't know, looks like an "O" with a "T" through it," Dillon said.

"And how about the funny looking "H"?" I asked. The "H" was wider at the top and bottom, narrower in the middle. "Looks like he turned a couple of them into butterflies."

"Yeah. A doodler." Dillon continued to thumb through the notebook.

"It all means something," I said.

Dillon and Sergeant Hiller looked at me like I was crazy.

"It expresses what was on his mind when he was killing time," I explained. "Most of us doodle when we're bored. This guy may have been on the phone, maybe calling about a part, and doodled on the page in the book while he waited. Everything in the book means something, all of the numbers and all of the doodling."

"Doodling is doodling as far as I know," Dillon said. "What makes you think it means something?"

"I knew somebody that did a thesis on it in grad school," I said. "The Bureau probably has some geek in a back room somewhere that could decipher it."

Dillon and Sergeant Hiller considered what I was saying but were noncommittal.

"Sergeant Hiller," I said, changing the subject. "You say you've been watching this place for several months. Any theory on where the cars are going once they get them back together and they leave here?"

Sergeant Hiller shook his head. "No telling, we haven't gotten that far yet," he said. "They could be shipping them to car auctions in another state, or even have a car lot of their own somewhere here in California. They could be going anywhere. We'll look through the files and see if something turns up, unless you want your people to look through it."

Dillon nodded his head affirmatively. "We'll want you to do that for us."

"How big an operation do you suppose they are running here?" I asked.

Sergeant Hiller shrugged his shoulders. "Hard to say," he said. "But I would guess that if they operate this day and night, using the same people to take the cars apart and put them back together again---then maybe ten cars or so a week. But that's just a guess."

"I'd say that it's a pretty big operation," Dillon said. "Ten cars a week, thirty or forty thousand-dollar per vehicle, that's three or four hundred thousand a week. They could easily be grossing a million dollar a month."

Sergeant Hiller stood a little straighter.

"Too bad the news cameras are already out front," I said. "Maybe we could've kept this quiet for awhile and see who else showed up.

Now it's going to be all over the news and anybody else involved won't come within a thousand miles of this place."

Sergeant Hiller shrunk a little.

"It still might work," Dillon said, trying to sound optimistic. "Let's get rid of everybody out front. Maybe the news people will hold this until the evening news tomorrow and we'll have twenty-four hours to see if anybody else comes in."

"Good luck with that," I said. "But it wouldn't hurt to try."

Sergeant Hiller said he would take care of the news crews personally.

"Sergeant, I'm going to want the names of everybody you have in custody," Dillon said. "And keep them here, don't take them in and process them yet because if you take them to jail, word may get out. We don't want to tip off any more people than we already have. Maybe we'll get lucky."

Sergeant Hiller quickly scratched a copy of his notes, tore the sheet from his notepad, and after presenting it to Dillon, hurried off to take care of the media.

Dillon walked out of the warehouse to make a call on his cell phone and so I decided to nose around the salvage yard a little more. The first thing I noticed was that two Channel 13 news trucks had arrived and they were setting up a satellite dish. Sergeant Hiller was going to have a hell of a time getting this quieted down. The world is always hungry for news and I was sure that any sound bite about the *Beleza* would be gobbled up as fast as it hit the airwaves.

The salvage yard was hot and dusty and I was just about to go back in the shade of the warehouse when I saw it. It was an "O" with a "T" through it and it was on the driver's door of a semi-truck and trailer in the salvage yard. Just like the doodle in the notebook recovered from one of the suspects. I walked over and wiped the grime away with my hand. Oaxaca Trucking. Hermosillo, Mexico.

I was going to find Dillon and tell him about the truck but he found me first with news of his own. Astal Kamran's minivan, or at least the Arizona license plates currently attached to it, had crossed the border from Mexico into Nogales, Arizona yesterday afternoon.

"So, they left the original license plates on the van for the getaway from the boat fire in Manhattan Beach, but they put another set of license plates on it and go to Mexico?" I said.

"Looks like it," Dillon said.

"Why would they keep this particular minivan? They have a whole auto theft ring here and are getting cars with clear titles. They could steal and drive anything they want. Why change just the license plates and then keep driving Kamran's van?" I asked. "It doesn't make sense."

"Arizona license plates to cross the border at Nogales? Maybe because it's low profile?" Dillon suggested. "A lot of people from Arizona cross the border every day. Besides, if they got caught doing something illegal with one of their own cars, it could be traced back here, but with a stolen vehicle, they could just dump it and nothing would tie it to this little operation."

"Maybe," I said and then I told Dillon about what I'd found. "We need to find out more about Oaxaca Trucking. This is the second time today that they've turned up in this investigation."

Dillon nodded and then answered an incoming call on his cell phone. He turned his back to me and walked a few yards away. The call was short and he didn't offer to tell me what it was about.

"What do you say we look in a few of these shipping containers?" I said. "Just to see what we'll find."

"Maybe we should get Sergeant Hiller's boys to open them. There's no telling what's inside," Dillon said.

"Anything in particular you're afraid of finding?"

"Rattlesnakes."

I looked around. The salvage yard had vacant land full of weeds on three sides. Dillon might be right. "Good point. Hiller's boys are probably used to dealing with snakes out here."

"Curiosity killed the cat," Dillon said and went to round up a couple uniformed deputies from the San Bernardino County Sheriff's Department.

"Do you get many snakes around here?" I asked as the deputy opened the first box for us and shined his flashlight inside.

"A few," he said with a smile. "You don't like snakes?"

"Not much."

Sergeant Hiller's theory turned out to be right on the money. The container was full of automobile parts. I watched as the deputy carefully lifted a sheet of plastic. A piece of paper taped to the plastic identified the parts as those to a 2008 Jaguar. Leather seats, front and back. Leather door panels. Carpet. A box that contained the stereo and all the speakers. Engine and Transmission. Nuts and bolts in marked baggies. Pirelli tires, still on Jaguar wheels, were stacked nearby. A box of lug nuts sat on the floor next to the stack of wheels. I was relieved not to find a rattlesnake coiled up under the plastic.

"They certainly have it down to a science," Dillon said.

"Yes, they do." I lifted the sheet of plastic again. "They get these guys with green cards to do all the dirty work. I'll bet they have a couple of guys lifting cars off the street full time. They can probably have a car taken apart and in a container before it's even reported stolen."

I wouldn't doubt it," Dillon said, looking under the plastic at the collection of Jaguar parts. Dillon hesitated and then looked directly at me. "Why Oaxaca Trucking though?"

"NAFTA," I said. "Since they passed the trade agreement, Mexican and Canadian trucking companies can get away with operating inside the United States."

"So?"

"So, they aren't subject to the same scrutiny as U.S. trucking companies," I said. "Local cops don't like to pull them over because it's a waste of time. Most of the time the drivers can't speak English, or at least they pretend they don't speak English, and then the tickets never get paid. These guys don't have local driver's licenses so there is no way to keep track of them. It's a mess. Using a Mexican or Canadian trucking company is the ultimate in low profile."

The deputy's walkie-talkie squawked. One of his partners was looking for the Feds.

"What do they have?" Dillon asked.

"Weapons," said the deputy. "They found a container with crates of weapons."

We sprinted four containers down where a deputy stood in front of the open container doors pointing at the contents.

Sunlight spilled inside and I could read what was on the boxes but Dillon aimed his flashlight beam at the words stenciled on the metal box anyway. SEP DARD 120. The words 'Anti-tank', along with precautions, were written in French.

"That's them," Dillon said. "That's what we're looking for."

I reached down and opened the first box. Empty. I looked at Dillon and then opened the second metal box. Empty.

Four of the metal boxes were empty; eight still had their rockets inside. There was also a cardboard box with food and a couple of gallon jugs of water inside the shipping container. An old stained twin sized mattress with a pillow and blanket was on the floor near the rocket boxes. Somebody had been living with the weapons.

Dillon made everyone stand clear of the container and then made another call on his cell phone. We inspected the remaining shipping containers but only found car parts. No snakes or SEP DARDS.

There wasn't much adding to do when the subtracting was done. Four rockets had been used on the *Beleza*. We had eight more still in their original shipping crates. That made twelve. We were still missing sixteen SEP DARDS and a couple hundred kilos of plastic explosives. I hate it when that happens.

13

Sunday afternoon turned out to be a glorious fall day in San Pedro Harbor. A large area of high-pressure was building over Nevada and the clockwise circulation of the weather system had cleared the smutty skies in Southern California. Arbitrary cumulus clouds, like white cotton candy caricatures, frolicked on a baby blue background, changing their shapes with every whisper of the fickle ocean breeze; the sun was a resplendent promise from heaven.

Dillon and I had taken the thirty-minute helicopter ride back to the Coast Guard base from Fontana once the weapon situation was contained. Homeland Security's Terrorist Task Force had been called in and ran all us mere mortals out of the salvage yard. FBI crime scene personnel towed Astal Kamran's minivan somewhere so they could go over it with a fine-toothed comb. Dillon spent quite a bit of time on his cell phone while we waited for the chopper to pick us up in Fontana. It was obvious that he had something else going on but he was still playing his cards close to his chest. An unmarked government car with tinted windows was waiting for him when we landed at the Coast Guard base and he got into the car without looking back or saying where he was going. Not even a goodbye, screw-you, or kiss-my-ass.

A little over fifty-six hours had lapsed since the tanker *Beleza* had been attacked at the entrance to San Pedro Harbor, and now she was at the end of a towline, outbound for Singapore. A lot had happened concerning the *Beleza* in just fifty-six hours.   Underwriters and surveyors from Lloyd's of London had inspected the ship while she lay in the mud off Berth 46 in the outer harbor where Captain Hannigan grounded her. Surviving crewmembers were flown home and new crew replacements that were needed to discharge the vessel's remaining cargo had arrived from the Isle of Man. A powerful Dutch salvage tug had pulled the damaged tanker from the mud and she'd been moved as a dead-tow to her unloading berth to discharge her cargo. Now she was leaving San Pedro for good.

The *Beleza's* owners ultimately decided that the damaged ship didn't fit into their long-range plans, so they offered her up for sale. As is, where is. An opportunistic ship operator from Hong Kong quickly closed the deal and made arrangements for the ship to be towed to Singapore for a complete overhaul. Before being put back into service, the ship would need extensive repairs to her hull and engineroom, a fresh coat of paint, and undoubtedly a new name. Her current name was now too famous.

Local and national news services monitored the progress of the empty tanker as she was slowly towed down the main ship channel toward the open sea. Local news helicopters plied the skies overhead, documenting the action while the salvage crew rigged the towing bridle on the foredeck of the *Beleza* in preparation for the ocean voyage. Just inside the breakwater, responsibility for the ship would be transferred from the harbor pilot and local harbor tugs to the master of the brawny salvage tug that would take her to Singapore.

There would be no formal ceremony to bid the ship and human victims of the attack farewell or to wish the vessel good luck on its perilous voyage across the Pacific. Nothing more than routine entries in the logbooks of the salvage and harbor tugs involved in moving the ship out to sea would indicate the *Beleza* was ever in the harbor and the only formality would be a friendly wave goodbye from a deckhand after he got his tug's towline back aboard. Tonight's sound bites on the evening news would probably the last anybody would hear about the ship's brief and eventful time in the limelight because the *Beleza* was old news now. Sunday's hottest stories included a prominent actress going to drug and alcohol rehabilitation and a Los Angeles city councilman that was photographed leaving a massage parlor in a seedy section of Hawthorne. Somehow, during her brief stay in San Pedro Harbor, the *Beleza* had been transformed from the victim into the problem, and everyone involved would be glad when she finally cleared the breakwater and disappeared into the sunset.

Less than two hours after the Fontana raid, Admiral Ballard gave a nationally televised news conference from the East Coast during which he explained how the multi-agency task force had taken only two days to get to the bottom of the attack that crippled the Port of San Pedro. Arrests had been made and illicit arms seized. He talked of the urgent need for enhanced harbor security and made a point of emphasizing that our nation's harbors are the primary lifeline to the entire world's economy. Admiral Ballard vowed to lobby Congress to increase the budget allocations for the Coast Guard and other agencies charged with maintaining port security.

I wasn't about to take a chance of the *Beleza* being attacked on her way out of the harbor so I'd caught a ride on the 86-foot Coast Guard Cutter that trailed the massive tanker down the main shipping channel. The cutter's captain graciously offered me his chair in the wheelhouse and brought me cup of hot and bitter black coffee. Normally, the captain is the only one in the ship's crew allowed to sit while in the wheelhouse; everybody else is required to stand and now I know why. The low pitch drone and steady vibration of the cutter's engines was putting me to sleep. I walked from bridge wing to bridge wing a few times to get my blood flowing, poured another cup of coffee, and then tried Calling Rita Velasco a few times but couldn't reach her. I was surprised she wasn't around for the *Beleza's* departure but several Sea Marshals I talked to told me she'd gone home after checking on the ship's security this morning.

Following the ship down the channel was about as exciting as watching grass grow. I had a lot better things to do this afternoon but being here right now was a cover-your-ass move learned best in government service and honed to a fine edge before retirement. Those in government employment that don't know enough to cover their own butts often find themselves in the civilian sector selling vacuum cleaners door-to-door and wondering where they went wrong. If somebody decided to take a long range pot-shot at the ship, there wasn't too much I could really do about it, but after what Admiral Ballard said, I was damn sure going to be on the scene.

Not enough sleep and too much caffeine do strange things to the human brain. I was leaning on the port bridge wing and the world was going by like some cheap B-movie where faces flickered and the words didn't quite fit the mouth's movements. It took me a moment after the cutter's captain spoke to me to realize that he'd asked me if I needed more coffee. My brain was out of synch with my surroundings; my hand gave him my coffee cup before my brain said to do it. When he handed my cup back full of steaming coffee, I heard myself ask him how fast we were moving. "Three and a half knots," he said and when I just stared at him because his words didn't register, he added, "About four miles an hour."

Four miles and hour! Shit, I walk faster than that. We'd shut down the whole damn harbor to move the *Beleza* past the breakwater. Ships at their berths were waiting to sail and ships at sea were waiting to come in and we were holding them up with a dead-tow moving four miles an hour!

I took too big a drink of the too hot coffee and that brought me around a little. The cutter's captain was talking to me again and although his words weren't registering, his lips and the sound he made were in synch this time. My brain was stuck in a pre-sleep type state where it was just freewheeling. Thoughts entered my head and departed just as quickly as they'd arrived, but an uneasy feeling began to emerge. I was missing something or something was about to happen. I could feel it. I just wanted to lie down and I told myself that as soon as I got off this cutter I wouldn't even go home, I'd just lock my office door and sleep on the floor until I was rested enough to drive home.

The anxiety turned to guilt as Elisha's memories entered my head. Her death was my fault as surely as if I'd put a gun to her head and pulled the trigger myself. Sure, the affair wasn't my fault because it was part of the undercover assignment. What happens undercover doesn't count in real life does it? If you ask an undercover cop if he's a cop and he says he isn't, then he's lying. So if you sell him the drugs and he arrests you, can your attorney get the charges dismissed because he lied? I don't think so. The whole thing was bad timing. First the affair. Then her cancer. Elisha wouldn't fight it. She didn't even want to try. The only control she felt she had over her life was to refuse medical care. If she couldn't control her life, she would sure as hell control her death. Her family begged her to get treatment and when they asked why she refused, she would only say, "Ask Jared." My affair devastated her and in return she'd laid a blanket of guilt on me so thick I'd never get out from under it. I couldn't remember any of the good times we'd had and we had plenty of good times. Great times. Now all I can remember about her is the pain and the hurt and her slow death at the hands of cancer and the broken heart I caused. Nobody should die like that or have to live with the residual guilt.

I forced myself to think of something else. What was it that bothered me about the Fontana bust? I got the feeling that something wasn't right but the heat, dust, confusion, lack of sleep, and the threat of rattlesnakes had distracted me. I forced my mind away from Elisha to go over the Fontana bust again. Twelve SEP DARD boxes. Four empty. Eight still had their contents. Obviously the reported shipment of twenty-eight rockets and plastic explosives had been split up. It didn't take a genius to figure that out. Did the four empty boxes belong to the rockets used in the *Beleza* attack? If not, there was another cache, maybe in the harbor. If the *Beleza* rockets had come from a different cache, then several hundred pounds of explosives and four SEP DARDS were missing from Fontana and part of another attack plot. That had to be it. Fontana was sixty miles as the crow flies from San Pedro Harbor. Why keep the munitions that far away from the attack? Fontana had to be close to the next attack. But where and why?

It hit me so hard my knees buckled. That had to be it. I wondered why Mike Dillon hadn't heard of the land bridge when I'd explained it to him at my house. He wasn't being friendly when he offered to take me out for a beer Friday night. He wanted to find out how much I'd figured out. He was playing dumb!   I tried to picture the national railroad system in my mind. The three major port areas on the West Coast were Seattle, the San Francisco Bay area, and the Los Angeles basin and they all fed into four major sets of tracks across the country to the East Coast. Take out a single bridge on any of those major systems and the whole rail line comes to a standstill. East of the Mississippi, traffic could be routed around a damaged area, but out west, only four major track systems exist and there are hundreds of bridges across creeks and canyons. A few hundred pounds of explosives strategically placed on a railroad trestle could bring it crashing down in a jumble of twisted steel and concrete. A couple of SEP DARDS into the lead locomotive and we'd have a derailment over a mile long with thousands of containers strewn everywhere. Clean up and the resulting disruptions could last weeks or months. The land bridge across the United States is one giant Achilles Heel in the global transportation system and somebody's got that figured it out.

I felt a hand on my shoulder and the cutter's captain was talking to me but his words weren't registering.

"What?" I said. "I was thinking of something else."

"They found another body, Commander," he said.

"Another body?"

"Yessir, just like the last one. Shot in the back of the head, execution style."

It took a moment for it to register what he was saying. "Malaysia-Pacific?"

"No sir. The Korea Line Terminal this time."

14

The elderly black guard greeted me from his seat inside the metal and glass guard shack that stood at the entrance to the Korea Lines shipping terminal. I flashed my credentials and smiled at the man that had that *I just want to go home* look of somebody that had worked all day.

"Got 'em backed up this evening," I said to the guard, nodding toward the long line of trucks waiting outside the terminal gate.

"Yessir," he said as he slumped back into his seat.

It was twenty past five and I hoped I wouldn't be too late getting to the crime scene. I threaded the blue Coast Guard sedan through countless rows and stacks of containers until I found the water and then looked up and down the dock line, not quite sure which way to turn. Finally, I saw an SPPD squad car screaming through the terminal with its lights flashing so I followed it. I parked near the other vehicles on the quay, stepped over the yellow tape, and held up my identification for one of the uniformed police officers at the scene.

I'd been to enough crime scenes over the years that I had could get a feel of who was who in no time at all. It didn't take long for me to spot Larry Jackson of the Pacific Shipping Association and he'd cornered someone dressed in the classic FBI uniform of the day. I could see that Jackson was furious, and since I was curious, I slowly circled around the pair and eased up to them from an angle that was behind their line of sight. When I was within earshot, I turned my back to them, took a notepad from shirt pocket, and pretended to study it while eavesdropping on their conversation.

"I know that." Larry Jackson said in a heated tone. "But we've been delayed for over three hours now. Do you have any idea how much money it's costing Korea Lines to have that ship steaming in circles outside the harbor while you've got longshoremen crews standing by doing nothing?"

"Well..." stammered the FBI agent.

"They've lost over a hundred thousand dollars this afternoon so far." Jackson said. "And now you have cargo backed up for miles outside the front gate."

Not wanting any part of their conversation, I tried to slip away in the direction of the crowd that was milling around the coroner's van and what was sure to be the recovered body.

"Commander!" shouted Larry Jackson before I could escape unnoticed.

I pretended to look around and act like I hadn't noticed the pair talking and feigned studying my notebook briefly before returning it my uniform shirt pocket. It didn't work. Larry Jackson stood in front of me.

"Mr. Jackson," I said matter-of-factly and then turned to greet the FBI agent. I recognized him as one of Dillon's clones but hadn't been introduced yet. "I don't believe we've met."

"Special Agent James Edmonds," said the youngster in the dark suit, white shirt and black tie. James Edmonds wore immaculately shined black Corfam shoes.

Edmonds had soft blue eyes and an even softer handshake to go with his sweet smile, straight teeth and manicured fingernails. I tried to pinpoint his accent that sounded like it originated somewhere near the Boston area. My first guess was that the Bureau had recently recruited Edmonds from an Ivy League law school.

"How long is this terminal going to be closed, Commander?" demanded Larry Jackson.

"You know," I said, trying to be as polite as possible, especially since Jackson had stormed away from our last conversation at the Marine Safety Office. "I just got here and I'm trying to get up to speed. Let me go over here and ask around and I'll get right back to you."

Larry Jackson didn't have time to respond because I turned quickly on my heels and moved toward the crowd lingering around the coroner's van. Neither Jackson nor Edmonds called out after me and I considered myself lucky.

A Coast Guard Sea Marshal patrol boat accompanied two police boats with flashing blue lights that secured a perimeter in the water about fifty yards off the dock. Several small civilian powerboats lingered outside the established perimeter. I looked to see if Rita Velasco was in the Coast Guard patrol boat but I didn't see her. She must still be asleep because she hadn't returned my calls yet.

I observed the crowd at the crime scene for a few moments and when I spotted the person that looked to be in charge, I politely maneuvered through the crowd, displaying my credentials and flashing my best smile.

"Commander Stanton," said the neatly dressed plainclothes detective. "I'm Lieutenant Bill Halverson," he said as offered to shake hands. "I've been to a couple of your meetings but we haven't met yet."

Halverson had an efficient smile that showed no teeth, hard dark eyes and a steel-like handshake. His neatly cut and thinning brown hair was graying around the temples and it was obvious by the way he conducted himself that this wasn't his first dead body. Halverson searched the pockets of his light blue sports jacket before finding what he was looking for in the left rear pocket of his tan slacks. He handed me one of his business cards.

I accepted the card, nodded politely, a habit I'd picked up dealing with Asian businessmen, and then looked at Halverson's shoes. Halverson wore weathered but comfortable brown Red Wings and I knew he spent more time on his feet than sitting behind a desk.

"What can I do for you this evening?" Halverson asked, smiling without a hint of cockiness or condescension.

"Just nosing around," I said, returning his smile. Professional courtesy. "What do we have here?"

"We've got a John Doe is what we got. A harbor tug with a bunker barge spotted the body floating about twenty yards off the dock," Halverson said. "Looks like a single gunshot wound to the back of the head. I'm guessing he's probably been in the water three or four days. We'll know more after we get the coroner's report."

I glanced around the West Basin of San Pedro Harbor where the Korea Line Terminal was located. The West Basin was more or less triangular in shape, about a thousand yards across at the widest point. The south end of the basin, one of the tips of the triangle, was open and a channel led to the main shipping channel under the Vincent Thomas Bridge. A large black-hulled containership was berthed on the north side of the basin and two small rusty coastal type freighters were docked on the east side. The body had been found floating just off the dock on the west side of the basin.

"Shot execution-style?" I said.

"Yep, just like that Custom's agent." Halverson squinted. The sun was low in the sky, just above the tops of the warehouses and was shining in his eyes, so he took a couple of steps away from the crowd and turning away, motioned for me to come closer.

"Do you have anything on this that I should know about, Commander?" he asked, eyeing me in a polite but suspicious manner.

"Not a thing," I said. "But I do wonder if the two are connected. Have you checked to see if Customs is missing anybody else?"

"I got a guy checking it out but haven't heard back from him yet."

I glanced around the West Basin again. "Any idea how the body got here?"

Lieutenant Halverson gave me a non-committal shake of his head. "We have a couple of canine units checking all the terminals in the basin," he said as he motioned towards the ships docked on the far side. "They're concentrating along the water line, looking for blood mostly. But heck, the body could have been dumped anywhere along here. Maybe even from a boat. And since the body has been in the water three or four days, I doubt they're going to find anything. Even blood scent fades in that time."

We stood silent, studying the growing number of curious civilian pleasure craft lingering outside the perimeter established by the police boats.

"So we could be looking at a murder that took place hundreds of miles from here and they just dumped the body in the harbor?" I asked.

"Could be," he said. "But why dump the body in the harbor instead of out in the ocean. I mean, if you have a boat, why not tie some weight to the body and send it to the bottom of the ocean where nobody but the crabs would ever find it?"

"Maybe somebody gets seasick."

"Maybe," he said. "Then again, maybe somebody wants to make sure we find the body."

"Maybe it's to send a message to someone."

Lieutenant Halverson nodded. He reached into his pants pocket and pulled out a pack of Juicy Fruit and offered me a piece.

"No thanks, chewing gum makes the fillings in my teeth hurt."

Halverson unwrapped a piece of gum and stuck it in his mouth.

"Is this going to be your case?" I asked.

"Yeah," he said. "Unfortunately."

"Who's got the Customs agent's case?"

"I've got that one, too." Halverson chuckled to himself, looked at his feet and shook his head. "Although the Feds have their noses into that one all the way up to their ankles. Everything goes through them."

"Are you being punished for something?" I asked with a smile. "You draw both these murders and get to work with the Feds."

Halverson looked pained. "The Captain tells me they give me these cases because I'm good," he said. "But I think he gives them to me so that when things get fucked up he has a good reason not to promote me."

"That's how it usually works, never be too good at your job, you'll never get promoted because your boss won't want to lose you. Screw up and maybe he'll recommend you for promotion in a different precinct."

"I'll keep that in mind," he said. "I'll try to screw up a few cases just to make it look good.

"Have you developed any leads on the murder of that Customs agent?" I asked.

Halverson squinted and looked away. "Not much."

"Are you having trouble getting Customs to cooperate?"

Halverson eyed me. "How'd you know that?"

"They're treating everybody like that," I said. "I can't figure out if they're trying to cover something up or if they're on the verge of breaking something wide open and don't want to share information."

Halverson chewed his gum and watched as the body was loaded into the coroner's van.

"Why don't I get your cell phone number," I said. "You've got both these cases and the guy from the Bureau looks like he's still wet behind the ears."

"It's on my card," he said. "So, I take it that you've met the Agent Edmonds?"

"Just briefly, a few minutes ago. He was talking to Larry Jackson so I didn't hang around."

"Yeah, Jackson was over here hounding me and I sent him over to talk to Edmonds to get him off my back."

"Larry Jackson seems pretty hot under the collar."

"Can't say that I blame him," he said. "It was just rotten luck that the body showed up here just before a ship was supposed to come in. It screwed up their scheduling pretty bad I guess."

I glanced around the West Basin again and could see that one of the canine teams was coming down the dock towards us. The dog, a large dark German Shepard with a lolling pink tongue, looked relaxed, like he was going for a walk in the park and I knew he hadn't turned up anything.

"How well do you know Larry Jackson?" I asked.

"What do you mean?"

"It's funny, but I have a feeling I know him from somewhere and I just can't place him."

Halverson smiled his efficient smile. "Teflon."

"Teflon?"

"Yeah, that's his nickname around here."

"Why Teflon?"

"Nothing sticks to him."

"I'm not following you."

Halverson took a couple more steps away from the crowd and glanced around to make sure no one was eavesdropping.

"That Simms Lines incident a few years ago," he said in a low voice.

"Simms Lines?"

"Yeah, there was a harbor commissioner that got busted for taking bribes."

"Okay," I said, finally remembering where I'd seen Larry Jackson before. The evening news. "That happened a few years ago, just before I got here, but I remember seeing something about it on television. What was that all about?"

"A few years back, Simms Lines wanted to move into the harbor," he said, pointing toward the two rusty freighters across the triangular basin. "Over there, I think."

The evening sun made the two ships look like derelicts waiting to sink alongside the dock.

"Anyway, the board of harbor commissioners had to approve the contract and the board was split. Some of them didn't want to tie the dock space up with a long-term contract like Simms Lines wanted. The vote went against Simms Lines and shortly after that, Steve Walcott, one of the harbor commissioners, was investigated for taking bribes. It seems like he got too good a deal on a forty-foot powerboat from down in San Diego."

"Somebody gave him a powerboat to vote against Simms Lines? Why would somebody pay him to vote against a long term contract for the harbor?"

"Well," Halverson said. "First of all, Walcott insisted he paid for the boat, but it turns out he actually paid way below market value for it. Secondly, Walcott claims he was being set up because he voted against the Simms contract."

"Set up by who?"

"Larry Jackson," he said. "Walcott claimed Larry Jackson came to him and asked him to be the swing vote on the Simms Line contract but that he didn't do it."

"But that's kind of Jackson's job isn't it?"

Halverson shrugged his shoulders. "Lobbying is part of his job but bribing public officials isn't. Anyway, the boat appraised for $160,000 but Walcott could only show proof of paying $22,000."

"So who blew the whistle?"

Halverson shrugged his shoulders and then glanced around to make sure no one was listening. "Walcott claims it was Jackson that turned him in but no one knows for sure. Walcott got busted on an anonymous tip."

"Why would Jackson turn Walcott in if he was the one that bribed him? Wouldn't that implicate Jackson in the bribery case?"

"Sure," said Halverson. "If anybody could prove it. Knowing something and proving it in court are two entirely different propositions."

"Ain't that the truth?"

"Anyway, the investigation showed that Walcott bought the boat through a third party, and that's where they got a little sloppy."

"Who got sloppy?"

"Jackson's firm. The whole sale was supposed to be hush-hush, but a young lawyer from the firm gave his phone number to the third party that bought the boat from the original owner. I guess there was a finder's fee involved, and the whole transaction was cash, except the $22,000 check from Walcott that was supposed to make the deal look legitimate. Anyway this young lawyer, I can't remember his name right off, gave his phone number out and the investigators tracked him back to Jackson's firm."

"Still, why would Jackson turn dime on the guy?"

"Revenge," said Halverson. "Or maybe to make an example out of him."

"So how did it all turn out?"

"Walcott got ten years with all but three months suspended, and I think he got out in about thirty days, but he got kicked off the harbor commission."

"How about the others?"

"Like I said, Jackson is called Teflon, so they never proved he had anything to do with it. The young lawyer got disbarred and I don't know whatever happened to him."

"Do you think it put a stop to bribe taking in the harbor?"

"I doubt it. Bribes and kick-backs are just a part of doing business in America."

"I hate to admit it, but I have to agree with you. We have the best government that money can buy," I said. "What about Simms Lines?"

"They ended up signing a long term contract up in the Bay Area, Oakland I think."

One of the German Shepards working the terminal walked up and wagged its tail at Halverson. Halverson scratched the dog's ears before the officer on the other end of the leash put the dog in the back of the black and white Dodge Durango that served as transportation for the canine unit.

"So what's your gut feeling, detective?" I asked.

"About what, Commander?"

"These harbor homicides. You've been around the block a few times. Do you have a theory yet?"

Lieutenant Halverson chewed his gum and hesitated while he formulated his answer. "You know what, Commander," started Halverson, pausing to re-formulate his answer. "There were over twelve thousand homicides that went unsolved in this country last year. Unless we have a clear motive or substantial crime scene evidence, like in a domestic dispute or somebody shoots a convenience store clerk and we get it on tape, we're pretty much shit-out-of-luck. I hate to tell you this, Commander, but we usually only get the dumb criminals, the smart ones get away with it."

I'd worked with the Bureau long enough to know he was right.

Halverson looked at me and forced an apologetic smile. "Then there's the bad news, Commander."

"What's that?"

"By the time I fill out this report," he said. "I'll be on my next case. I'll just add this John Doe's file to the stack already on my desk. Unless something falls into my lap, this one will probably go unsolved. I hate to say it, Commander, but it's true."

I knew what he meant. Law enforcement agencies all have limited resources and more and more of their resources were being dedicated to anti-terrorism these days. Unfortunately, most of their anti-terrorism activities are largely undercover and not obvious to the general public who is becoming increasingly frustrated with the rise in street crime. It's frustrating for everyone, especially local cops, and there's no end in sight.

"This John Doe will lay in the morgue with his toe tag on and we'll hope that somebody eventually claims him and gives us something to go on," he said. "If not, well, the morgue only has so much room…and you know what happens then."

Halverson and I watched as the coroner's van drove off and the yellow tape began to come down. Larry Jackson was making a beeline for us. James Edmonds was talking on his cell phone.

"I'm all out of time here, Commander," Halverson said, watching Larry Jackson draw closer. "He's all yours."

"Sure," I said. "Thanks for your help. Next time you're over my way, stop in and I'll buy you a doughnut."

"I'll do that," he said smiling efficiently again. "I'm always looking for a new place to hide from the Captain."

Larry Jackson was closing at a rapid pace. Just as Jackson began to speak, Halverson turned to him and said, "Bring your ship in Mr. Jackson, we're all done here." Halverson promptly turned away and began barking orders to both uniformed and plainclothes officers at the scene. Almost immediately, policemen disappeared into their cars and started driving away like it had been rehearsed a thousand times before.

Unfortunately, I was left alone to face Larry Jackson.

"Commander Stanton," Larry Jackson said. "This is exactly what I was telling you about! Unnecessary delays!" Jackson looked at his watch. "Four hours! This is ridiculous!"

"Let me stop you right there," I said. "Don't mistake my naturally easygoing nature for weakness or stupidity, Mr. Jackson. We all have a job to do here, you need to understand that."

"I understand it all too well," he said. "I have a job to do here, also. And that job is to make sure our shippers are represented and not saddled with unnecessary delays while you and your people take all day to do your jobs!"

"I think we're getting off on the wrong foot. We should all be working together on this, not pointing fingers at one another assigning blame. Things happen that none of us have any control over, and these things need to be dealt with."

"I won't argue..." said Jackson as Agent Edmonds suddenly interrupted him.

"Commander Stanton," Agent Edmonds said. "I really need to talk to you."

"Not again!" Larry Jackson said. "Don't tell me..."

"Please, Mr. Jackson," said Edmonds. He danced from foot to foot like he needed to use the restroom. "This doesn't concern you."

"That'll be a first!"

Edmonds and I moved aside and then waited for Larry Jackson to leave.

"What's up?" I asked when we were finally alone.

Edmonds looked nervous and glanced over at Larry Jackson who luckily found a longshoreman willing to listen to his tirade.

"Astal Kamran has been shot."

"What?" I asked. "When, where, how?"

"Just a while ago. We'd picked him up again after he showed up to represent those illegals found in the container over at Malaysia-Pacific. We were moving him when he got shot?"

"Go on."

"Anyway, we had to move him for security reasons," Edmonds said, his eyes darting to and fro. "I just got the call from Special Agent Dillon and he said to tell you that Rita Velasco visited

Kamran and that's why they decided to move him. They figured if she could find him, somebody else could, too."

"They moved him because of Rita Velasco?"

"Exactly, and now they want to talk to her," he said. "Do you know where she is?"

"No. She has today off. She's worked a lot of hours and I sent her home."

"Well, you need to find her."

"I'll do that," I said, my mind racing. "How's Astal Kamran? Did they get the shooter?"

"They're taking him to the hospital now," Edmonds said, speaking excitedly. "But it doesn't look good, the sniper shot him with a high powered rifle as soon as they brought him out the front door. Somehow, somebody found out they were going to move him. And no, we didn't get the shooter yet."

"I'll find Lieutenant Velasco and give you a call," I said.

"You better come with me now," Edmonds said. "Agent Dillon wants us to meet him at the hospital right now."

15

The red Honda Accord in front of me braked for the light and I almost rear-ended it while trying Rita Velasco's cell phone number again. Agent Edmonds was two cars ahead of me in the Sunday evening traffic on Pacific Coast Highway enroute to the Veteran's Administration Hospital in Long Beach. I doubted Kamran was a military veteran so the FBI must be using the VA hospital for security reasons. Rita didn't answer and I left another message for her to call me and then I tried her home phone again. Still no answer.

Why did Rita visit Astal Kamran this afternoon? I had no doubt she could find him even if the FBI had him hidden somewhere. All it would take is a few phone calls and of course she had a Department of Homeland Security identification that would get her in to see him. Had Astal Kamran used her to get information about harbor operations or security and she wanted to confront him about it? Why did she look so shocked when I told her he was implicated in the *Beleza* attack? More importantly, what did Astal Kamran know that was so important somebody wanted him dead?

When traffic stopped again, I punched in Admiral Ballard's cell phone number.

"Good evening, Jared," he said. "I hope you're calling me with good news about that damn ship leaving."

"Yessir, she's clear of the harbor and safely on her way Singapore."

"Damn fine job, son," he said. "Damn fine job."

"Thank you, sir."

"And a damn fine job finding those weapons, Jared."

"It wasn't me, Admiral, it was the San Bernardino County Sheriff's Office that got lucky."

"But you had enough sense to take a closer look, Jared. Hell, those clowns may have left everything just lying there. They were busting up a chop shop, not looking for anti-tank rockets."

"I'm sure they would have found them eventually," I said. "I want to talk to you about something I think is strange about that, sir"

"What do you mean by strange?"

"We didn't find all the weapons or any of the explosives and I think that maybe…"

"I'm flying out of here tomorrow afternoon," he said, cutting me off. "We'll talk about it then. Anything else? I'm my way out to dinner."

"We found another body in the harbor this afternoon."

"Another body?"

"Yessir, we recovered another floater, shot in the back of the head like Mick Biller, the undercover Customs agent. This guy's been dead three or four days."

"Hell, Jared, that could be anybody, some pot smoking low-life for all we know. I doubt it means anything."

"And Astal Kamran was shot today," I said, somewhat frustrated by the Admiral's apathetic attitude. "I'm following the FBI over the VA Hospital right now."

There was a pause before Admiral Ballard spoke again. "You must be on your cell phone, Jared. You're breaking up. I'll swing by when I get in tomorrow, damn fine job on this case, son. Damn fine job."

Admiral Ballard disconnected before I could say anything else. It was obvious that he didn't want to talk to me. Why? Then it hit me. We were talking on our cell phones, which meant our conversation could be picked up if somebody were listening in. Unlike the average Joe-citizen's cell phone, of which there are about a hundred million, our government phones were encrypted and our conversations were quite secure unless another government agency was listening in. Is that why Admiral Ballard didn't want to talk to me? Was Homeland Security monitoring our conversations?

My brain was functioning at only a fraction of its normal speed. I needed sleep and I needed it bad. It was instinct and not rational thought that made me ditch Agent Edmonds. He was still two cars ahead of me in traffic when I made a quick right turn into a McDonalds burger joint and went out the back exit. By the time he got turned around I was long gone.

Thinking was making my head hurt so I knew I'd have to operate on instinct. Right now that instinct was telling me that I had to find Rita before the FBI did.

Rita Velasco lived in a small yellow two-bedroom house in Hawaiian Gardens just off the 605 Freeway. She'd hosted a couple of barbeques for the Sea Marshal unit over the summer. I'd been invited and made brief appearances to be polite but the Sea Marshals seemed to relax a little more when I wasn't around so I hadn't stayed long. I knew the exit off the freeway and that she lived on Manapua Way but I couldn't remember which house was hers. It was close to dusk, which didn't help because I'd only been to her house in the in the daytime and the area looked different to me now. The third time I drove down the street I checked names on the mailboxes and then finally found her yellow bungalow. The house had looked white to me in the low light the first two times I'd driven past. Rita owned a red Mazda Miata but it wasn't in the driveway and she didn't answer her front doorbell. A clapboard one-car garage was on the side of the house. I looked through a small dusty side window but her car wasn't inside.

What should I do now? She wasn't home or at work and wouldn't answer her cell phone. It's amazing how little you really know about people you work with. I knew Rita on a professional basis and had a good grasp on her abilities, but as far as her personal life, I didn't have a clue. She never mentioned a boyfriend. What were her hobbies? Who were her friends outside of work? Other than her ill-fated relationship with Mike Dillon when she worked for the Bureau and the fact that she knew Astal Kamran, I didn't really know a damn thing about her. My thinking was muddled and slow right now and I was too damn tired for this. Eddie Taylor. She knew Eddie Taylor, the security guy from Malaysia-Pacific, but I didn't know his phone number. Where did he live? Where the hell could Rita Velasco be at eight o'clock on a Sunday night?

I rang her doorbell again and was thinking about going around back to see if I could find a place to break in when the neighbor across the street let his Schnauzer out the front door to take care of dog business. Suddenly I became aware of how quiet the neighborhood was and what a bad idea breaking and entering would be. The Schnauzer finished his business and when he spotted me standing across the street, he started barking so I just got back in my car. I fished Detective Halverson's card out of my shirt pocket and punched his number into my cell phone.

"Halverson," he said.

"Working late?" I asked.

"I have two ex-wives getting alimony checks so I work all the overtime I can get." Halverson sounded exhausted. "Fortunately, the department has figured out that it's cheaper to work the shit out of the few detectives they have on the force than it is to hire more. What can I do for you, Commander?"

"I need a favor."

"Shoot."

"I can't find one of my Sea Marshals and I was wondering if you could run her name through the system to see if anything has turned up."

"Sure."

"Her name is Rita Velasco and she drives a red Mazda Miata."

"How long has she been missing?"

"Too long and I need to talk to her."

"Do you want to file a missing persons report?"

"I haven't got time."

"Since she's with Homeland Security, I think the FBI would be your best bet, Commander."

"I'm not on the best of terms with them right now."

There was enough silence on the other end to make me think I'd been disconnected.

"Do you have her driver's license number or the Miata's license plate?"

"Sorry."

"Give me a few minutes. I'll call you back."

"Sure."

I watched as the Schnauzer's owner brought the dog inside and after a few moments I could see somebody pull the drapes back to peek out the window.

It was about ten minutes before Halverson called me back.

"We don't have anything, Commander. She hasn't been in an accident or been arrested as far as I can tell."

"Thanks."

"I flagged her in our system so if one of our patrol officers spots her or her car, they'll call me."

"Thanks."

"Good luck, Commander. See you around the harbor."

Where the hell could she be on a Sunday night? The movies? Dinner? I damn sure was going to meet some of the local cops if I stayed here because the Schnauzer's owner kept looking out the window at me.

Church. I remembered she went to church on Sunday night. She often worked during the day on Sunday and would go to church at night. The guy's name was Pastor Jim. He'd been at one of her barbecues and I'd talked baseball with him. He was a California Angels fan and I told him I would pray for him.

The Schnauzer's owner watched me as I drove away. Back on the main drag, I stopped at a Gas & Grub convenience store and asked for a phone book. The clerk behind the counter was a twenty-something kid with bushy black hair, wiener arms, and a facial expression that said he wasn't very happy to be working there in the first place. He was even less happy when all I wanted was his phone book. I showed him my Homeland Security Identification and gave him a choice of handing me a phone book or getting handcuffed while I found it myself. Bushy-hair wasn't impressed but gave me the phone book anyway.

There are a lot of churches in the Yellow Pages and it took me awhile to find Pastor Jim Elliot's listing for a non-denominational Christian church. I threw the phone book back to the clerk and thanked him on my out.

The old white stucco Spanish Mission style church was at 4th and Elm in Westminster, about five minutes from the Gas & Grub on side streets and in a quiet residential neighborhood. The parking lot, sans any red Mazdas, was fairly empty but had enough cars to convince me that something was going on inside so I parked the government sedan and cut across the lawn to the church. A broad hedge-lined veranda with a red Mexican tiled roof stretched the width of the building and two massive oak doors marked the entrance. I paused to listen before entering and Sunday smells lingered in the air; a pelagic ocean breeze mixed with the scent of freshly mown grass and steaks cooking on the grill. The door creaked on its hinges as I slipped inside.

"In the Old Testament, wealth was regarded as evidence of God's favor," said Pastor Jim. "Let's consider our good friend Job for a minute."

Pastor Jim was a compact man, an ex-Marine if I remembered right, with disheveled gray-brown hair and thick black-framed glasses. He looked more like a mad scientist than a pastor.

I sat in one of the dark oil stained pews by myself, three rows from the back, and Pastor Jim acknowledged my arrival with a consenting nod. I was one of about twenty people in the church for the evening service and a quick glance around the room told me that Rita Velasco wasn't here either.

"Our friend Job was a very wealthy man," Pastor Jim said. He held up an open hand, waving to one side of the congregation and then quickly turned to face the other. "The bible says he had seven thousand sheep, three thousand camels, five hundred yoke of oxen, five hundred female donkeys, and a very large household, so that this man was the greatest of all the people of the East."

I turned my cell phone off and tried to decide what to do next. It was a long shot, but maybe Rita had confided something useful from her personal life to her pastor. It was well past eight o'clock and with any luck the service would end before I fell asleep.

"In verse six it says, 'Now there was a day when the sons of God came to present themselves before the Lord, and Satan was among them. And the Lord said to Satan, 'From where do you come?'" Pastor Jim paused for effect. He didn't stand behind the pulpit and read from the bible. He obviously knew the scriptures by heart so worked the stage, engaging the sparse but resolute congregation as he gave his sermon. "And Satan said, 'From going to and fro on the earth, and from walking back and forth on it.'" Pastor Jim scowled and glowered menacingly at the congregation to show them what Satan must have looked like.

The sanctuary was cool and dark; the archetype of the Spanish Missions that dotted the California coast, but this sanctuary had an indistinct musty odor. The pews were hard oak and creaked as people fidgeted, trying to find a comfortable spot on the unforgiving hardwood. A stained glass window towered behind the pulpit. Inlaid in the window was a cross with Jesus on it and I knew that at one time the church must have been Catholic. This church was much smaller and simpler than the one where Elisha and I were married. Had it been that long since I'd been inside a church? It seemed a lifetime ago.

"Then the Lord said to Satan, 'Have you considered My servant Job, that there is none like him on the earth, a blameless and upright man, one who fears God and shuns evil?'" Pastor Jim paused to roll up one sleeve and then the other. He was about ready to get serious with the sermon.

A baby began to cry to my right and I involuntarily looked over. The young mother used her large brown eyes to apologize to me and then quietly shushed the infant, rewrapping it in a soft blue blanket. The child continued to fuss and the mother rose to leave.

"Don't go, Emily," Pastor Jim said. "Babies are precious unto the sight of the Lord and their voices joyous sounds unto his ears."

Emily paused, tentative, then eased back into the pew and another woman drew alongside her to help comfort the infant.

"And Satan said to the Lord, 'Does Job fear God for nothing? Have You not made a hedge around him, around his household, and around all that he has on every side? You have blessed the work of his hands, and his possessions have increased in the land.'" Pastor Jim seemed to be on the verge of frenzy. He paused to catch his breath and again assume his Satan-like scowl. He stretched his open right hand toward the congregation. "And then Satan said to the Lord, 'But now, stretch out your hand and touch all that he has, and he will surely curse You to Your face!'"

Pastor Jim obviously loved doing Satan's lines.

"And the Lord said to Satan, 'Behold, all that he has is in your power; only do not lay a hand on his person.'"

Pastor Jim went into great detail about what Satan did to Job in an attempt to have him curse the Lord, and when Job wouldn't, Satan was allowed to touch Job's person. Pastor Jim told the congregation, in great detail again, the grievous afflictions suffered by Job and how Job's friends were convinced that Job must have sinned greatly against the Lord to deserve such malicious treatment. Job was now poor, sick, and abandoned by his wife and friends.

"And Job said 'Naked I came from my mother's womb, and naked I shall return there. The Lord gave, and the Lord has taken away; Blessed be the name of the Lord.'" He paused to let the congregation consider Job's remark. "And when Job's wife said, 'Do you still hold fast to your integrity? Curse God and Die!'"

Pastor Jim paused again, sighed, and then let his chest collapse to emphasize his point.

"Job asked her, 'Shall we indeed accept good from God, and shall we not accept adversity?' And in all this Job did not sin with his lips."

My mind wandered, I stifled a dozen or so yawns trying to stay awake, and before I knew it, the sermon was over. I didn't even hear how it ended. The young woman with the baby approached me sheepishly.

"I'm sorry..." she started. Her soft brown eyes seemed to be on the verge of crying. The baby was quiet now and she held him close to her breast, the blanket covering his face, and she bounced almost imperceptibly from foot to foot. Her light brown hair was pulled back into a ponytail, several loose strands hung in her eyes and she

pursed her lips and tried to blow them away from her face. She
wore no make-up other than a hint of light pink lipstick and her
flawless skin was alabaster. She smelled of baby powder and oil and
she looked tired.

"No, please," I said. "Don't be sorry, it's just that…"

"He's been so colicky lately, usually he's really good. I'm sorry
if…"

I felt a hand on my shoulder and when I turned, a non-descript
middle-aged gentleman that welcomed me to the congregation
greeted me. The conversation was short and when I turned back,
Emily had disappeared.

I waited outside near the hedges until the church was almost
empty and then went back inside to find Pastor Jim. He hadn't
moved more than fifteen feet from where he'd given his sermon and
was praying with an elderly couple.

Pastor Jim motioned me to his office when I was the only other
person left in the church.

"Coffee?" he asked as he poured himself a cup of the scalding
black liquid.

"No, thanks. I'm about coffeed-out."

"What can I do for you?" he asked as he slumped into the chair
behind his desk. The tiny office was on the east side of the building,
adjacent to the sanctuary, and had two overstuffed cloth chairs
against the near wall, just inside the door. The far wall was nothing
more than a massive bookshelf. Pastor Jim's desk faced the two
overstuffed chairs and held only a lap top computer and a bible. The
coffee pot was on a small table next to the office door.

"I'm worried about Rita Velasco," I said. "I thought maybe you
could help."

Pastor Jim hesitated and looked thoughtful for a moment. "I
don't recall seeing her in church today."

"She wasn't here," I said. "I was hoping you might have some
idea where she is?"

"No." He gave me a curious glance. "Why would you think I would know where she is?"

Playing the long shot I said, "She mentioned she was doing some counseling with you."

"Yes," he said. "But of course that would be confidential. You know that, right?"

"Yes, and I hope you will keep this conversation confidential also."

"Of course." He rose from his desk and closed the office door.

"Rita works for me and she's missed some work," I said, intentionally being vague. "She's not at home and we can't contact her on her cell phone."

Pastor Jim sipped his coffee and listened while I talked, his eyes never leaving mine.

"I was hoping that something in her counseling sessions with you would be helpful in locating her."

"I'm sorry," he said, after a moment's consideration "I don't think I can help."

"Maybe something..."

"Really," he interrupted. "There's not anything we talked about that I think can be helpful to you. Quite frankly, and I shouldn't even be saying this, but, it wasn't so much counseling as it was she just needed someone to talk to. Somebody she could trust. A friend to confide in."

"I see," I said. "Did she ever mention someone by the name of Astal Kamran?"

I could see by the look on his face that he'd heard the name before. He wouldn't be much of a poker player.

"Really," he said as he took another sip of his coffee and looked away. "I can't discuss what goes on in our counseling sessions."

"I understand that," I said. "Again this has to remain confidential..."

Pastor Jim nodded affirmatively.

"The last time anyone saw her was earlier today when she went to visit Astal Kamran, who incidentally was in the custody of the FBI. Astal Kamran has been linked to the Friday morning rocket attack of a British tanker outside the San Pedro breakwater. Rita was aboard that ship while it was burning, she lost one of her Sea Marshals in that fire and as a result, is very distraught."

Pastor Jim set his coffee cup down and leaned forward, resting both arms on his desk.

"This afternoon, Astal Kamran was shot while being transferred to another location. The FBI is looking for Rita and I need to find her first, for her own good."

Pastor Jim rubbed his temples with his right hand and contemplated. He looked genuinely concerned.

"I'll tell you this much," he said. "She called me this morning to ask my advice on something concerning him."

"I know that they're old friends," I offered. "They went to law school together."

"Yes, I recall her mentioning that," he said. "And she wanted to help him. Again, I shouldn't be telling you this, but given the circumstances..."

"Naturally this is just between the two of us, Pastor. I think she needs our help"

"She wanted to help him but was afraid it would be a conflict of interest with her work. She seemed to be torn between the two."

"Did she happen to mention what she was planning to do?"

"No," he said. "You don't think that the FBI feels she had anything to do with him being shot, do you?"

"I doubt it. I think they are more curious about how she found him and what the two of them talked about. He was supposed to be in a secure location and she was able to track him down. She's pretty resourceful that way."

"I see."

"So, she didn't give you any indication of what her plan might be, or if she was going to drop out of sight for awhile?"

"No," he said. "But from talking to her, I think she had a strong sense of loyalty to him, so her dropping out of sight as you call it, might be a possibility."

I considered that for a moment.

"That's not like her," I said. "I really think she would have called me or asked for time off. She's pretty much by the book when it comes to things like that."

"Maybe she didn't think you would approve of her actions or maybe you wouldn't give her the time off."

"I don't think so," I said. "Unfortunately, I'm afraid something has happened to her."

"I hope you're wrong."

"Me, too," I said, standing up. "I'd like to leave you my phone numbers just in case you hear from her. If she calls you or comes by the church, tell her that she's not in trouble with me. I'm just concerned about her welfare."

"I'll do that," Pastor Jim said. "And I'll keep her in my prayers."

My car was the last one remaining in the church parking lot and after getting behind the wheel I turned my cell phone on. What should I do now? What could I do? All I knew is that we'd found two guys floating in the harbor and Astal Kamran had been shot.

My cell phone showed one missed call but the caller's number had been blocked and that started my paranoia moment. Was the government behind this?

I'm not really big on conspiracy theories but some of them are interesting. Why did Jack Ruby shoot Lee Harvey Oswald? Who was afraid Oswald would talk and what would he have said? Conspiracy theories were rampant concerning the Oklahoma City bombing and the attacks on the World Trade Center's twin towers. Our own government has been known to delve into some shady areas, the Iran-Contra affair, Manuel Noriega in Panama, and of course our backing of Afghan rebels during the Soviet occupation of that country-the very same rebels we once trained and supplied are the ones we are fighting now. Was the attack on the *Beleza* a CIA operation sanctioned by our own government or was it a part of a larger cover-up?

"You're paranoid," I said aloud as I started my car, half expecting it to turn into a massive fireball. When I was a quarter mile down the road, I noticed the young woman with the ponytail who had talked to me in church. She was pushing her baby down the sidewalk in a stroller. It took me a couple of blocks before I thought to offer her a ride; she'd seemed so tired in church and it was dark. I went around the block and drove past where I'd seen her last, but she was gone.

I made a u-turn in the street and headed for home. What else could I do? I didn't know where Rita was and there wasn't a damn thing I could do about it tonight. Tomorrow I'd track down Eddie Taylor and then talk to a few of her Sea Marshals. They might know something. And who knows, Rita might just walk into work all bright- eyed and bushy-tailed and saying she'd fallen asleep on a friend's couch.

The conversation I'd had with Admiral Ballard began to bother me again. Why didn't he want to talk to me? What did he know that he would only say to me in person? Paranoia settled over me like a cloud of mosquitoes. Why did Jack Ruby really shoot Oswald? Why would somebody execute one of our Custom's agents? Were the two harbor homicides related? They were damn sure similar.

I tried to force myself into thinking about something else when Pastor Jim's sermon struck home. Job said, "Naked I came from my mother's womb, and naked I shall return there. The Lord gave, and the Lord has taken away."

16

Where the hell was I and who was singing so damn loud? I recognized the song as Jimmy Buffet's *A Pirate looks at Forty* and it was playing my on radio. I threw a pillow at the radio alarm clock but it just knocked a few things off my dresser. Jimmy Buffet was still crooning.

I'd slept like I was in a coma and could fall back to sleep if the radio wasn't blasting. The pillow over my head didn't work so I got up, checked the time on the red digital display, six-thirty, pulled the plug on the radio, and then crashed face first back in bed.

Shit. It's Monday morning and I've got to go to work. Seriously, I need a different job. My brain was slowly coming online and I knew there was no way I'd get back to sleep now. The night's rest had cleared my paranoia for the most part. The *Beleza* was gone and out of my hair. I hadn't found Rita but maybe she would be at work this morning with a plausible explanation for her actions and whereabouts. Maybe I could row before work. Shit. My boat was in the back of my truck back at the Coast Guard base, I was driving the government sedan. Astal Kamran being shot was the FBI's problem, not mine. Hell, I'd never even met the guy.

There was a fresh set of gray Coast Guard sweats in my dresser and I pulled them on. I'd eat breakfast, grab a quick run on the beach, and then go to work. Monday. Seventy-two hours since the *Beleza* had been set on fire to ruin my whole weekend. Shit, I hate Mondays.

Making coffee in the morning is pure reflex action. So is putting a fire under the skillet and gathering the makings for breakfast. Jimmy Dean is my morning best friend and I put four of his pre-cooked sausages in the microwave and then melted a chunk of butter in the skillet. The three eggs were sizzling in the skillet and I was buttering my toast when my doorbell rang.

"This can't be good," I said, opening the door to find Mike Dillon standing there.

"Always with the sarcasm," he said.

"Who's being sarcastic?"

Dillon looked at his feet and shook his head.

"So, what's up?" I asked.

"I just came by to tell you that I'm taking off."

"Where are you going?"

"Back to D.C. and then to Puerto Rico probably. You know the Bureau."

"Why?"

"I'm being reassigned."

"So the Bureau thinks they have this thing all wrapped up?"

"They think that it's routine now, and that there's no need for extra agents being wasted on it."

I couldn't believe what I was hearing and Dillon could read it in my face.

"It's not my call, you know that," he said.

"I know."

We stared at each other for what seemed a long time

"What do you want from me?" he asked.

"I don't want anything from you."

"Then what's your problem?"

"This thing isn't over with, that's all."

"Sure it is. We found the weapons, have eight people in custody from Fontana, and have enough evidence to link Astal Kamran to the conspiracy."

"What did you charge him with?" I asked. "Just out of curiosity."

"We didn't charge him with anything, we were bringing him in to formally charge him when he got shot. If you'd have come to the hospital last night like you were supposed to, you would know that he's dead."

"Dead?"

"Graveyard dead."

"Did you get the shooter?"

"We have some leads."

"Some leads? That's it? That's Bureau-speak for you don't have shit."

"We're working on it."

"What were you going to charge him with?"

"Conspiracy to commit acts of terrorism."

"Based on what?"

"A couple of the guys in the Fontana raid were on his client list, his minivan was used in the getaway, and then his vehicle was found on the same property as the weapons."

I laughed in Dillon's face. "You were going to charge a lawyer because his clients did something illegal? Since when is that a crime?"

"The crime lab is turning up evidence from his minivan, too."

"But his minivan was reported stolen. How were you planning to link him the actual weapons and the attack?"

"Don't forget, he also showed up to represent the illegals that were found in the shipping container at the Malaysia-Pacific Terminal," he said defensively.

"So what?" I said. "The way I heard it, Astal Kamran said that somebody from the Immigration office called him and asked him to come down. What's wrong with that?"

"That didn't happen. Nobody from Immigration ever called him."

"Get real, Dillon," I said. "You're not going to get anybody from Immigration to admit they called Kamran now that his name is all over the news. I know for a fact that Immigration calls lawyers all the time to help expedite deportations. With no identification to tell us who they really are and no family members to help get them out, those guys could be sitting there for months plugging up the system."

"Nobody from Immigration called him, we checked it out."

"Not that you can prove, but I'll bet you ten bucks that somebody in that Immigration office called him to come down and look into the situation. He didn't just go down there on his own. Remember, we're still looking for somebody known as El Jefe."

"Maybe Kamran is El Jefe," he said. "Did you ever think of that?"

I considered that option for a moment. "I still say the call came from Immigration. But you'll never get anyone to admit it now that Kamran is dead."

Dillon shook his head. "Besides, El Jefe may have nothing to do with this. He may just be somebody running illegals across the border."

"You've got nothing on Astal Kamran," I said. "Everything you've got is circumstantial and if he were still alive, he'd be on the street in a New York minute."

"We'll never know."

"That's right," I said. "What about Hannigan and the Hansen boys? Are you just going to drop those investigations?"

Dillon shrugged his shoulders. "We're turning everything we have over to the locals, the SPPD and the County Sheriff's office. We'll keep an eye on Hannigan ourselves, he's been red-flagged because of his ties to the IRA. But if the Hansens are guilty of anything, it's a matter of local jurisdiction as far as we're concerned. Besides, Hannigan is going to have his hands full dealing with your agency because he brought that tanker into the harbor. He may do some serious jail time for that. "

"What exactly did you find out about the Hansens?" I asked. "Do you think they were running drugs or illegals up from Mexico?"

"Could be. But it's a problem for the locals now, the Bureau is turning it over to them, we have other things to move on to."

"What did you come up with on Oaxaca Trucking?"

"We're still looking into it. It's ongoing, but they're operating out of Mexico so it takes a little longer to check it out. Hands across the border and all that, so the State Department is handling it for us now."

"The State Department?" I looked at Dillon and just shook my head. This investigation was mired down in bureaucratic bullshit so deep we'd never get anything done.

"So, you'll send me a copy if you ever make out a report?" I asked.

"You're going to be liaising with a new guy from our L.A. office. You met him last night, Special Agent James Edmonds, you'll be running everything through him from now on. He'll get a copy of the report and you can get it from him."

"What about the rest of the weapons...and the plastic explosives?" I asked. "We can only account for twelve of the twenty-eight SEP DARDS that were supposed to be in the shipment, and if my math is right, there's still sixteen anti-tank rockets out there somewhere that we can't account for."

Dillon tried not to look flustered but I could tell I'd hit a nerve.

"Come on, Jared, we don't even know if they're in this country," he said "They might be overseas someplace."

"But what if they are here?"

"Look, Jared," he said. "We're still working on it, we haven't forgotten about them."

"So what happens when two days from now another ship is blown out of the water with the rockets we didn't get back?"

"What do you want from me?" he asked. "There's nothing I can do. It's not my call."

"I know how it works," I said. "My point is that this thing is not over with. There are still sixteen rockets out there and you knock on my door first thing in the fucking morning and then and act like this thing is over with and it's bullshit. We recovered less than half the rockets, you put together a circumstantial case against a guy you let get killed while he's in your custody, and now he can't even defend himself because he's laying on a slab, but everybody in the Bureau is walking around patting themselves on the back saying what a good job they've done.

"What's your point?"

"Have you got shit in your ears? How many times do I have to say it?"

"Come on, Jared, be realistic, you know it's never really over with," he said. "You know that better than anybody. Every day something new comes up, a new threat we have to look at, there's thousands of plots every year nobody ever hears about."

"I know that. But what irritates me is that nobody ever finishes anything. They do a half-ass job and then congratulate themselves. But they haven't done anything. Nothing's solved. Astal Kamran and a few Mexican Nationals weren't behind the rocket attack on the *Beleza*. I'm not stupid enough to believe that."

"You may be right, I'm not going to argue with you, but it's not my call. I'm being reassigned, and if you think there's a threat to San Pedro Harbor, you need to talk to the Admiral about it."

"You bet your ass I will."

There was another awkward silence and Dillon just looked at me with lost puppy eyes.

"So why did you really come by?" I asked. "You could have called and told me you were leaving, you didn't have to ring my doorbell before I ate breakfast. Better yet, you could have written me a letter and mailed it from the airport on you way out of town."

"You don't like me much, do you?"

I couldn't keep myself from laughing out loud. "What difference does it make, Dillon? I ain't sleeping with you."

"I'm just curious about what you have against me, that's all."

"Dillon, you brown-nosed your way to the top. Now that you're there, you don't like being called what you are," I said. "You're an incompetent kiss-ass, and even worse, you're a one-way buddy-fucker."

"I resent that," Dillon said.

"Hey, you made your choices."

"Don't blame me just because you got run off…"

"That's got nothing to do with you."

"I think you still have hard feelings," he said.

"Forget it, Dillon. That's water under the bridge now."

"But you still don't like me, right?"

"What's that got to do with anything?" I asked. "I work with a lot of people I don't like, that's just the way it is. It's not bad, it's not good, that's just the way it is. Dillon, I hate to say this to you, but you and me are probably never going to go bass fishing together."

"What's that supposed to mean?"

"It's self-explanatory. Think about it."

"You're an asshole."

"That's what I've heard," I said. "Do me a favor though, will you?"

"What's that?" he asked Dillon.

"Tell them what I said when you get back to D.C. Tell them I said that it's not over. I want that officially on the record with the Bureau."

"Okay," he said and then he stood silent, waiting.

"So, let's try this again," I said. "You could have called. Why come over in person?"

"I just thought I should tell you face-to-face what was going on, that's all"

I wasn't buying it. "If it has to do with Rita, forget it. I'm not getting involved. She thinks you sold her out to save your career. A person like Rita doesn't get over something like that. Ever."

"But she doesn't understand."

"Oh, she understands," I said. "That's your problem."

Dillon started to talk, thought about it again and stayed silent.

"She hasn't been stabbed in the back by somebody like you as many times as I have," I said. "She'll get used to it in time, if she stays around long enough."

Dillon was silent.

"Look, I hate to throw you out, but I have other things to do today," I said.

Dillon turned and walked back to his car and I waited until he drove away before closing my front door.

My breakfast was cold when I finally sat down to eat but I didn't even notice because I was busy wondering if I'd been too hard on Dillon. The Bureau's case against Astal Kamran was completely circumstantial and he wasn't even alive to defend himself. They were framing a dead guy. Why? Why was the State Department handling the investigation into Oaxaca Trucking? It sounded like a classic case of the Bureau passing the buck and covering its own ass and there wasn't a damn thing I could do about it. Some of the Bureau's new agents like James Edmonds would be cutting their teeth by wrapping up the details and handling the prosecution on this case. It was a bullshit case. Unless Dillon wasn't telling me everything.

I drank another cup of coffee and hashed everything over in my head one more time. Still, none of it made any sense.

My phone rang and it was Chief Petty Burke of the Sea Marshal unit.

"Sorry to bother you, Commander Stanton, but Lieutenant Velasco isn't here to make the duty assignments and we we're wondering if she was going to take the day off."

I'd answered the phone the night the hospital called to say my grandfather was in intensive care. They said he might not make it through the night and we should come right away. I'd stood there with the phone in my hand, my blood had turned cold, my heart dropped, and I'd felt like throwing up.

I choked back my Jimmy Dean's and tried to sound calm. "I'm not sure what her schedule is today, Chief, but why don't you get the Blacklist from the Comm-Center and make today's assignments."

"Yessir."

I brushed my teeth and changed from my sweats into my working blues. Anxiety welled up inside me. The shit was going to hit the fan. I could feel it coming.

17

Monday morning traffic was only moderately heavy on Pacific Coast Highway and I figured that was because a lot of other people woke up today feeling the same way I did about work. A damp silver mist floated over commuters as it drifted in off the Pacific and I suspected when the inland desert began to heat up and the onshore flow surged, the coastal fog would get thicker before the sun finally burned it off some time this afternoon.

When I got to the Coast Guard base I discovered that during the night a mild inversion layer had combined with the weak onshore breeze, creating a dense gray fog that had already enveloped the harbor. An unidentified voice called my name from out of the fog to remind me that my headlights were still on and I had to double back to the car to shut them off.

"Commander Stanton," Yeoman Jenkins said as I unlocked my office door. "Agent Edmonds from the FBI has called several times already this morning and wants you to call him back right away."

"Sure," I said. "Hold my calls and bring me a cup of coffee."

"Yessir," he relied. "And Commander, there's a Captain Hannigan waiting to see you, he's looking for Lieutenant Velasco."

"Hannigan?"

"Yessir."

"Where is he?"

"Waiting in the front lobby."

"Okay, bring me some coffee," I said. "Give me five minutes and then send Hannigan in."

"Yessir."

"And hold my calls."

"Yessir."

I tried Detective Halverson's cell number but he didn't answer so I left him a voice mail explaining that Rita Velasco was still missing. I ran my finger down the Blacklist and saw we had three tankers, two passenger ships, and a refrigerated fruit ship from Chile on it. Hopefully Chief Burke had enough Sea Marshals to cover the jobs.

"Good morning, Commander Stanton," Captain Hannigan said when he entered my office. Hannigan appeared to be freshly showered, shaved, and sporting a new haircut. He wore a tan corduroy sports jacket, brown slacks, and a white shirt with a neatly knotted dark brown tie that matched his socks. The burns on his face were starting to heal.

"How are you this morning, sir?" he asked.

"Where the hell have you been?"

"What do you mean?"

"You heard me," I said. "Where the hell have you been? We've got an active investigation going, which you're smack-dab in the middle of, and then you disappear without a trace."

"I was..."

"You didn't leave a phone number, or tell anyone where you were going to be. You just took off. The FBI was going to issue a felony warrant for your arrest."

"I didn't think..."

"That's right." I said. "You didn't think, Captain Hannigan. You didn't think before you brought that burning tanker into the harbor and you didn't think before you left town without a trace."

"I thought that…"

Yeoman Jenkins knocked on the door and stuck his head in the office.

"Commander, Agent Edmonds is on the phone and I told him you were in a meeting but he said it was urgent. He needs to talk to you."

"Put him through."

The phone on my desk rang and I raised my left held up to signal Hannigan that our conversation was not done, merely on hold.

"What is it Agent Edmonds?"

"We still need to talk to Lieutenant Velasco and you never got back to me," Agent Edmonds said.

"Well, she's not here right now," I said. "Which you probably already know, because you've tried to call her and when you didn't get her you called me."

"Well, yes."

"I'll have her call you as soon as she gets in."

"Thank you, Commander," Agent Edmonds said. "Pardon my saying, sir, but I'm guessing that you're not quite sure where she is."

"She's not in yet," I said. "I'll have her call you."

I glanced up at Hannigan and saw that he was trying to appear like he wasn't listening to my phone conversation.

"Commander, Rita Velasco's car turned up at an impound lot in Garden Grove," Agent Edmonds said. "If you don't know where she is, we need to know that, and right now, I can't get a straight answer out of anybody working for the Coast Guard as to her whereabouts."

"What?"

"We need to locate Lieutenant Velasco…"

"I know that part," I snapped. "What do you mean her car turned up in an impound lot?"

"The Garden Grove police found it abandoned in the Von's grocery store parking lot," Edmonds said. "When her car wasn't moved overnight, the store manager had it towed as an abandoned vehicle and it ended up at the city's impound lot. We have some people down there going over the car right now."

"Have they found anything?" I asked, almost afraid he was going to say they'd found blood or other evidence of a struggle.

"We don't know anything yet," he said. "But Commander, let me ask you again. Do you know where Lieutenant Velasco is?"

"No," I said, my voice trailing off. "I don't know where she is."

"Thank you, Commander, that's what I thought," he said. "Just a moment, Commander..."

There was a pause and I could hear a muffled conversation over the phone that sounded like Edmonds talking to someone else in the background.

"If you hear from her, contact us right away," he said and then the phone line went dead.

It took me a moment to register what I'd just heard. Rita's car was abandoned? Why would she leave her Miata at a grocery store?

"Are you still here?" I asked, finally looking up to see Captain Hannigan still in my office.

"I didn't think we were done," he said.

"We're not," I said, refocusing. "Where have you been?"

"I took my sailboat to Catalina for the weekend," he said. "I didn't know it was going to be a problem. Nobody said I couldn't leave."

"Yeah, well, we had a few more questions for you."

"Like what?"

"Like do you know William Hansen?"

"Who?"

"William Hansen. He owned the twenty-eight foot Donzi that was used in the attack on the *Beleza*."

Hannigan pondered the question. "I don't think I know him."

"He identified you as somebody who looked at his boat."

"Looked at his boat?"

"Is there an echo in here?"

"He said I looked at his boat?"

"Yes, he said you looked at his boat. He had it up for sale before it was stolen and he identified you as someone that looked at his boat."

"What does that have to do with anything?" he asked. "I thought the case was closed. I saw on television that you found some rockets and took the people responsible for the attack on the *Beleza* into custody."

"Well, there are still a few loose details. Did you look at Hansen's boat or not?"

"There was a guy at the marina with a Donzi and he kept in the slip across from mine," he said, appearing to choose his words carefully. "It had a for sale sign on it, and I saw him hanging around one day, so I walked over and talked to him. That's all. I never looked at it with the intent of buying it."

"How about stealing it?"

"Like I said, I was just killing time one day and walked over to look at it," he said. "Besides, I thought you caught the guys that stole the boat. That's what they said on television."

"Like I told you before," I said. "There are still some loose details."

"Okay."

"You mean to tell me that you didn't recognize William Hansen's Donzi as the boat that attacked the *Beleza*?" I asked, getting more specific with my line of questioning. "That Donzi was kept in a slip near your own boat, and you even walked over to talk to the owner and looked at it on at least one occasion that you admit to, and now you're trying to tell me that you didn't recognize that same boat the morning it fired four rockets at a ship you were piloting?"

"There are a lot of boats that look like that one, Commander," he said. "And I never saw rockets being fired, I was busy lining the *Beleza* up for the breakwater entrance."

Hannigan appeared calm and I wondered if he had rehearsed his responses.

"Not that I'm trying to change the subject," he said. "But, I couldn't help overhearing your conversation about Lieutenant Velasco."

"That doesn't concern you."

"Begging your pardon, Commander," he said. "But, I came here today looking for her."

"She's not in."

"That's what I gather," he said. "But, I have an official Coast Guard hearing coming up, a hearing that is going to determine whether or not my pilot's license is going to be permanently revoked. Lieutenant Velasco is the only available witness to my actions that day."

"That may be..." I said before a loud knock on my office door interrupted our conversation.

Yeoman Jenkins stuck his in my office. "Commander, I have two more people out here that say it is urgent that they see you."

Yeoman Jenkins lingered with his head stuck through the door, waiting for my response.

"If Lieutenant Velasco can't make it to the hearing my attorney needs to know that," he said.

"Just a moment," I said to Hannigan and then told Jenkins I'd be right out. I could hear the phone on the yeoman's desk ringing again before the door was closed.

"Captain Hannigan," I said. "We have a lot going on right now and I don't really have time to address your problems at this time."

Hannigan started to protest.

"But given the circumstances of the case," I said. "I'll give Admiral Ballard a call on your behalf..."

"I don't see..."

"Captain Hannigan" I said curtly, cutting him off. "Today is the wrong day to argue with me. I said I'd make a call on your behalf."

Hannigan's flushed. I wasn't sure if it was from anger or embarrassment but it didn't really matter. Hannigan and his license hearing would have to wait until another time.

"Thank you, sir," he said in a hushed a hushed tone, but the look in his eyes said something else.

The Yeoman Jenkins knocked on the office door again and stuck his head inside. Just as the yeoman began to speak, Larry Jackson pushed his way inside.

"Your Sea Marshals have the entire harbor shut down," blurted Larry Jackson.

"Excuse me," I said. "But I'm in the middle of a meeting."

"The entire harbor is shut down and you are costing us hundreds of thousands of dollars an hour." Jackson said.

I'd had enough and charged around my desk at him.

"Out of my office," I said, pointing the way out the door.

Larry Jackson stood his ground.

I took another step toward him. "You can leave the easy way or the hard way!"

Jackson's face pinched and he reluctantly moved toward the door.

Yeoman Jenkins grinned at me as he closed the door behind Larry Jackson.

"Now, where were we before we were so rudely interrupted." I said, sitting at my desk to address Captain Hannigan. "Do you know Mr. Jackson?"

"I haven't formally met him," Captain Hannigan said. "But I know the name because it's well known fact that he's quite critical of the San Pedro Harbor Pilot Service."

"In what way?"

"Well," he started, glancing over his right shoulder to make sure the office door was closed before leaning forward in his chair. "Mostly complaints about delays."

"Delays?"

"Yeah, every time he thinks a ship is late getting to the dock he complains."

"What kind of delays?"

"That's the thing. There really aren't any delays to speak of," he said. "When a ship arrives at the sea buoy, we go right out to get it and bring it in. Sometimes ships will get backed up at the entrance and there will be more than one ship the pilot boat has to put a pilot on, or sometimes, a ship arrives late to the sea buoy and the pilot doesn't get it to the dock as fast as Jackson thinks he should."

"Anything else?"

"I don't think Jackson really knows how things work. He tries to time ship movements like NASA times their rocket launches. It just doesn't work that way with ships."

"So why do you think he is upset this morning?" I asked.

"Probably because ships are being delayed in the fog."

"Why would he blame the Sea Marshals for that?"

Hannigan grinned. "They just got caught holding the bag, that's all."

"Meaning what?"

"Well, nobody likes to move a ship in the fog," he said. "Except the shore side people who have nothing to lose."

"Explain."

"Sure," he said. "Pilots don't like to move ships in the fog because if there is an accident, they get blamed for it and will lose their licenses. So, they tell the ship captain that it's not safe, but that the captain has the option of bringing the ship in by himself if he wants to, which of course would be suicide for the captain because if anything happens, the pilot has already said it wasn't safe."

"The pilots can do that?"

"Sure, the captain has the ultimate legal responsibility for the ship in the eyes of Admiralty courts, the pilot is merely his adviser. There's always a lot of expense involved when ships get caught in the fog and nobody wants to take the blame so they pass the buck if they can."

"So the captain passes the buck to the pilot who passes it back to the captain…"

"And they both pass it to the Coast Guard," grinned Hannigan. "Excuse my saying so, Commander, but the Sea Marshals don't really understand the dynamics of the situation and are usually more than willing to say the ship can't proceed."

"I see," I said. "Is that going to be your defense, Captain Hannigan?" I asked. "Are you going to say that the captain of the *Beleza* was responsible for bringing the ship into the harbor?"

Hannigan hesitated, looked at the floor, and then looked directly into my eyes.

"That's not my intention," he said. "But quite honestly, I may be forced to take that course of action if Lieutenant Velasco can't testify at my hearing. "Between you and me, Commander, I brought that ship into the harbor on my own. The truth is that I had no choice. The *Beleza* was too close to the breakwater to abort the approach, but nobody can testify to that fact except Lieutenant Velasco. The *Beleza's* captain flew back to England and the mate on watch and helmsman were so badly injured that they can't testify to anything."

Hannigan had a dead serious look in his eye.

"After the fire was out, Lieutenant Velasco told me she thought I did the right thing," he said. "But if she can't testify at my hearing, my lawyer and I will have to figure out some other way to save my license, and ultimately my career."

"I understand," I said, standing up to signal Captain Hannigan that the meeting was over. "I appreciate your honesty."

Hannigan and Larry Jackson passed in the doorway.

"Now, Mr. Jackson, what can I do for you," I said.

"I was on my way here to see you on another matter," Jackson said. "When I was informed that the Sea Marshals had closed the harbor."

I motioned for Jackson to be seated but he chose to remain standing.

"It's my understanding that the fog has the harbor shut down and not the Coast Guard," I said. "The Coast Guard doesn't control the weather."

Jackson's face turned red.

"That's not my understanding," snapped Jackson. "I was told that the pilots were willing to bring the ships in but that the Coast Guard wouldn't allow it."

"Well, Mr. Jackson," I said. "When it's foggy at the airport, the planes don't land either. I'm sure that the airline pilots would be willing to land their planes, but somebody has to make the call as to when to close the airport for safety's sake. Somebody made the call to shut down the harbor because of the fog and you can't blame the weather on the Coast Guard. There are certain safety guidelines that must be adhered to in this port, and unfortunately, navigating ships in the fog is one of them."

Anger welled up in Larry Jackson's face. "Well," he stammered. "I came here to talk to you about something else anyway."

"What might that be?"

"Your Sea Marshal's are routinely delaying our ships at the sea buoy."

"How are they delaying them?"

"They are taking too long to make their inspections and give clearance to proceed into the harbor."

"This is the first I've heard of the problem," I said. "How long are the delays?"

"Sometimes they are taking up to an hour."

"Again, this is the first I've heard of it, but I'll certainly look into it," I said.

"Well, I want to know what you're going to do about it," demanded Jackson.

"Mr. Jackson, you and I seem to have gotten off on the wrong foot here," I said, trying to be as diplomatic as possible. "It is certainly not the Coast Guard's intention to delay ships or cost shipping companies money. However, there are certain security precautions that must be taken and…"

"I understand that Commander, but I want to know what you are going to do about these totally unnecessary delays."

"Let me explain something to you, Mr. Jackson," I said, leaning across my desk and lowering my voice, abandoning my polite approach to the situation. "I am one big government monkey that you don't want on your back."

Jackson was startled by my comment.

"I'll work with you if I can, but if you come in here again with your snotty attitude, you're going to hit the biggest bureaucratic brick wall you've ever seen," I said. "I'll see to it that every crew member on every ship is drug and alcohol tested before a ship gets to come inside the harbor…and we'll send search teams out to the sea buoy with drug dogs and microscopes."

"I…I…" stammered Jackson.

"You don't want to get on my bad side, Mr. Jackson," I said. "But you're well on your way. Now get out of my office with your petty complaining because I have work to do."

Jackson's face flushed bright red. "Maybe I should…"

"Maybe you should."

Larry Jackson stormed out of my office and slammed the door.

"Uh-oh," I said to myself. "I'm going to get a call from the Admiral on this one."

Yeoman Jenkins knocked on the door again. "I've got somebody here about Lieutenant Velasco."

"Lieutenant Velasco isn't in today," I said before I recognized who was standing in my office.

"I know," Eddie Taylor said. "She's been kidnapped."

18

"What do you mean Lieutenant Velasco has been kidnapped?" I said as I stood up, leaned across my desk, and eyeballed Eddie Taylor. "How do you know?"

"They called me and said they had her," he said.

For some reason I was having trouble grasping exactly what he'd just said to me. I'd had a nagging feeling something happened to Rita once I found out her Miata had been abandoned. Ever since I got that news, the little voice in the back of my head was screaming something was wrong, but actually hearing the words was altogether different. Eddie wore a pained expression on his face reminiscent of a Van Gogh painting and I knew what he was going to tell me wasn't going to be good. He'd said kidnapped, which meant Rita Velasco might still be alive instead of turning up as a floater in the harbor like Mick Biller the Customs agent.

"Okay, Eddie. Now, who called you?" I asked, trying to organize my thoughts and only ask one question at a time. "And why did they call you?"

"I don't know," stammered Eddie as he played with the Dodger baseball cap he had in his hand.

"What did they say when they called? When did they call you? And why you?"

Eddie Taylor looked like he was on the verge of falling apart. I sat down again and motioned for him to be seated in one of the chairs on the other side of my desk but he didn't move a muscle. I was just trying to breathe normally and knew I'd need to calm myself down in order to question Eddie in a logical and systematic manner.

Organizing my thoughts, I studied the young security guard on the other side of my desk with an element of suspicion. "Why are you coming to me?" I asked.

"Because I know that you're Rita's boss and I didn't know who else to go to. I don't know what to do. They said they'd kill her." He was on the verge of tears.

Eddie Taylor was still standing, toying with his hat, and I again motioned for him to be seated. He finally perched on the edge on one of the chairs but looked at the floor instead of making eye contact with me.

"Let's start at the beginning"

"Okay," he said softly.

"Look at me."

Eddie hesitated and when he finally looked at me, his eyes were glassy.

"This is very important," I said, trying to use a calming tone. "I need you to give very straight and very complete answers to my questions?"

"Okay."

I took a couple of deep breaths while collecting my thoughts. "When did you get the call?"

"Last night."

"Sunday night? What time Sunday night?"

"I don't know," stammered Eddie as he looked down and toyed with hat again. "It must have been about ten o'clock. I didn't really look at the clock, I was panicking and all."

"Okay, look at me. Ten o'clock last night and you panicked when they called," I said. "What did they say to you?"

Eddie hesitated, glanced at his shoes and toyed with his hat some more.

"I need straight answers," I said again. "If I'm going to be able to help, I need to know what you know."

"Look," stammered Eddie. "This is going to make me look bad, but it really isn't what you think. And I don't care what happens to me, we have to help Rita."

"Okay."

"I'm in a lot of trouble and that's why they have her."

"Just answer my questions and we'll sort through this."

"Sure."

"If you're in trouble that's one thing, but if you can help me find Rita, I may be able to help you out in return. But, I need to know all the facts first."

Eddie looked a little relieved.

"You came to the right place," I said to reassure him. "Tell me exactly what they said when they called."

"They said that unless I wanted her to end up like Raney, I should do something for them," he said, his voice cracking.

"Rainy?" I asked. "Who is Rainy?"

"John Raney, R-A-N-E-Y," he said. "The dead guy that was floating in the harbor this weekend. He worked as a security guard over at the Korea Lines terminal."

"So, they said Rita would end up like John Raney unless you did something for them?"

"Yes."

"They said that she would end up dead in the harbor?"

"Yes." Eddie choked up. "It's my fault."

"Now, wait a minute," I said. "I'm not understanding this at all."

Eddie wiped a tear from his cheek with the back of his hand.

"So why did they call you about Rita? I'm missing something."

"They want me to do something for them."

"Why would they think that kidnapping Rita would get you to do something for them?"

"They know that Rita and me are friends," he said. "I think they spotted her with me the other night at the terminal, and they must have figured they could get to me by grabbing her."

"You're talking about when Rita and I rode with you at the Malaysia-Pacific Terminal the other night?"

"Yes."

Yeoman Jenkins knocked on my door and stuck his head in the office. "Admiral Ballard is on the phone and wants to talk to you right now!"

"Tell the Admiral I'm in the middle of a crisis right now but that I'll call him back within a half hour with the details…and make sure you get the phone number where I can reach him."

"Yessir."

Larry Jackson hadn't wasted any time going over my head and it pissed me off but I knew I needed to focus on Eddie Taylor. "Now, let me get this straight," I said, turning my attention back to Eddie. "You and Rita are friends, and when we rode with you at the terminal the other night, the people who kidnapped her found this out, and now they are threatening to kill her if you don't do something for them."

"Yeah."

I carefully considered my next question. "What does your trouble have to do with Rita and the dead guy in the harbor? Raney isn't it?"

"They killed Raney because he wouldn't help them, he wanted out just like me," he said. "So when I told them I didn't want to help them, they took Rita and said they would kill her if I didn't do what I was told. She should have never come down to the terminal to see me."

"What exactly do they want you to do for them?" I asked.

Eddie looked at the floor again and played with his hat.

I fought the urge to grab Eddie by the throat and shake the information out of him.

"They want me to help them take a container from the Malaysia-Pacific Terminal."

"Aaah," I said, finally starting to put two and two together "I'm guessing that you know these people and have dealt with them before."

"Yes," he said as he hung his head.

"And this must be the trouble you spoke of?" Helping them take containers?"

"Yes. But it's not what you think."

Eddie Taylor was formulating his explanation and I did my best to be patient. I was afraid if I were harsh with him, he would shut down altogether.

"They suckered me into it and now it's too late to get out," he said defensively. "I was in too deep before I knew what I was getting into."

"How did they sucker you into it?"

"They had me change some numbers on a couple of containers and I thought it was legitimate. I work night security as you know, and sometimes the owner of the container changes, or something else changes, and we have to re-mark the containers. We do it legitimately all the time, it's part of our job, he said. "But ever since that ship was attacked, everything at the terminal has been crazy and it's too dangerous. I told them that I wanted out, but they said that it was too late for me to get out because I was already involved and I would go down with the rest of them."

"They got you to change the numbers on a few containers and you didn't know you were helping them steal them?" I asked, trying to subdue my skepticism. "You were just doing your job?"

"Yeah."

"And then what happened?"

"Well, one afternoon this guy Bill, but he calls himself Ken now, anyway, he comes over to my house with a couple other guys," he said. "They unload this big flat screen digital television and a home theater system and then Ken hands me twelve thousand dollars in cash. He said it was my cut!"

"Did you know this Bill, or Ken as he now calls himself?"

"Yeah, he used to work at the terminal with me but he quit a while back. He was with the longshore clerk's union and they handle the paperwork for the cargo."

"So, he was working at the terminal, and telling you which containers to change the markings on, and you were doing it and thought it was all legitimate, and then he shows up one day and tells you that you've been helping them steal containers?"

"Yeah. I'd change the markings and somebody at the front gate would help with the paperwork and they'd just drive the containers out of the terminal."

It didn't sound right to me. Surely Eddie must have known better.

"And after Bill quit working at the terminal, you still changed the markings on the containers for him?"

"I had to," he said. "Like I told you, I tried to quit, but I was already involved and they threatened to turn me in to the cops if I quit. I'd be facing jail time or worse, look at what they did to John Raney."

I took a clean sheet of paper and an envelope out of my desk. "I'm going to need names."

"They said they would kill her if I talked to the cops," he said. "That's why I came here, they said they would be watching me."

"Were you followed here?" My friend, paranoia, raised its ugly head again.

"I don't think so, I drove around a lot before I came here, and I kept checking my rear view mirror to see if anybody was following me. I don't think I was followed."

"Good," I said. "I need names. Who is this Bill or Ken?"

"I just knew him as Bill when he worked for Malaysia-Pacific, he was a longshore clerk, but he goes by the name Ken Jacobs now. I'm pretty sure that's not his real name, I think he stole somebody's identity."

"That's a possibility," I said. "Anything else about him that you can tell me? Height, weight, hair, race, tattoos, or other marks?"

Eddie Taylor told me as much as knew about the guy going by the name Ken Jacobs and I wrote it down on the sheet of paper. Then he gave me the low-down on the man known as Larry Raney that had turned up floating in the harbor off the Korea Line dock.

"And Ken Jacobs has a tattoo of a dagger on his right forearm," Eddie added. "Oh yeah, and he has kind of a self- given tattoo on his left hand, I'm not sure what it is, maybe some initials."

"Was he ever in prison?" I asked. " Because sometimes those tattoos are done in prison to mark gangs."

Eddie considered.

"He never specifically mentioned it," he said. "But I think maybe he was in prison because of the way he acts."

"How does he act?"

"He's mean," he said as tears began to form in the corners of his eyes. "He won't have any problem killing Rita. I know that."

"What did they say about releasing her?"

"Nothing. They just said to do what they want or they'd kill her."

"When do they want you to change the markings on the container?"

"Today, I mean tonight, when I go to work." Eddie wiped a tear away from his face with the back of his hand. "They said it had to be tonight."

"And you know which container it is and where it is located in the terminal?"

"Yes."

I leaned forward and put my elbows on the desk and rested my face in my hands while rubbing my temples with my thumbs. My heart thumped in my chest and my mind raced as I contemplated what course of action to take. I looked up at Eddie Taylor and knew he was scared shitless. He had the scattered look of somebody way over his head with no way to get out.

"How are they going to know when you've done it?" I asked.

"They said they'd be watching and that they'd know."

I rubbed my temples with my thumbs again and tried to think "This guy, Ken, the one you've been working with," I said. "Is he the top dog or is he working for somebody else?"

Eddie paused, his eyes rolled back in his head as he considered his answer.

"Sometimes he mentions another guy," he said. "He calls him the Spaniard."

"The Spaniard?"

"Yeah."

"What do you know about this Spaniard?"

"Nothing," he said. "Other than I've heard his name."

"Do you know what's in the container they want you to help steal?"

"I don't have any idea," he said. "And I don't want to know. I never asked any questions, I always figured that the less I knew the better off I was."

"Okay," I said as I stood up. "I want you to wait outside while I make a couple of phone calls…"

"They said they would kill her if I called the cops," sobbed Eddie.

"I know," I said calmly in my best *trust me* voice. "I've handled situations like this before. I want you to wait outside my office and don't talk to anybody."

I had Eddie write down the location and identification numbers of the container he was supposed to change and then gave him a piece of paper so he could make a sketch of Ken Jacob's tattoos.

When I had all the information organized, I turned Eddie over to Yeoman Jenkins for safekeeping and then closed my office door.

As much as I hated to do it, I dialed Mike Dillon's cell phone number.

"Yeah," was all the voice said when it answered on the third ring.

"Dillon?"

"Who is this?" asked the person on the other end.

"It's Jared Stanton you idiot," I said when I finally recognized his voice "Where are you?"

"Commander, how nice of you to call. I'm on a plane to Miami. What's up?"

"I have a problem," I said. "But if you're on a plane to Miami, I don't think you can help me. I thought you were going to Washington."

"Things changed. What's going on?"

"Rita Velasco has been kidnapped."

There was only silence on the other end of the phone.

"Dillon?"

"Yeah," he said. "Did you just say that Rita has been kidnapped?"

"That's what I said."

"How do you know?" he asked. "Are you sure?"

"The last time anyone heard from her was Sunday morning, and a guy just walked into my office saying somebody called him and threatened to kill her if he didn't help them steal a container out of a shipping terminal."

"Let me get this straight, somebody just walks into your office with information that Rita has been kidnapped? Are you sure about this guy?"

"Yeah, he seems to be on the level and appears to have pretty good information. Not only that, but Edmonds called a few minutes ago to tell her car was in an impound lot because it was found abandoned."

"Who has her? Did this guy say?"

"He thinks it's some people that are part of the hijacking ring here in the harbor," I said. "And I think they work for somebody called the Spaniard."

There was another extended moment of silence. "Did you say said *the Spaniard*?"

"Yes."

More silence and then, "Where is the guy now? The one with all the information?"

"Right outside my office."

"Keep him there. I'll be there in thirty minutes."

"What? How can you be here in thirty minutes if you're on a plane to Miami?"

"I'm in L.A."

"You asshole."

"Calm down, Jared," he said. "I'll be there in a half hour, keep the guy there."

"Dillon, I told you not to double-cross me. You're a lying piece of shit and you've been lying to me all along you son-of-a-bitch. I'll handle this myself."

"Calm down, Jared, you can't handle this by yourself…it's too big. You don't know what's involved."

"That's right, Dillon, I don't know what's involved because you've been holding out on me again. You're up to your same old tricks and you're going to leave Rita hanging out to dry just like you did the last time. You're going to get her killed."

"Just hold onto the guy and I'll be there in a half hour."

"Forget it, Dillon," I said. "You're out of this now. I have the information and I'll handle it myself."

"You don't know have any idea what's involved here, Jared. You've only seen the tip of the iceberg. Don't go down there," Dillon pleaded. "You'll get Rita killed for sure. We don't have any jurisdiction down there."

"What do you mean *down there*?" I asked. "Down where?"

"Nothing. Just keep the guy there," he said. "I'm on my way. Don't do anything stupid, wait for me."

I slammed the phone down to end the call and summoned Eddie Taylor back into my office.

"Somebody mentioned Rita might be *down there*," I said as soon as my door was closed. "Does that make any sense?"

Eddie thought about it for a few moments.

"Ken Jacobs has a place in Mexico, just across the border from San Diego, near Rosarito Beach."

"Do you know where his place is?"

"Yeah."

My mind was racing now. If I was going to cut Dillon and the FBI out of whatever I was going to do, I needed to do it quick. Dillon would be here in a half-hour. Maybe less. "I don't think he would take a chance driving her across the border, it would be too dangerous," I said. A hostage in your trunk might attract too much attention and I knew Rita would be howling like a scalded cat.

Eddie's face brightened. "He has a plane! He could have flown her down there."

"How do you know he has a plane?"

"He's flown me down there a couple of times," he said, glancing toward his shoes. "I bought a place down there, too," Eddie said, his voice trailing off.

I must have given him a judgmental look because he added, "I didn't want to deposit the money Ken gave me in my bank account here so I just kept in a safety deposit box and when I had enough money, I bought a place on the beach in Mexico. The surfing is good down there."

I wasn't worried about his illegal activity at this point. Rita was my priority. Eddie Taylor could pay the fiddler later.

"Can you describe the plane?" I asked.

"A Cessna, I think. It has the high wings, and it seats four people."

"How about the color or where he keeps it?"

"He keeps it out at John Wayne Airport, and it's white and I think it has blue and red trim."

That made sense. John Wayne International Airport was conveniently close to the harbor.

"White with blue and red trim," I said, repeating it back to Eddie as I wrote it down to make sure I had it right. I checked the time. Eight-thirty-eight. Dillon was on the way and time was running out.

"And I know some of the numbers on the tail," added Eddie.

"Numbers?"

"Yeah, 747, you know like the big commercial jets, the 747's," he said. "The last three numbers are 747. He always joked about taking his 747 to Mexico."

I wrote the tail number on the paper with the description. "I need your address and phone number," I said. "And then you're going to help me get Rita back."

Eddie wrote his address and phone number on the same sheet of paper with all the other information I'd gathered.

"Those guys are bad news," stammered Eddie.

"They haven't got a clue what bad news is," I said. "I'll give 'em bad news."

"I don't know..."

"What time do you have to be at work?" I asked.

A plan was forming in my head. A crude plan, but a plan no less.

"I've got to be at work at Malaysia-Pacific at four o'clock this afternoon."

"Okay, you leave here right now and stop by the grocery store," I said. "Buy two or three bags of groceries, just in case they were watching your house and wondered where you went."

"Okay."

"If they call, you tell them that you'll do it. Tell them anything they want to hear, okay?"

"Okay."

"Tell them you will do anything they want, for as long as they want, if they don't hurt Rita. We want them to think they have you right where they want you."

"Okay."

"You convince them that you're their man and that you're loyal to the death."

"Okay."

"Then you tell them that you're really sick today, the stomach flu or something, but that you'll go into work and do what they want."

"Okay."

"Eat a big meal before you go to work."

"Why?"

"Because after you change the markings on the container, you're going to get sick and have to go home. Make a big deal of being sick...try to throw up in front of somebody if possible."

"How am I going to do that?"

"Drink dish soap."

"Dish soap?"

"Yeah, it's an old trick.

"Dish soap?"

"After you change the markings, drink a cup of dish soap and it will take about thirty minutes until you're puking your guts out. But you'll be okay in a couple of hours after the soap is out of your system."

"Okay."

"Pack for Mexico this afternoon, you'll be too sick later."

"Then what?"

"You go to work as usual, re-mark the container, get sick, then go back home and wait for me. I'll be in contact with you and then we'll go get Rita back."

"Okay."

"Get going," I said.

I escorted Eddie to the door, warned him not to talk to anyone, and then started to dial the Admiral's number, but aborted the call and dialed Lieutenant Halverson's cell phone number instead. Halverson answered on the second ring.

"You busy?" I asked.

"Up to my eyeballs," he said.

"Do you want to get promoted to captain so you can sit at your desk eating jelly doughnuts all day?"

"Who doesn't?"

"Where are you now?"

"Pedro."

"Shake yourself loose and meet me in an hour at that Yugoslav place on Sixth. Do you know it?"

"I know it, but I'm really kind of busy," Halverson said. "Are you sure this is important?"

"If you're too busy, that's okay, I'll give it to somebody else. But I think you'll want in on it."

"What is it?"

"You remember that floater we had in the harbor over the weekend?"

"Yeah. What about him?"

"Do you know who he is yet?"

"Not yet. Like I told you, he's just another file on my desk"

"I'm pretty sure he's a guy by the name of John Raney that used to work security at the Korea Lines terminal," I said. "Check it out and if our floater is John Raney, I'm sitting on something big and you can have it."

Halverson was silent for a moment. "I'll tell you what, I'll make a couple of phone calls and if this guy John Raney checks out, I'll meet you at the Yugoslav place, otherwise I'm too busy to chase blind leads."

"Fair enough."

Terry Baldwin at the Immigration office was my next phone call.

"I need a favor," I said.

"Well, hello to you, too," she said.

"Sorry," I said. "But I'm really pressed for time and I need you to do me a favor some kind of bad. I'll owe you."

"What do you need?"

"Do you have any of those new tracking devices, you know, the small microchips that just stick on something?"

"I can get them," she said. "There's some paperwork and I'll need to know…"

"Start the paperwork," I said "I'll be there in ten minutes."

I checked my watch again before dialing the Admiral's number. Time was running out if I was going to stay ahead of Dillon and my gut told me it was Rita's only chance.

"What's going on, Commander?" Admiral Ballard asked.

I quickly briefed him about Rita Velasco's car being found abandoned in a grocery store parking lot and Eddie's story about her kidnapping; not caring if our conversation was being listened to by another government agency. I told him how the FBI had been holding out on us all along and that I was sure they considered Rita Velasco to be expendable. Acceptable loss is the term used in the Bureau. A certain amount of collateral damage is expected and certainly acceptable if the ultimate goal is achieved.

"I'm pretty sure she's being held in Mexico and I need to get to her before they get their hands on the contents of that shipping container."

"I don't know, Commander," he said. "Maybe the FBI is right. If it's out of their jurisdiction, it's definitely out of ours."

"I'm not asking your permission, Admiral," I said. "I'm just giving you a warning so you can distance yourself from me in case this gets really fucked up."

There was only silence on the line.

"I'm taking full responsibility, sir." I added.

"I appreciate that, Commander," he said. "Anything else?"

"Yeah, one more thing," I said. "I bounced a guy by the name of Larry Jackson out of my office this morning. He's the head of the Pacific Shipper's Association and he was in here complaining about the delays caused by increased security in the port and this morning's fog. He got on the wrong side of me and so I tossed him out. You'll probably get a call about it and I wanted to give you a heads up on that one."

"That's funny."

"Why?"

"I've never heard of Larry Jackson before today, but I've heard his name twice this morning already."

"Really?"

"Yes. I was talking to a Senator friend of mine here in Washington and he mentioned that Larry Jackson of the Pacific Shipper's Association has been lobbying him pretty hard to provide *more* security in the West Coast ports."

"More security?"

"Yes, Commander, the Senator said Larry Jackson wanted more port security."

"That's strange," I said. "Why would he want more security?"

19

A brilliant red arc reigned over the parking lot behind the Coast Guard's Marine Safety Office on Terminal Island and when I stepped out the door, the sun's energy was already heating the harbor, slowly warming the fog above its dew point. The radiation type fog, always thickest closest to the water and ground, was internally diffracting the sun's light, forming the brilliant red arc above the parking lot. Looking skyward as I walked to my truck, I watched the bands of the rainbow form their colors. The outer band was bright red, with concentric arches of orange, yellow, green, blue and violet inside the red band. A secondary rainbow formed, outside and somewhat paler than the primary rainbow. The order of the colors of the secondary rainbow was reversed from that of the primary rainbow. The pelagic aroma of the morning's falling tide was held captive by the remnant fog.

"Commander Stanton," said the voice behind me. I turned to face Captain Hannigan.

"I want to help," he said.

"Pardon me?"

"Lieutenant Velasco is in trouble," he said. "And I want to help."

"It doesn't concern you."

"Yes, it does."

I walked closer and faced him. "What makes you think Lieutenant Velasco is in trouble?"

Hannigan glanced around the parking lot before speaking again. "I figured it out from the things you said on the phone." He wiped accumulated mist from his face with his right hand. "And I heard what that other guy said to your yeoman."

"It doesn't concern you." I turned to walk away.

Hannigan grabbed my left forearm. I stiffened and faced him, then took my arm back.

"Captain Hannigan, you may be correct in your assumptions, but you are way out of your element and area of expertise. I suggest you go home."

"Maybe you're right, but I don't have a job to go back to and nothing but idle time on my hands until after my hearing. She's my only witness and I'm possibly facing charges of criminal negligence. Besides that, my lawyer told me that if my harbor pilot's license is revoked at the Coast Guard hearing, every tree-hugging environmentalist within a thousand miles of here could name me in a civil suit. My career will be ruined, I'll lose my house to pay legal fees, and my retirement fund will be history. I can't just go home and do nothing if there is something I can do to help her."

Hannigan's demeanor said he was serious but there was something else going on. I checked my watch again. Dillon was on his way to the Marine Safety Office and time was running out if I was going to avoid him.

"There's something you're not telling me, Captain," I said. "You don't need Lieutenant Velasco for your hearing, you need a good lawyer. If she doesn't show up, there's not going to be anyone that can possibly dispute your side of the story. A good lawyer will get you off."

"I'm seeing her."

"What?"

"I'm seeing her," he said. "We're dating."

"Shit."

"I don't know," he said, struggling to find the right words. "We'd been out a few times… and it was all right…but ever since the *Beleza* accident, well, I just feel different about her. I can't explain it."

I looked away from Hannigan. There it was. He was dating her and I wasn't quite sure how I felt about it. My relationship with Rita had always been professional but I guess in the back of my mind there was the possibility of something else. Hell, she was beautiful and smart. But Rita worked for me and I still wasn't over Elisha; there was still way too much baggage involved with her death. Suddenly I realized my professional relationship with Rita had grown more personal without me really knowing it.

"I'll do anything," Hannigan said. "I don't care what I do as long as I do something to help."

Captain Hannigan looked as screwed up as Eddie Taylor did when he told me about Rita being kidnapped. Adding me to the list now made three clowns in the same ring. "Anything?" I asked, automatically looking at my watch. Dillon could pull into the parking lot any second.

"Sure," he said.

I wasn't quite sure how I was going to get Rita back. I knew Eddie Taylor needed to keep her alive until we could get down to Mexico and I had to dodge Dillon and his gang of FBI thugs in the short-term. Other than that, I was making it up as I went along. Maybe I could use Hannigan. He cared about Rita and his back was to the wall legally. Criminal charges could mean jail time and that was still on the table. He was right, future charges would depend on the outcome of the Coast Guard hearing. Maybe, just maybe, Hannigan could come in handy.

"What are you driving?" I asked.

"That black Jeep Wrangler over there," he said, pointing across the parking lot.

Switching vehicles couldn't hurt and it might buy me some time. Dillon would be looking for me in a government car or my pickup.

"Good." I fished my truck keys from my pocket. "Let's trade, you're driving that now."

I pointed at my pickup with the rowboat still tied down in the back of it.

"Why?"

"How many people are in command of a ship at sea at any one time?"

"Just one."

"That's right," I said. "And I'm in charge here. If you want to help, you have to follow my orders without question. If you can't do that, go home, because you won't be any good to me or Rita."

"No problem." He handed me the keys to his Jeep.

"Do you know that Yugoslav restaurant over on Sixth Street in San Pedro?"

"I've eaten there before," he said.

"Good. Go over there and wait for me. Park on Sixth Street, about a half block from the restaurant if you can," I said. "People might recognize my truck, I'll want to know if anybody comes by to talk to you or if you're being followed."

"Okay."

"I have a couple of things to do but should be over there within the hour. Wait for me."

I started to walk away, then stopped and turned toward Hannigan again. "Just so you know what you're getting into," I said. "There's nobody else on our side. We're on our own and I'm not sure where we're going to end up."

Hannigan shrugged his shoulders. "I've got nothing more to lose."

"Just so you know," I said. "You may end with a shitload more trouble than you're already in."

***

My first stop in Hannigan's Jeep was the U.S. Immigration offices to see Terry Baldwin. I gave her a quick rundown on the situation and then the location and identity of the container Eddie Taylor was going to help steal. Terry Baldwin assured me that she would have an undercover Immigration officer put the tracking device on the container before noon. I wrote down the description and partial tail number of the Cessna Eddie Taylor told me about and she agreed to check with the FAA and Border Protection to find out if they had a record of the plane crossing the border into Mexico recently.

"You're going to Mexico looking for Lieutenant Velasco?" she asked. "What if she's not there? You're not really sure where she is."

"True," I said. "If she's still on this side of the border, I'll have to trust Mike Dillon to find her. But I have a hunch she's in Mexico, and if she is, then nobody's going to help her down there."

"You'll be outside the law."

"Pretty much. Ain't much law in Mexico anyway."

Terry Baldwin shook her head. "Do you have any idea what's in the shipping container these guys want to get their hands on?"

"I can only guess," I said. "Although, I'm pretty sure we don't want them to get anywhere near it."

Terry Baldwin handed me a small cardboard box with two battery powered digital receivers that had already been set up with the tracking code for the microchip device that was going to be attached to the container.

"Try not to lose these. I'm not supposed to loan them out."

"Sure," I started to leave

"Jared."

I turned to face her.

She walked over, stood on her toes and gave me a kiss on the cheek. "Be careful."

"Always."

Terry Baldwin gave me a slap on the butt. "Try not to lose this either."

"That's the plan."

***

It was ten fifteen by the time I drove the black Jeep Wrangler past where Hannigan was parked on Sixth Street. I turned right at the corner, then right again on Seventh Street and parked the Jeep in the middle of the block. I put the box with the receivers under my arm, shoved a buck and a half worth of loose change in the parking meter, and walked around the block where I could watch Sixth Street for a few minutes. I stood on the corner, in the doorway of a clothing store, and when I was sure it was clear, I walked up to my pickup and knocked on the passenger window. Hannigan leaned over and rolled it down.

"Anybody watching you?" I asked.

"I don't think so," he said. "Except the parking cop that put a chalk mark on the front tire. I've gotta' move in two hours."

"No problem, I'll be done before then."

I looked up and down Sixth Street on both sides for anything that jumped out at me. It looked clear. So far so good. Hannigan and my truck with a rowboat in the back of it stood out like a sore thumb and would be easy enough for Dillon to spot.

"You look a little paranoid, Commander," he said.

"Just because you're paranoid," I said. "Doesn't mean that they're not after you."

"Who are they?"

"It's a long story, I'll explain later. I'm going into the Yugoslav restaurant through the back door, if anybody comes by and talks to you, give me three honks on the horn and then drive off."

"Okay."

"Don't answer any questions about me or my truck."

"I'm not that stupid. I got it the first time."

"After I'm done inside, I'll come out the front door," I said. "I'll wave if I need to talk to you. If I don't wave, just drive home and pack for Mexico."

"Mexico?"

"Yeah. And don't pack any clothes that make you look like a tourist, or wear anything that will make you stand out in a crowd." I looked at Hannigan's red hair. "And wear an Oakland Raiders hat over that hair."

"Why?"

"In Mexico, your hair is going to make you easy to spot. We want low-profile, the less we look like gringos, the better off we're going to be."

"Okay. You're going to need my address so you can pick me up," he said.

"I already know where you live, be ready to go when I come by."

"What time?"

"Late this afternoon. Sometime after four."

I walked down the block, crossed the street at the light and then strolled toward Fifth Street. I pretended like I was window shopping, paused at the entrance to the alley between Fifth and Sixth, checked the street one last time to make sure I wasn't being followed, and then slipped down the alley to the backdoor of the Yugoslav restaurant.

Halverson was sitting at a small, well-worn wooden table that was covered with a stained red and white checked tablecloth. He was drinking black coffee from a heavy white mug, his back to the wall so he could watch both the front door and the kitchen. He saw me immediately.

I quickly scoped out the restaurant. This time of day there were only a few natives of the old country that stopped by to drink coffee and talk about the way it was and still should be. Maybe play some checkers or pinochle. Occasionally, when the mood struck, a rowdy game of dominoes would break out. The soothing smell of dinner rolls baking in the oven emanated from the kitchen behind me.

"Using the back door I see." Halverson said. "You're late." He looked annoyed and when he sat forward in his wooden chair it let out a mournful groan.

"Just keeping a low profile." I said, taking a chair on Halverson's left, keeping the front door in view. "You showed up."

Halverson nodded. "I'm still waiting for positive identification," he said. "But it looks like your tip about John Raney is going to check out."

"Good."

"What's in the box?" he asked.

"A present for you."

"You shouldn't have."

I glanced over my left shoulder as the squat wife of the restaurant's owner came through the kitchen door with a glass of water. She set the water down in front of me and pulled a tattered notepad from the front pocket of her soiled white apron, withdrew the pencil from behind her ear, and looked at me with one raised eyebrow. Her graying hair was pulled back into a bun and covered with a hairnet. Without speaking, she waited to write something down.

"Water's fine," I said. "I'm not staying."

Her sneer informed me that I was wasting her time. She shuffled over to the checker game, refilled coffee cups, and then sat down to watch the contest.

"What do you have for me?" Halverson asked, peering over his coffee cup.

"A big break on the container hijacking ring in the harbor."

"You don't say?"

"We've got one marked that's due to go out of there by truck sometime tonight." I rattled the receivers in the box and set it on the table in front of Halverson. "You can track it with these."

Halverson pulled back one flap on the box and peered inside.

"Ever use these?" I asked.

"I've got someone that has. Not a problem."

"Good."

Halverson hesitated. I could see he was considering his next question.

"Why are you giving this to me?" he asked. "Why not take it yourself or give it to the Feds?"

"I'm leaving town this afternoon on something else," I said. "And me and the Feds aren't seeing eye to eye these days."

Halverson cocked his head only so slightly. "You're not getting along with the Feds? You're a Fed."

"I'm talking about the Bureau."

"Look, Commander," he said. "It's not that I don't appreciate what you're trying to do for me. But long after all this is over, I'll still be stuck working with the those guys from time to time, and I'm not too anxious to get in the middle of your little feud with them. That's the type of shit that always comes back to bite me in the ass."

"I can understand that."

"I'm not going into this blind," he said. "I'm not that stupid…I need to know what you and the Bureau are bickering about."

"Okay."

Halverson took a sip of coffee, peered over his cup, and waited for me to explain myself.

"They aren't playing nice."

"Welcome to the real world, Commander."

"One of my Sea Marshals has come up missing and I think she's been taken to Mexico. I want her back but the Bureau has different priorities, and besides, they have no jurisdiction down there."

"Is this tied in with the Mick Biller murder?"

"That's my guess."

"How are you going to get her back?"

"I'm going after her."

"You're going to Mexico?"

"Yes."

"That ain't smart."

"I not thrilled about it," I said. "But how many other options do I have? Once the hijackers get their hands on that container you're tracking, she's as good as dead."

"Maybe the CIA has some operatives that can help."

"The Bureau wants to turn it over to the State Department and that's sure as shit her death warrant."

 Halverson was deep in thought for a minute or so. "Are you sure you want me to handle this instead of one of the other agencies? You're going to piss off a lot of people by doing it this way."

"I'm on my way out of town and my people can't handle it because we're not set up for it. That leaves the Bureau, Customs, INS, or the boys from the BATF. The Bureau is the most logical choice but I don't like the way they'll handle it."

Halverson toyed with his cup. "So you're giving it to San Pedro Police?"

"San Pedro Harbor is your home turf, Detective," I said. "I figured that you'd want to handle it and that you'd have enough personnel to cover it."

Halverson took another sip coffee and then licked his lips.

"Customs has already lost one undercover agent on this and I got Immigration to tag the container and give me these." I said, tapping the cardboard box with a knuckle.

"What exactly is it that you want me to do?"

"The container is in the Malaysia-Pacific Terminal and could go out of there anytime after four o'clock today."

Halverson looked at his watch and shook his head.

"Not going to work for you?" I asked.

"Not really." Halverson considered. "I'll have to change some things around. What's in the container you want me to watch?"

"My guess," I said. "Is that you'll be sitting on the rest of the anti-tank rockets, the French Sep Dards, used in the attack on the *Beleza*."

Halverson whistled softly.

"I could be wrong and it could be something else inside that shipping container, but it doesn't really matter, you just have to follow it and find out where it goes. Once it leaves the terminal, it's a stolen container, and that means you get to make some arrests."

"Since you suspect it contains illicit arms, are you sure you don't want the Bureau of Alcohol, Tobacco and Firearms to handle this? That's the protocol."

"Between you and me, Detective," I said. "They're idiots. They shoot first and ask questions later. That won't work this time. If I let them handle it, my Sea Marshal ends up dead."

Halverson nodded.

"This is all yours," I said. "But you have to do one thing for me."

"So there is a catch after all," he said. "There aren't any free lunches are there?"

"It's not like that."

"How is it?"

"You have to give me twenty-four hours after that container leaves the terminal before you make any arrests."

"Twenty-four hours?"

"I need twenty-four hours before they find out that you're on to them," I said. "That's why I need somebody I can trust not to screw it up. I gotta' have twenty-four hours."

Halverson rolled his eyes. "That's easier said than done. The way it usually works is we catch the bad guys in the act and them cuff 'em. We don't usually sit around eating doughnuts and wait for them to get away."

"Sorry. That's how it has to be. I need to find her before they know we have that container."

"What happens if they try to move the rockets somewhere else once they get the container?"

"Do what you have to do, but try to give me twenty-four hours before you take them down."

"What happens if I don't take this?"

"People die. Rita Velasco will be the first. Then probably me if I'm anywhere close to her."

"You're laying a lot of shit on me with damn short notice."

"Sorry about that, but I didn't create this, I'm just want my Sea Marshal back and unless you got some friends south of the border to handle it, it's up to me."

"What if I lose track of it somewhere along the way? They might take it outside my jurisdiction."

"Mexico is way out of my jurisdiction by a long shot."

Halverson smiled. "Sometimes those lines of jurisdiction get a little fuzzy. Hot pursuit and all that. But what if I lose track of that container for some reason?"

"We're screwed. We'll miss our chance and another load of shoulder fired rockets gets into the wrong hands," I said. "No telling what they have planned next time. Maybe another attack on the harbor, or maybe even the airport or some Federal buildings downtown. The next attack could happen anywhere on the West Coast."

"Where are you going in Mexico?"

"I don't know yet."

Halverson finished the last of his coffee.

"I need something else," I said.

Halverson nodded and then looked over at the waitress to see if he could get her attention. She was in a heated discussion with the old men playing checkers and refused to look our way.

I showed Halverson the piece of paper with the sketch Eddie Taylor drew of the tattoos. "I'm following this guy and I need to find out who he is."

"You have a name to go with the ink?"

"He's going by the name Ken Jacobs now," I said. "That name is more than likely just an alias, probably a stolen identity."

"You're not giving me much to go on," he said. "It's a big world out there."

"I'm thinking that you could start by running the name through DMV, then comparing the DMV photos with the prison records here in California," I said. "It's a long shot, but we may get lucky and match up faces and get a real name."

Halverson looked skeptical. "Like I told said, it's a big world out there."

"Do what you can."

Halverson nodded.

"If you come up with anything on this Jacobs guy, leave it on my cell phone voice mail." I stood up to leave. "Don't let that container get away."

"My biggest concern," he said. "Is how it got here in the first place."

20

As soon as I stepped out the front door of the Yugoslav restaurant, I discovered that the sun had returned. Somewhere in the harbor below, a cargo ship was clearing its berth and the long blast on her steam whistle rattled windows up and down the narrow traffic filled streets of San Pedro. Skyward, cotton candy clouds celebrated against a melancholy backdrop. A hundred miles to the east, the sun was relentlessly heating the high desert, causing the air to rise vertically, drawing cool sea air inland to replace it. It was turning into a classic fall day.

The amatory fragrance of a woman's perfume lingered in my nostrils and I quickly glanced up and down the sidewalk, first for the woman, and then for anyone else loitering on the street that might be waiting for me to come out of the restaurant.

Across the street, Hannigan was watching for me and when our eyes met he gave me a thumbs up. Parked at the curb a few cars behind my pickup was a white Ford Crown Victoria four-door sedan with black-wall tires and dog-dish hubcaps and I knew it was a government car so I ducked back into the Yugoslav restaurant. Halverson was paying his tab.

"Back so soon?" he said.

"Forgot to use the backdoor." I brushed past Halverson and the table of locals playing checkers.

When I got to the alley, I pulled two bags of garbage from the dumpster outside the restaurant's back door and hurried toward the street. Hannigan had followed my instructions and left his parking spot when he saw me come out the front door. Now he was sitting at the stoplight waiting for it to change. The white sedan had pulled into traffic and was three cars behind Hannigan at the traffic light. I ran across the street before the light could change, threw the two bags of garbage in the bed of the truck next to my rowboat, and then slid into the cab on the passenger's side of the truck.

"What's that?" Hannigan asked.

"Garbage. Take a right when the light changes."

"Garbage?"

"You have a white car behind you, the third one back. Do you know this town good enough to lose him?"

"No problem."

When traffic moved, Hannigan made a right turn, keeping his eyes glued to the rear view mirror. "They're still behind us," he said.

"Take another right at the next corner and slow down, I'm hopping out."

"Okay."

"Try to lose them, but if they pull you over, just tell them you were running errands with me," I said. "Whatever you do, don't tell them about Mexico."

Hannigan cruised up to the corner of Seventh Street and as soon as we rounded it, I opened the door and slid out. "Drive fast and good luck."

Hannigan gunned the pickup's engine, shifting gears as he roared up the street. I crouched between two parked cars and watched for the sedan to turn the corner. When it did, I hopped to the curb, staying low and out of sight. After the sedan passed me, I hustled up the block to where I'd parked the Jeep Wrangler, started it, and then made a quick u-turn in the middle of the block that resulted in a cacophony of horns, verbal insults, and obscene gestures.

How did they find me so fast? Did they follow Hannigan from the Marine Safety Office or had Halverson tipped them off? The worst-case scenario that ran through my mind had Halverson working with the FBI, playing both ends against the middle, and that meant the Bureau would soon know about the container in the Malaysia-Pacific Terminal. If that were the case, I'd be screwed because Dillon wouldn't give me the twenty-four hours I needed to get to Rita and help her.

As I drove the Jeep toward my house in Huntington Beach, I amused myself with the thought of Dillon spending hours digging through the two bags of garbage I'd thrown in the back of my pickup as a decoy. Midway across the Vincent Thomas Bridge spanning the main shipping channel of San Pedro Harbor, I saw a massive container ship lumbering in the turning basin below. Three tugboats were assisting the ship and a strange, mournful symphony evolved as they sounded their whistles in acknowledgement to commands given by the harbor pilot. Caustic black smoke billowed skyward as their diesel engines labored to muscle the massive ship into her berth.

If the Bureau caught up to Hannigan in San Pedro, it would only be a matter of time until they figured out that I was driving his Jeep and they put out an all-points-bulletin out on it. The white sedan meant that they were on to me, and it was only a matter of time before they would be watching my house as well as monitoring my cell phone calls. I turned my cell phone off so they couldn't track me, threw it in the passenger seat, and began to develop a plan on how to get inside my house without getting nabbed.

Traffic was heavy on Beach Boulevard all the way through Long Beach. Beach Boulevard turns into Second Street, crosses the slough twice and then merges with Pacific Coast Highway just outside Seal Beach. As soon as I was on PCH, I pulled into a strip mall to look for a pay phone and a place to eat. I found both at Ashmatrak's, a small family owned Greek restaurant. At least that's what the sign in the window said.

The aroma of rosemary roasted souvlaki lamb, honey sweetened baklava, and stale cigarette smoke greeted me at the door. I took a small table where I could watch the front door and slid into a chair. A grizzled old-timer in a Greek fishing hat sat at the table next to mine. He gave me a toothless grin, tipped his hat with one hand and raised a small glass of Ouozo with the other. The motherly Greek waitress sighed disapprovingly when I turned down the offer of Greek coffee in lieu of a glass of ice water, but smiled when I ordered a gyro with extra feta without even looking at the menu.

The pay phone was down a small hallway at the back of the restaurant, near the restrooms and across from the entrance to the kitchen. Glancing into the kitchen as I walked past, I saw three cooks working feverishly, yelling at the tops of their lungs, attempting to be heard above one another and the ventilation fans. Mystery meat laced with olive oil sizzled and popped on the grill, occasionally bursting into flames, only to be whisked away and flipped with a spatula.

I was running low on loose change but had enough to dial Hannigan's home phone. No answer. Did he get caught? He should have been home by now. I hung up and my money clanged into the coin return. My next call was to Terry Baldwin but she had gone to lunch. The phone ate my money.

I ducked into use the restroom and regretted it. The place was filthy.

The gyro was disappointing and I left without finishing it but left a five-dollar tip so I wouldn't offend the motherly Greek waitress even though I couldn't imagine ever coming to the restaurant again.

Since I hadn't been able to reach Hannigan on the phone at home, I decided to go on the assumption that Dillon and company had him in custody. If I was going to Mexico tonight, I was going to need to pick up a few things from my house so I took the back streets home, watching my rearview mirror the whole time. Dillon probably had somebody watching my house by now so I parked the Jeep on a side street two blocks west of where I lived and cut through backyards, avoiding those that looked like they had people at home or dogs in the yard. I crept as I approached my backyard and peeked over the four-foot high cedar slat fence. My house looked quiet and there was no one was in sight so I hopped the fence and worked my way across the recently cut grass in the backyard to the bedroom window. I paused to listen for noise coming from inside the house, but dogs barking down the block kept me from hearing anything else. Moving to the back door, I slipped my key into the lock, turned the latch slowly, and then began to ease the door open. The door hinges emitted a raspy squeak so I changed my grip from the doorknob to the side of the door and quickly pushed it open. No squeaking. I stole a look into the laundry room and listened for sounds inside the house. Nothing.

There was an unfamiliar smell in the small laundry room. Was it shoe polish and cologne? The laundry room is separated from the kitchen by a door that I always leave open. A quick glance told me that nobody was in the kitchen either. As I stepped into the laundry room, the old wooden floor groaned under my weight. There was a sound from the living room. I could hear the faint creaking of someone was getting out of my recliner and then there was only silence.

With a slight squeak, I eased the back door closed. My plastic laundry basket was on the floor in the two-foot gap between the wall and the washing machine where I kept my dirty laundry. I set the basket on the washing machine and squeezed into the gap, pressing myself against the wall behind the doorjamb. I was out of the line of sight between the kitchen and the back door and I listened so hard my ears began to ring. Then I smelled it again. The faint scent of shoe polish.

About the time I'd convinced myself I was imagining the smell, I heard the almost imperceptible sigh of the kitchen floor.

Now I could scent and sense the intruder. There was no sound other than the barking of dogs outside and my heart pounding in my ears. I could smell the cologne again so I clenched my right fist as I pressed my back into the wall. When I saw the barrel of the ten-millimeter Smith & Wesson, I brought my clenched right fist up and swung a wild wide arc, just clearing the plastic laundry basket, no destination yet chosen. I rolled to my left, putting all my power into the wildly arcing right fist. As my line of sight cleared the doorjamb, I searched for a location to land the blow already in motion. Then I saw her. Sky-blue eyes that widened and then got huge. The ten-millimeter Smith & Wesson jerked toward me and I tried to stop the punch in mid-flight. Too late. She was blonde. I'd never seen her before. The wild haymaker landed on the left side of her face and she went down like a sack of potatoes, the Smith & Wesson clattered to the floor.

She lay flat on her back in my kitchen. Blood began to trickle from her nose and I wondered if I'd killed her. I'd damn sure hit her hard enough. She still had a pulse and her breathing was shallow, but at least she was still breathing. Her FBI identification was in her jacket pocket. Yolanda Carter. She was young, fragile, just a kid, and unconscious on my kitchen floor.

I picked up the Smith & Wesson and pulled out the clip. The safety was off and a live round was in the chamber. Yolanda had meant business. I jacked the round from the chamber and slipped in back into the top of the clip for her.

Taking a clean dishtowel from the drawer next to the sink, I ripped it vertically into strips, then turned her on her side and loosely tied her hands behind her back. I carried her into the living room, gently set her in my rocking chair, and bound her feet with the remaining strips of cloth. Blood ran from her nose, across her cheek, and dribbled onto her white blouse.

"Sorry," I said before moving into my bedroom to pack.

A small black nylon equipment bag from my days with the Bureau was on the top shelf in the closet I and unzipped it and turned it upside down on the bed to make sure it was empty. I tossed in two pairs of socks and changes of underwear from the dresser. Two clean white t-shirts, one blue and one white dress shirt. Toothpaste, toothbrush, razor from the bathroom. In the bottom of the closet, I found my old FBI field boots and set them aside.

Yolanda Carter stirred in the living room and I checked on her. Blood continued to ooze from her nostrils but she was still unconscious.

I pulled on clean white socks, slipped into a pair of blue jeans, and threaded a black western belt through the loops. The belt had a four-inch silver cowboy buckle with a money clip behind it. I lifted the corner of the heavy mahogany dresser, swung it away from the wall, and studied what I'd hidden in the void beneath the bottom drawers. Weapons and money. I counted out a thousand dollars - six hundreds, four fifties, and the balance in twenties, folded the bills in half and hid them in the money clip behind my belt buckle. I took the slim, bone-handled Henry folding knife with a five-inch blade and put it in the sheath sewn inside my left boot. The High-Standard .22 magnum derringer went inside the right boot. After setting my reliable nine-millimeter Browning Hi-Power and two clips of ammo on the bed, I lifted the dresser back in place, making sure it lined up just right with the marks on the carpet. When I laced up my boots, the knife and derringer pressed against my legs just above my ankles. I doubled checked what I'd packed in the black bag and then zipped it shut. After wrapping the Browning in a blue nylon Dodgers windbreaker from the closet, I placed it on top of the bag so it could be carried between the two loop handles.

In the living room, Agent Yolanda Carter was still unconscious in the chair. It occurred to me that since I was going to Mexico, it might be a good idea to take a hat so I returned to the bedroom and retrieved my fishing hat, an old straw Stetson. I had everything I came back for and started to leave the house but on my way out I looked at her again. The blood had started to dry on her face. I went to the bathroom and wetted a washcloth with warm water to wipe it off.

"Can you hear me?" I said as I nudged her shoulder.

She stirred and then tugged at her bindings when she discovered she was restrained.

"I'm sorry, Yolanda."

She blinked at me. "You assaulted a Federal Officer."

"Let's not forget about that you were breaking and entering," I said. "And you had a loaded weapon in my face."

"The weapon wasn't for you. We're trying to protect you."

"Did Dillon send you here?" I asked.

She nodded. "He wanted me to stop you."

"I'll bet he did."

I checked her bindings and made sure they weren't too tight.

"Sorry, but I'll have to leave you like this," I said. "I'll call Dillon and let him know that you're here."

Blood oozed from her nose again and I wiped it away with the damp towel.

"Let me give you some advice," I said. "Get away from Dillon as soon as you can. He's bad news for pretty young women."

She looked up at me with her big blue eyes but said nothing.

"I gotta' go now. Your weapon and badge are on the kitchen table."

I walked out of the living room, paused in the kitchen, and looked back at her.

"I'll tell Dillon I got his message."

She tugged at her bindings. "Don't do it," she screamed. "Don't go down there, you'll get her killed!"

21

I ran the stoplight at Beach Boulevard and Kent in Huntington Beach. I didn't do it on purpose; it's just that I was thinking about what Yolanda Carter said before I left my house with her tied up in my living room. She'd told me that they were trying to protect me. Who were they trying to protect me from? Did I have somebody coming after me and I wasn't even aware of it? I'd expected Dillon to have somebody watching my house, maybe staked out down the block in an unmarked car. That's standard operating procedure and the reason I'd parked two blocks away and cut through backyards. But to have somebody sitting inside my house? What was that all about? Yolanda Carter must have been expecting somebody other than me to come through the back door if she had her weapon drawn, a live round in the chamber, and the safety off.

I began to wonder if Rita Velasco was already dead. The only reason I could think of for them to keep her alive was to put pressure on Eddie Taylor. Maybe, just maybe, they needed Eddie for something more than that one container and they would keep her alive a little longer. There wasn't a doubt in my mind that as soon as they got what they wanted that Rita Velasco would be history.

I was westbound on Pacific Coast Highway and at the next stoplight I powered up my cell phone and punched in Mike Dillon's number.

"Where are you?" he asked.

"I just left my house." I could tell by his hesitation he was surprised.

"Let's meet and talk about this."

"Talk about what? Are we going to talk about who nabbed Rita Velasco and why you had Yolanda Carter sitting in my house?"

"What did she tell you?"

"Nothing I don't already know. Except maybe why you need to protect me."

"Tell me where you are and I'll meet you. We can talk about it."

"We're talking now. Why waste time setting up a meeting?"

"It's complicated."

"Isn't it always? What are you doing to get Rita back?"

"We're working on it."

"Not good enough. You might want to drop by my house and give Yolanda a hand, she's a little tied up right now." I turned my cell phone off and put it in my shirt pocket. They probably had enough time to track me but it was no big secret that I'd just left my house.

Dillon said they were working on getting Rita back. I know all too well how it works at the Bureau. By the time they finished jumping through all the bureaucratic hoops necessary to do something, Rita would be in a shallow grave somewhere in the Mexican desert.

Needing to put some distance between Huntington Beach and myself as fast as possible, I decided to drive the thirty-five miles or so to Eddie Taylor's neighborhood to scope it out. When I got to Long Beach, I took the 405 Freeway heading north. It was one-fifteen in the afternoon when I exited at Crenshaw Boulevard in Torrance, made a left turn at the bottom of the freeway ramp and headed south. The Denny's parking lot looked fairly empty so I pulled around back where Hannigan's rig couldn't be spotted from the street, locked the Wrangler, and went inside. The counter was empty so I took a seat, ordered an iced tea from the waitress, got change for a five-dollar bill from the cashier, and then sought out Denny's pay phone. Terry Baldwin was my first call.

"We have a problem," she said.

"Already?" I turned my back to the restaurant and hunched over, phone close to my ear just in case somebody walked by. "What happened?"

"I got a call from the FBI, your buddy Agent Dillon," she said. "He's looking for you."

"Why did he call you?"

"Well, I found out from the FAA that your Cessna filed a flight plan from John Wayne airport to Ensenada on Sunday evening," she said. "I figured that you were on to something so I checked out the owner of the plane."

"Good. What did you find out?"

"It turns out that the Cessna is registered to a guy by the name of Ronald Cordoza."

"Did you check him out?"

"Yeah, I ran him through the system," she said. "It turns out that Ronald Cordoza is the nephew of the guy that owns the salvage yard in Fontana where the missiles where recovered."

"Really?"

"Yeah, but the San Bernardino Sheriffs Office already has him in custody."

"For what?"

"I didn't get that far, all I found out was he was picked up on outstanding warrants."

"That's pretty vague, they could have arrested him for almost anything."

"Anyway, within minutes of me trying to access Cordoza's arrest information, Agent Dillon called me and wanted to know why I was checking out Ronald Cordoza's file?"

"What did you tell him?"

"I didn't know what to say," she said. "I was surprised to get the call. I told him that it was just routine because Cordoza owned an airplane that turned up in one our ongoing investigations."

"Did he buy it?"

"Not even close. He pretty much accused me of working with you and then warned me off."

"Did he accuse you of interfering with an active FBI investigation?"

"That's what he told me," she said. "Are you sure you know what you're getting yourself into?"

"I'm beginning to wonder," I said. "But now I'm sure that the kidnapping of Rita Velasco is connected to the attack on the *Beleza*. I'm guessing that since Cordoza is in custody, somebody else grabbed up Rita and now they're desperate."

"That makes sense."

"Is there anything else you can tell me?"

"I got the feeling that Dillon didn't know Cordoza had an airplane," she said. "He got quiet when I mentioned it."

"Well, he knows now."

"Sorry about that."

"It's not your fault. Dillon should have known about the plane a long time ago."

"I didn't say anything to him about the container at Malaysia-Pacific," she said. "And just so you know, we've got it tagged already. You can start tracking it any time now."

"Good," I said. "Thanks, Terry, I owe you another one."

"Can I ask you a question?"

"Sure."

"Why not just share what you have with Dillon and work together?"

"I don't know where to begin."

"Anywhere."

"Well, first of all, Dillon left Rita Velasco hanging out to dry once already, a few years ago when she was with the Bureau," I said. "Now he's lying to me and cutting me out of what's really going on, not to mention how sloppy his investigation is. Dillon should have known about Cordoza's airplane."

"Okay," she said. "I was just wondering, but it sounds like you have your reasons."

My next call was to Hannigan. I let it ring about a dozen times and was about to give up when Hannigan finally answered the phone.

"Were you able to lose them this morning?" I asked.

"Yeah, but that truck of yours is a real dog."

"You didn't wreck it did you?"

"No."

"Good. Where is it now?"

"Come on, Commander," he said. "I'm not an idiot. I've got it parked in my garage and out of sight."

"Good. What have you been doing?"

"Packing like you told me."

"I called a little while ago and nobody answered. I thought maybe they caught up to you."

"No," he said. "I haven't been answering the phone. I don't want anyone to think I'm home."

"You just answered it."

"I had a feeling it was you."

"Are you ready to go?"

"Sure," he said. "But I have one question."

"What's that?"

"You said to pack for Mexico. Where in Mexico are we going?"

"Does it matter?"

"It does if we're going into the hurricane," he said.

"What hurricane?"

"Don't you ever watch television, Commander?" he said. "Hurricane Kendra, it's beating the daylights out of Cabo San Lucas right now."

I pictured the map of Baja Mexico in my mind and the NOAA report yeoman Jenkins had given me about the hurricane. "That's way south of where we're going," I said.

"If you say so. But Kendra is moving north at twenty-five to thirty knots."

"It won't be a problem," I said. "Just be ready to go."

"When are we leaving?"

"Later," I said. "I have a few other details to take care of."

Halverson's cell number went to voice mail but I didn't leave a message. Back at the counter, I put two sugars in my ice tea and stirred it with the long spoon. Denny's was still empty and I could hear the waitresses talking in the kitchen.

What was I getting myself into? Maybe Dillon was right. Ronald Cordoza owned the airplane but he was in custody. So who kidnapped Rita and why was Yolanda Carter at my house to protect me? Maybe this was a wild goose chase after all. If I ended up in the shit in Mexico I'd be on my own. Nobody in the U.S. Government would come down and vouch for an illegal and unsanctioned rescue operation turned terribly wrong.

"More tea?"

I looked up at a set of big brown eyes and friendly waitress smile. "I'm fine."

Her nametag said 'Becky' and she couldn't have been over twenty-one. Her whole life was ahead of her. Just like Elisha had her whole life ahead of her before I let her die. And then it really hit me. If I didn't do something, Rita Velasco would die, too.

"Have a nice day," Becky said as she slid my bill across the counter.

"I'll do that." Becky had drawn a smiley face on the back of my bill.

It was two o'clock on the nose when I dialed Halverson's cell phone again from the Denny's pay phone. Halverson answered on the second ring.

"Did you come up with anything on the tattoo for me?" I asked.

"As a matter of fact," he said. "I did."

"What'd you get?"

"We got the DMV photos of everybody named Ken Jacobs and crossed it with the prison database on tattoos," he said. " Then we matched up photos, and it turns out your Ken Jacobs is really Terrance Hinkle, a two time loser out of Phoenix."

"Tell me more."

"The initials on his hand turned out to be tattooed on the middle two knuckles of his left hand. He has an 'L' and a 'D', the initials stand for Los Diablos, a prison gang."

"What was Hinkle in for?"

"Grand theft auto."

Now it made sense to me. Hinkle and Cordoza were probably involved in the chop shop together and now that Cordoza was in jail, Hinkle had Cordoza's airplane and took it to Mexico. It was just lousy luck we didn't bust them both in Fontana.

"You said he was a two time loser," I said. "What was he in for the other time."

"The same thing both times. Stealing cars."

"Sounds like he's a slow learner."

"We're all set up on that container at the Malaysia-Pacific Terminal," he said. "Whenever it goes out, we'll be on it."

"Good," I said "Stay with that, but remember to give me twenty-four hours."

"Sure. If it works out that way."

"I have another question."

"What?"

"This morning at the Yugoslav restaurant," I said. "The Feds were waiting for me as soon as I walked out."

"Yeah?"

"You didn't turn dime on me did you?"

Halverson paused. "No. It wasn't me."

"You don't sound so sure."

"I was just thinking," he said. "I was trying to remember if I said anything to anybody that would have tipped them off."

"Did you?"

"I don't think so."

I wasn't sure if Halverson was lying, but there wasn't anything I could do about it now. I'd set a plan was in motion and there was no turning back now.

"Somebody is tipping the Feds off and they're trying to step on my toes," I said.

"It wasn't me."

I was suddenly struck with the realization that I'd been at Denny's too long. If the FBI was monitoring Terry Baldwin's phone calls they could have tracked the pay phone number back here.

"I've got to run," I said. "But I'll be in touch."

"One other thing," Halverson said.

"What's that?"

"The tattoo of the dagger on Terrance Hinkle's forearm."

"What about it?"

"It's a Los Diablos tattoo. It means he's killed somebody with a knife for the gang's initiation. He's a cold-blooded killer."

22

The situation was different now that I knew Hannigan had given the Feds the slip. I'd been developing a plan in my head without using him until now. Originally I was going to wait for Eddie Taylor to come home from work and then head straight to Mexico in search of Rita. I knew I needed to lay low for a few more hours so Dillon wouldn't find me. I figured that he wasn't watching Hannigan's house anymore and that would be the last place he'd expect to look for me.

The afternoon traffic on Crenshaw Boulevard was heavy. Against my better judgment that told me I might accidentally tip off whoever was watching Eddie Taylor, I decided to drive past his house to check it out anyway. I was careful to drive the speed limit, staying in the right-hand lane through the intersection at Sepulveda, and three blocks later turned right on Sycamore. Four blocks later I made a left on Howard Street and slowed down, scrutinizing the neighborhood for anything that seemed out of place.

Eddie Taylor lived in a small tract house at the end of the cul-de-sac on Hummingbird Way, just off Howard Street. The neighborhood was mature, having been built in the midst of the post World War Two manufacturing and housing boom in Southern

California. The homes were all small, economy minded, two, three and four bedroom dwellings, built to house growing families and factory workers for the local aerospace industry. They'd been built close together and had neatly trimmed lawns utilizing hedges instead of fences to separate the properties. Lofty sycamore and cottonwood trees shaded the sidewalks, their root systems lifting and breaking the concrete every few yards.

I eased the Jeep down Howard Street past Hummingbird Way and glanced into the cul-de-sac. It looked quiet. Three blocks later, I made a right turn and ended up in another dead end cul-de-sac where I turned around so I could drive down Howard Street the other way. There was a spot along the curb at the corner of Howard and Hummingbird where I could observe Eddie's house so I cut the engine, pulled a California map from above the passenger's sun visor, and tried to look lost. There were a total of six houses in the cul-de-sac and Eddie lived at 632, near the back, in a modest ranch style house that was white with green trim. A mature rose garden grew under the large window in front of the home and the front lawn was ready to be cut again. The concrete driveway, complete with oil stains where cars normally parked, was empty and the garage door closed.

The sweet fragrance of gardenias drifted through the open driver's window of the Jeep. A bent old man, two houses down the street from Eddie Taylor's, was moving the water sprinkler on his front lawn, his arthritic knees an obvious handicap. The old-timer waved a big knuckled hand in my direction but I pretended to be studying the map and didn't return his greeting. Two blue-gray haired women shuffled up Howard Street toward me on the far side of the street. There was no sign of life at Eddie Taylor's house so I folded the map, put it back over the sun visor, and started the Jeep's engine.

Back on Crenshaw Boulevard, I drove through the small town of Lomita and then up over the densely populated Palos Verdes Hills, cursing the traffic and the Jeep's vague clutch. At the top of the hill, I glanced down over the grassy rolling hills of Portuguese Bend and descended the sloping thoroughfare toward the azure-blue Pacific Ocean that spread from horizon to horizon in front of me. The ambient temperature dropped considerably on the windward side of the Palos Verdes Hills and the air was crisper. Crenshaw Boulevard dead-ended into Palos Verdes Drive South and at the stoplight I went left toward San Pedro.

Hannigan's white stucco Spanish style house was on a quiet street just up the hill from the Point Fermin lighthouse. I drove around the immaculately manicured neighborhood several times, to get the feel of it and to make sure there were no FBI vehicles parked on the street. When I was sure it was clear, I parked the Jeep in Hannigan's driveway and knocked on the front door.

"Are we leaving?" he asked when he opened the door. Hannigan wore blue jeans, running shoes, and a black and silver Oakland Raiders t-shirt. "I'm ready."

"Not yet," I said, pushing my way inside. "Nice place."

"Thanks. When are we leaving? I'm ready to go anytime."

"Take it easy. We have to wait awhile."

"Sure," he said. "Can I get you something to drink?"

"I'm fine. What's the latest on the hurricane?"

"Sit down and I'll get the Weather Channel for you."

There was a large leather recliner in front of the big screen television that seemed to swallow me when I sat in it. The woman on the Weather Channel was talking about the drought in Florida and how it was adversely affecting the water levels and wildlife in the Everglades.

"They talk about the hurricane every half-hour or so," Hannigan said. "What's the plan?"

It was two-thirty, an hour and a half before Eddie Taylor had to be to work, and then he would need time to change the markings, get sick and drive home.

"We have to wait for another guy," I said. "He thinks he knows where we can find Rita."

"Are you talking about the longshoreman I saw in your office this morning?"

"That's the guy."

"So what's the deal with the car that was following me this morning?"

The woman on the Weather Channel switched from the Everglades and was talking about the lack of rainfall in the Great Plains and how it would affect the winter wheat crop.

"It's kind of complicated," I said. "But I'm pretty sure that it was the FBI following you this morning."

"Were they after me or did they want you?"

"Me."

"Why?"

"Let's just say that I have some information they want and we don't agree on how that information should be used."

"Are you talking about Rita?"

"Yes." I reached down and lifted the lever on the right side of the chair. The footrest popped up and the chair reclined.

"I'm confused," he said. "Why wouldn't you share your information about Rita with the FBI?"

"We have different priorities and agendas."

"Why wouldn't you and the FBI have the same priorities and agendas?"

"In the big picture," I said. "Rita is an acceptable loss, and the FBI is looking at the big picture. She's probably in Mexico and there's no way they're crossing the border for her, so I'm going to let the FBI worry about the big picture and I'm going to get Rita back alive."

Hannigan weighed what I said. "I'm definitely for getting her back alive."

"I knew you would be."

"So, who has her and why?" he asked. "And what makes you think she's in Mexico?"

"Have you heard about the two bodies we pulled out of the harbor since the *Beleza* attack?"

"I saw it in the paper."

"I'm pretty sure that the same people that dumped those bodies in the harbor have her."

"But why would they kidnap Rita?" he asked. "It doesn't make sense."

"They dumped the bodies into the harbor to send a warning to anybody who might want to cross them, and they've grabbed Rita because now they want to pressure somebody who knows her. The odds are that she'll only be alive until they get what they want."

"So time is of the essence."

"Exactly."

"Yeah, but how do you know…" started Hannigan.

"Look," I said. "I need a little rest right now, the last few days have been really fucked up and it's going to be a long night. We'll have plenty of time to talk later."

"Sure."

"Wake me up in an hour or so," I said as I closed my eyes.

The woman on the Weather Channel gave a run down on the hurricane. Cabo San Lucas had been hit with hundred mile an hour winds and more than fifteen inches of rain. Hurricane Kendra was on a roll.

Hannigan woke me in an hour but I needed more rest so I told him to give me another hour. My eyes popped open at twenty past six. It was time to get moving.

"Are you ready?" I asked as I got out of the chair.

"I'm ready," he said. " I was going to ask you before. This sounds like it might be dangerous. Should I bring a gun with me?"

"Do you have one?"

Hannigan nodded.

"Better not," I said. "It might get you in trouble. I've got one, but I've also got Homeland Security identification."

Hannigan grabbed the bag with his gear and pulled a Raiders baseball cap low over his head.

"You drive," I said.

We rode without talking in the heavy evening traffic toward Eddie Taylor's house. The drive took almost forty minutes and we parked on the same corner where I'd stopped earlier in the day.

The sun was setting behind the Pacific's cloud strewn horizon and a weak offshore flow was developing, bringing warmer dryer air from inland toward the ocean. Lights were beginning to come on inside houses in the neighborhood and the sweet bouquet of lovingly tended flower gardens and damp grass filled the evening air. I assumed Eddie Taylor wasn't home yet because there wasn't a car in the driveway or a light on in the house.

"What time are we meeting him?" Hannigan asked.

"He should have been here by now."

We watched as an older Ford four-door sedan passed us going south on Howard Street and drove several more blocks before turning left.

As the darkness grew I became more worried, checking my watch every couple of minutes. At seven-thirty, there were still no lights on in Eddie's house.

"Do you have a cell phone?" I asked.

"Sure."

"I need to make a call." I didn't want to use my own phone because I knew Dillon would be tracking me.

I punched up Halverson and he answered on the third ring.

"Anything happening on your end yet?" I asked.

"Not yet," Halverson said. "We're sitting on it, but it hasn't moved as far as I can tell. Are you sure about your information?"

"I'm beginning to wonder."

"Maybe we're being set up."

"I hope not. Maybe they're waiting until after midnight."

There was a moment of silence on the open phone line.

"Anything happening on your end?" he asked.

"I'm still waiting."

"By the way, I talked to Terrance Hinkle's parole officer this afternoon."

"What did he have to say?"

"If you're going after him," he said. "Be careful. Hinkle is a two-time loser, and if you catch up to him, it'll be his third strike. His parole officer seems to think that going back to prison is not an option Hinkle embraces."

"Guys like him rarely do," I said. "Gotta' go. I'll be in touch."

"Buh-bye."

Maybe Halverson was right. Maybe we were being set up. Maybe Eddie Taylor had been followed to my office or I'd been spotted here earlier in the day. Maybe Terry Baldwin's people marked the wrong container. Or maybe once Eddie got to work, somebody had him change the marks on a different container and now Halverson was sitting on a decoy. Maybe Rita was already dead. That's one helluva a lot of maybes.

I couldn't wait any longer. I needed answers.

"I'm going to take a walk," I said to Hannigan. "You stay here."

I grabbed the Dodgers jacket wrapped around my Browning Hi-Power from the back seat and searched my bag for a flashlight. Slipping out of the Jeep, I donned the blue Dodgers jacket and tucked the Browning in the small of my back. The flashlight went in my right jacket pocket.

"How long are you going to be gone?" Hannigan asked.

"I'm just going to check out the house, give me fifteen minutes."

I crossed the street into the darkness that was descending on Hummingbird Way, paused to adjust my boots because the knife and derringer were chafing my legs, and then walked purposefully toward Eddie's house, watching my peripheral vision for movement. Eddie's front door was locked and I put my ear to it so I could listen for sounds inside. Nothing. I lingered on the front porch for a moment, carefully observing the surroundings, the smell of the roses in the bed under the front window, the sound of traffic several blocks away on Crenshaw. Other than the muffled sounds of a television from one of the nearby houses, Eddie's neighborhood was quiet. When I was sure nobody had seen me me, I ducked around to the back of the house. The backdoor was locked but it was an old style device that was merely a minor deterrent, manufactured in a gentler and more trusting time, not a fool-proof security measure like most modern day dead-bolt door locks. My Sears credit card easily fit between the doorjamb and the latch and the door popped open. Inside, I listened and let my eyes adjust to the darkness.

Pale yellow light from the next-door neighbor's house shone through the window and I could see I was in the kitchen. The odor of bananas was the first thing I noticed, then the smell of rancid grease and onions.

As I stood in Eddie Taylor's kitchen I began to consider the possibility that I'd been set up from the beginning. Maybe Eddie Taylor's story was nothing more than a diversion. Magicians are masters at diverting attention from the real action. Was that what this was? A diversion? Customs agent Mick Biller and security guard John Raney turned up dead in the harbor. Astal Kamran was shot while in custody. Rita Velasco kidnapped. Was it too easy? Eddie Taylor just walked into my office with information about Rita Velasco being kidnapped and I'd run off half-cocked. How easy was that? The FBI said they wanted to protect me. From what or who? Maybe they wanted to protect me from myself.

I took the small flashlight from my jacket pocket, adjusted the Browning in the small of my back, and cupped my hands as I turned the flashlight on, letting only a small stream of light escape between my fingers. The linoleum kitchen floor had been laid on a concrete slab and so I was able to move around without making the floor squeak. There were four chairs at a small table that still had dirty dishes and a newspaper on it. Today's paper. Sports page on top. There was an old refrigerator in the corner humming quietly and an old gas range with a cast iron skillet on one of the burners; the faint flicker of the blue flamed pilot light beneath the skillet emitted the ever so subtle smell of natural gas.

Staying as close as possible to the wall, I peered into the next room. The small flashlight beam escaped through my fingers, bleeding light into the room. There were couches and a television on a table against the wall. No sound. Stale air. The room looked like someone had tossed it. Or maybe Eddie Taylor was just sloppy. I moved to the front window and pulled the curtains back just enough to see down the street to where Hannigan was parked. The black Jeep was in the shadows and unless you knew it was there, you probably wouldn't notice it.

There was no sound in the hallway leading to the other rooms. My ears were ringing as I strained to hear any sound at all. The hallway was dark and completely absorbed the small amount of light that slipped between my fingers so I opened them a little to let more of the beam escape. The hallway was musty and stale. Eddie Taylor needed to air out his house sometime soon. The first bedroom door was closed and I pressed my ear against it but could only hear the ringing in my ears. The filtered flashlight beam traveled up the hallway, past the open bathroom door toward two other doors, opposite each other at the end of the hall. Passing by the first bedroom without opening the door, I checked the bathroom. It was empty, toilet seat up, shower curtain pulled back. Pale yellow light spilled into the hallway from the open door on the left. I cupped the flashlight tighter, choking back more light. With my back against the wall and the cool hard steel of the Browning pressing into my flesh, I peeked into the room. It too, looked like it had been tossed. I stole into the room, letting my eyes adjust to the light. Bed, dresser, clothes and shoes on the floor. Locker room smells of sweat and mildew. Several dresser drawers half open, clothes spilling out. The smell of dirty socks. Opposite the door was a closet with sliding mirrored doors, one side open halfway. I eased forward, walking over the clothes strewn about on the floor, and then let my light illuminate the dresser where several bowling trophies were on display. The bed was unmade, covers carelessly thrown back. The closet was dark and littered with old shoes and clothes that had fallen from their hangers. Between the bed and the closet was a nightstand that had a phone, alarm clock, and a paperback book left open, pages down, front and back covers up.

I worked my way back around the bed, stepping on clothes. Then a sound. Where did it come from?   All I could hear could now was my own heart beating, my breathing, and the ringing in my ears. Had the noise come from inside the house or outside? Unless my eyes were playing a trick, more light seemed to come from the hallway now. I began to navigate the clothing strewn bedroom floor toward the hallway. Between the bed and the door I kicked something. A shoe? I lowered the flashlight beam and saw a sock with a foot in it. Letting the full beam illuminate the floor, I first saw the leg, and then the entire body that lay on the floor on top of a pile of clothes.

23

Kendra chose the path of least resistance and was dying. I'm not sure why the Weather Channel's prognosis was coming to mind at this moment. Maybe it was the forecaster's choice of words when I'd listened to the last storm update at Hannigan's house. She said Kendra was dying. Mick Biller and John Raney were dead. The body on the floor looked dead and if it was Eddie Taylor, Rita Velasco wouldn't be far behind him.

The Baja California weather forecast kept rattling through my head. Hurricane Kendra was generating gale force winds for more than three hundred miles in all directions of the eye that measured a mere sixteen miles across. The center of the storm had passed directly over the resort town of Cabo San Lucas nestled on the tip of Baja and was now traveling northeastward up the Sea of Cortez at twenty-five knots. With land on both sides of her eye and cut off from the very forces that sustain hurricane life, Kendra was dying.

I let the full beam of my flashlight shine on the motionless body at my feet, instinctively looking for a wound or blood before illuminating the face. It took me a moment to recognize Eddie Taylor. Kneeling next to the body, I checked for a pulse. He felt cold but had a pulse. A strong pulse. I pulled back an eyelid with my left thumb and shined my light in it. The pupil contracted and Eddie Taylor stirred.

"Eddie." I said, rolling him over on his back. "Wake up Eddie."

"What?" he said, shielding his eyes from my flashlight.

"Are you okay?"

"No."

"What's the matter?"

"I'm sick as a dog."

"From drinking dish soap?"

"Yeah."

"How much did you drink?"

"A coffee cup full...just like you told me."

"I meant a measuring cup, you idiot," I said. "Did you dilute it?"

"Dilute it?"

"You didn't drink a coffee cup full of straight dish soap did you?"

"That's what you said to do."

"I wanted you to drink a small amount of liquid soap diluted in water. It doesn't take much to make you throw up."

"Go away," he said and then closed his eyes.

"Did you do what they asked?" I shook Eddie's shoulder. "Wake up. Did you change the markings on the container?"

"Yeah." Eddie tried to sit up but groaned and flopped back on the pile of clothes.

"We need to get going then," I said. "You need to come with me."

"Maybe later. I'm sicker than shit right now."

"I'll bet you are, but we need to find Rita. We don't have much time."

"They said they would let her go," he said. "They promised me."

"They're lying. There's no way they'll turn her loose alive, she knows too much."

I tried to lift him but the dead weight was too awkward. I needed help. Hannigan saw me when I came out the front door and waved to him. Without turning the Jeep's headlights on, he pulled into Eddie Taylor's driveway. The two of us dragged Eddie to his feet and out of the house.

"He doesn't look so good," Hannigan said. "He's not going to puke in my Jeep is he?"

Eddie crawled into the small, awkward backseat of the Wrangler, groaned, and then doubled over, clutching his abdomen.

"I think all that's behind him now," I said optimistically. "He'll start feeling better soon."

But just in case it wasn't all behind him, I grabbed my own bag from the back floorboard and threw it up front on the passenger's side.

"You drive," I said, climbing in and adjusting the bag between my feet.

"Where're we going?"

"South toward San Diego and then across the border. If you get tired, let me know, I'll drive."

We stopped at a convenience store before getting on the freeway to buy some Gatorade, jars of applesauce, plastic spoons, bananas, and box diarrhea tablets so I could nurse Eddie back to health. I could handle a little vomiting, but if Eddie shit himself in the backseat, I was going to have all kinds of trouble with that. Once Hannigan was back in traffic, I opened the box of diarrhea tablets and gave Eddie four of them, double the adult dose listed on the box.

"Take these," I said to him. "They'll help with the cramping."

Eddie held the tablets in his shaking hand.

"Wash them down with this," I said, handing him a bottle of strawberry Gatorade. "You're dehydrated. Let me know when you start to get hungry, I have some applesauce and bananas."

Eddie groaned and clutched his abdomen. "No food."

"It'll pass in a few hours. The sooner you can eat the sooner you'll regain your strength."

Hannigan drove in the frustrating stop-and-go traffic of the southbound San Diego Freeway. We rode in the Jeep without talking, toward the Mexican border at San Ysidro, some 120 miles to the south. By the time we reached the town of Del Mar, just north of San Diego, it was a quarter past eleven and I told Hannigan to get off the freeway so we could find a place to eat and get gas for the Jeep before crossing the border.

Louie's was a small family style restaurant on the main drag that was open twenty-four hours a day. Eddie headed straight to the restroom and I went with him to make sure he was all right. Back at our booth, I ordered chicken noodle soup and a side order of dry toast for Eddie. Hannigan and I went with bacon cheeseburgers, fries, and coffee.

Eddie spooned the soup past his lips and looked like he was getting stronger.

"Where are we going when we cross the border?" I asked.

"Get on the toll road going toward Rosarito Beach. Ken Jacob's place is near Las Palmas, south of Rosarito," Eddie said.

"How far is it once we cross the border?"

"About fifty miles or so. The roads are good so it'll take less than an hour once we get clear of Tijuana."

"Where exactly is Ken Jacob's place?"

"His house is on the beach, inside a gated community called Villa Hidalgo."

"Are we going to have any trouble getting through the front gate?"

Eddie shook his head. "Not unless you're Mexican. They wave us gringos right through."

"You said you had a place down there, too," I said. "How far is it between Ken Jacob's house and your place?"

"Mine is south of Ensenada," he said. "It's twenty or thirty miles south of where we're going. But it's about another hour drive because we have to go through downtown Ensenada."

"Do you think they would be holding Rita at your place?"

"I doubt it. I don't think Ken has ever been there."

"Have you ever heard the name, Terrance Hinkle?"

Eddie hesitated. "No, I don't think I know that name. Why?"

"How about Ronald Cordoza?"

"No."

"Ronald Cordoza owns the plane you told me about and Ken Jacobs is really Terrance Hinkle."

Eddie considered what I said and then shook his head. "I don't know those names. I thought Ken Jacobs owned the plane, at least he always acted like it was his."

I studied Eddie's face, looking for a sign that he might be holding something back.

"So, you're pretty sure this place south of Rosarito is where they'll be keeping her?"

Eddie shrugged his shoulders. "Ken Jacobs has a place on the beach, and every time I've seen him down there, that's where he is."

I fought back the nagging feeling that I was making a big mistake. Self-doubt hung over my head like a thick black cloud of mosquitoes. This could be a wild goose chase. Mexico is a big place and Rita could be anywhere. They might not have even taken her south of the border. Desperate people usually aren't very logical. I forced myself to think about what Dillon said to me about not going down there and that the plane owned by Cordoza had filed a flight plan for Ensenada. Rita was missing and my best guess was that she was in Mexico. My only choice was to play the cards in my hand.

"We can start looking there," Eddie said. "If he's not there, I know a few other people and places in Ensenada to check."

"Okay," I said. "Let's do this."

When we got to the parking lot, I crawled into the backseat of the Jeep. I knew that Dillon might have somebody waiting at the border, checking faces and descriptions of people crossing into Mexico, and I didn't want to make it any easier than it had to be. The Mexican authorities wouldn't be looking for me; they'd have no reason to. But Dillon and the FBI might try to keep me from leaving the United States and I wanted to make sure that didn't happen. Hopefully nobody was looking for Hannigan's Jeep and the FBI couldn't possibly check every vehicle crossing the border.

Getting into Mexico is easier than getting out and the long line of vehicles at San Ysidro moved quickly. I wore my cowboy hat low across my face and slumped down in the back seat. Judging by the number of sailors crossing the border into Tijuana with us, I figured that an aircraft carrier and her picket ships must have docked in San Diego recently. The authorities were waving everyone through and we breezed past the check station without a hitch.

Within yards of crossing into Mexico, things changed. Sights, sounds, smells. Tijuana has become more tourist and family oriented since the passage of the North American Free Trade Agreement, but unbridled sin still runs rampant on the side streets and in the back alleys. The neon illuminated main streets of Tijuana were crowded with tourists, music, prostitutes, hustlers, and the smell of food being sold by street vendors. Any given night in Tijuana is like a low budget version of Mardi Gras in New Orleans with a lower moral standards.

Hannigan navigated the Jeep across the steel and concrete Tijuana River Bridge before pulling onto a side street so Eddie could change some of my money for us. We easily found a black market hustler that was happy to make the money transaction. After the money exchange, the hustler tried to sell us some girls, then screamed Mexican obscenities at us when we declined his offer and drove away.

Southbound traffic on the toll road was fairly light once we cleared the outskirts of Tijuana. On a quiet stretch of the highway we pulled over and switched places. Hannigan went in the cramped back seat, I drove, and Eddie sat up front to give me directions.

"Hunter's moon," Hannigan said as we all settled into our new places.

"What are you talking about?" I asked.

"This month's full moon will be the hunter's moon."

"Yeah," I said. "I guess so."

"Ironic isn't it?" Hannigan said.

"How so?"

"We're hunting somebody, that's all."

I released the parking brake, put the Jeep in gear, and pulled back on the road, spinning the Jeep's tires on the loose gravel on the shoulder.

"The full moon closest to the autumnal equinox is the harvest moon," said Hannigan. "That was last month. This month's full moon will be the hunter's moon."

I rolled the driver's window down, trying to flush the lingering smell of Tijuana from the inside of the Jeep. "It's not a full moon yet."

"No," Hannigan said.

"So then what's your point?"

"No point. I was trying to make conversation. I guess I'm a little nervous."

"Well relax, I'll let you know when to be nervous." I looked over at Eddie and saw he was resting his head against the window.

"Are you awake, Eddie?" I asked. "Because you need to be awake to tell me where I'm going."

"I'm awake," Eddie said. "Stay on the toll road and I'll let you know where to turn off."

I varied our speed, watching the rear view mirror as much as I looked through the windshield so I would know if any of the other cars on the toll road were tailing us. After we'd gone twenty miles I was pretty sure we weren't being followed.

My thoughts went back to Rita. Was she still alive? Was Halverson still waiting for the container to be moved from the

Malaysia-Pacific Terminal? Had somebody seen us take Eddie Taylor from his house?

Forty-five minutes of tires humming on tarmac was about to put me to sleep.

"Slow down," Eddie said after another five minutes of what already seemed like an eternity. "The turn's coming up."

My pulse quickened as adrenaline began to churn through my bloodstream.

"Take the Las Palmas exit and go right as soon as you get off," he said.

The drone of the Jeep's tires slowed as I eased onto the exit ramp. A small sign with an arrow read, *Av. Hidalgo,* and I turned right on the smooth and freshly paved asphalt road.

"How far now?" I asked.

"A couple of miles."

The smell of the ocean blew through the open driver's window of the Jeep. The night air was warm and moist with a heavy saline scent. Nobody spoke, but tension was so thick inside the Wrangler's cabin that you could cut it with a knife. Palm trees suddenly began to line the sides of the darkened road and the pavement curved to the right, then left, and suddenly we were at the front gate to Villa Hidalgo.

Ground-level spotlights hidden in the immaculately landscaped portico punctuated the front entrance to Villa Hidalgo. A small, white stucco guard shack sat atop an elevated grassy knoll in the middle of the paved two-lane road. Palm trees frolicked in the ocean breeze and a ten-foot high white stucco wall, capped with red Mexican brick, lined both sides of the entrance.

As I slowed the Jeep, a wiry young Mexican guard stepped from the shack.

"Drive though," instructed Eddie.

"Buenas noches," I said, waving as I gunned the motor.

"Buenas noches," said the guard, returning my salute.

"Go straight," Eddie said.

The moon provided just enough illumination to see some of the Villa Hidalgo development. It looked new. Immense white stucco Mexican-style houses with red tile roofs were liberally scattered on generous sand dune lots. The smell of fresh asphalt drifted through the Jeep's windows. The crashing of ocean surf was audible over the sound of the motor.

"Turn right here," Eddie said. "It's going to be the second house on the left."

Once we were past the first house, I pulled the Jeep into the sand on the side of the road, cut the engine, and turned the headlights off.

"What's the plan?" Eddie asked.

"I don't know yet," I said. "What kind of people live here?"

I could vaguely make out the house by the light of the moon. There weren't any lights on inside. A warm, moist breeze drifted through the open Jeep windows and the night was quiet except for the sound of the surf.

"I don't know," Eddie said. "Mostly retired Americans I would guess. Maybe some business owners from Ensenada."

"What's the house like inside?"

"Four, maybe five bedrooms. There's an office upstairs and a huge living room with a lot of windows that look out on the beach. He has a big deck on one side of the house with an outside shower and some patio furniture."

"Okay."

I checked my watch. It was almost two o'clock. We'd made good time and I wondered if this was near the hour that the marked container would be moving from the Malaysia-Pacific Terminal.

"Not many lights on around here," Hannigan said from the back seat.

"It's the middle of the night," I said. "Eddie, do you know if they have security patrols here or just the guard at the gate?"

"I couldn't tell you."

"Here's what we'll do," I said. "Captain Hannigan and I will get out here and work our way over towards the house. Eddie, you wait here until we get close and then you drive up in the driveway and knock on the front door."

"Okay," Eddie said.

I grabbed my Dodgers jacket and Browning Hi-Power from the bag on the passenger's floorboard, slid out of the Jeep, and held the door open for Hannigan. When Hannigan was out, I eased the door closed, slipped on my jacket, and jacked a live round into the chamber of the Browning.

"Give us a few minutes to get close to the house," I said. "Then drive up in the driveway."

"Okay."

"Take your time getting to the front door. You'll be distracting them while we slip up to the house from the opposite direction."

"Okay."

"Follow me and be quiet," I said to Hannigan.

Staying low, Hannigan and I snaked across the sand dunes toward the darkened house ahead of us. To our left, large ground swells crashed to the beach, sending white foam rushing shoreward before they dissipated in the sand. The night air was thick with sweet saline mist from the surf.

"Star-dogged moon," Hannigan said in a hushed tone.

"What?"

"Star-dogged moon." He pointed at the silvery sphere overhead. "See how it's distorted and it has the pins of light that look like stars?"

I knelt in the sand and looked skyward.

"It's caused by high altitude ice crystals," he said. "The hurricane draws moisture from the surface and sends it thousands of feet up where it turns to ice."

"That's nice," I said. "Now shut up and let's move."

"A star-dogged moon is bad luck," he said. "Always bad luck."

24

Crouching on the beach, I made sure to keep the Browning out of the sand because the last thing I needed right now was a jammed action. The moon cast an eerie, silvery light over the house and down the shoreline; enough light to see, but at the same time, not enough to see clearly. The only sound was the intermittent pounding of the surf less than fifty yards away. The stench of rotting seaweed, stranded by the falling tide, combined with the clammy seaspray from the breakers to saturate the night air. Emptiness overwhelmed me. What if I died here tonight?

Hannigan squirmed in the sand next to me.

"What are you doing?" I whispered.

"Trying to get comfortable."

"Well, hold still. You're going to give us away."

Another comber crashed to the beach, white foam hissed as it rushed forward, then slowed and disappeared as the beach sloped upward, and then I heard Eddie start the Jeep's motor. The headlights came on and he pulled back onto the pavement as I tried to calculate the timing of my next movement with his arrival at the front door.

"One by one, by the star-dogged moon," Hannigan said. "Too quick for groan or sigh, each turned his face with a ghastly pang, and cursed me with his eye."

I looked at Hannigan in disbelief. His face was a pale argent outline in the light of the moon. "What the fuck are you talking about?"

"It's a poem," he said. "About the star-dogged moon."

"Are you mental? I should've left you in the Jeep."

"Why?"

In twenty-twenty hindsight, I should have left Hannigan in the Jeep, or better yet, in San Pedro. But it was too late now because Eddie pulled it into the driveway and cut the motor

"Are you nervous again?" I asked.

"Yeah."

"Good, because it's time. Stay low and follow me."

We approached the house at an angle and I dropped into a prone position in the sand about thirty feet from the back deck. Hannigan flopped next to me, breathing hard.

"Quiet," I said. "You're making more noise than a busted muffler."

The whites of Hannigan's eyes, luminescent in the moonlight, telegraphed his fear.

I strained to hear noise from inside the house but the adrenaline-induced pounding in my ears drowned out all other sound. A light came on in the house and I got to my knees, left hand in the sand for balance, Browning forward. I motioned for Hannigan to stay still and then crept closer to the back deck.

Eddie Taylor came to a sliding glass door in the back of the house, paused, and then unlocked the door and slid it open.

"Nobody's home," Eddie yelled into the darkness. "You can come in."

Hannigan and I climbed the two brick steps up to the red tile deck in the back of the house.

"There's nobody here," Eddie said again. "But the front door was unlocked."

"Unlocked?" The hair went up on the back of my neck and I suddenly had the feeling we were walking into a trap. "Let's turn some of these lights out."

Eddie was right. The house was big. The cavernous living room had vaulted ceilings, Spanish style white stucco walls and red tile floors. The ocean side of the living room was semi-circular with windows from the floor to the rafters that gave a 180-degree view of the Pacific Ocean outside. Three sliding glass doors made access to the deck and beach easy. My first impression was that nothing but the finest furnishings graced the room; leather furniture, hand woven rugs, artwork on the walls. I walked over to a table near one of the couches and touched a two-foot high ebony carving of an African antelope.

"I don't think Ken Jacobs would leave his front door unlocked," Eddie said. "That's not like him."

"I don't think so either," I said. "But let's look around while we're here."

Hannigan sat on a leather barstool at the counter separating the expansive kitchen from the living room. A wicker basket filled with seasonal fruit was on the counter and Hannigan picked through it. "Mangoes," he said, holding one for me to see.

"Quit touching things, " I said. "You're leaving fingerprints."

Eddie came with me as I explored downstairs. There were three bedrooms with their own full baths, a laundry room, and a small library in addition to the living room and kitchen. None of the doors were locked and it was obvious that nobody was home.

"Stay here in case somebody shows up," I said to Eddie. "I'm going to check upstairs and then we need to get out of here."

Using my flashlight to probe the darkness, I found an open sitting area with four leather couches at the top of the stairway, a master bedroom to the right, and to the left, a spacious office with an elaborate bathroom and ocean view. I lingered in the office. It had a large cherry desk, generous leather chairs, and a wet bar. Thick carpet. Expensive smells. Cool air blew from the air conditioning vents even though it wasn't needed. My flashlight illuminated three chest-high rows of file cabinets across the room from the wet bar. Something was wrong. I walked over to the huge bookcase that occupied the entire south wall of the office and thumbed at some of the volumes. Why was the front door unlocked? Why would Ken Jacobs, a car thief and lowlife, have an office like this? There weren't any signs of the house being used recently; no dirty dishes, wet towels, or out of place clothing. A beach house should have wet towels and sand somewhere. But nothing was out of place. Everything was perfect. Maybe that was it. I scrutinized the office again in the beam of my flashlight. Everything was in its place. Suddenly I knew what I was looking at and the hair went up on the back of my neck again. That's why the front door was unlocked. They had to be close, watching us right now.

There was the muffled sound one of the sliding glass doors opening downstairs and then I heard voices. Were Eddie and Hannigan talking that loud? No, the voices were different and I instantly knew we'd walked smack-dab into the middle of a set-up. Instinctively, I took a defensive position behind an overstuffed leather chair and crouched behind it. I could still hear them talking downstairs but couldn't make out what they were saying. Eddie said something. Then Hannigan. Someone was asking them questions. Had Ken Jacobs come home? Was he walking on the beach when he saw the lights come on in his house?

Straining to hear the conversation downstairs, I waited for someone to come looking for me. How many different voices were there? Seconds seemed like hours, but when I was sure nobody was coming up the stairs, I moved to the office door in order to hear better. The voices were reverberating off the stucco walls and tiles floors of the living room and I still couldn't make out the conversation so again I moved closer, this time to the top of the stairway, Browning ready, fourteen rounds in the clip and one in the chamber. I'd distinctly heard two different voices, but had others come in the house that weren't talking? The stairs were carpeted over cast concrete and didn't squeak or groan under my weight. The knife and derringer in my boots were irritating my legs now, maybe wearing blisters.

At the bottom of the stairs, I could hear everything being said.

"Like I told you, I'm a friend of Ken Jacobs," Eddie said. "I have a week off and I came down here to do a little surfing."

"You don't have a surfboard in your Jeep," said a voice I didn't recognize. "That's going to make surfing tough."

"My buddy Ken has a lot of surfboards," Eddie said confidently.

"The guy that lives here doesn't have any surfboards," said the voice. "You better try again."

A freestanding partition wall separated the hallway at the bottom of the stairs from the kitchen and living room. From the bottom of the stairs, I could see into one side of the living room and the reflections in the tinted glass windows showed two men standing, one with a handgun pointed at Eddie and Hannigan who were seated at the counter.

"He keeps them in the garage," Eddie said.

"There aren't any surfboards in the garage," said the man without the gun.

"Sure there are. At least there used to be."

I eased across the red tile floor of the hallway, the rubber soles of my boots making an almost imperceptible squishing sound on the floor. Staying low and balanced, I kept the partition between me and the kitchen. A few feet more and I could still see into the kitchen by looking at the angled reflections in the glass of the living room.

"No, there are no surfboards," said the voice. "Let's see your identification."

"Why?" Eddie asked.

"Let's just say that you have one foot on a banana peel and the other foot in a Mexican prison. Have you ever been in a Mexican prison?"

"No." Hannigan emitted a squeaky, nervous laugh.

I studied the reflections from the glass and made a mental note that they were reversed from what was actually happening. Eddie and Hannigan were sitting next to each other on stools at the counter and the man doing the talking was standing in the kitchen while the one holding the handgun was facing the living room windows with his back to me. I knew that as soon as I came from behind the partition, the intruder with the handgun would be able to see my reflection in the windows.

"Let's go," said the voice. "I want to see your driver's licenses and passports if you have them."

When I burst from behind the partition partition, the man in the kitchen jerked his head instinctively and the one with the handgun started to turn towards me. Keeping my weight low and forward, balancing with my left foot, I drove straight through the guy with the handgun, hitting him hard with a right forearm and elbow to the base of the skull, driving his forehead into the kitchen counter. His head plopped like a melon and he fell to the floor on top of his weapon.

"Don't even think about it," I said as I leveled the Browning at the other stranger's face. "Now I get to ask you questions."

The stranger's dark brown eyes darted back and forth, quickly assessing the situation.

Eddie got up from his barstool and started around the counter toward the man in the kitchen and the stranger stood with his left foot slightly forward, weight low, hands loosely clenched into fists; a non-aggressive defensive position.

"Stay back, Eddie," I said. "I don't want to have to shoot both of you."

Eddie returned to the counter but remained standing. Hannigan hadn't moved at all and was still squeezing the same mango.

I studied the darkly dressed stranger and mentally connected the voice I'd heard to the distinct Latino features and closely cropped black hair. He was in his middle to late twenties and had white teeth. Too white. His English was more polished than I'd expect from a local Mexican and he wore boots similar to mine. Two and two added up to him working for some branch of the U.S. Government.

With my left foot, I nudged the man on the floor. A small pool of blood formed on the clay tile next to his nose.

"I know what you're thinking," I said to the Latino in the kitchen. "You're thinking that I'm old and slow and that you can get the drop on me…and that these other two are unarmed and that you can probably take them both out without any trouble."

The stranger answered with his eyes.

"Don't try," I said.

The stranger relaxed his defensive position. "You must be Jared Stanton."

"That's right," I said. "And you'd be?"

I nudged the man on the floor again just to make sure he wasn't playing opossum.

"I have a message for you," the Latino said.

"Sit," I told him, motioning toward the kitchen floor with my weapon. "And keep your hands in sight. You know the drill."

He kneeled and then sat on the red tile floor with his legs crossed, resting his back against the kitchen cabinets, hands opened, palms upward on his knees. I was right, he knew the drill.

"Eddie," I said, motioning with my free hand toward the unconscious man on the floor. "Get this guy into the living room and see if he's okay."

Eddie's eyes met mine.

"And be careful, he may not be as hurt as we think," I said. "Get his weapon, too."

The Latino sitting on the floor has his eyes locked on me.

"What's your message?" I asked.

"Stay out of it. Let us handle it."

"If this is the way you handle things, it's a damn good thing I'm here."

Eddie dragged the unconscious man into the living room by his feet. "He's breathing."

"Good."

Eddie slapped the man's face a couple of times and then opened an eyelid. "He's out like a light."

I nudged Hannigan. "Get a towel out of one of the bathrooms and wipe this blood up."

The Latino watched Hannigan as he moved.

"I don't have a lot of time here," I said to the Latino. "Where is Rita Velasco?"

"Who?"

"Are you here with the sanction of the Mexican government?" I asked. "I know who you work for."

The Latino was poker faced but I had my answer.

"Okay, let's try this," I said. "Why are you watching this place and what are you looking for?"

The Latino just stared at me.

"You're making this harder on yourself than it has to be. I just need a few simple answers. I haven't decided what to do with you yet."

I rested the Browning on the counter.

"I'm not your problem," I said. "Your problem is going to be your superiors when they find out that I got the jump on you."

The Latino blinked.

"I got your message," I said. "You took care of that part of it, but I'm guessing they also wanted you to grab me up and keep me somewhere. Right now you're not in too deep to get out. When you get back, you'll be able to talk your way out of this little fuck-up."

The stranger blinked again.

"On the other hand, if I take your weapons and leave you tied up, that's going to be awfully hard to explain. Just imagine your weapons being mailed back to headquarters. That's a shitload of explaining you'd have to do."

He still said nothing.

"Or I can let you get your partner to the hospital. He's going to need medical attention."

I could see in his eyes I'd struck a nerve.

"Answer a few questions and give me a head start out of here," I said. "I won't take your weapons with me. I know that you're just taking orders, but I also suspect that you fell asleep out front and now this whole thing is out of control for you. You need to be thinking about how you're going to get out of this predicament and how bad you want your report to look on paper. You're making a career decision."

"What do you want to know?"

"Have you seen Rita Velasco?"

"No."

"Do you know who she is?"

"No."

"How long have you been watching this place?"

"On and off for a week or so."

"A week or so?" It didn't fit. They'd been staked out here before the *Beleza* was even attacked. "A week or so?" I asked again, just to confirm what I'd heard him say.

"About that."

"Why? What were you looking for?"

"Just surveillance. Pictures, times, people who come and go."

"And what have you seen?"

"Nothing."

"Who do you report to?"

The Latino blinked.

"Are you working along with the Mexican government? Do they know that you're here?"

"This guy is starting to wake up," said Eddie from the living room.

"Look," said the Latino. "We have a surveillance assignment on this place and a couple of others down here, watching a few guys. As far as anybody is concerned, we're just tourists. I don't know what's going on, I just report back. They e-mailed me your picture this afternoon and said you may show up. If I saw you, I was supposed to tell you to stay out of it because we're on it."

"And apprehend me?"

"Hold you," he said. "They said to hold you if we could."

"Okay, what about Rita Velasco? Did they send you a picture of her?"

"Nobody said anything about her."

"I'll explain this once, so listen closely," I said. "I'm looking for Rita Velasco and the people you're watching are holding her somewhere near here. If she's not dead already, she'll be dead soon, and I don't want that to happen. Time is critical."

The stranger nodded.

"Here's what I'll do," I said, pointing my Browning at him again. "You carefully slide your weapon over here, and I'll need your car keys. I'll toss everything out the window as we drive away. Then you clean this blood up and get out of here before somebody comes back."

The Latino nodded, slowly extracted his weapon and keys, and then slid both across the floor to me.

"Just a warning," I said. "Take care of your partner and don't try to follow us. I won't hesitate to shoot you if you get in my way. You've had your warning."

"Deal," the Latino said.

"Load up boys," I said to Eddie and Hannigan. "Let's go."

"I told you a star-dogged moon was bad luck," Hannigan said. "Plain, shit, bad luck."

25

Star-dogged moon or not, I knew we'd been lucky. The two guys at the beach house could have very easily turned Mexico into a dead-end disaster.

"How far now?" I asked.

"A few more miles," Eddie said as he navigated the Jeep down the narrow pitch-black coast road toward the next bar he wanted to check. The first place, a small open-air palapa on the beach, had been a bust.

The fruit basket. I'd been in such a hurry to get out of Ken's Jacob's beach house before somebody else showed up that I'd overlooked the fruit basket. Fatigue was taking its toll on me and I'd missed the obvious. If nobody had been to the beach house in a week or so, the fruit would have been rotten.

"Those guys were lying," I said to Eddie. "I think Rita was there."

"How do you know?"

"If she was never there, they'd have no reason to lie to me."

"Why would they lie about Rita being there? They knew about you, and you made a deal with them."

"They don't want us walking into the middle of their little operation."

"What operation?"

"I don't know yet, but a have a feeling we're about to find out."

It was starting to make sense now. Dillon had shown up in my office right after the *Beleza* attack. He'd said he was working near the border, but in morning rush hour traffic it would have taken him three hours to get from the Mexican border to my office. He had to have been near the harbor when the *Beleza* caught those rockets. How big was this operation they were running? So far, I knew it stretched from at least Ensenada to San Pedro. The Latino at the beach house said they were watching a few other places. Were they watching Eddie Taylor's house? Or was Eddie Taylor working with them and keeping an eye on me?

Suddenly I didn't trust Eddie anymore. "Tell me about this next place that we're going," I said without trying to sound suspicious.

"It's just another place the guys hang out sometimes."

"The guys?"

Eddie shrugged his shoulders while he drove.

"It's been a few miles. How much farther is this place?" I studied Eddie's facial features in the light from the dash gauges while I waited for him to answer. Did he try to walk me into a trap at the beach house to get me out of the way and was he leading me into another set-up at the next bar?

"We're almost there."

Hannigan was asleep in the back seat and I fished a pair of thick white athletic socks from my gear bag on the front floorboard. After unlacing my boots, I massaged the spots where the knife and derringer were rubbing. No blisters yet, but the areas were sensitive to the touch. Fresh socks went over the old ones and I hoped the extra thickness would give me a greater level of comfort but it just made my boots tighter. I probed the bag for my bottle of ibuprofen and swallowed two capsules without water.

"This is it," Eddie said as he abruptly hit the brakes and threw me into the dash.

"Same as before," I said, looking at the bar that had seemingly come out of nowhere on the coast road. "You go in alone, I don't want to get recognized."

"I'll go, too," Hannigan said in a sleepy voice from the back seat.

"No. You stay with me." I was really beginning to regret my decision to let Hannigan come along because he was getting on my nerves.

Eddie made a right turn and eased the Jeep into the small gravel parking lot of the bar. Even though it was almost three o'clock in the morning, the lot was full of cars and there was no place to park. Eddie finally found a place along the highway, south of the bar, and pulled up behind a large flatbed truck.

"Give me fifteen minutes to check it out," Eddie said as he slipped out of the Jeep.

It was unusually warm when I got out of the Jeep and so I took off my Dodgers jacket, pulled out my shirttail out, and slid the Browning into the sweaty small of my back to keep it out of sight.

Hannigan started to climb out of the back seat.

"Stay inside," I said.

"Why?"

"We don't want to attract attention. Let's keep a low profile. Three gringos attract a lot of attention."

Stepping into the shadows along the highway, I focused my attention on the activity at the bar. Drunks laughed and swore in the parking lot. There was a lot of boasting going on, most of it in English. Were they gringos on vacation or American ex-patriots? The boom-boom bass tones of the music from inside the concrete building echoed off the cars in the parking lot and the smell of fajitas sizzling on the grill wafted in the breeze.

A car was coming up the highway from the south so I moved over behind the flatbed truck to stay in the shadows and out of the oncoming headlights. The car passed, going up the highway without stopping at the bar. The frame of the truck was tilted downward because the shoulder of the road was lower and I had a clear view of the two concrete structures on the flatbed. Somehow they looked familiar but I knew I'd never seen anything like them before. The structures were of cast concrete, about ten feet tall and had four legs. Each side looked like the letter 'H', narrower in the middle than at the top and bottom. A large loop made of two-inch diameter steel protruded from the upper end of each leg, making a total of four loops per structure. Why did these look familiar?

The sound of laughing from the parking lot attracted my attention as a group of seven men came out of the bar. Suddenly, one drunk took a swing at another and a loud scuffle broke out as the others tried to subdue the combatants. The fight ended as quickly as it began.

When I turned my attention back to the flatbed truck, I noticed that both concrete structures had the letters 'PE' spray-painted on them in several places. What did that mean? I eased my way toward the cab of the truck and looked at the door. I wiped the dirt away from the printing on the door and found that the letters 'O-T' were painted above the name Hermosillo on the door. Oaxaca Trucking. The same trucking company that was involved in the Fontana raid. Suddenly I knew why the concrete structures on the flatbed looked familiar. They were similar to the odd sketches in the notebook recovered from Astal Kamran's minivan in Fontana.

Back at the Jeep, I leaned in the window. "Hannigan. Are you awake?"

"Yeah. Why?"

"Come here."

Hannigan climbed from the Jeep and slammed the door.

"Try to be quiet," I said.

"Sorry."

"What are these things?" I asked, pointing to the concrete objects on the flatbed.

Hannigan studied the structures and tugged at the chains that secured them to the bed of the truck. Two chains were secured through the middle of the 'H' on each one and pulled tight with turnbuckles and shackles.

"I don't know," he said. "Looks like they're used in construction somehow."

"Obviously."

"If it weren't for those lifting eyes, I would say they could be used to set something on."

"You've never seen something like this before?"

"Not really, and it almost looks like they would have to be set upright, because the way they're built, the legs would break if you laid them on their side," he said "But they have the lifting eyes on top so you couldn't set anything on them."

"Unless once you put them where you wanted them, you cut the lifting eyes off."

"Maybe."

A car approached from the north, slowed, and then turned into the gravel parking lot of the bar.

"This can't be good," I said.

"What?"

"That's a police car," I said. "Let's not stand out in the open."

I pulled Hannigan under the flatbed truck with me and sat in the gravel on the shoulder of the road. The Browning dug into my back so I removed it and rolled over on my right side to watch the bar.

The marked cruiser prowled through the parking lot. The front side windows were rolled down and in the light from the moon and the bar, I could see that two uniformed officers were inside. The car stopped where the group of bar patrons had gathered and the scuffle took place. After a few moments the drunks began to disperse and the police car rolled across the gravel lot toward the highway.

"If they turn this way," I said. "We need to get out of here. They might have a description of the Jeep."

The driver cruised the parking lot; gravel crunching under the tires, both officers looking out their open windows. The car stopped when it got back to the highway. Waited. Started to move. Stopped and waited again. When it finally pulled onto the highway, it headed north in the direction it had come from.

"I didn't care for that," I said. "I wish Eddie would hurry up, I'm getting a bad feeling about this."

I crawled from beneath the flatbed truck and Hannigan followed.

"I wish I knew what these things were," I said.

"Why?"

"Just curious," I said, not wanting to explain the sketches found in the notebook.

I climbed up and looked through the passenger's side window into the cab of the truck. When I couldn't see anything, I tried the door and found it locked.

"Curiosity killed the cat," Hannigan said.

"I'm a tough old cat," I said, shining my flashlight through the window.

"See anything?"

"Nope."

Another car was approaching from the south and its headlights illuminated the area between the flatbed truck and the bar.

"Is that Eddie?" Hannigan asked.

"I don't know," I said, watching the figure walking toward us. "Get down and stay out of the light."

The car slowed down as it approached the entrance to the bar parking lot, took the turn too fast and slid on the gravel. There was laughing from inside the car. Drunks looking for another drink.

Eddie walked to the driver's side of the Jeep and started to get in. "Where are you guys at?"

"Over here," I said. "Did you find out anything?"

"Yeah," he said. "I found Fred Murphy."

"Who the hell is Fred Murphy?" I asked.

"The pilot," Eddie said. "He's Ken Jacob's pilot."

"Did he know anything?"

"Yeah. He knew a lot."

"Spit it out," I said, drawing close to Eddie. "Does he know where Rita is?"

"He said he flew a woman and Ken and a guy named Lupe over to Hermosillo to meet with The Spaniard."

"When? What else did he say?"

"He flew them over this morning, actually yesterday now I guess," Eddie said. "And then he flew a couple of Mexican businessmen from Hermosillo back here to Ensenada for The Spaniard."

"Monday morning? He flew Rita to Hermosillo on Monday morning?" I did the math in my head. We were less than twenty-four hours behind her.

"Yeah."

"Do you know where The Spaniard is in Hermosillo?" I asked. "Do you know how to find him?"

"No," Eddie said. "I've never been to Hermosillo, but I know that it's inland, just up the coast from San Carlos on the mainland side."

"I know where Hermosillo is," I said impatiently. "We need to get over there and find out where The Spaniard is."

"That's where Fred Murphy comes in."

"What do you mean?"

"It's going to cost us a thousand bucks. But Fred said he would fly us over there. Do you have any money?"

"I have some," I said   "How is Rita? Did he say how she looked?"

"He said she was sick and that she puked all over the inside of the plane."

"But she's alive?"

"She was when he last saw her."

"Good," I said. "What else did he say?"

"Not much," said Eddie. "Fred Murphy doesn't ask a lot of questions. That's why they like him."

"People are going to be waiting for us to show up at the airport," I said. "They're already watching the beach house and by now they know about the plane."

"That's what Fred said. That's why he keeps the plane up in El Tigre."

"El Tigre?"

"It's a small landing strip not far from the beach house," Eddie said. "The local Federales can't keep up with all the small landing strips down here now, so they just watch the major airports like the one in Ensenada."

"So he'll fly us over to Hermosillo for a thousand dollars?"

"He wants a thousand bucks and says he needs to fly us over pretty soon because he needs to be back in Ensenada late this afternoon to pick up the same two guys he brought over from Hermosillo yesterday."

"I'm ready right now," I said, even though I still had that lingering feeling of impending doom. Had Eddie talked to somebody in the bar to arrange another set-up?

"Let's go," Eddie said. "Fred says to meet him at El Tigre in thirty minutes and I'm not sure I can find it in the dark."

"Okay, but before we go," I said. "Do you have any idea what these concrete things are on the back of this truck?"

"Sure," he said. "They're using them to build the new breakwater for Ensenada harbor. They truck them down this highway by the thousands."

26

El Tigre turned out to be a plywood and tin slum precariously built on a small plateau across the highway to the east of the wealthy Villa Hildalgo beach resort below. Eddie had to put the Jeep into low-range four-wheel drive in order to climb the rocky trail that probably saw mostly foot and donkey traffic. The landing strip was easy enough to find because there was only one road in El Tigre. The voice in the back of my head told me to have Eddie park the Jeep before we got too close to where the aircraft was tied down. Hannigan grumbled when we left him behind to guard the vehicle while Eddie and I walked over to check out the airplane.

"This is it, all right," Eddie said, tapping n the aluminum fuselage of the high wing aircraft with his knuckles.

The tail number of the four-place Cessna was 'N32747'. Ken's 747. A large tarp covered it and the doors were locked but I searched the inside with my flashlight without finding anything unusual.

The luminescent hands on my watch said it was half past three. "He should be here soon," I said.

"Yeah."

"So, who is this Fred Murphy guy?" I asked as I motioned Eddie into the shadows of a large cottonwood tree about thirty yards from the Cessna.

"Like I told you, he flies the plane for Ken. Supposedly he's an ex-army helicopter pilot that flew two combat tours in Afghanistan."

"An ex-army helicopter pilot?" I asked, easing myself to ground where I could lean against the trunk of the tree.

Eddie sat on the ground next to me. "I don't know what happened to him in the war," he said after a moment. "But Fred is a little different."

"What do you mean by different?"

"I don't know. He drinks a lot for one thing…and I think he's kind of unstable."

"Unstable in what way?"

"I don't know. The way he acts I guess. He's pretty much socially dysfunctional if you ask me."

"And you arranged for him to fly us to Hermosillo?"

"He's a good pilot," Eddie said defensively. "Besides, we don't have a whole lot of options do we?"

I couldn't make out Eddie's face because of the shadows beneath the tree and the clouds that were thickening in front of the moon. I fingered the Browning and wondered how valuable Eddie Taylor would be as a hostage if he were in fact setting me up. I was trapped on top of a Mexican plateau in the middle of the night and if they were going to take me out, this would be a nice quiet place to do it.

"Did Fred Murphy say anything else about Rita?" I asked, still searching for a clue about what was really going to happen.

"No, just that there was a girl and she was sick," he said. "I guess Fred asked Ken who she was and Ken told him to mind his own business."

"How can we be sure it was Rita and not somebody else?"

Eddie considered the question for several silent moments. "I guess we don't know for sure."

"Shit." We might be tying to rescue Ken Jacob's girlfriend for all I knew.

"This is third-hand, but according to the two guys Fred flew to Ensenada yesterday, the Spaniard was pretty mad at Ken for bringing the girl to his house."

"What do you mean?"

"Fred heard them talking in Spanish and they were discussing the Spaniard and how he was furious about how things were turning out."

"The way what things turned out? What does that mean?"

"I don't know," Eddie said, sounding defensive again. "Look, I didn't have a whole lot of time to talk to Fred in the bar. I only had enough time to find out that he flew Ken and a girl, who I assumed was Rita, over to Hermosillo. I had to think quick, so I told Fred that I was supposed to meet with Ken, but we'd missed each other, and that it was urgent that I catch up to him as soon as possible. Then Fred said he would fly me to Hermosillo for a thousand bucks and that Ken could pay for the gas."

"I know you didn't have a lot of time," I said, hoping to put Eddie at ease. "You did good."

"Thanks."

I checked my watch again. "Where is this guy?"

"No telling," he said. "Fred promised he would meet us here in a half hour."

"Well, it's been over a half hour. Let's move the Jeep out of sight just in case we're getting into more than we've bargained for."

"Sure," Eddie said. "Stay here and I'll move it."

"Tell Hannigan to stay in the Jeep."

Eddie nodded and then disappeared into the darkness in the direction of the Jeep. After a few moments I could hear him talking to Hannigan and then the motor started. Eddie didn't turn the headlights on and I could hear the tires crunching the ground as he moved it a short distance and then cut the engine.

"Hannigan ain't too happy," Eddie said when he came back and took a position on the ground next to me.

"Why?"

"He's tired of sitting in the Jeep. He says it's too hot in there."

"He wanted to come with us and I told him upfront he'd have to follow orders. It's hard but it's fair, he had a good home but didn't stay there."

"Fred should be here by now. He said to meet him in a half-hour."

My watch told me that it had been almost an hour since we'd left the bar. "I'm going to shut my eye for a little bit," I said. "If I fall asleep, wake me up as soon as anybody comes up the road."

The stars had disappeared from the sky and the twin halos around the moon were getting more intense. The fickle breeze brought the sound of crickets to the otherwise silent night and I wondered what I was doing here. It seemed surreal, sitting on the ground under a cottonwood tree in Mexico, like I'd been plucked from my real life and deposited here by some strange alien force. The only thing that felt real to me right now was the guilt in my heart because of my role in Elisha's death. She said she didn't want to fight the leukemia but I know what she really wanted was for me to show her how much I wanted her to fight it. She hated me for what I did and her way of showing it was to refuse to live. But I saw the fear in her eyes, the hurt and confusion, and now I know what she really wanted me to do. She wanted me to fight to the death for us and I didn't do it.

***

Fred Murphy never showed up and it was the crowing of a rooster that finally brought me out of a deep slumber. Eddie Taylor was asleep on the ground, curled up on his right side like a little baby. The Jeep was parked behind another massive cottonwood with the doors open. I rolled to my knees and crawled over just to make sure Eddie was breathing and not dead. The rooster crowed again, inciting a donkey to bray. The rugged outline of the mountains to the east was backlit by the crimson dawn sky. The wind was picking up and a small dust devil whirled dirt and weeds into the air near the ridge that dropped off toward Villa Hidalgo.

The airplane was still here; wings and tail tied to the ground, covered with military style camouflage tarps, sitting in the shelter of a massive shade tree where it would be invisible to aircraft or satellites flying overhead.

"Get up." I gave Eddie a shove with my boot.

"What time is it?" Eddie sat up and blinked at the sunrise.

"Way past time for your friend to show up."

The Jeep was about sixty yards to the south and I walked over to wake Hannigan. I found him slumped in the passenger's seat and when I banged on the hood, the rooster crowed again.

"Rise and shine, princess," I said.

"What's going on?" he asked, rubbing his eyes.

"I wish I knew."

Rummaging through the gear in the back seat, I found a bottle of Gatorade and took several large gulps.

"This is not good," I said, staring at the blood red dawn that was breaking. "Not good at all."

Eddie walked over. "He said he would be here, I don't know what to tell you."

"You said he was unstable," I said. "It's almost seven o'clock, do you know where we can find him this time of day?"

"No," Eddie said. "Whenever I see Fred, he's always at the plane, a bar, or at Ken's beach house. I don't think he has his own place."

"Well, we're at the plane, the bars are closed, and there isn't any way we can go back to the beach house now. We're pretty much fucked."

"I wonder if he went back to the beach house before coming here," Eddie said. "Maybe those two guys grabbed him. Fred was pretty drunk when I saw him in the bar."

"Great," I said. "Our whole plan depends on an unstable drunk that doesn't show up."

A long row of cottonwood trees lined El Tigre's primitive road and they swayed to the restive morning wind while singing a mournful song with their branches. A peasant man with a donkey and two boys was coming down the road in our direction. We stopped talking when they got close and the old man flashed us a toothy grin from beneath a large straw sombrero before continuing toward the large green field towards the north side of the plateau.

I drank from the bottle of Gatorade and studied the terrain. Baja California, for the most part, is a rugged, mountainous, and desolate region with very little water. But the small plateau above Villa Hidalgo was lush and green. Cottonwood trees need a lot of water, and for some reason, they thrived in this area. A ridge of rugged mountains punctuated the sky a mile or so to the east. A large, jagged brush-lined ravine led up the mountain on the far side of the small plateau. As I studied the geology of the plateau closer, I saw that it was actually a large circular catch basin, three or four miles wide, located at the foot of the mountains. What little rain fell in the area washed down from the mountains and collected beneath the soil of the plateau.

Wind howled through the cottonwoods and tugged at the plane's moorings. One corner of the camouflaged cover on the plane tore loose and began flapping in the breeze.

The plywood and tin tenement was built on the edge of the plateau's west side, overlooking the ocean below. The cool ocean breezes surely provided welcome relief from the summer heat. The villagers were probably nothing more than poor dirt farmers, scraping out a modest living from the earth, maybe trading with local fishermen from below. A tall wood and steel water tower stood to the east of the village. It was too new, shiny and expensive to belong to the villagers and I concluded that it must be the water supply for Villa Hidalgo. As I sipped my Gatorade, I wondered how long the underground water in the small basin would last if it were being used to water palm trees and fill swimming pools for the wealthy tenants of Villa Hidalgo. What would happen to the village and the people in it when their water supply dried up?

The wind gusted, seeming to come from all directions at once, not knowing which direction it wanted to blow. Then I heard something. The wind blew again, drowning out the sound for a moment. Then I heard it again. It sounded like an engine, revving, running hard. Coming closer. Then the sound of an undercarriage scraping rock.

"Let's take cover," I said.

Eddie Taylor and Hannigan scrambled in the loose dirt and finally found a hiding spot behind a cottonwood tree.

As soon as it came into sight, I knew the distinctive grill of the dark blue convertible belonged to a BMW. As the car came closer, the sound of Mariachi music blared from the stereo and I could see that a blonde haired man with mirrored sunglasses and a handlebar mustache was driving the car. Four young Mexican women in various stages of undress rode in the car, laughing and giggling.

"That's Fred Murphy," Eddie said, darting from behind the cottonwood to wave down the BMW.

Fred hit the brakes, throwing everyone in the car forward, evoking another round of giggles.

"Where have you been, man?" Eddie asked.

Fred Murphy stood up in the driver's seat, wearing khaki shorts and a blue flowered Hawaiian shirt, put a bare foot on the door and hopped out of the convertible.

"I've been busy, as you can see," he said, thumbing his shoulder length hair behind his ears.

The girls giggled. A girl from the back seat threw Fred his sandals.

"We've been waiting," Eddie said.

"Are these your friends?" Fred asked.

"Yeah. This is Frank," Eddie said as he motioned toward me. "And the other guy is Tom."

Fred twisted both ends of his handle bar mustache, then took his sunglasses off and studied us. "Frank and Tom? You two don't look like no Frank and Tom."

I could see that Fred's eyes were wild, blue, and glassy. Eddie's assessment of Fred being a little strange was an understatement.

"You're a big dude," Fred said to me, involuntarily spitting on me as he spoke. "Are you a football player?"

"No."

"Football is great game. You don't know what you're missing," he said. "How much do you weigh?"

"About two-twenty," I said. "Why?"

"Because we need to get the aircraft off the ground and weight is always a factor," Fred said with a disturbed look in his eye. "On days like this, I need all the help I can get."

I shrugged my shoulders and looked at Eddie.

"Oh well, you can't live all your life," Fred said and then turned to Eddie. "You got my money?"

I took eight hundred from behind my belt buckle and Eddie and Hannigan each kicked in another hundred.

"Thanks, man," Fred said as he walked back to the car and handed the money to the girls. "You ladies go buy something pretty and I'll be back tonight."

The girls giggled. A raven haired beauty in a yellow flowered sundress climbed up front and took the driver's seat, started the motor, stalled the car twice, and then made a big U–turn in the green field before making her way back down the hill. The girls laughed and waved the money as they drove away.

"Sweet ladies," Fred said to Eddie.

Eddie nodded.

"Let's get going," Fred said, gesturing toward the aircraft. "This wind is going to be a bitch."

Fred untied the camouflage sheets from the plane, crumpled them up on the ground as best he could in the wind, and then rolled several large rocks on them so they wouldn't blow away.

"Better let me start the plane before we release the tie downs," Fred said.

"What about my Jeep?" Hannigan asked, looking in my direction.

"I don't know what to tell you," I said. "You can drive it back to San Pedro now if you want to."

Hannigan ruminated.

"Or you can come with us," I said. "We'll have to come back for it later."

Hannigan nodded. "I want to come."

"Leave the keys in the ignition," I said.

"Why?"

"A present for them," I said, pointing toward the ramshackle peasant village. "Just in case we don't come back."

Hannigan thought about it, smiled and then ran back to the Jeep. "Do we need anything out of here?"

"No," I said, feeling for the Browning in the small of my back. "I've got everything, let's go."

Eddie and Hannigan climbed into the cramped rear seat of the Cessna and Fred started the engine. It sputtered at first, idled unevenly, and then roared to life. Fred did a quick check of the instruments and then gave me the thumbs-up. I released the wing tie downs and hopped into the front right-hand seat, slamming the door as the plane began to taxi. Fred leaned forward, studying the wind direction for a moment, and them jammed the throttle forward, heading the plane up the dirt strip along the field towards the mountains. Just as the plane became airborne, a gust of wind caught it, forcing the left wing to clip the foliage in the field.

"Hot damn!" Fred said as he slammed his open right hand on the top of the dash. "If you don't believe in God, now's a damn fine time to start!"

27

Eddie Taylor was right. Fred Murphy was a good pilot, but that didn't mean his flying didn't scare the shit out of me.

Once airborne, we entered a tight circle to the left, the wind buffeting the fragile aircraft mercilessly, and as we left El Tigre's plateau, Fred pushed the yoke forward and flew the small Cessna not more than twenty feet off the ground, just above the tops of the cactus. After a few miles, we banked left and flew up through a small gorge in the rugged Sierra de Pedro Martir mountains, wheels just above the rocks as we climbed through the rocky terrain, the wingtips almost touching the sides of the narrow mountain pass that was really not much more than a ravine. A small band of Desert Mountain Sheep was startled by the sudden appearance of the plane and scrambled effortlessly up the nearly vertical sides of the mountain pass. I was close enough to see the spooky look in their yellow-green eyes. My stomach rose to my throat as we dropped down the other side of the mountain range toward the Sea of Cortez, some twenty or thirty miles away and visible on the horizon. Fourteen minutes later we flew over a broad sandy beach and the seaside village of San Felipe before turning southeastward and out to sea.

"There's some dirty weather knocking about," Fred said, trying to be heard above the drone of the engine and the howling of the wind outside.

We were literally skimming the surface of the water. White caps spread from horizon to horizon, the wind streaking the tops off the waves while pummeling the small plane even more brutally.

"It makes me nervous up there," explained Fred, pointing an index finger skyward when I asked him about the low altitude flying. "And they don't shoot at you down here. Besides, up there you have time to think about dying. Down here you live for now, a mere kiss away from eternity."

This guy is nuttier than a fruitcake I thought to myself as I checked my watch. It would be noon before we crossed the Sea of Cortez and landed in Hermosillo according to Fred. Maybe longer if the wind picked up any more. Time was running out for Rita Velasco if it she wasn't already dead. The container Eddie Taylor marked for us had probably left the Malaysia-Pacific terminal sometime during the night. I'd asked Halverson to give me twenty-four hours and I felt he would do his best, but I know things don't always go as planned. Halverson would have to do what he had to do. There was no way I could count on Mike Dillon's help because he was trying to take me out. Besides, Rita had been at the beach house and those two guys didn't lift a finger to save her. I realized now that the Latino lied to me because he knew I was after the girl and he wouldn't have a chance of making a deal if I thought he had some information about her.

Once out over the Sea of Cortez and steadied on the southeasterly course, Fred began nodding off, jerking awake to correct the plane in the gusty wind. I nudged him a few times to ask him if he was all right. Fred just smiled behind his mirrored sunglasses, played with his mustache and said, "You look nervous, brother," and then he took a small plastic bag from his shirt pocket and swallowed a couple of small white pills.

"Vitamins," he said.

About ten minutes after Fred took the pills, he got talkative. Very talkative. Of course, I could hear very little of what he was saying because of the noise from the engine and the wind outside. From what I could make out, most of Fred's ramblings dealt with Afghanistan and combat flying. I nodded and smiled a lot and wondered if death would be quick or I'd have to swim for it when he plowed the small Cessna into the sea.

***

It was just past eleven-thirty when Fred nudged me and pointed out the windshield at the brown smudge on the horizon. "Isla de Tiburon," he yelled as he banked a little to the left. "The wind is picking up."

Eddie and Hannigan were wide-awake and bug-eyed in the cramped back seat.

"The hurricane is that way," hollered Fred as he pointed out the side window behind me.

"How do you know?"

"Buys Ballot's Law."

"What?"

"Buys Ballot's Law," he said. "In the northern hemisphere, face into the wind and the center of the low pressure is to your right, slightly behind you. You can tell which way the wind is blowing by looking at the white caps. See the way the wind is knocking the tops of the waves off? That means the eye is getting closer."

"How close?"

"Too close, but we'll be on the ground soon," he said, grinning wildly.

I reached into the back seat a poke Eddie in the knee.

"What?" Eddie asked.

I pointed to my watch and the island that was growing larger.

Fred looked over his shoulder at Eddie. "Do you want me to land at The Spaniard's place?"

Eddie deferred to me.

"We're going to need a car," I said, leaning closer to Fred so he could hear me clearly. "Let's land at the airport in Hermosillo and we'll drive the rest of the way." Obviously, we'd be taking a chance by landing at the airport, but I hoped Dillon's boys wouldn't be expecting us on this side of the Sea of Cortez.

Fred flashed me a toothy grin and I wondered why. Our landing at The Spaniard's place would be sure death for everyone involved, and I firmly believed that discretion is the better part of valor.

"But maybe you should fly by The Spaniard's place so we can see who's there," I said into Fred's ear. I wanted to get a good look at the layout of the place from the air so I'd know what I was getting into.

"The Spaniard don't like people flying over his place," Fred said. "He shoots at any plane that gets near him and I got this thing about getting shot at.

"Of course," I said. "Just fly by without getting too close, we're in enough trouble with Ken as it is."

Fred acknowledged me with a crooked smile and then twisted his moustache.

We were still low to the ground as we made landfall on the Mexican mainland near a sleepy fishing village north of Punta Esteban. Fishermen mending their nets on the beach gawked and waved as we flew by. Within yards, the sandy Sea of Cortez beach changed into the sparse, prickly vegetation of the Sonora Desert.

Fred eased the yoke back and added more throttle, forcing the plane to climb, and after donning his headset, he toyed with the radio. "They're funny about some things around here," he explained. "Traffic control and all that."

There was a better view of the surrounding area as we gained altitude. Fred leveled the Cessna off a couple of thousand feet above the ground, checked the compass and then banked left. "A lot of crosswind, a helluva lot of crosswind."

The wind seemed to buffet the plane even more at higher altitudes and my stomach was doing flip-flops.

Fred leaned back and poked Eddie. "That's The Spaniard's place over there," he said, pointing out his window to the north.

Eddie made a large circle in the air with his finger.

Fred nodded and banked the plane to the left, starting a large circle around The Spaniard's place.

The Spaniard's place was near the base of a small mountain, along a dry creek bed. A tall white wall surrounded the main house and two other smaller structures that were also constructed of white stucco and red Mexican tile. A swimming pool and green lawns were inside the compound, and outside of the wall, there was a small golf course and a dirt landing strip. No people or cars were in sight and there weren't any aircraft at the landing strip. After making a wide circle around the estate, we banked to the right and followed Highway 15 toward the sprawling city of Hermosillo that was still some distance away.

"That's the manufacturing plant," Fred said as he pointed out the window. "The Spaniard owns that, too."

The facility looked to be about a square mile in size and set off from the surrounding desert by chain link fencing. Several large greenish ponds were in the southeast corner of the property and a huge metal building was in the center. Hundreds of the same concrete 'H' shaped structures I'd seen on the flatbed truck outside the bar were stacked in neat rows outside the building. A mobile crane was in the process loading one of the concrete structures onto a flatbed truck and numerous trucks of all sizes and shapes were going in all directions in the facility, stirring up dust. It looked like The Spaniard was doing a bang-up business.

I was never so glad to get on the ground in all my life. The wind made landing especially precarious. Just as the plane was about to touch down, a gust lifted it skyward, almost stalling us midair, but Fred dealt with the near-disaster routinely.

"I'm getting a beer," Fred said as he taxied past two Aero Mexico jets at the terminal and cut the engine. Terminal attendants rushed from the building and quickly tied the plane's wings down. "How about you?" Fred asked as he looked at me.

"Sure," I said. "I'll buy."

Eddie took Hannigan with him to rent a car.

Fred stayed outside to watch the Cessna being re-fueled and I went inside the terminal to order two beers from the grungy airport bar. The plastic glasses of beer were warm and flat and we found a convenient seat on the edge of a square concrete planter that was home to a ten-foot palm tree.

"I gotta get back before this weather gets bad," Fred said, beer foam clinging to his mustache.

I sipped my beer and tried to see his eyes behind the mirrored sunglasses.

"I don't think I'll be flying back here again tonight like I was supposed to," he said and then a grin broke across his face. "I sure hope those girl's bought something pretty."

My beer was pitiful and not worth the fours bucks gringo I paid for each of them.

"Ken's a good guy," Fred said. "He gave me that BMW."

"Oh yeah?"

"Yeah, that's the second one, too," he said. "Those girls are rough on cars. I love Beemers."

"Ken just gave you the BMW?"

"Yep. He asked what kind of car I wanted and a few days later he brings this ice blue ragtop with white leather interior. I love ragtops. He says it's all mine cause I'm so loyal to him." Fred sipped his beer and watched the Cessna being re-fueled. "Of course the girls wrecked that one, so Ken had to get me another one."

"That is nice."

"I don't ask questions," he said, looking at me from behind his sunglasses. "You're military."

Not knowing what to say, I said nothing.

"You're an officer," he said. "I was a warrant officer, but you're commissioned. I can tell."

I was busted so I just smiled acknowledgement.

Fred grinned a strange toothy grin and played with his mustache. "You ever hear the voice?" Fred took his sunglasses off and looked at me.

Our eyes met and his were wild and bloodshot.

"You know that voice," he said. "The voice that tells you to go to sick call instead of flying and you do, and then that's the very same day that your mission gets shot up." Fred's blue eyes were piercing now. "I listen to the voice, man, and it's usually right."

"What's the voice telling you now?"

Fred looked away. "You ain't no friend of Ken's."

I flicked a swimming fly out of my beer and took a sip.

"Looks like they're about done with my plane," he said, taking two more pills from the plastic baggie in his shirt pocket and washing them down with the last of his beer.

Fred stood up and faced me, put on his sunglasses, and tried in vain to slick his long blonde hair back with both hands in the wind.

"Judge not, lest ye be judged," he said. "I gotta go." Fred walked back to the plane, climbed in and started the engine. As he taxied away, he gave me the thumbs up.

Eddie was arguing with a young dark haired man at the rental counter when I walked up. The man renting cars had coal black eyes and popped his chewing gum as I leaned on the counter.

"Problem?" I asked.

"No problemo," said the young man.

"Yeah, there's a problem," Eddie said. "I speak the language, I'm not a gringo, I live here and I know that you're cheating me. You think I'm some stupid gringo tourist."

"Did you get us a car?" I asked.

"Yeah, but…"

"Then let's get out of here," I said. "Just forget it, Eddie."

"Yeah, but…"

"Forget it, Eddie. Focus. Focus on what we're doing and forget about whether he thinks you're a gringo or not." Eddie was still steaming mad and I grabbed his arm. "Get the keys and let's get the fuck out of here, we've got a lot to do and time is running out."

Eddie signed the papers and the young man slid the keys across the desk. "A-10," he said, pointing toward the parking lot.

"What's the plan?" Eddie asked once we were outside.

"I don't think they'd keep her at that concrete factory," I said. "If she's still here and still alive, she's probably at the house."

Eddie nodded.

Hannigan played with his cell phone as we walked through the parking lot looking for our car. "We don't have cell phone reception down here," he said. "That sucks."

The bright red rental car in A-10 was a well-worn Ford Escort.

"Great," I said. "We'll stand out like a sore thumb."

"So, are you just going to walk up and knock on the door and say where's Rita?" Hannigan asked.

"No, I want to climb that hill behind the house and watch it for awhile," I said. "Do you think you can find your way back to the house?" I asked Eddie

"I think so," he said. "I got some landmarks while we were flying by in the plane."

Eddie fought the erratic Hermosillo traffic and cursed while I navigated from the rental company map. The air conditioning in the rental car didn't work and there was no comfortable place to hide the Browning on my person so I slid it under the front seat. Hannigan sat in the back seat and said nothing while he tried to get reception on his cell phone.

Forty-five minutes after renting the car, we finally pulled off Highway 15 and onto a gravel road. Pebbles flew up and hit the undercarriage as we sped down the winding and uneven rural road.

"I think we're getting close," Eddie said about five minutes after leaving the main highway.

I scrutinized the cactus-ridden landscape. "I think you're right. That looks like the hill behind the compound."

Thunderheads towered skyward to the south and west, their sinister white anvils scrawled from horizon to horizon across the troubled sky. The wind blew dust and tumbleweeds in all directions at once. My own sweat had me stuck to the passenger's seat of the car.

"I think the house is coming up on the right," Eddie said.

"Drive past it and we'll get out on the other side of that hill," I told him.

Eddie slowed the car as he approached the driveway to The Spaniard's house but the buildings were barely visible above the desert terrain. We slowed to a crawl near the well-maintained driveway.

"Keep going," I said, still studying the hill behind the house. The gravel road didn't curve around the hill as much as I thought it would. I was hoping that we could keep the hill between us and the Spaniard's estate, but the road looked different from the ground than it did from the aircraft when we did our flyby.

"Might as well stop here," I said. "We're going to have to hike anyway."

Eddie pulled over and I climbed out of the car, pulling my sweat soaked clothes away from my body.

"What are we going to do with the car?" Eddie asked.

"I'll tell you what let's do," I said, retrieving the Browning from under the front seat.. "Let's split up for awhile. I'll take Captain Hannigan with me and we'll climb that hill and try to get a good look at the house."

"What about me?" Eddie asked.

"You take the car and go back up the road toward the highway," I said. "Find a place to get off the road where you can watch things from that end. You know what Ken looks like and if he comes or goes from the house, we'll know Rita is somewhere close."

"Okay," Eddie said. "But how do we communicate? We got no cell phone service."

"That's going to be a problem," I said. "I guess if Ken comes to the house, come up the hill and find us, but of course, maybe we'll have seen it."

"And what do I do if I see him leave? Do I follow him?"

"Good question," I said. "I wish I had a good answer for you."

"If I see him with Rita, I'm going after him."

"Maybe you could follow him to find out where he takes her and then come back for us so we can help you. You don't want to try taking him one on one." What I wasn't telling Eddie was that if Rita left the compound, she would be wrapped in plastic and riding in the trunk of a car on her way to be planted at the foot of a cactus plant in the middle of the Sonoran Desert. "It's ten past two now, give us some time to get behind the house and watch it. If nothing happens by five o'clock, come up the hill and find us."

"Five o'clock," repeated Eddie. He slammed the Escort's door, made a quick u-turn, and then kicked gravel in all directions as he sped back down the road.

I started out across the desolate Sonora, Hannigan stumbling along behind. It was brutally hot and humid and in less than a hundred yards I was beginning to think I'd made a big mistake.

"I'm thirsty," Hannigan said.

"I hear you. I kind of wish we'd grabbed a couple of those Gatorades from your Jeep before we left."

"Oww!"

"Be careful where you step," I said, turning to watch Hannigan pull cactus spines from his left ankle. "Everything out here either bites you or sticks you."

"So I found out."

We cautiously climbed the hill behind The Spaniard's house, trying to use the terrain and vegetation to stay out of sight. The hill was steeper than it looked and the footing was terrible because of the loose rocks. A covey of Gamble's quail exploded from a cat claw thicket to our left and I instinctively drew down on them with the Browning.

Hannigan puffed and tried to catch his breath.

"Let's take a break over there," I said, pointing to an area overgrown with fibrous broad-leafed agave plants. "Watch for snakes."

"Snakes?"

"Yeah. Rattlesnakes."

"I hate snakes."

"Who doesn't?" I carefully picked my way through the agave patch, keeping a close eye on the house. When I found a clear spot on the ground, I sat down and motioned for Hannigan to sit next to me.

Hannigan toyed with an agave leaf that was wide and thick at the base and tapered upward into a needle-like point. "These things are wicked," he said. "If you ever fell on one, it would kill you."

"I'll keep that in mind."

Hannigan picked up a small stone and absently threw it at an agave plant. "I have the feeling that this rescue is not very well organized."

"Yeah, well that's how it happens sometimes. I'm doing the best I can. Nobody else is trying, that's for damn sure."

I tried to determine the layout of the compound below but we weren't in a very good position yet. After studying the terrain, I decided to move from spot to spot until we had the best view and cover possible. Before moving from where we sat, I picked my next stopping point, a large boulder with several barrel type cactus around it.

The heat and humidity were brutal. Dust blew from the top of the hill and the wind whistled through the agave plants, making it impossible to hear anything else.

"I'm thirsty," Hannigan said again.

"There's a lot of barrel cactus here," I said. "They're supposed to have water in them."

"Is it good?"

"How am I supposed to know?"

We stayed low to the ground as we crept to the spot near the boulder and the barrel cactus. The view of the house wasn't much better than we had before.

"Are these the barrel cactus?" asked Hannigan.

"Yeah."

"Let's open one up."

"Let's wait until we get to a better spot and can sit for awhile." I wanted to get higher on the hill and work my way closer around to the back of the house. I surveyed the hill above and to my left and saw there was a large cat claw thicket about seventy-five yards away that would provide good cover.

"Look, a bird's nest." Hannigan stood up and toyed with the small stick and mud nest built on top of a barrel cactus. He probed the nest with his fingers and withdrew a feather.

"Sit down, we don't want to be seen," I said. "It's probably just a Cactus Wren nest."

"Cactus Wren?" Hannigan said, twirling the feather between his fingers. "This is good luck then."

Hannigan sat next to me, eyeing the feather fondly.

"I've been meaning to ask you something," I said. "What is it with you and feathers?"

"What do you mean?"

"That bookmark you showed us when we questioned you after the *Beleza* incident. You had a business card and a feather encased in plastic."

"Yeah."

"So what does the feather mean?"

"There are a number of meanings, but usually it is considered a good luck charm," he said. "It's kind of like a rabbit's foot."

"I've never heard of it before."

"It's an old sailor's superstition. The feather of a wren is supposed to save a sailor from death by shipwreck and drowning."

"A superstition?"

"It's an old legend that started in the Isle of Man centuries ago," he said. "Supposedly there was a mermaid who lured seamen to their death by singing to them in a voice so sweet that they had no choice but to follow her and then their ships would wreck on the rocks and they would drown. Finally, a knight-errant, in a desire to save the seamen, discovered a means of counteracting her siren charms but she escaped capture by turning into a wren. The mermaid supposedly appears as a wren on New Year's Day every year, and if a seamen can get a wren's feather, he is safe from drowning for another year."

"You're kidding? That's why you carry a feather encased in plastic?"

"You don't believe in superstition?"

"Kind of ironic, that's all."

"How's that?"

"You found a good luck charm that keeps you from drowning."

"So what?"

"Take a look around," I said. "You're in the middle of the desert."

"Yeah, well take a look at that sky," he said, pointing to the sinister weather system that was rapidly approaching. "Before too long there's going to be enough rain to drown a fish."

28

The twenty-four hours I'd asked Lieutenant Halverson to give me were about up and there was still no sign of activity in the house. My gut told me I had to make a move soon or it would be too late.

"I'm hungry," Hannigan said.

"Me too." I wiped the folding knife on my pants leg and put it back in my boot. "How's your cactus?"

"It tastes terrible and there's not any water in it, just sticky slime. It tastes like hot snot." Hannigan nibbled at the piece of barrel cactus I'd cut for him. "And there's a lot of small stickers that get in your fingers," he said, throwing the pulp on the ground in disgust. "I wonder where Eddie is?"

"No telling." If Eddie had followed my instructions, he would still be parked down the road because we hadn't seen anybody come or go from the residence. I decided I was finished sitting in the heat and watching The Spaniard's place. "There's nothing going on down there, let's go check it out. If Rita's not here, we need to figure out where she is."

"What's the plan?" Hannigan asked, scrambling to his feet.

"Look at the sky over there," I said, pointing to the south, toward Hermosillo.

"I've been watching it. It'll be on top of us before long and it's going to rain like a bad dog."

Hermosillo had disappeared into a sweeping malevolent black squall punctuated by airy blue and white electrical discharges. The wind on the hill behind The Spaniard's house had inexplicably stopped blowing and the sweet humid smell of rain was heavy in the air. A bolt of lightning, leading the approaching weather, split into multiple arcs that struck the desert floor a dozen miles to the south and soon the thunder rumbled by us like a thousand freight trains.

"What's the plan?" Hannigan asked again, this time with more urgency.

I looked Hannigan in the eye. "There is no plan, haven't you figured that out yet? We go down the hill, hop the wall, look in the windows, and maybe break in so we can look around."

"Break in? I thought you'd have a plan."

"It's hard to make a plan when you don't know what you're getting into," I said. "If you have any bright ideas, now's the time to share them." I started down the hill, sliding on the loose rocks, trying to avoid the cactus. "Stay here if you want."

Hannigan followed. "I thought there would be a plan."

"You wanted to come," I said over my shoulder. "So quit moaning."

We moved deliberately, trying to be quiet and stay behind cover when we had it, constantly watching the house for activity as we descended the hill.

"This wall is taller than it looked from up there," Hannigan said when we finally reached the cinder block and stucco barrier. "How are we going to get over it?"

I looked around for a large boulder to roll against the wall, or maybe a log or board to prop against it to get a foot up. Nothing was in sight.

"I can give you a boost and then you can pull me up," he said.

"That might work."

Hannigan got on all fours and I gingerly put a boot between his shoulder blades, stood up, and grabbed the top of the wall.

"How much do you weigh?" he grunted.

"Quit belly-aching." After pulling myself onto the wall, I straddled it. "Give me your hand."

Hannigan reached up with his right hand, put a foot against the wall, and I pulled him up. He struggled at the top of the foot-wide bulwark, trying to get his balance, and then rolled over it, landing in a heap on the brick patio. I dropped to the ground with a little more grace.

There were four windows and two doors along the backside of the house. In keeping with the barren desert theme, there was no landscaping, only the brick patio that stretched from the wall to the house, a distance of about twenty feet.

Hannigan was still on the ground rubbing his right knee and I was reaching down to help him when I first saw the dogs. Dobermans. One dog ahead of the other, coming around the corner of the house at a dead run. Why hadn't I thought about dogs? I lunged for the nearest door, tried the knob, and it opened.

Hannigan yelped.

I turned and kicked the dog in the ribs hard as I could and when it released its grip on Hannigan, the second Doberman attacked. My kick caught the dog in the chest just as it lunged for Hannigan, sending it reeling backwards. Both dogs sat on their haunches, a little stunned, glowering, contemplating another attack. I've seen a fair share of guard dogs in my day, but this pair didn't seem all that committed to their job.

I grabbed Hannigan by the shirt and started through the door. "Let's go." I didn't even have time to blink before the rifle butt caught me in the face.

***

Throbbing pain in my head. The taste of blood in my mouth. Hands that wouldn't move. My eyes wouldn't open either. Not that I wanted them to. I tried desperately to crawl back into the pleasant state of unconsciousness but the discomfort was too great.

"…thy will be done on earth, as it is in heaven…"

I was on my left side and when I tried to change positions to ease the pain in my ribs, my feet wouldn't move. The concrete floor was hard and pleasantly cold and I imagined myself melting into it.

"…forgive my trespasses, as I forgive those that have trespassed against me…"

"I think he's alive."

"Commander. Commander."

A foot nudged me as I tried to descend into the darkness again.

"He is alive."

"Are you all right?" asked a female voice.

My stupor was ebbing and there was more pain to go with the sticky taste of blood in my throat. "Do I look like I'm all right?"

"Thank you, Lord," said the female voice.

I forced an eyelid open. "Rita?"

"Yes."

"You're alive?"

"Yes."

"How about Hannigan?"

"I'm here too."

I tried to move but couldn't. "Where's Eddie?"

"He's not here, " Hannigan said. "I'm bleeding, those damn dogs. I hate Dobermans."

I tried to move again but couldn't.

"Your hands and feet are bound with plastic ties," Rita said. "Who's Eddie?"

When I forced my other eye open I saw that the only light in the room was coming from beneath the door. "Where are we?"

"In some sort of storeroom," Rita said. "And Captain Hannigan says we're at some guy's house that you called the Spaniard."

"Oh, yeah," I said. "Now I remember."

"It's not looking good," Hannigan said.

"Ya think?" I tried to spit the blood out my mouth but it had coagulated.

"My hands are numb," Rita said. "I've been tied up for a long time."

"We were trying to get to get the knife out of your boot," Hannigan said.

"They'll be coming back to give me another shot," Rita said. "They've been keeping me drugged."

I was drifting back to sleep but a foot nudged me again.

"We need your knife," Hannigan said.

"What happened?" I asked.

"They were waiting for us," Hannigan said. "They beat the crap out of you...kicked you about twenty times while you were down. One of those fucking dogs bit me again."

"I'm sorry," Rita said. "It's my fault you're here."

"Not really," I said. "You were kidnapped. How did they get you?"

"It happened when I was coming out of the grocery store. I had two bags of groceries in my hands...I should have known...the van was parked next to my car and the parking lot was all but empty. They hit me with a stun gun before I even had a chance...they've kept me drugged ever since. Why me?"

I couldn't have been out that long because Hannigan hadn't told Rita about Eddie.

"You were taken hostage so Eddie would help these guys get a container out of the Malaysia-Pacific Terminal," I said.

"Are you talking about Eddie Taylor?" she asked.

"Yeah, they must have spotted you the night he showed us around the terminal and they probably figured you were his girlfriend."

"Eddie is involved with smuggling containers?"

"It's a long story," I said. "But Eddie helped us find you."

"Kind of funny that he's not here with us now," Hannigan said. "That worked out good for him."

"What do you mean?" Rita asked.

"He dropped us off and was supposed to watch the road to the house, but they were waiting for us when we jumped the wall and let the damn dogs loose," Hannigan said.

Moving what body parts I could, I assessed how much damage I'd sustained. My ribs felt like a truck hit me, and although I had a screaming headache, my tongue told me I still had all my teeth. Headache or not, it didn't take a rocket scientist to figure out we'd all be dead in short order. Hell, Hannigan and I would probably have to dig the graves and then they'd make us watch Rita die before we knelt next to our holes in ground to take a piece of lead to the brainpan.

"I know you have a knife in your boot," Hannigan said. "If I can get it, I can cut these plastic ties and we can jump them if they come back."

I didn't bother telling Hannigan it wasn't a matter of 'if', it was a matter of 'when'.

"How many are there?" I asked.

"I saw four and Rita says when they give her the shots to make her sleep there are two of them."

"Armed?"

"Oh yeah," Hannigan said.

"Mexican?"

"Of course."

"Big?"

"Not really. I'm pissed off, we can take them," he said. "If we can get your knife, I can cut us free."

"Okay."

"Which boot?"

"Left."

Hannigan was trying to back up to my feet when we heard a key in the lock. Light shattered the darkness as the door swung open and when the overhead light was flicked on I closed my eyes against the brilliance. Boots heels clicked across the concrete and then I got kicked in the legs.

"Arriba," said the voice and I got kicked again.

There was another set of boots coming across the floor and I heard that voice say something I didn't understand but I didn't miss the metallic click of a folding knife being opened. I felt the tugging on the plastic tie binding my feet and then my legs were free. I opened my eyes just a crack against the glare, hoping to see someone I could kick back but I took a boot to the ribs first.

"Arriba."

I rolled left onto my stomach and I felt someone grab my arms and drag me to my knees. I paused for a moment and then was being lifted to my feet, hands still bound behind my back with a zip-tie that was now cutting into my flesh, my fingers already tingly numb.

"Vamanos," said the voice and I was being poked in the ribs with what I assumed was a rifle.

I forced my eyes open enough to see a dark man dressed in khakis holding an AK-47 semi-automatic rifle. He looked about thirty years old, shy of six feet tall with a slender build, bandido moustache, and dark cruel eyes that told me he didn't have a sense of humor. I was poked from behind again and I stepped into the hallway, my steps sluggish and weak, and I followed the Bandido down the marbled corridor. I opened my eyes wider as I was escorted past a kitchen area and several closed doors. We turned sharp right at a large open room with lavish Spanish style décor and entered another marble-floored hallway, finally pausing at a massive mahogany door while one of my guards knocked.

After a moment, I heard a voice on the other side of the door and was promptly escorted into the room. The first thing I noticed was the wall of windows overlooking the pool area and the sinister sky outside that spread across the horizon like it had been painted by Satan himself. A man, wearing an expensive silk Hawaiian shirt that was embroidered with red and white flowers, was standing with his back to me, holding a tall icy drink, looking out the windows in the direction of the approaching storm. To my left was a chrome and mirrored wet bar against the wall, and nearer the windows, was a large teak desk with manila file folders stacked several feet high. A shredder sat on the near corner of the desk and the wastebasket was overflowing with ribbons of paper. To my right was a large conference table with a dozen chairs and next to it was a large multi-colored and three-dimensional model of what looked like a construction project. The model was about ten feet square and sat on two oak tables that had been shoved together.

The man at the window squeezed a slice of lime into his drink and then with an airy gesture waved my guards out of the room. I waited for him to speak but he stood, looking out the window. After a moment I moved closer to the desk but he only glanced over his shoulder at me without letting me see his face. One of the file folders near the shredder was open and saw the letterhead for MARPONA, Inc.

"You must be the Spaniard," I said to break the silence.

"No," he said and then took another sip of his drink. "But we are associates."

The voice was familiar but I couldn't place it.

"Looks like rain," I said.

Larry Jackson turned around to face me. "What are you doing here, Commander Stanton?"

I was trying to comprehend Larry Jackson's presence and didn't know what to say but, "Business," involuntarily came out of my mouth.

Larry Jackson winced. "Business?"

"Sure. I guess I'm ruining you little party," I said, nodding toward the pile of shredded documents in the thrash can.

"You know nothing."

"You're probably right. I never expected to see you here. You got me with that one".

An arrogant smirk crossed his faced before he asked me again, "So what are you doing here? This is way outside your jurisdiction, Commander."

"The woman you're holding is Rita Velasco."

"So?"

"She's with the Coast Guard. She works for me and some of your goons kidnapped her so I followed her trail here. I just want her back and then I'll be on my way."

"That won't be happening."

"Like you said, I'm outside my jurisdiction, hell we're in Mexico, let us go and we can pretend this never happened."

Larry Jackson shook his head. "It's more complicated than that."

"Can I ask you something?" I said. "Why kidnap Rita? I don't get it."

"You know nothing," he said with a snarl.

"No shit, Larry." A surge of adrenalin hit my system for some reason and suddenly my pain faded and my thinking became more astute. I love adrenalin sometimes. "I hope you don't mind me calling you Larry, but if I knew what the fuck was going on I wouldn't be standing here all beat to shit and tied up. It's kind of obvious that I know nothing."

Larry Jackson walked back to the window.

"Why grab Rita? If you hadn't taken her I'd still be sitting on my ass in San Pedro waiting for you to come by and give me a ration of shit about some ship being delayed."

His back was still to me so I eased over to look at the large model.

"Come on Larry, you killed the customs agent and the security guard, and I'm figuring we're not walking out of here alive, so why don't you tell me what's going on."

"It wasn't me."

"What do you mean it wasn't you? Was it the Spaniard?"

"No. It was those stupid clowns that work for us."

"Ken Jacobs?"

"Call him what you want, but, yes, it was him."

"Why Rita?"

"Because he's stupid, that's why. This…" Larry Jackson said, gesturing to the files and shredder on the desk, "Is because he's stupid."

"He's been smuggling containers out of the terminals in San Pedro, I know that much."

Larry Jackson sighed. "We caught him. Containers were missing from the terminals and nobody was helping, not Customs, not SPPD, not the FBI, so we hired a private security firm and within a week we caught him and infiltrated their operation."

"You busted the smuggling ring? Why didn't you turn them in?"

"You know nothing."

"Come on, Larry, we've already established I know nothing and that I'm going to end up in a shallow grave in the desert. Give me a break and satisfy my curiosity before I die. I didn't want to end up here any more than you wanted me here."

He considered my comment for a moment and then set his drink on the table with the model. "This is our little project," he said, pointing to the construction model while trying to contain his cockiness.

"Do you mean Marpona?"

"How do you know that?"

"I know a few things." I scanned the room for something sharp I could back up against in order to cut my hands free.

"What do you know about Marpona?"

"I've heard the name, it's a construction company." I was winging it on adrenaline, the obvious, and pure bullshit. I'd never heard of Marpona until I saw the letterhead a minute ago.

Larry Jackson eyeballed me suspiciously.

"Exactly what am I looking at?" I asked, moving closer to the model.

"The new Ensenada container terminal," he said flatly.

There was a stack of manila envelopes and a letter opener on the conference table so I moved around the model of the harbor where I was between Larry Jackson and the weapon.

"Quite a project," I said feigning interest in the mock-up.

"We'll be handling five million containers within a year, and in ten years, sixty percent of the Pacific Rim trade will flow through the port of Ensenada."

I forgot about the letter opener. Now the attack on the *Beleza* made sense. "That's a lot of cargo. I'm assuming Marpona will be the main contractor?"

"Naturally."

"And you and The Spaniard are Marpona."

Larry Jackson nodded.

"The Spaniard must be the brains. What do you do?" I was trying to piss him off and it worked. Larry Jackson clenched his jaw but didn't speak. "Come on Larry, this is a big project, I know you didn't think it up. I'll be dead before long, humor me. Who is this Spaniard guy? Some big-shot real estate developer from Spain? You're a nickel and dime maritime lawyer. How did you hook up with the Spaniard?"

"You're right about one thing, Commander," he said, looking at his watch. "You'll be dead soon and none of this will be of concern to you."

"Then humor me. What do you have to lose? Are you the brains and the Spaniard your pawn?"

"The Spaniard isn't Spanish, he's Russian, the former KGB Bureau Chief in Madrid, hence the nickname."

"So he's the money and you're the brains?"

"Something like that."

"If you're the brains, why are you working with a two-bit loser like Ken Jacobs?"

"Convenience. Like I said, we caught him in the act, and since it was going to be his third strike, he was facing a life sentence as somebody's girlfriend in a California correctional facility. We made a deal."

"There's always dirty work to be done."

"Of course."

"It didn't hurt that he also had a little hot car operation going, did it?"

"It turns out these Mexican officials are partial to luxury cars, and he just so happened to have some inventory he needed to move."

"NAFTA, GATT, and Oaxaca Trucking. Free trade is a wonderful thing."

Larry Jackson smiled.

I studied the model of the new Ensenada harbor and mentally compared it to San Pedro. The area inside the proposed breakwater was huge and the concrete structures I'd seen on the back of the flatbed were being used to build it. The container terminals would put San Pedro out of business and the savings in labor would be huge. Cargo could be transported to the East/West rail system in California just north of the border by truck or existing Mexican railroads.

"How did you get the land?"

"A bribe here, a bribe there, and the government was only too glad to see us bulldoze the slums. After all, we are bringing thousands of jobs to their port. Their cut of revenues will be substantial."

"Five hundred billon dollars worth of international commerce and it all flows through Marpona."

"That's the plan."

"Too bad it's all ruined now."

"Not quite, Commander."

"Then why the shredded documents?"

"There are a few things we don't want wandering eyes to see, but our influence here is too great. For instance, within the hour, the Federales will be here. I know because I arranged the time. I'll be gone, of course, and so will you and your friends. The Federales will find little, it's mostly a show for the American diplomats poking their noses into affairs south of the border that don't concern them. In a week, this unfortunate incident will be forgotten and it will be business as usual. After all, this is Mexico, Commander Stanton, and there is little you understand about business in Mexico."

There was a knock on the door before it opened. The same two guards came in and walked over to me.

"You know what must be done," Larry Jackson said to the Bandido.

The Bandido nodded.

"I'm sorry, Commander Stanton," he said, the look in his eyes indifferent. "But you really should have stayed in San Pedro."

29

The Bandido kicked my legs out from under me and I dropped to the concrete floor like a sack of potatoes. "Asshole," I said after he turned out the lights and locked the door.

"Where did they take you?" Hannigan asked.

"No place good," I said. "We don't have very much time left. Can you get the knife out of my boot?"

"I'll try."

I rolled toward Hannigan's voice and we fumbled for position in the dark. He'd seen where I put the knife after cutting up the cactus but was having a hard time with the laces because his hands were bound.

"You must be a big disappointment to your girlfriend," I said when I thought he was taking too long.

"Do you want me to use my teeth?"

Rita laughed from somewhere in the dark.

"Quit screwing around and get the knife. When they come back we're dead."

Holding my legs out sent razor sharp pain through my ribcage and it seemed like Hannigan was taking forever to get the knife.

It started slowly at first and I didn't know what it was. It was almost a sizzling sound that quickly changed into a loud hiss and finally a drone. Rain. A lot of rain. The wind wailed a mournful song as it tore at the building. A door slammed and someone was yelling and then I could feel the wind blowing damp cool air under the storeroom door.

"Hurry," I said to Hannigan.

"I am."

One of the back doors must have been open because I could hear rain hitting the patio and when the thunder cracked it was like it was on top of us.

"I got the knife." Hannigan said. "I'll free your hands and then you get mine."

"Wait," I said as I rolled onto my back and sat up. "Let's go back to back and you hand me the knife. If you try to free me you'll probably slash my wrists."

It seemed like an eternity while Hannigan and I positioned ourselves for the knife exchange but he finally slipped me the knife. I cupped the knife between my hands and flicked open the blade with the fingers on my left hand. I had to set the knife on the floor before turning it in the upward position between my wrists.

"I can't do it," I said. "I don't have enough leverage to cut the plastic. See if you can grab the blade and pull it toward you."

"Shit."

"What?"

"I cut myself," Hannigan said.

"Pull the end of the blade toward you."

"I am."

I felt my wrists pop free and the knife clattered to the floor. "Got it."

There was more yelling in the hallway outside the storeroom, the sound of a door being slammed shut, and then the rain's fury sounded muted. The breeze beneath the door stopped. I massaged my wrists long enough to get the blood flowing and then began unlacing my other boot to get the derringer.

"Are you going to cut me loose?" Hannigan asked.

"I'm getting to it." I said, working furiously with the bootlaces, but my fingers had a mind of their own. My first thought was to get the derringer before cutting Hannigan free and finally helping Rita. If they came back for us I would have a weapon although it occurred to me that the .22 magnum derringer with only two shots was no match for the weapons we were up against. A .22 magnum slug between the eyes is effective, but the same bullet a foot or so to the side of somebody's head would only aggravate them and derringers are reputed to be accurate for about as far as you can throw them.

"Is Eddie really involved in stealing containers?" Rita asked.

"Let's talk about that later," I said, still fumbling with the laces. "Are you all right, Rita? Because when they come back, I'm betting they're coming to kill us."

"I think you're right," she said. "I'll be a little stiff and could really use a drink of water, but I'll be ready. Dying is not on my list of things to do today."

"How are you doing, Captain Hannigan?" I asked. "Can you fight?"

"That dog bit me up pretty good," he said. "And I'm still bleeding, but I'm not ready to die either."

"Good." I said, slipping the derringer from my boot. I quickly laced both boots so I wouldn't trip on the strings. On my knees, I advanced to Hannigan, cut the ties that bound his feet and then those on his wrists. My eyes had adjusted to the small amount of light shining beneath the door and I found Rita. Her constraints were rope, probably a soft Dacron, and her limbs were securely wrapped.

"What do they do when they come in?" I asked her.

"They just come in and turn on the light," she said. "Then they give me my shot and leave and then I go back to sleep again."

"How many come in?"

"Two. One has a weapon and the other brings the syringe. I don't know what'll happen this time because there's three of us."

"We need a plan this time," Hannigan said. "We didn't have a plan last time."

"How about we grab the first guy through the door and kick his ass?" I said.

"What if there's more than one?" he asked.

"I have a two shot derringer. I'm hoping they don't send three."

"Where did you get a derringer?" he asked.

"It was in my other boot."

"What else do you have in there?" Hannigan asked. Is there a flask of bourbon? I could treat these dog bites internally and externally."

"Is there anything to eat?" Rita asked. "I can't remember the last time I ate."

"No food," I said. "But dinner is on me when we get out of this."

I put the derringer in my right rear pocket and searched the room for something else that could be utilized as a makeshift weapon but there wasn't much. I found an old refrigerator that was unplugged and smelled like something died in it, some bedroom furniture, and a couple of television sets. I knew the darkness would be to our advantage because our eyes had adjusted to it. It took me awhile, but I found and removed the light bulbs from the ceiling fixtures.

"I don't want them to be able to see you two when they open the door," I said. "So stay where the light from outside the door won't hit you."

We assumed our ambush positions. I stood in the corner where I'd be out of sight when the door opened. Rita and Hannigan crouched along the wall behind the door. The rain pounded the roof outside and a couple of times every minute thunder shook the house. We waited without speaking, my mind trying to anticipate what I'd do in every possible scenario.

My mind was dwelling on how they planned to kill us and the possibility of poison gas being piped into the storeroom was rattling through my brain when I heard the door being unlocked. The doorknob turned and gray light from the hallway streamed into the room as a hand reached for the light switch. The hand flipped the switch several times trying to get the light to come on and then the body attached to the hand, a small man holding an assault rifle, stepped into the room. I lowered my shoulder and drove him into the doorjamb and could feel bones break. He groaned as he exhaled, went limp, and the automatic weapon skittered to the floor. It had only taken a second to neutralize the first guy and I stepped into the corridor, squinting into the light. His buddy hadn't expected the ambush, but was now wide-eyed as he began to raise his weapon. He was small, like the first man, dark, probably Mexican, and too slow. I grabbed his shirt and slammed him against the doorjamb. As he went limp, I grabbed his weapon with my left hand and let him fall. His head thumped like a watermelon when it hit the concrete. The Bandido poked his head out of the kitchen when he heard the racket and when he saw me he bolted down the hallway toward the front of the house. I didn't have time to use the weapon in my left hand so I drew the derringer from my pocket and slipped the safety off. I rushed my first shot and knew it went wild, probably high and right, but by the way the Bandido flinched, I knew the second shot hit him.

A gunshot thundered in the hallway and I ducked back into the storeroom. The automatic weapon in my hand was a Russian made AK-47. Checking the weapon, I found the 20-round magazine full and that a live round was chambered. I stole a quick look down the hallway and another gunshot thundered, splintering the doorjamb next to my head. Slipping the safety off, I knelt, blindly stuck just the

AK-47 out the door with my right hand, and squeezed off a short burst from the fully automatic weapon. There was no return fire.

"Everybody okay?" I asked.

"Yeah," Hannigan said. "Damn, that was slick."

"I went to a special school for that," I said. "Rita, are you okay?"

Rita had the other AK-47 in her right hand and my Browning in her left hand. "I'm fine. Is this yours?" she asked, holding out the Browning.

"I wondered where I left that," I said as I checked the assault rifle's magazine. I had twelve rounds left.

Both men were conscious but hurt and neither one had any more ammunition for the assault rifles. "Tie these guys up," I said to Hannigan.

"With what?"

"Their belts if you have to. Just find something."

"It's dark in here, somebody took the light bulbs."

"Then use their belts. I just don't want them to get loose." I stole another glance into the corridor to make sure we weren't under attack.

"Here," said Rita, yanking at one of the victim's pants. "I'll show you."

Keeping watch on the corridor, I waited while Rita and Hannigan bound our two hostages with their own belts.

"Do you know how to use this?" I asked, handing Hannigan the Browning Hi-Power.

"I know."

"Good, let's move these two guys over by the door and you wait here in the dark. Shoot anybody that tries to help them."

"Where are you going?" he asked.

"Rita and I are going after Larry Jackson."

"Larry Jackson?" he asked. "What's he doing here? I thought this was the Spaniard's house. Is he The Spaniard?"

"It's a long multi-billon dollar story," I said. "I'll explain later."

"Since these guys are tied up," he said. "Can I come with you and Rita? I have my own gun now."

"No. Stay here. Take care of your bites and we'll be back in a few minutes."

I peeked into the corridor again and it was still clear. "Ready, Rita?"

She slipped her weapon's safety off. "Ready."

"I'll go first, cover me, and watch our backs."

"Right."

"If you see those dogs," Hannigan said. "Shoot them."

I crouched and darted into the hall, staying low to reduce my target area, but nobody shot at me. I moved forward and Rita sallied into the hallway behind me. When I checked on her position, I noticed her eyes were glassy and I wondered if I should have left her behind.

"You don't look so good, maybe you should stay here," I said. "I didn't come all the way down here to save you and then have you get shot while getting away."

"You don't look so good yourself," she said. "I'm going with you."

Staying down and against the wall, we advanced steadily. The brutal winds outside made it impossible to hear footsteps and I knew our survival would depend on getting the first shot off. I approached the kitchen door, glanced inside, and when I saw it was empty I motioned for Rita to follow. I stood guard while she drank a bottle of water from the refrigerator.

"You really do look like shit," she said, scraping dried blood from my cheek with a fingernail.

"Good to see you, too," I said. "Let's go, I'll lead, you cover our backside."

We stayed close as we moved through the house, me on point and Rita taking drag. When we got to the central marble-floored foyer, I saw two massive wooden doors that marked the front entrance to the house.   A carpeted semi-circular stairway to the upstairs floor was on our immediate left and a number of other rooms were off the foyer, some had doors open, others had closed doors. There was a breeze blowing through the house and sound of rain coming through one of the open doors. Safety off, finger on the trigger of the AK-47, I nodded to Rita and we did our best imitation of a sprint across the foyer to the open-door hallway. Once we were in the corridor, I could see it led to a four-car garage. When I checked it out, I discovered all the vehicles were gone and that the vertical doors had been left open. Rain was blowing inside onto the concrete floor.

"I think our shooter high-tailed it," I said. On our way out I locked the hallway door that led from the garage. "Are you okay?" I asked.

Rita nodded. "I'm pretty weak, but I'm okay."

We systematically checked the downstairs rooms in the house. There was a formal dining room, an extravagant bar area, several small meeting rooms, another large kitchen, and the large office where I'd talked to Larry Jackson.

"How about the upstairs?" Rita asked.

"I think they're gone," I said. The adrenaline was wearing off and fatigue was setting in. My ribs made it painful just to breathe. "I want to show you something," I said, leading her into the large office.

"What is it," she asked as we stood in front of the model.

"The new Ensenada container terminal. Larry Jackson and his buddies have been buying up land down here to develop the port. He was behind the *Beleza* attack."

"Why?"

"To put San Pedro Harbor out of business. There are lower operating costs here and with a few extra miles of railway, they can tie into the land bridge across the United States to get cargo to Europe. All he needed was a reason for the shipping companies to use Ensenada instead of San Pedro, and by sinking the Beleza at the harbor entrance, shipping companies would be climbing all over themselves to get dock space down here to unload their ships."

"What about the long-term contracts they have with the container terminals in San Pedro?"

"Larry Jackson is a maritime attorney representing the Pacific Shippers Association and I'm sure he'd be able to get them out of their contracts if the harbor was closed. Besides, I'm guessing the explosives the CIA told us about were intended to blow up strategic railroad trestles in the desert just east of Los Angeles. With no way to get cargo out of San Pedro, shippers would have to use Ensenada."

"Convenient," she said, looking around the office. "What's with all the trash on the floor?"

The files on the desk were gone. Larry Jackson must have taken them with him, but the pile of shredded documents had grown since I was last in the office.

"Destroying evidence," I said, walking over to the file cabinets. They were unlocked and I opened a few drawers. Some of the cabinets still had files in them while others were pretty barren. I thumbed through a couple of the files looking for evidence of Marpona and Larry Jackson's involvement.

"Well," said a husky male voice that interrupted my rummaging. "This didn't work out half-bad after all."

The unshaven man in jeans and a dirty white t-shirt had a gun to Rita's head and his left arm around her neck. I recognized the dagger tattoo on Ken Jacob's right forearm because Eddie Taylor had sketched it for me. Jacob's was wet from head to toe and his black windblown hair highlighted the wild look in his depraved eyes.

"Now I can finish this little errand once and for all," he said.

30

Ken Jacobs pressed the revolver into Rita's temple and she let her assault rifle drop to the floor. I'd leaned my own weapon against the desk and it was at least three steps away. Rita would be greeting Jesus before I could even get a finger on the trigger.

"We need to talk about this, " I said. "We're on the same side."

"Are you shittin' me?" Ken Jacobs shuffled his feet while randomly eyeballing the rest of the room.

Why hadn't I seen him come into the office and how did Rita let him get behind her? Another shot of adrenaline surged through my body and my mind raced. I hadn't come this far to let some two-bit ex-con take me out.

"Really," I said. "Larry Jackson and I have worked together on this for years."

"How stupid do you think I am? He told me to take care of you and that's what I'm going to do."

"Exactly," I said. "It was a test. You passed with flying colors. Congratulations."

"What the fuck are you talking about?" he asked, nervously shuffling his feet again.

"I've got to tell you, Larry was pretty pissed off about the way you and your guys handled the attack on that tanker in San Pedro. We went to a lot of trouble to get those rockets and then you missed with two of them and you didn't even destroy the ship."

"Those things were pieces of shit, they're French. What did he expect? Besides, I never shot anything like that before. We did the best we could."

Rita's eyes were focused now and Ken Jacobs had relaxed his grip a little. She would know when to make her move. I just needed to keep distracting him.

"Right, right. We know that, but those were the best we could get. It's a tough market out there." I tried to appear relaxed but my heart was pounding in my ears and my mouth was bone dry. When I started to move toward the desk he tensed up again, pressing the revolver into Rita's temple with more resolve.

"You're choking me," Rita said.

"Relax, she's with us, too," I said.

"Bullshit, I know who she is."

"She's not Eddie Taylor's girlfriend," I said. "Think about it. How long have you known Eddie and have you ever seen her before?"

"She's a Coast Guard Sea Marshal, she's a fucking Federal pig."

"She's with us," I said. "The Coast Guard doesn't pay worth shit, Jackson has had her on the payroll for months. How do you think he targeted the *Beleza* that morning? She's on the inside giving us information."

Ken Jacobs was having trouble processing what I was saying and he looked antsy.

"Larry wants to make sure you're still loyal, that's why he's giving you this test."

"Bullshit."

"Why did you steal that guy's minivan? What was his name? Astal Kamran?"

Ken Jacobs tightened his grip and started pulling Rita toward the door.

"Of all the cars you could have stolen, why take his?"

"I hate lawyers."

"That's it? You hate lawyers."

"I especially hate that lawyer."

"Why?"

"He's a money-sucking bastard that's why."

"But he helped you get green cards for the guys in Fontana."

"He knows how long it takes to train somebody, and when we needed him to help keep one of the mechanics from being deported, he charged us out the ass for it. For him, it was all about the money."

"Larry Jackson is a lawyer. You know that don't you? You might want to take it easy on lawyers."

Wind and rain pounded the windows so hard I thought they were going to cave in. Ken Jacobs was dragging Rita toward the door again.

"Eddie Taylor is working with us, too," I said. "Larry Jackson knew you'd been using him to change markings on shipping containers and brought him onboard as a back-up in case you didn't work out."

"What?"

"It's true."

Ken Jacobs stopped dragging Rita while he tried to process what I'd just told him. His grip relaxed just a bit and Rita made her move. She caught his right forearm with her left hand across her body, moving the revolver away from her head with a swift powerful blow, and then elbowed him in the ribs as hard as she could. He still had her around the neck with his left arm but she squirmed free. He was leveling the revolver on her when she knocked it from his hand with a roundhouse kick, sending it skittering across the marble floor toward the conference table. He tried to grab her again but she kicked for his crotch with all her might. The blow landed off the mark, hitting him on the thigh, and he backhanded her hard enough to knock her off her feet.

By the time Rita hit the floor I had my AK-47 leveled between his eyes. Ken Jacobs saw me pointing the weapon and much to my surprise, he charged me. I pulled the trigger but nothing happened. When did I put the safety on? Damned government weapons training, I'd automatically placed the firearm on safe without thinking. I fumbled for the unfamiliar safety but he had the assault rifle by the barrel and was pulling it from my hands. His grip was stronger than mine and I knew he was going to get it so I rushed into him, swinging my right elbow into his head. I hit him hard enough to knock him to one knee and I kicked at the assault rifle as hard as I could, connecting with enough force to send it flying in the same direction as he revolver. As he stood up I landed a good right hand to his left ear and he went all the way down. I rushed in for a kick to the head but he rolled away and came up with a knife. Ken Jacobs slashed at the air and by the way he handled the knife I knew he was good. I had some FBI self-defense training but his skills had been honed to a fine edge in prison yards. He strategically put himself between the firearms on the floor and me, advancing while slashing and probing the air. I retreated to the desk, looking for something I could use to protect myself. When I shoved the desk chair at him he just kicked it aside and kept coming. There were liquor bottles on the wet bar but they were out of reach. I grabbed a thick manila file folder with my left hand thinking it would afford me some protection but he just laughed and came at me faster. I was backed up to the windows and he jabbed the knife at my stomach but it was a fake and I fell for it. His real move was a backhand slice at my throat. Time slowed to a crawl as I saw the silvery blade dissecting the air. I jerked my head away but was too slow and I felt the icy hot agony of razor sharp steel lacerating the flesh next to my mouth and along my jawbone. Blood spurt onto the manila folder and I ducked to my left away from the windows. The letter opener was still on the conference table and I grabbed it. I tried to get on the other side of the table but he anticipated my move and shoved it against the wall, cutting me off. Blood was running into my mouth and dripping down my left arm all the way to my hand. I crouched and stabbed at the space between us with the letter opener. When I tried to go to my right he switched the knife to his left hand and cut me off again. He slashed wildly at my face with a backhand motion and I tried to block it with the blood-soaked manila folder. His forehand stroke sliced deep into my stomach muscles and I dropped the folder to clutch my abdomen. Holding the letter opener low, I waited for him to approach and finish me off but he just grinned and walked away. Looking down, I saw my boots were covered with blood and when I looked up, Ken Jacobs had Rita by the hair and was ready to slit her throat. Lightning and thunder pierced the room at the same time and I dropped the letter opener and fell to my knees, trying to keep the blood inside my body with both hands.

The blood was sticky and warm in my hands, salty in my mouth, and I knew I was going to die and it wasn't all that unpleasant. I imagined Rita holding my head, pressing a towel to my stomach, and then I was in a boat rowing while Elisha sunned herself in the transom.

***

Four days in a Mexican prison isn't an eternity, but almost. Rita and I shared a cell away from the general population and Hannigan was somewhere else. I figured the Federales weren't quite sure what to do with us because they knew Rita and I worked for the U.S. Government. Of course there was that little problem of another U.S. citizen, albeit an ex-con illegally in Mexico, that was dead by way of a gunshot wound to the head with my Browning. Apparently

Hannigan disobeyed my orders and came looking for us when he thought we'd been gone too long.

Somewhere along the line I'd been stitched-up, filled with Mexican blood and painkillers, then dumped into a prison cell. Rita was adamant that she be allowed to stay with me and we were in the prison infirmary for a day before they moved me out for my own safety. Rita called our cell the honeymoon suite but I wasn't up to laughing at the joke yet. We'd been interrogated, first by the Captain of the Federal Police and then by someone from the Ministry of Justice and as far as I could tell we were stuck in a holding pattern.

Rita filled me in as best she could. The Federal Police had stormed The Spaniard's villa shortly after Hannigan shot Ken Jacobs. She was sure I was going to die because I was losing so much blood but they got me to the Hermosillo emergency room without a lot of time to spare. I don't even remember the hospital visit; my first memory was the prison infirmary.

Our six by eight foot cell was constructed of cast concrete with steel bars in the front and a small open barred window in the back that let heat and dust in during the day and biting insects at night. There were two military surplus metal cots with thin lumpy mattresses pushed against the walls. A dirty commode and even dirtier sink that trickled brown water was between the cots along the back wall. We didn't have electricity or a mirror in the cell but we got three meals a day, which I suspected, was a lot more than the general population was treated to. The meals were room temperature by the time they got to us. Breakfast was some sort of brown congealed meat with corn tortillas; lunch was beans and tortillas, and dinner the biggest meal because we got beans, congealed meat, flour tortillas, and a slice of tomato. A tin cup of coffee that tasted like mud came with each meal. It was awkward sharing the commode at first, but Rita and I learned to roll over and face the wall while the other was using it. The food made sure we got plenty of practice.

My stitches itched. Since there wasn't a mirror in the cell, the only view of the wound on my face was Rita's expression when she saw me touching it so I knew it was bad. I counted eighteen stitches on my stomach and they were swollen purple and black. On the second day they'd begun to ooze yellow liquid and the prison doctor started me on antibiotics.

When I slept I dreamed of Elisha. Not the pleasant dreams of us being together in happier times, but horrific dreams of me cutting her heart out with a knife. Rita and I talked for hours; nonsense mostly, religiously avoiding a discussion of what had happened or what we thought was going to happen. She told me about her grandmother's cookie and brownie recipes and I talked about fishing and camping even though I'd only been a couple of times in my entire life. We kept track of the bugs we killed. We each had a separate pile and I was ahead 237 to 142, mostly because I tried not to sleep. I was afraid of my dreams.

Rita was asleep facing the wall and I was sitting on the edge of my cot, watching flies crawl over the lunch plates I'd set next to the cell door for pickup, when I heard someone coming. I recognized the metallic clang of the main cellblock door and two sets of footsteps. One set of footfalls belonged to a guard's heavy leather boots but the other was softer like more expensive footwear. It had been two days since we'd been interviewed by the representative from the Ministry of Justice and I wondered if he was coming back to ask us more questions.

"Aqui' esta," said the guard and then Mike Dillon stepped into view.

I waited until the guard left and heard the cellblock door clang shut before I stood up. Dillon wore a rumpled version of the FBI uniform of the day and was unshaven. Sweat glistened on his face and he looked tired.

"Are you here to get us out?" I asked, speaking softly so I wouldn't wake Rita.

"The State Department is working on it," he said. "You're in some deep shit."

"You don't say?"

Dillon stared at the cut on my face. "That's nasty," he said.

I lifted up my prison shirt and showed him my abdomen.

"Damn."

"If you're not here to get us out of this shithole then why did the Bureau send you?"

"They didn't. I had to take vacation days."

"Vacation days? What the fuck for?"

Dillon shrugged and clasped the bars with both hands.

I looked over my shoulder at Rita. "She hates you."

"She should."

"Don't tell me you're getting a conscience in your old age."

"It is what it is."

"I think you're feeling guilty about us being here."

"I tried to warn you, I even tried to stop you."

"If you had stopped me, Rita would be dead now."

Dillon looked at the floor. "I know. You were right about that part."

"You were just going to write her off as an acceptable loss."

"There was nothing I could do. I was told it was being handled. She was in Mexico."

"You could have told me where."

"I couldn't."

"Yeah, I know. It would jeopardize your precious fucking career. Well, I jeopardized the shit out of mine. Does Admiral Ballard even know we're alive?"

"We told him."

"No doubt my ass is fired."

"It depends on how you write up the report."

Looking over my shoulder again, I saw Rita was still sleeping, or at least pretending to sleep.

"So did you get the Spaniard? I heard he was ex-KGB."

Dillon got a shifty look in his eyes. "Kind of."

"What does that mean?"

"We're not so sure he's ex-KGB. We think he's still working for them."

"Doing what?"

"Our satellites began picking up radiation readings in Ensenada harbor last year. We checked it out and followed the trail back to Hermosillo where the breakwater interlocks are being made."

"Radiation?"

"The EPA had been tracking hazardous waste disposal in the States and found that a significant amount was being shipped across the border and dumped into pits outside Hermosillo. It turned out that the waste was being mixed with the concrete to make the interlocks."

"Are we talking about the Spaniard's manufacturing plant?"

"That's the one."

"So the Spaniard was making big bucks disposing of hazardous waste for American manufacturers that didn't care if their pollution ended up in somebody else's back yard. Where did the radiation come from?"

"Once he had his toxic waste dump set up and all the local officials bribed, he sought out radioactive waste worldwide."

"Even more money for the illicit dumping of radioactive waste. Nobody wants nuclear waste in their own backyard. Just ship it out and dump it in the Mexican desert."

"It goes a little farther than that."

"What do you mean?"

"He was involved in expansion and development of Ensenada harbor."

"I know all about that. He and Larry Jackson were bulldozing slums to put in a big container terminal so they could put the port of San Pedro out of business."

"The long-term plan was a little more elaborate than that."

"Meaning?"

"By introducing radioactive waste into the concrete breakwater interlocks, they could mask the movement of nuclear weapons into the harbor."

"But wouldn't the satellites pick that up?"

"Not necessarily. There are naturally occurring radioactive hotspots all over the earth and we adjust our satellites to ignore them so we can concentrate on new areas. By slowly building the breakwater, the entire area becomes a hotspot, and when we re-zero our satellite readings to make the harbor disappear, we wouldn't be able to detect nuclear weapon movement."

"So Larry Jackson was just a pawn after all."

Dillon nodded.

"Did you get him?"

"The Ministry of Justice picked Jackson up at the Hermosillo airport. His flight had been delayed because of the weather. They also seized all of Marpona's assets here and overseas so they can they can use the money to tear the breakwater apart. It all has to come out and be properly disposed of."

"How about the Spaniard?"

"He had a private jet."

We stood in silence for a few moments and I knew he wanted to talk about Rita.

"How about Captain Hannigan?" I asked.

"I hear he's okay and that the State Department is working on his release."

"How about Eddie Taylor?"

"Border Protection grabbed him a few days ago. He tried to walk across the border at Nogales."

"Where is he now?"

"The Bureau has him in custody. Charges are pending in relation to his involvement with the San Pedro hijackings."

"He was working undercover for me."

"I hadn't heard that."

"Now you are. I'll testify in his behalf." I looked over my shoulder at Rita. "She's alive because he helped us."

Dillon was doubtful.

"Look at me," I said. "If Eddie Taylor was responsible for me ending up in this cell and all cut to shit like this, would I be vouching for him?"

Dillon nodded. "I'll take care of it then."

The sound of the cellblock door clanging open echoed down the corridor.

"I've got to go," he said. "Give her this."

Dillon handed me a slip of paper through the bars. He'd written the name Jack Cameron and a phone number with a Washington D.C. prefix on it.

"What's this?"

"Her friend, Astal Kamran."

"I thought he was dead."

"He might as well be, he's in Witness Protection, working as an attorney for the Justice Department."

"That doesn't sound like him."

"It wasn't his idea."

"Got drafted?"

"That's what happens when you're too good of a lawyer."

The guard walked up and looked at Dillon.

Dillon started to walk away and then looked over his shoulder at me, "Don't tell her where you got that. It could jeopardize my career."

"Yeah," I said. "I'd hate to see you end up in deep shit."

31

Admiral Ballard told me to take some time off and when the Coast Guard shrink heard what happened to me in Mexico and the dreams I'd started having about killing Elisha, it was a done deal. Besides, even though my stitches were out, I wasn't able to shave yet and my homeless shelter style beard wasn't in keeping with the Coast Guard's professional image.

Rita got some time off as well and made a trip to the East Coast, probably to Washington D.C. to visit Astal Kamran, but she was going to have to be back in time for Captain Hannigan's hearing. Unofficial word around the office had Hannigan getting nothing more than a slap on the wrist for his actions aboard the *Beleza*.

Halverson treated me to lunch at the Yugoslav restaurant in San Pedro and brought me up so speed on the hijacked container they'd seized at a Compton warehouse. The balance of the missing Sep Dards were mixed in with a load of rattan furniture and I found out that while I was lavishing in prison south of the border Halverson's face had been plastered on the front page of the L.A. Times. "It's not all good," he'd said. "Now they expect me to make a bust like that every week."

When I told Halverson I was thinking about taking a fishing trip to kill some time he loaned me a wall tent and some saltwater gear so I could camp at his favorite surf-fishing spot six hours up the coast near Morro Bay. I lasted a day and a half before packing up and coming home. Come to find out, the concept of a fishing trip is a lot different when you're in a prison cell. When I returned the tent and fishing equipment, I presented Halverson with the two small sand bass I'd managed to hook.

I spent the next couple of days knocking about Huntington Beach looking for something to occupy my mind. After a sidewalk lunch near the pier one day, I saw an ad in the window of a travel agency touting low airfares to Greece. I'd stepped inside just to get a brochure but ended up booking a round-trip flight that was a screaming deal if I stayed a full month and left the next day. When I got home I cruised the Internet and found a room over a small taverna in Athens near the harbor for just 95 Euros a week

I boarded the flight with little more than some toiletries and the clothes on my back. After landing in Athens, some thirty-eight hours and four connections later, I caught an airport cab and my first stop was a clothing store. The cabbie helped me select some attire that would help me blend in with the locals. I didn't want to do the American tourist thing. The room turned out to be just like the pictures, small and basic, with a cool Aegean Sea breeze that blew through the windows in the afternoon. It proved impossible to sleep until after midnight because of the noise from the restaurant below but that worked for me because I was still having the nightmares about Elisha.

The first two weeks in Athens I wandered the streets stuck in the middle of an identity where the locals knew I was American but the tourists thought I was Greek. Since I didn't speak the language anyway, I eventually discovered that I could survive by just nodding and gesturing. I'd walk into a restaurant and point to something another person was eating or drinking and that's what

I'd get. After a week of practice, I had my mute routine down pat and I blended inconspicuously with my surroundings. I could sit on a bench, ride a bus, or spend the evening in a bar and nobody would notice me.

Afternoons were the best time for me to sleep because I didn't dream. I could nap until six or seven when the taverna below my room filled with customers and the noise woke me. I'd grab a light meal and then ride buses around the city until they stopped running, walking back to my room or catching a cab if I was too far away. I made no friends and shunned human contact.

If I was going to fall asleep by one o'clock in the afternoon, I needed to start drinking at eleven. Since drinking alone in my room was a road I didn't want to start down, I looked for a quiet place to medicate myself. Oddly enough, the Intercontinental Hotel bar turned out to be just the place to do it. Dagla was the bartender and he was content to bring me drinks and get his tip without engaging me in conversation. Other than an occasional tourist dropping in for a morning Bloody Mary, Dagla and I usually had the place to ourselves. The bar wasn't as large as one would expect for an Intercontinental Hotel. It consisted of an L-shaped bar with ten black leather and chrome stools and six matching tables that were crowded into an angular foyer just off the fourth floor elevator lobby. I particularly liked the sweeping view it had of the Acropolis contrasted by rugged hills and the brutal blue Greek sky.

It was Tuesday, six days before I was scheduled to fly home, and I was sitting on the corner stool sipping ouzo from a water glass and wondering if it was worth the money to change my ticket so I could stay for another month when a refined older-looking businessman in an expensive gray suit walked into the bar and took a stool. He set a black leather briefcase on the floor next to his stool, glanced over at me, and then waited for the bartender to take his order.

"Metaxa," the gray suit said. "Seven Star."

Dagla nodded and went to pour the drink.

The new customer retrieved his room key card from the wallet he kept in his left breast pocket and when Dagla returned with the drink, the man slid the key card across the bar with his left hand. I noticed his left hand had only the small and ring fingers remaining. A jagged red scar in the skin indicated where the others used to be.

Dagla set the drink down and scooped up the card key so he could charge the drink to the man's room.

"Gracias," said the man, stroking his goatee with his right hand. He glanced at me again and the look in his eyes told me I was insignificant.

I stared into my glass of ouzo, looking into my future and minding my own business.

After recording the transaction, Dagla returned with the key card and nodded acceptance as he slid it back across the bar.

The man in the gray suit sipped his drink, put the key card back in his wallet, and then retrieved a small feather before returning the wallet to the left breast pocket of his suit jacket. He sipped his drink from time to time with his right hand while he toyed with the feather between the two fingers on his left hand. He looked neither right nor left, but occasionally glanced at the mirror behind the bar.

In due course, a dark man, with black wavy hair and a graying moustache that drooped to the corners of his mouth, came to the bar and sat down several barstools to the right of the man in the gray suit. He wore tan dress slacks and a black silk shirt with the two top buttons undone. He ordered Greek coffee. Two sugars. Paid Dagla with cash.

Neither man looked at the other.

"You have a feather," the dark man said.

"Feather of a wren."

The dark man slid his coffee toward the gray suit, leaving one stool between them.

"As we agreed?" asked the dark man.

"As we agreed." The gray suit hesitated. "But I am troubled by your price."

"This cannot be helped. There are many causes these days and the supply is short. I have many expenses."

"Of course." Gray suit sipped his drink. "I understand. It is business." With his right foot, he slid the black leather briefcase across the floor between the bar and stool toward the dark man.

"It was not my fault," the dark man said. "About your last purchase."

"Of course not. These things happen."

The dark man smiled into the mirror behind the bar and finished his coffee. "I must go," he said as he retrieved the black leather briefcase from the floor.

The gray suit turned, held the feather between the two fingers on his left hand and offered it to the dark man.

The dark man took the feather and twirled it with his fingers.

"What is this feather of a wren?"

The gray suit turned away and faced the bar. "Long ago, all of the feathered creatures got together to decide who was greatest."

The dark man held the briefcase, swiveled on his stool, checked the lobby, and then faced away from the bar.

"They decided whoever could fly highest would become the greatest. The eagle soared higher than all the others, and just as he was going to boast himself the greatest, the lowly wren emerged from beneath the eagle's wing where he had been hiding and flew higher. The wren declared to the others that he was greatest, because he was the most clever."

The dark man smiled. "The wren is the most clever."

"Si'," said the gray suit. "The lowly wren is the greatest because it is the most clever."

The End

About the Author

The author, a graduate of the U.S. Merchant Marine Academy at Kings Point, is the former president of the pilot's association and member of the harbor safety committee in one of the nation's largest ports. Much of what he experienced during his twenty-five year career in the maritime industry can't be told. Fiction, unlike the truth, must make sense.

www.ingramcontent.com/pod-product-compliance
Lightning Source LLC
Chambersburg PA
CBHW031104030726
47496CB00002BA/374